"Sorry, I didn't know you were out here."

"I didn't mean to be."

"I love sitting on the porch swing at night."

He scooted to the end, patted the slats beside him. "Feel free."

She hesitated a moment, but headed his way in the end.

"I don't know why I like it out here." She shuddered. "There're probably snakes lurking. Or bats. Or bears, for that matter. But I love the night sounds. You don't get that in the city."

"I imagine not."

"And the stars are so bright here. So many of them."

He scanned the horizon, ashamed he often took the stars for granted. "So why do you stay there?"

"It's where I belong. It's nice to visit the country, but I could never live here. I'd be bored to tears."

With all his worries over his friends and her reminder that she was a city girl through and through, why did he feel so pulled toward Devree? Despite the warm night, a chill settled in deep. He had absolutely nothing in common wi̶̶̶ ̶̶̶ ̶̶̶ ̶̶̶ ̶̶̶ ̶̶̶ter tread carefully.

Shannon Taylor Vannatter is a stay-at-home mom/pastor's wife/award-winning author. She lives in a rural central Arkansas community with a population of around one hundred, if you count a few cows. Contact her at shannonvannatter.com.

Jill Lynn is a member of the American Christian Fiction Writers group and won the ACFW Genesis Contest in 2013. She has a bachelor's degree in communications from Bethel University. A native of Minnesota, Jill now lives in Colorado with her husband and two children. She's an avid reader of happily-ever-afters and a fan of grace, laughter and thrift stores. Connect with her at jill-lynn.com.

Counting on the Cowboy

Shannon Taylor Vannatter

&

Her Texas Cowboy

Jill Lynn

LOVE INSPIRED

INSPIRATIONAL ROMANCE

LOVE INSPIRED®
INSPIRATIONAL ROMANCE

ISBN-13: 978-1-335-45618-2

Recycling programs
for this product may
not exist in your area.

Counting on the Cowboy & Her Texas Cowboy

Copyright © 2020 by Harlequin Books S.A.

Counting on the Cowboy
First published in 2018. This edition published in 2020.
Copyright © 2018 by Shannon Taylor Vannatter

Her Texas Cowboy
First published in 2018. This edition published in 2020.
Copyright © 2018 by Jill Buteyn

This edition published by arrangement with Harlequin Books S.A.

For questions and comments about the quality of this book,
please contact us at CustomerService@Harlequin.com.

Love Inspired
22 Adelaide St. West, 40th Floor
Toronto, Ontario M5H 4E3, Canada
www.Harlequin.com

Printed in U.S.A.

CONTENTS

COUNTING ON THE COWBOY

Shannon Taylor Vannatter

To my parents. I hate getting dirty, refuse to grow a vegetable garden and will never own farm animals, but I'm thankful y'all made a country girl out of me. Even though Logan says I'm too city.

And be ye kind one to another,
tenderhearted, forgiving one another,
even as God for Christ's sake hath forgiven you.
—*Ephesians* 4:32

Chapter One

Help! There's a goat on the roof!

Devree Malone typed the frantic text to her brother-in-law while edging the engaged couple she was showing around the ranch closer to the chapel.

If the goat would just keep quiet up there, maybe the soon-to-be newlyweds wouldn't notice and she wouldn't lose this gig. At least it was still April, as the cooler not-quite-seventy degree temperature meant the farm animal odors were at a minimum.

A dark truck turned into the drive and a cowboy climbed out: Stetson, Wranglers, boots. *Maybe a ranch hand?* His gaze went to the goat, then met hers as a smirk settled on his lips. One so charming she almost forgot about the goat.

Almost. *Do something, cute cowboy.* Hopefully, her mental plea would span the thirty or so feet between them. She guided the couple inside the chapel and tried to concentrate on the bride's excited chatter.

"Imagine burgundy roses on the lattice arbor with tulle trailing down the sides." If only she could have gone ahead and decorated. But the wedding was still two weeks away. "We'll put big poufy bows on the end of each pew."

For now, she needed to wow them with what she could. She flipped the switch, setting off a sea of twinkle lights woven among the exposed rafters above.

"Oh." The enchanted bride leaned her head against her groom's shoulder.

Why put so much into the wedding when the marriage would probably be history in less than a year? In her eight years of wedding planning, just under half her couples had divorced. And then there was the ceremony that got canceled when Devree discovered her boyfriend of six months was the groom-to-be.

Just stomach this last wedding.

A month in Bandera serving as the event planner at the Chasing Eden Dude Ranch would provide Devree the chance to help her brother-in-law. It would help make sure his very pregnant wife stayed on bed rest and brought Devree a healthy niece or nephew into the world.

If she nailed this nuptial, maybe the bride's wealthy father, Phillip Brighton would hire her to plan his Brighton Electronics company retreat. And she just might be able to leave her *I do* planning behind.

Something caught her eye out the window. The cowboy, feed bucket in hand, walking backward toward the barn. The goat clambered from the top of the pavilion, across the storage shed, onto the old storm shelter and then down to the ground.

Her gaze bounced back to the couple. Still enthralled with the twinkle lights.

"Instead of walking off to the side for the unity sand

ceremony, what do you think about having a couple of groomsmen move it here in the middle of the aisle?" Devree positioned herself where she thought it should go. "That way all you'd have to do is turn around."

It would be difficult enough to maneuver the bride's mile long train up and down the aisle once without adding the possibility of it getting tangled up in vases of sand.

"I love it." Miranda Brighton's eyes lit up. "That way I won't have to fight with my dress and our families and friends will be able to see better if we're up front and center." She pressed her face into her groom's shoulder. "I can't wait to be Mrs. Joel Anderson."

"I can't wait to be Mr. Joel Anderson."

The couple's giggles mingled, ending in a sweet kiss.

Devree looked away. She used to love weddings. Almost as much as the brides and grooms she'd worked with. Until Randall.

Just one more ceremony. If the goat didn't ruin it for her. Then, if she never got another glimpse of tulle and twinkle lights, she'd be a happy woman. And maybe, just maybe, this charming couple would make it.

"There are a few side rooms along the foyer connecting the fellowship hall in the back. Plenty of room for the wedding party to prepare for the ceremony."

"Thank you so much for meeting with us, Devree." Miranda never took her eyes off her groom-to-be. "I wanted Joel to see the chapel since he's only seen pictures online."

"I don't care where the ceremony takes place. The married part is all that matters to me." The requisite sappy response from Joel.

It would be nice if he kept feeling that way. But odds were—he wouldn't.

"Okay, I'll see you both for a consultation in a week." *Please let the goat be all lassoed and out of sight.* She led the way to the exit, praying as she went. Guilt stabbed. She shouldn't ask God for anything after ignoring Him for so long. Closing her eyes, she hesitated at the double doors, then swung them open and scanned the area. No goat. Her breath rushed out.

"Thank you." The giddy bride hugged her and the couple held hands as they strolled to their car.

"Excuse me." The cowboy behind her. "You work here?"

"Yes." She turned to face him. His Stetson shadowed pale green eyes, dark hair and a cleft chin. Enough to make a girl weak in the knees. Thankfully, she wasn't a girl anymore. She was a battle-scarred woman. "I'm the new wed—I mean—event planner." At least she hoped to leave nuptials behind. "Thanks for getting rid of the goat."

"I love goats." His gaze locked on hers, as if he had all day.

"Do you work here?"

"Not yet. Don't s'pose you'd know where I might find the owners? Do the Donovans still own this place?"

"My sister and her husband, Chase Donovan." She checked her phone. Chase hadn't responded to her frantic text.

"I used to be best buds with Chase."

"Really?"

"I lived here as a kid. You and your sister from around these parts?"

"No. We're from Aubrey. I live in Dallas, technically anyway. I'm just here for six weeks." Why was she telling him all this? Those magnetic eyes held her prisoner, kept her running at the mouth.

"What about Chase's little sister, Eden? She still around?"

"Um…she died three years ago."

"No." His shoulders drooped. "Not sweet little Eden."

His genuine sadness got under her skin. "A few years back. Scuba diving accident. She and my sister were friends. That's how Landry and Chase ended up together." She shoved her hands in her back pockets. "Speaking of which, he's leading a trail ride, but Landry's inside. I'll take you to her."

"I'd appreciate that."

She headed for the ranch house. His footfalls trailed behind her.

Despite her sister's difficult pregnancy, the yard was still a well-kept green oasis in the middle of yellowed drought-ridden Texas Hill Country. Thanks to a nightly dousing by sprinklers Chase had set up. She hugged herself, staying in the middle of the walkway, keeping as much distance as possible from any lurking poison ivy or rattlesnakes hiding in the suspicious-looking crape myrtle bushes lining each side.

Would the cowboy disrupt Landry's calm? She stopped, spun to face him.

He skidded to a stop.

"You're not going to stress her out, are you?"

The corner of his mouth hitched up. "Not planning on it. Unless applying for a job does that to her."

"She usually doesn't hire the ranch hands. Chase does that." She chewed on the inside of her cheek. "But he should be back soon." She turned back toward the house. But what had he done with the goat? She halted again and swung around.

More space between them this time. He grinned, deepening the cleft in his chin and awakening dimpled cheeks. A dangerous combination. "Learned my lesson. Don't follow too close."

"Where is the goat?"

"Put him in that pen." He motioned to the rail fence near the barn out back.

No goat in sight.

"Didn't think it would hold him long." He adjusted his hat. "Goats are notorious for getting out. Especially if they're alone. And I didn't see any others. Unless they all got out."

"I don't have a clue how many there are. I didn't know they had any until I saw the one on the roof. Thanks again for taking care of that. If my bride had seen him, she may have freaked out and changed venues."

"Count on me for goat wrangling." He searched the area. "If you find him again that is."

"I don't have any other appointments, so we'll let Chase worry about the goat." She strode toward the house again. Made it all the way this time.

As she stepped onto the porch, he passed her, opened the door and held it for her.

"Thanks." Why did her cheeks warm?

His boot heels clanked behind her as she led him through the lobby into the great room.

"Landry?"

"Oh, I'm so glad you're here." Landry lay on the couch, the mound of her seven-and-a-half-month pregnancy obvious. "I'm so bored. Tell me all about your meeting."

"We have company."

Landry craned her neck until the cowboy stepped into her line of vision.

"Sorry to bother you, ma'am."

"I'd get up, but my doctor insists I lay here like a bloated heifer."

"This is…" Devree faltered. She didn't even know the cowboy's name. What if he'd made that whole story up from stuff he'd found online? What if he was some robber or escaped convict? Why hadn't she thought of that? Constant guests at the dude ranch and the laid-back country lifestyle where everybody knew every-body had lessened her suspicious nature. Thankfully, Chase's chef dad was in the kitchen, only a scream away.

"Brock McBride. I'm here to apply for the handy-man position."

"Oh, good. Please tell me you're qualified." Landry paused as she worked something on her phone. "I'm Landry Donovan, and this is my sister, Devree Malone."

"Nice meeting you, ma'am." He tipped his hat.

"My husband is leading a trail ride, but I just texted him and he should be back any minute."

"You might have a goat out." His gaze roamed the room, from the barn-wood ceiling and walls to the mas-sive stone fireplace.

"Again?" Landry rolled her eyes.

"The crazy thing climbed up on the chapel roof. It's a wonder my jittery bride didn't see him, run scream-ing and cancel everything."

"I found the feed bucket and it went right in the pen." Brock took his hat off.

Landry grinned at Brock, then Devree. "Your hero."

Her skin heated to boiling. "I said thank you." She shot her sister a look. "But I'm not in the market for a hero."

"Good. Because the goat was out again by the time they left." His mouth twitched. "Besides, my cape's at the dry cleaner, and in my experience, damsels are more trouble than they're worth."

"How's my princess?" Chase entered the great room, his focus solely on Landry. Worry evident in his furrowed brow. "Are you following orders?"

"I've been here all day, I promise. And baby Donovan is kicking up a storm." Landry motioned to Brock, introduced him and explained why he was here.

Chase's frown relaxed and a wide grin took over. "Brock McBride?"

"The one and only."

The two men hugged with lots of back clapping.

So he'd told the truth about knowing Devree's brother-in-law.

"Guess y'all know each other." Landry rolled onto her side.

"Brock used to live here. We grew up together. He's Becca's son."

Landry's eyes widened.

"Becca, the housekeeper?" Devree turned to Brock. But her last name wasn't McBride.

His face went ashen.

"She'll be so excited to see you." Landry's mouth curved into a smile. "Does she know you're here?"

"Uh—maybe I should come back some other time." Brock took a step back.

"No. Timing's perfect." Chase slapped him on the back again. "Let's go to the office. Unless you want to let your mom know you're here first."

"No," he replied, a hint of dread in his tone. He cleared his throat. "I should have called first. And I have another appointment. I'll have to get back to you."

"But you can't leave without seeing your mom." Chase steered him to the foyer. "She's just upstairs cleaning the guest rooms."

Seconds later, the great room door closed.

"What was that all about?" Devree sank into the chair facing her sister.

"I didn't make the connection when he first introduced himself, but Becca mentioned she was married before Ron and worked here back when Chase was a kid. Chase told me he and Brock were friends until Brock's dad died when he was young and Becca moved away." Landry scrolled down her phone, tapped and pressed it to her ear. "Becca came back several years ago, but she and Brock have been estranged. She's longed to reconnect with him for years. And now, he's here. She'll be so excited."

"Maybe we shouldn't get involved in their private business. Besides, I think he's leaving."

"He's probably nerv—Becca. You won't believe who's here. Brock," her sister said, ignoring Devree's words of caution. "Yes, I'm sure. Chase is in the foyer talking to him as we speak."

An audible squeal came through the phone.

"Hurry, Devree," Landry begged. "You have to stop

him. If he leaves before Becca can get to him, it'll break her heart."

Surely, he wouldn't leave without seeing Becca. Always so sweet and pleasant—who could be estranged from her?

She should stay out of it. But if she did, she knew Landry would try to stop Brock from leaving. And her sister didn't need any more stress. On top of that, the ranch badly needed a handyman.

Devree dashed toward the foyer.

"Please don't leave without seeing your mom." Chase stepped in front of the exit, cutting off Brock's escape.

"It's been a while. I should have called first," Brock repeated through gritted teeth.

"Look, I don't know what happened between y'all. All I know is your mom has pined for you—the entire fifteen years since she came back here."

Fifteen years. His mom had been at the dude ranch for that long. Miss City Girl—who'd nagged Dad to move—had come back willingly and stayed? Probably the only place she could find a job, considering her habit. But if his mom was still using, would Chase keep her on? Surely not. Unless she somehow hid her addiction.

Footfalls behind him; he braced himself.

"Wait!" The wedding planner.

He'd enjoyed talking to her, despite their being from different worlds. Until Chase mentioned his mom.

"Landry called Becca. She's on her way. You can't just leave."

"I'll leave when I'm good and ready." He spun to face her. "And I'm good and ready."

She gasped at his outburst and something flashed in her eyes. Hurt.

"I'm sorry." He hung his head. "I didn't mean to snap at you. It's just—there's history to wade through. And I didn't bring my muck boots." He turned and strode for the door, intent on going through Chase if he had to.

"Brock!" The voice he dreamt about too often for peace of mind echoed down the staircase behind him and took him back in time. Ten years old, sobbing on the social worker's shoulder, wondering when his mom would come back for him.

Never.

For the last fifteen years, she'd been here. And never lifted a finger to try to find him.

The sound of hurried footsteps descended on his ears.

Pressure built in his chest. He didn't turn around.

"Please wait!" A small hand grabbed his arm. "Please." Pleading, tearful. "At least look at me."

She stepped in front of him. Much the way he remembered her. Rail thin, long brown hair. Eighteen years older. But somehow she looked better. Healthier. No telltale sunken shadows beneath her pale blue eyes. The hand on his arm was steady.

"Sure hope you'll stick around, Brock." Chase gave him a beseeching smile. "The job's yours."

"You didn't even look at my résumé." He focused on his friend, mainly to escape his mom's imploring gaze. Why did he still think of her as his mom after she'd abandoned him?

"I'm familiar with your work and you're overqualified. Your mom found an article about you building luxury cabins in a magazine a few years back."

"I still have it." She squeezed his arm.

Why did she think she had the right to touch him? He pulled away from her grasp, took a step back.

Her hand fell to her side. "Please stay."

"We'll give you some privacy." Chase stepped away from the exit, motioned Devree to follow.

"I need to stash my wedding paraphernalia in the chapel loft." A pinched frown drew her brows together. Her gaze clashed with his, and then she whirled away and disappeared outside. Was she embarrassed to witness their turmoil? Did she feel sorry for him? Or for his mom?

"Please, Brock, can't we talk? You came here for a reason. Don't back out now."

His mom's plea clanged in his head. He'd come for the job. But also because the eight years he'd spent at the dude ranch were the best of his life. When his dad had been alive. When his mom hadn't been catatonic and actually cared if he ate or not. Before their move to Dallas. Before they lost their apartment and ended up moving in with his alcoholic grandfather. Before she got hooked on drugs.

He'd returned to come to terms with his past and his mom's abandonment. To remember his dad. He'd expected to come face to face with the memories that haunted him. But not with her.

"Please come to the office with me." Tears streamed down her cheeks.

But not as many as he'd cried over her. "I didn't know you were here."

"Or you wouldn't have come." She hiccupped a sob. "I get that. Can't we just talk for a few minutes?"

"Do the Donovans know everything? I mean, about you."

She sucked in a big breath, shook her head. "Granny did, but she's been gone several years. I told everyone else your father's family turned you against me and we haven't spoken in years."

"So you expect me to stay and live your lie with you?" He glanced at the door, seeking escape. "I don't think so. Tell Chase bye for me."

"But you can't leave." She blocked him off, set her hand on his arm again.

"I'm leaving now. Please get out of my way. I think I've had enough of memory lane."

"I wish you'd stay. Jesus forgave me. For everything. Can't you give me a chance?"

How dare she pull the Jesus card.

"If you stay, I'll give you space. And if you give me some time, I'll summon up the courage to tell the truth."

"I'll think about it." If it would get her out of his way, he'd think about all she'd said. All the way to his truck. All the way back to Waco.

She stepped aside.

He practically bolted out the door, down the porch steps and across the pristine yard to the parking lot.

But Devree, with the sun setting her cinnamon hair aflame, waited by his truck. Blocking his escape.

"Could you tell Chase I'll call him?" He willed her to step aside.

Her brilliant blue gaze locked on his. "Please don't go."

A heartfelt plea from a beautiful woman. Normally he couldn't resist that. Even though it was obvious the redhead was just the type he needed to steer clear of: a city girl.

Just like his mom. And he certainly didn't want anything to do with her. He needed to get out of Dodge. Fast.

Chapter Two

Devree's face heated when she realized he could have taken her plea for him to stay as her own. "I mean, Chase could use you around here."

"I'm sure he can find someone else." Brock shifted his weight, obviously wanting her to move out of his way.

But she had to convince him to stay. For her sister's sake. And Becca's too. "The chapel's completed, but they're still in the middle of expanding the ranch. Their new house, along with honeymoon and hunting cabins are in progress. Chase is up to his eyeballs with all of it and the handyman bailed."

"Surely there've been other applicants."

"Several who would be great as ranch hands, but painfully inexperienced when it comes to fixing anything other than fences." She drew in a long breath.

"I can't stay here."

"I have a wedding scheduled next month. Plus, they've got more weddings starting in June and wild boar hunts booked through fall with guests expecting cabins ready for their stay. Meanwhile, there are a dozen projects that need attention and a very pregnant lady who'd like to be in her new house before the baby comes. Please say you'll take the job."

"I can't do this. Not with—"

"Landry had a stillbirth last spring." Her vision blurred at the memory of the tiny casket.

His shoulders sagged. "I'm sorry. Chase didn't say anything."

"They don't like to dwell on it. It's too hard." She blinked the moisture away. "She's almost lost this baby twice and is still having complications. She can't handle any more stress. Chase needs to spend more time keeping her calm. Just stay until Chase can find someone else. My niece or nephew's life could depend on it."

His eyes softened. "No pressure."

"Sorry." Devree kicked at the gravel drive. "They're scared to death. And so am I." She managed to get a hold on her emotions, looked back up at him. "Here's your chance to help an old friend. With a baby's life hanging in the balance."

"You drive a hard bargain." He looked skyward. "I'll stay on one condition."

"Which is?"

"I don't want to talk about my mother. And I don't want any of you pushing me toward her."

"We owe you." She offered her hand. His rough, calloused palm dwarfed hers.

"And only until Chase can hire someone else."

"Come on. Let's go tell them." She jogged to the ranch house.

With his long stride, he stayed right with her even though he was only walking. He beat her to the porch, climbed the steps and opened the door for her.

"Do you think your mom is okay?"

His gaze went steely. "Don't know."

And obviously didn't care.

"And that counts as talking about her."

"I can't help it if I'm worried about her." In the last year since the dude ranch started hosting weddings, Devree had planned a handful here. Becca helped decorate and clean after each one—a real sweetheart. How could he not care about her?

"You're still talking about her."

"Sorry." She stepped inside, hurried across the foyer to the great room.

Landry was right where she'd left her—laying on the couch, feet in her husband's lap.

"Good news. Brock agreed to take the job."

"Wonderful." Landry's relief whooshed out in a heavy sigh.

"Glad to hear it." Chase's smile went a mile wide.

"Where should I bunk?"

"Go out to the barn, ask for Troy. He'll get you settled in a room at the bunkhouse where a lot of the hands stay."

"Sounds like a plan. I'd like to tackle the goat problem. Exactly how many are missing?"

"Eleven. Six does—one is gestating with a kid due in the next few weeks—and five bucks. All pygmies. We're planning a petting zoo by the time school's out."

Does and bucks? Weren't those deer? Gestating with a kid due? Did that translate into pregnant goat? Devree was desperately behind on her ranch and farm animal lingo.

"They need something to occupy them so they'll stay in the pens."

Apparently, Brock knew a thing or two about goats. Or does and bucks and kids. Or whatever they were.

"Use whatever you need out of the lumber pile in the barn." Chase adjusted the comforter around Landry's feet. "I'd also appreciate it if you'd arrange for demolition of that old storm shelter on the east side of the chapel. It's an eyesore and goat magnet. Besides, we have a basement so we don't need it."

"Sure. First thing in the morning."

"And, Devree, since we have a handyman now, I need to add to your load."

"Okay?" *Hopefully, nothing dirty or stinky.*

"Our event schedule is kind of dead between spring break and June. Which will leave you at loose ends. With Landry down for the count, our last handyman's wife was supposed to handle decorating the chapel and the honeymoon cottages. I was wondering if you could help with that."

"Um, I'm a wed—event planner. Not an interior decorator." Especially not a rustic one. Country-themed weddings were always a challenge for her.

"Please don't let Chase do it." Landry groaned. "Everything will end up looking just like the hunting cabins. With dead wild boar heads on the walls."

And cause her sister stress. "I guess I could try."

"You'll do great." Landry sounded so certain. "With all your experience at decorating venues for weddings. For the chapel, just a few decor items. Keep it simple and rustic with a few crosses and burlap. And for the cabins, pick some paint colors, tile and flooring. We get all our decor items, furnishings, drapery and bedding from Resa's store. She'll give you good advice."

"I'm on it."

"Great." Chase relaxed, ran his fingers along the bottom of Landry's toes, eliciting a giggle out of her. "I'll need you and Brock to focus on the chapel and Gramp's fishing cabin to begin with."

"Why the fishing cabin?" Devree tried not to cringe. She'd much rather work in one of the new structures instead of an old abandoned one.

"With a wedding in two weeks and the new cabins unfinished—" Landry adjusted her pillow "—it'll be quicker to transform the fishing cabin into a honeymoon hideaway than finishing one of the others."

"But no one's lived in the cabin since I moved out after our wedding. Becca cleaned it—" Chase winced as he obviously realized he'd brought up a sore subject "—but it needs caulk around the plumbing and trim work."

Right on cue, the muscle in Brock's jaw had flexed at the mention of his mother. "I'll check it out and tackle it in the morning." His words came out clipped, his mind still obviously on whatever his issues were with Becca.

"It should be vacant by now." Landry cringed. "Chase set mouse traps."

That bit of info almost stopped Devree's heart. She squelched a shudder. Surely, there wouldn't be any critters. Not live ones, anyway.

"I'll try to find where they're getting in," Brock promised.

"We'll be fine," she assured her sister and Chase. But would *she*? With mice? If there were rodents, there might be snakes or worse…spiders. "Don't worry about a thing. Y'all just concentrate on baby Sprint."

"Sprint?" Landry squinted one eye, her thinking mode.

"I figure his or her dad is Chase, so she or he is Sprint."

Landry's giggle mixed with Chase's chuckle. A nice relaxed sound. Just what she wanted to hear from her sister.

She turned to see that she'd even elicited a grin out of Brock.

"No matter what y'all name the baby, that's what I'm calling him or her." She shot her sister a wink. "I've still got boxes of wedding decorations to stash in the chapel."

"You'll need help." Landry smoothed her hands over the roundness of her belly.

"I'm on it." Chase moved Landry's feet, started to get up.

"Stay put," Brock ordered. "I'll help her."

"That's not in your job description."

"She's your top priority." Brock pointed at Landry. "I'm here. Let me help."

Chase settled Landry's feet back in his lap. "I appreciate that."

So, Brock could be caring—just not toward his mother. Despite the tension, it would be nice to have someone else take part of Chase's load so he could focus on Landry. And given time, maybe Becca and Brock could work things out.

He followed her to her car where they each grabbed a stack of plastic containers and headed for the chapel.

She hadn't anticipated working with the broad-shouldered, way too good-looking cowboy. But she couldn't let him distract her.

Without shifting his load, he shouldered the door to the chapel open and held it for her. "Where do you want these?"

"On the back pew will be fine."

He set down her containers. "Is that all?"

"Yes." It would help if he stashed everything in the loft for her, but that would mean having him stick around. "Thanks. I can take it from here."

He tipped his hat and exited. Through the side window, she saw him hurry toward the long building that housed a dozen hands and the foreman, Troy. His temporary home.

She had to concentrate on the chapel and the fishing cabin. Not the cowboy.

Barely daylight, Brock nailed the final board into place on the play station in the goat pen. A buck, barely two feet tall, nibbled his elbow. And they said cats were curious.

"Just give me a minute, little guy, and I'll get out of your way." He gathered his tools, slipped them in his belt and took a step back. Just as soon as he was out of the way, all five bucks climbed on the station, wrestling their way to the top. The matching structure in the doe's pen was getting used as well. He slipped out the gate, fastened it back.

He'd never built such a thing, but he'd gotten ideas off the internet last night. Apparently, good ones. With wire fencing in place and two more wooden rails at the top, they should stay in now.

Next on the agenda, he planned to caulk the fishing cabin and make the repairs there. He needed to keep busy. Keep his mind off the pretty redhead. And his mother. On his first official day as handyman, he'd already set up a time for the demolition of the old storm cellar by the chapel.

He loaded an assortment of lumber he hadn't used into his truck and drove over to the barn. Once the fishing cabin and Chase's new house were complete, getting his friend moved before the baby came would be his priority.

After that, he'd focus on whatever else needed fixing. But hopefully, he wouldn't be here long.

As he stacked the wood neatly back where he'd found it, a prickle of awareness swept over him. Someone watching. He glanced around and saw movement in the loft. A moment later, a child's head popped up, then ducked again.

"Are you supposed to be up there alone?"

Busted, she came out of hiding, peered down at him. "My grandpa had to take guests to their room and I sort of slipped out. But I'm real careful when I climb in the loft and I can hear the bus when it gets to Cheyenne's house. She lives next door. Once I hear it, I can run to the road. And I'm real fast." She climbed down to reveal light brown hair and freckles. First grade maybe.

"You shouldn't slip out on your grandpa like that. He'll worry."

"I'll be back before he knows I'm gone. I'm Ruby."

"I'm Brock."

"I know who you are." She plopped on a hay bale. "You're my uncle."

A hollow weight settled in his chest. Had his mom had another child—his sibling?

"But I'm not supposed to tell anybody. It's me and Mama's secret. I'm real good at keeping secrets. I figured you already knew, so I don't gotta keep it from you."

He swallowed hard. "So who's your mama?"

"You haven't met her yet. Her name's Scarlet. My

grandma's favorite color was red. So she named Mama Scarlet and Mama named me Ruby to memorialize her."

"Like I said, you best get back before your grandpa misses you."

She gasped. "There's the bus." She waved, then bolted for the ranch house as fast as her little legs would carry her. Minutes later, he heard the bus stop at the end of the drive. It didn't tarry long before driving past.

Scarlet? Did he have a sister? But red had never been his mom's favorite color. At least when he'd lived with her anyway. Maybe the child was confused? Or playing a game?

A scream echoed through the morning stillness.

Brock bolted in the direction it came from.

Another shriek from Gramp's old fishing cabin.

He charged full force.

On the porch, Devree held something small with pliers. She dropped both with a screech and did a little dance in her high heels.

"What's wrong?"

She whirled in his direction, her business-style skirt slim-fitting at her knees. Wild-eyed, mouth open and pulled down at the corners, she looked ready to let out another blood-curdling shriek. She sucked in a breath, shuddered. "A mouse. Its tail was caught in a trap."

"Where?" He climbed the porch steps, tried to hold in his laughter.

She propped her hands on her hips. "It's not funny. I turned it loose." She pointed to the end of the cabin. "It ran off over there."

He took in the trap laying nearby along with two sets of pliers. "You know," he said, unable to control his grin. "If you turn it loose, it'll most likely come right back in."

"I couldn't take all that squealing." She covered her ears with both hands. "From the moment I got here. Snap! Snap! Snap! And the poor little thing went to squealing."

"What's wrong?" Chase sprinted in their direction still wearing his robe.

"Nothing." Her hands dropped away from her head. "I didn't wake Landry did I?"

"No." His brows rose. "Why were you screaming about nothing?"

She repeated her story, shrugged as if it was no big deal. "When I turned him loose, he darted toward my foot. I might have yelled a bit. Just a little adrenaline kicking in. But I'm fine. And the mouse is too."

"You should have killed him." Chase tightened the belt on his robe. "He'll only come back inside."

"I know, but he was crying. And he was kind of cute."

Chase cut his gaze to the sky, as if trying to keep from rolling his eyes. "Are there any dead ones in other traps?"

She pulled in a shaky breath. "I think so."

"I'll empty them for you."

"I'll take care of it." Brock stepped up on the porch. "Just tell me where they are."

"Under the kitchen and bathroom counters, behind the trash can in the kitchen, living room and bedroom."

"I'm on it. What about getting some cats?"

"Good idea." Chase ran a hand through his bed head. "If you have any more live ones, call me."

"I'm fine." She pulled on a brave smile.

"And try not to scream. It scares the guests." Chase strolled back toward the ranch house.

Poor guy—completely stressed out.

"Let's just say I'm not the most serene person when it comes to rodents."

"I noticed." Brock smirked. "Guess you won't be helping me with the traps."

She shot him a look, then hung her head. "I think I'll hide in the closet while you take care of things. Landry can do anything—help birth farm animals, decapitate a rattlesnake with a hoe, bait her own fishing hook. But I'm not like that. Not at all."

A definite understatement from what little he knew of her so far.

"Sounds like it'll be a challenge to keep Landry occupied for six weeks." He peered down at her. "You really here for events? Or to help Chase babysit her without her knowing it?"

"Chase called, wanted me to help out here. They happened to have the first wedding booked in the new chapel." She shrugged. "It worked out perfectly."

"Kind of sounds like you were meant to be here." He hooked his thumbs through his belt loops.

"Except that I'm trying to go in a new direction as an event planner—company retreats, family reunions, conferences, corporate Christmas parties—that sort of thing. But my sister needed me, so I'm doing this *one last wedding*." Bitterness edged her words. "And that's it." She stepped inside.

Her distaste for nuptials didn't detract from her beauty. Not at all.

He followed. Several large white-tailed and axis deer preserved in taxidermy mounts hung on the wall. A large glass display box full of fish hooks of every size and style, from hand-tied fly to vintage wooden lures. It had always fascinated him as a kid when he'd come here with Chase and Gramps.

"This place creeps me out." Devree shivered, hugged herself tighter.

"I always loved it. Gramps—he insisted everyone call him that—used to bring us here for early morning fishing." The smell of Pine Sol and lemon cleaning supplies tickled his nose. Took him back.

Since he always wanted to help when he made the cleaning rounds with his mom, she'd let him dust the guest rooms. He could almost feel the damp, worn terry cloth in his hand. The way he got two nightstands and a headboard dusted in the time it took her to clean an entire room and bathroom. But she'd never hurried him or reprimanded him for taking too long.

He shook the memories away. But his brush with Ruby settled in his empty spaces. "Do you know a little girl named Ruby?"

"Sure. She's Ron's granddaughter. She comes here to catch the bus some mornings and gets off here in the afternoon part of the time."

"I met her in the barn this morning. And Ron is?"

"Your um—Becca's husband. He's a bellhop and wild boar hunting guide here at the dude ranch."

So Mom had remarried. The muscle in his jaw twitched. "And Scarlet?"

"Ron's daughter."

His stepsister. It all clicked into place. Well, Ruby was cute and all, but he had no intention of getting to know his blended family while he was here.

"They're really sweet people." Devree settled on the

plaid couch. "I need to get a feel for the space." She must have sensed he didn't want to talk about it. She tucked her feet up beside her. Probably trying to avoid varmints.

He scanned the room. With the blinds open, sunlight streamed into the main living area. There were wood floors, ceilings and log walls with a dozen marble eyes staring at them.

"It's perfect as is for a hunting cabin. Why not take the personal items out, spruce it up a bit and use it for that?"

"We need a honeymoon cottage up and running ASAP. And the guest cottages are all on the front of the property while the hunting ones are on the back of the acreage."

"But this is such a personal space. Why are they opening it up to guests?"

"Chase doesn't want it to go unused and eventually rot away. A ranch hand is coming sometime to take all these poor dead animals to the new house. Along with those." She gestured to the fishhook display with another shudder.

Snap! Another trap went off and she jumped. "Great. Another victim. Isn't there any other way?"

"I could buy some poison. But you take the chance of one dying in the wall. Trust me, you don't want to go there."

"Ugh." She closed her eyes. "Something humane?"

"There are live traps that don't hurt them. I'm going into town later to buy lumber. I could pick up a few."

"Say you do that and we catch them. Then what do we do to keep them from coming back in?"

"I could feed them to my pet boa constrictor."

Her eyes popped open wide, revealing a hint of green amidst the blue.

Captivating. "Kidding. I'd find some place deep in the woods."

"But what would they eat?"

"Seeds, berries. Don't worry, I'll find a good place for them."

"I'd appreciate it."

He went in the kitchen, came back with two traps.

She clasped a hand over her mouth.

"Sorry. You might not want to watch." He hurried to the door, emptied the traps several yards from the cabin and returned.

She buried her face in a pillow, stayed huddled on the couch while he made another trip with the remaining traps. Finished, he returned to the kitchen and washed his hands.

"You don't want me to reset them?"

"Definitely not." She peeked from behind the pillow.

"Okay, I'll bring the live traps by later. Anything else I can do for you before I start caulking?"

Her gaze darted to the glass display case hanging on the wall. "Could you do something with that?"

"The fishhooks?"

"Yes, please. If you laugh, I'll die, but I'm terrified of them."

Seriously? But the terror in her eyes kept his humor at bay. He opened the case.

"No!" She screeched. "Just take the whole thing." She closed her eyes. "I mean, it would be awful if you lost one."

"Or if one fell out."

"Stop." She pressed her face in the pillow again. "You'll give me nightmares."

"Relax. I was only checking to see how it's mounted. Have you been hooked?"

She lowered the pillow. With a slow nod, she rubbed the skin between her thumb and forefinger on her right hand, a slight scar. "My father promised to take Landry and me fishing when we were little. But someone called in sick and he had to work in the Christian bookstore our parents own. I got a hook out and tried to put it on my line so we'd be ready when he got home."

"And hooked yourself."

She pinched the skin. "It went through right here. All the way through, barb and all. It had to be cut out in the emergency room. I can still feel it."

Her vulnerability tugged at him as he shut the display case, carefully lifted the brackets off the screws holding it up. "I'll take it to the new house when I finish insulating. For now, how about I put it out of sight, maybe under the bed?"

"Thanks."

"So, do you like to fish?"

Her laugh came out ironic. "No. I'm afraid of hooks, worms are slimy and fish are stinky. I just wanted to be with my dad."

"Did you not get much time with him?"

"He was great at setting up outings with us. But we'd have these awesome plans until someone called in sick and he'd end up at the store. Sometimes, I went to work with him, just to be with him."

She was way too charming when she showed this soft side. "My dad died when I was barely eight."

"I bet that was tough." Her gaze met his.

"It was. He was my hero." The loss burned fresh in his heart. He tucked the display case under his arm and headed for the bedroom.

"Thanks."

"Let me know if you need anything else."

"Thought your cape was at the dry cleaners. And I'll remind you, that despite circumstances, I'm not a damsel." A small smile slipped out. "Just slightly out of my element."

"Got my cape back this morning and we're in dire straits here. Mice and traps and fishhooks! Oh, my!" He mimicked the classic *Wizard of Oz* chant and got a chuckle out of her. And coming to her rescue might have its perks. She certainly wasn't a chore to look at.

"Just for the record, I'm afraid of flying monkeys too."

"Let me know if you see any of those." He shot her a wink and stashed the display box under the bed. "Typical city girl."

"I may be a city girl." Her tone turned sharp. "But there's nothing typical about me."

Definitely overly sensitive. And now he'd offended her. Maybe that was a good turn of events. The last thing he needed was to develop a soft spot for her.

Besides, he wouldn't be here long. And she wouldn't either. They were just biding their time stuck here together. Both itching to get back to their real lives.

Chapter Three

Devree drove past the ranch house and pulled into the cabin parking lot. Maybe she could do this. Once the ranch hands had removed all the dead animal heads yesterday, ideas for the cabin's decor took shape. A mix of rustic and shabby chic. This morning, her visit to Rustick's Log Furnishings had been productive.

Resa—store owner, neighbor and friend—had been extremely helpful. And, so Landry wouldn't feel useless, Devree had texted her pictures of her choices. With her sister's approval, she'd purchased a back seat full of curtains, pillows and a bedspread while the furniture would arrive next week.

Arms laden with goodies, she stepped up on the porch and reached blindly to insert the key into the lock. But the door opened.

Brock. "Here, let me help you." He tugged the bags out of her hands.

"Thanks." Why did his accidental touch send a shiver through her? Even after he'd called her *typical* just yesterday.

"You've been busy. Me too. I caulked all the plumbing and popped all the trim to seal the joints. Where do you want this stuff?"

"On the couch. New furniture will arrive next week. Will it be in your way?"

"I should be done with the messy stuff by then." He stashed the bags, then grabbed a putty knife, scraped a spot on the log wall and wiped the area with a cloth. "What about the old furniture?"

"Chase is sending ranch hands. Most of it will go in his man cave at the new house. What doesn't will go to charities. Will you be doing any work in the bedroom or bathroom? I thought I'd put curtains up in there."

"Go for it. Need a screwdriver?"

Why did he have to be so helpful? And appealing? "Come to think of it…"

"Have you ever hung curtains?"

"Hello? I have my own apartment."

"Just offering my help. And a step stool."

"That might be useful."

He picked up a small stool from the corner, dug around in his toolbox. "Flat or Phillips?"

"Phillips."

"You know your way around a screwdriver." He handed it to her.

"I have a dad, you know." When she saw his gaze drop, she wished she could take that back. She hadn't meant to hurt him; it had just slipped out. "Thanks." She grabbed the bag, hoofed it to the bedroom.

Brock followed, carrying the stool. "Sure you don't need any help?"

"I've got this." She turned to take the stool from him. Something scampered across her sandaled foot. She screamed, dropped the screwdriver and the stool.

"What?"

But she was too busy clambering onto the bed. Safely off the floor, she stood in the middle, scanning for movement.

"What?" His tone exasperated.

"I think—" she did a whole body shudder followed by a heebie-jeebies dance "—a mouse just ran across my foot."

"Okay." He reached for her hand. "Just calm down. Sit and relax before you fall off there and break your neck."

"I'd really like to get out of here." She gingerly sat down in the center of the bed, keeping her eyes on the edges, half expecting a mouse to come climbing up the bed skirt.

"Maybe that's best." He gestured toward the door.

"I'm afraid to put my feet on the floor." She squeezed her eyes closed. Great. She'd just proven every city girl notion he had about her to be true.

"Do I need to carry you?"

Her eyes popped open, surveyed him for a moment. Feet on the floor with the mice? Or carried out by the handsome cowboy she barely knew? Which was worse? Definitely rodents. With a slow nod, she scooted toward him.

He scooped her up.

With no choice, she put her arms around his neck, tried not to cling too tight.

As he stepped out on the porch, an elderly couple hand in hand rounded the walking trail thirty feet away.

"Look, Henry, newlyweds."

"In my day, you carried her inside, young man." The man frowned. "Not out."

"Thanks for the advice."

As her cheeks flamed, she felt the deep rumble of Brock's laughter. "You can put me down now."

He bent to lower her. "You know it was probably the same mouse you let go yesterday."

"Not funny." She smacked him on the shoulder.

"That little dance you did sure was." When she didn't smile, he sobered. "Once we get the furniture out, it'll be easier to get this place mouse-free with fewer places for them to hide."

"I'll be back post-evacuation." She headed for the ranch house.

"Watch out for flying monkeys." His chuckle echoed across the field.

What she really needed to watch out for was Brock.

He'd carried her out as if she weighed nothing. His strength had felt too comforting. Too safe.

And she knew from experience, the least safe place she could be was close to a man.

With a thousand things on his mind, Brock had awakened early. He strolled toward the fishing cabin with only birdsong and horse whinnies to greet him.

Past the cabin, he could see the chapel in the distance. The wood on the exterior was grayed with age. One of the hands told him it had come from an ancient barn a windstorm had toppled on the property a few months back. With a high peak in the middle and slanted roof on each side, the structure was a cross between a rustic chapel and a barn. Church always soothed him, no matter what was going on. He looked forward to attending services there.

But for now, he needed to focus. Maybe he could get

some work done before Devree showed up to distract him. Two full days of working with her and he felt as if he'd barely gotten anything done. At least she'd held up her end of the bargain. She hadn't tried to talk about his mother anymore.

And his mother had been true to her word. She'd steered clear of him. If they'd both just stick to their promises, he could stay. Help his old friend out, finish the cabins, get Chase moved into his new house. But it would never work. He'd run into her eventually. A new handyman was the only solution. Though Chase hadn't gotten any more applicants. Yet.

"You're stirring early." Devree's voice.

His feet stalled as he glanced around.

Over by the goat enclosures. Her foot propped on the bottom rail of the fence.

"I could say the same thing." He counted the goats—all eleven of them. Right where they were supposed to be—males in one pen, females in the other.

"Who could sleep around here with that stupid rooster on duty?"

"Aw, come on. Rusty's just doing his job. And a fine one at that." Just as he'd tagged her—classic city girl through and through. Even if she didn't want to admit it.

"I'm gonna buy him a muzzle."

The image made him chuckle. "I don't think that works on a rooster. I take it you're not a morning person?"

"I'm fine with morning. But this is the wee hours in my book." The sunlight picked out honeyed strands amidst her cinnamon hair.

"It's daylight." He tore his gaze away, checked his watch. Six thirty-eight to be exact.

"Yes. But it wasn't when he started up."

A goat clambered to the top of the play station, nudged the current resident out of his way. "So that first day, I'd have never taken you for a goat lover."

"I'm not."

"Then why are you standing here watching them instead of holding your nose and running the other way?"

She laughed a little at that. "I've been here long enough my sinuses are burned out and no longer detect farm animal smells. And goats are kind of fun. It's like they're playing king of the mountain. I want to see who wins."

"Knock yourself out." He tipped his hat, continued on to the cabin. Typical, but with a few surprises.

"I'll be there once you get it all evacuated."

He hurried down the path, eager to escape the scent of her apple shampoo. A scent that he was starting to recognize as uniquely hers. Just one more reason Chase needed to find another handyman and Brock needed to go on down the road.

As he stepped up onto the porch of the fishing cabin, a thud sounded at the back. Not Devree. Maybe the ranch hands were moving the old furniture out today.

He turned the knob, but it was still locked. He inserted the key, clicked the latch, opened the door. Just inside, a tightly woven wire cage with the grid open, a dozen mice still inside. "Huh?"

It was a live trap for larger animals, not the kind he'd bought. And besides, he'd put his traps in the bedroom and kitchen. He shut the wire grid, keeping the rodents locked inside, hurried toward the kitchen.

The window in the top of the live trap he'd set revealed it was empty, the release open. The back door stood ajar. He hurried out, looked around. Caught a glimpse of a man wearing a baseball cap a hundred yards away.

"Hey! What are you doing?"

The man bolted for the woods.

Brock shot after him, down the trail, past the barn and into the pine thicket behind it.

The runner stayed off the trail. Briars clawed at Brock's jeans. Some jabbed into tender flesh. The trees and undergrowth were so dense he couldn't see the guy anymore, just followed the sound of his escape. Prayed he didn't blindly step on a rattler.

A branch swatted him in the face. Eyes tearing up, he couldn't see a thing. Still, he was caught off guard when he stepped in a hole, his knee buckling, and he went down. He jumped up quick, but it was quiet as he peered into the dense sea of green. Nothing, as he stood there and listened for several minutes.

Why would the man put mice in the cabin? He headed back toward the structure. It explained the constant infestation. And brought up a whole host of new questions.

Devree kept her eyes on the ground. Aware that snakes slithered in the cool of the morning and evening this time of year, she stayed on the path to the fishing cabin.

The rooster crowed again, close by. Surely, the guests hated him as much as she did.

"I'm up already," she growled. "Can't you just sleep in sometimes?"

A flash of red to her left. The rooster running at her. She bolted for the fishing cabin, snakes forgotten, but the rooster cut her off. A flap of amber-colored wings, blue-and-green tail feathers, spurs aimed at her as he lunged/flew in her direction. She dodged, bit her tongue to keep from screaming. No waking Chase again or alerting Brock to come to her rescue. She scrambled around Rusty. He crowed in hot pursuit. Okay, maybe she wouldn't mind if Brock showed up about now.

"You stupid bird, leave me alone." She made it to the cabin porch, grabbed a broom, spun and jabbed it at the rooster.

He paced back and forth, looking cocky, crowed again, then turned and headed up the path back to the barn.

"Take that, you stupid rooster." But as much as she wanted to, she couldn't just leave him loose to attack guests. She followed at a distance. Not a ranch hand in sight to help her.

Instead of going to his coop, the rooster stopped near the goat pen, pecked at the ground. Though she'd never been inside the barn, if she could find some feed, maybe she could lure the foul fowl back into his lair.

At least he was the only one out. She rounded the goat pen, found a bucket near the chicken coop with seeds in it, opened the wire door of the pen, and jogged back to the huge bird. But not too close.

"Look what I got, big fella."

The rooster cocked his head, strutted in her direction. Faster than she was comfortable with, but she still had the broom. She backed all the way to the pen, then threw the bucket inside. Thankfully, the rooster went in and she fastened the door in place.

She blew out a big breath, closed her eyes, leaned her forehead on the hand that was still holding the broom.

A noise behind her. She jabbed the broom as she spun around.

And almost gouged Brock in the chest.

His arms went up in a defensive stance. "I never would have pegged you for having such impressive rooster wrangling skills."

She dropped the broom, covered her face with her hands. "Sorry. I thought Rusty had a friend."

"I doubt he has any with that attitude. Whoa! Get back in there." Brock scooped up the broom, darted around her. "No wonder he got out, there's a hole in the pen."

By the time she turned around, Brock had the broom clamped over the hole. The rooster flapped his wings and crowed, but at least he wasn't going anywhere.

"That's weird." Brock knelt, inspected the wire.

"What?"

"It's been cut. With wire cutters." He ran his fingers along the slit. "See how it's crimped—dull wire cutters do that."

"Why would someone cut the wire?"

"I have no idea. But probably for the same reason they'd bring a live trap full of mice to the cabin."

"Huh?" She shuddered. "Someone opened the trap you set?"

He told her about the extra trap and chasing the man he'd dubbed Ball-Cap into the woods.

"He broke in?" Her voice cracked. "Do you know who he was?"

"I couldn't get a good look. He was too far away. But I don't know many folks around here, anyway."

"So someone's been bringing mice to the fishing

cabin. And they cut the wire, so the rooster would get out. Why would anyone do that?"

"I'm not sure. But once I get this wire fixed, we need to tell Chase. Can you hold the broom while I find something to repair the hole?"

"Sure." She took the broom from him. As soon as he stepped away, the rooster flapped at the hole. But she kept him at bay.

Brock hurried back with a spool of wire and cutters. He threaded the wire to make a seam across the hole, with the rooster flogging the broom through the whole procedure. By the time the repair was finished, she was shaking.

"That should keep him." He raised up, took the broom from her. "Hey." His hands settled on her shoulders. "You okay?"

"I just don't know who would want to hurt Landry and Chase. She can't handle this."

"We won't tell her. But Chase has to know someone has it out for this place. Maybe he'll know who we're dealing with. Or it could be teenagers playing pranks. Whoever it is, we'll get to the bottom of it. And it'll be okay." He squeezed her hand.

Gentle, calloused palm. Soothing, comforting. And suddenly, the effect the cowboy's touch had on her was much more worrisome than dude ranch hijinks.

Chapter Four

"We can't tell Landry about this." Chase paced the office.

"That's why we asked to talk to you alone." If only Brock could take away his friend's stress. But instead, he was adding to it.

"What about a competing dude ranch?" Devree picked at her nails. "Any owners capable of pulling something like this to steal business?"

"No. The other owners are stand up people. They might undercut our prices, but not purposely try to sabotage us. I can't imagine anyone I know doing this."

"Anyone got a bone to pick with you?" Brock pressed on. They had to figure this out. "An ex-employee maybe?"

Chase snapped his fingers. "There was a ranch hand. Nash Porter. I fired him shortly after Landry and I met. A real troublemaker."

"Is he still around these parts?" He glanced at Devree.

Fiddling with her phone? Was she trying to play it calm, ease Chase's worries?

"He's in jail." She caught his gaze.

"He is? How do you know?" Chase zeroed in on her.

"I just googled him. Assault and battery, stemming from a bar fight."

"I'm not surprised." Chase tunneled his fingers through his hair. "There's no one else I can think of. Here's what we're gonna do. Not a word to Landry. I'll have the locks changed for the cabin. Only y'all get keys. No one else."

"I'll change them out today."

"And I'm sorry about the rooster, Devree. He won't bother you again."

"I'm fine."

"You should have seen her. She handled him like a pro." Maybe she was tougher than she realized. And Brock was beginning to suspect she didn't hate the country as much as she thought she did. Trouble was— she'd probably never realize it.

Besides, his mom had toughed it out once. Then returned to the city just like Devree would.

"Come to supper with us tomorrow night, Brock. Landry's been wanting to have you join us."

"I reckon I'm always up for good grub."

"Six o'clock. But no talk of live traps or wire cutters or disgruntled saboteurs."

"My lips are sealed. But does that mean I can't tell about watching this one run from Rusty?"

Chase chuckled. "As long as you don't mention how he got out."

"I bet y'all wouldn't laugh if his spurs were aimed in your direction." Devree's cheeks went pink, but her good-natured smile revealed only affection for her brother-in-law.

"You're right." Chase sobered. "He could have easily hurt you."

"No harm done. Except for two years he shaved off my life expectancy." She stood. "We better get to work. The hands are coming to move the old furniture out this morning."

"I emptied the interloper's live trap and reset both." He followed her lead. "Maybe the mouse population has decreased during our absence."

Devree closed her eyes for a second, then headed for the door. "Don't worry, Chase. We're on it. This wedding will go off without a hitch and the happy couple will have a pristine cabin ready for their honeymoon."

"I still think we should report it to the police." Brock adjusted his hat.

"No!" Chase cleared his throat. "It would get around town and Landry would hear of it for sure. Just keep an eye on things."

"Will do." Brock followed Devree out. The guy he'd chased into the woods worried him. But he wanted to keep an eye on Devree most of all. What if she'd gotten to the cabin first? Caught Ball-Cap in the act. He could have hurt her. Once they were outside, he grabbed her elbow.

She turned to face him with a puzzled frown. "What?"

"I'm going to the hardware store to get new locks. I don't want you going to the cabin alone."

"Trust me, I won't. Too many mice for my comfort." But her attempt to make light of the situation didn't disguise what he saw deep in her eyes.

Fear.

The dude ranch dining room was hopping with guests as the drone of multiple conversations filled the room. Typical Friday night. Devree sat in a secluded corner with Landry and Chase, as Brock gave a detailed recount of her bout with Rusty.

"I wish I could have seen it." Landry giggled. "I can't believe you got him back in the pen all by yourself."

Devree shrugged, as if her rooster wrangling was nothing. "You expected me to turn into a screaming ninny?"

"Well—yes."

It was good to hear her sister laugh, even if it was at her expense.

But then Landry frowned. "I wonder how he got out."

Devree's gaze met Brock's, then shifted to her brother-in-law.

"It doesn't matter how." Chase refolded his napkin. "It can't happen again. What if he'd gone after a guest? Or a child?"

"I guess you're right." Landry groaned. "But he's the prettiest rooster I've ever seen. I hate to part with him."

The kitchen doors opened and Chase's parents entered, headed their way with his chef dad carrying a covered roasting dish.

"What's this?" Landry's hand went to her chest. "I thought we were having buffet along with our guests."

"We always try our new dishes out on family." Chase's dad, Elliot, took the lid off with a flourish to reveal a large Thanksgiving-worthy turkey.

"Brock, I'm so glad you're back." Chase's mom, Janice, squeezed his shoulders. "We always thought the world of you. And your folks."

"Thanks. It's good to be back." There were so many mixed emotions on his face Devree wasn't sure she could keep up. A frown marred his brow, and she could tell his smile was forced. But his pale green eyes shone with happy memories. He seemed genuinely glad to be here, but jumpy as if he expected Becca to pounce on him at any minute.

"We'll leave you to your meal. I'll need honest opinions." Elliot wiped his hands on his apron, headed back to the kitchen, Janice trailing him.

"What were we talking about?" Landry frowned.

"Rusty." Chase picked up the large carving knife and fork, started to work on the bird. "I've already taken care of it. He won't bother anyone else around here."

Devree's gaze dropped to the bird as Chase made a deep slice across the breast. On it's back, all fours in the air. *Why would Elliot try a new turkey recipe so far away from Thanksgiving? Or was it Rusty?* Her eyes widened.

As Chase doled out slabs of meat, her appetite fled.

"Give me your plate, Devree." Chase held a large slice of meat between the carving set.

Mute, she shook her head.

"Are you okay? You look rather pale." Landry touched her hand.

"I can't eat him." Her vision clouded. He may have been mean, but she hadn't wanted him to die.

"Who?"

"I can't eat a rooster I knew by name."

Chase guffawed. "I can assure you, this isn't Rusty. It's turkey."

Her eyes met his. "You promise?"

"It's turkey." Landry squeezed her hand. "Rusty may

be ornery, but he's much too pretty to eat. What did you do with him, Chase?"

"I gave him to the Whitlows. He's alive and well and far enough away you'll be able to sleep in tomorrow morning."

A relieved sigh whooshed out of her.

"Can I have your plate now?" Chase grinned.

She lifted her plate to accept the slice of meat as he lost his struggle with laughter. Again, at her expense. But she joined him. Soon Landry and Brock did too.

Appetite returned, she bowed her head as Chase prayed over the meal. Amens rounded the table and she muttered hers.

"The vegetables are on the buffet." Chase picked up his and Landry's plates, headed that way.

Devree caught Brock's gaze as she stood. She saw something different in his eyes—respect maybe?

Whatever it was made her pulse kick up a notch.

Dread weighed heavy on Brock's shoulders as he folded his napkin, set it by his plate. At least Chase and Landry hadn't harangued him about his mom during the meal. Or invited her to join them.

Though he'd have been more at ease if they hadn't included Devree. He couldn't seem to escape her presence and she always did a number on his peace of mind.

It was nice to see Chase's parents again. They'd always been such nice and welcoming folks. And the meal was mouthwatering. He thought of the moment Devree was sure the turkey was Rusty and almost lapsed into another bout of stomach-cramping laughter. How could a woman be so empathetic she didn't want to eat a rooster who'd tried to impale her?

"I don't mean to rush, but I need to get this lady back to her couch." Chase rose to his feet.

"Don't mind me." Brock picked up his hat, scooted his chair out. "That was the best meal I've had in some time. Is it always buffet here?"

"It depends on how many guests we have. When we're heavily booked, buffet is easier. I sure miss the kitchen." Landry stared longingly at the doors. "Your parents could probably use my help."

"They're fine." Chase scooped her up.

A few guests smiled; no one seemed to think it odd to see a pregnant woman carried out.

"I'll break your back." Landry giggled as Chase walked toward the foyer with her cradled in his arms. "Hey, Brock, don't run off. Join us in the great room."

He'd have loved to come up with an excuse. He was afraid, despite their deal, they'd bring up his mother. For that matter, if he went back to his bunk, he could avoid running into her. But he worked for the Donovans. He couldn't really refuse their offer.

"Sure. I'll get the door." Brock opened the double doors into the lobby. Chase carried his wife through.

As Devree trailed them, she glanced back at Brock. Her rich blue dress matched her eyes, caused his breath to stutter.

Landry smacked Chase in the chest. "If I could eat laying down, you'd make me, wouldn't you?"

"Whatever it takes." The seriousness in his tone silenced her protests.

She patted her stomach. "We're fine. Don't worry."

He set her down—oh, so gently—on the couch. The

care and love in his eyes reminded Brock of just what was at stake. Making the situation with his mother seem trivial.

"Happy Trails" started up, Chase's ringtone. He dug his phone from his pocket, sighed and turned it off.

"Who was it?"

"That real estate developer. You'd think as many times as I've rejected his call, he'd realize he's barking up the wrong tree. This place has been in my family for decades." Chase took his place at the end of the couch with Landry's feet in his lap. "How's the fishing cabin coming?"

Despite Chase's attempt to change the subject, Brock's brain was stuck on the real estate developer. Took him back to his days of hounding landowners during his short-lived and ill-fated business partnership.

"It's overrun with mice." Devree clamped a hand to her mouth, cut her gaze to Landry. "But we're handling it."

"I won't faint." Landry rolled her eyes. "I can handle the truth. I just don't understand where they're coming from. It's like somebody's trucking them in or something."

Devree's gaze met Brock's.

"I caulked all the plumbing, around the windows and doors, and underneath the baseboards and trim. With it airtight, we'll conquer them." And changed the locks so Ball-Cap couldn't bring in more. "We got the old furniture out today. That should help."

"I'm so glad you're here." Landry plumped her pillow. "I have to admit, I was getting worried."

"We'll have the cabin ready. I promise." Devree sat

down in a cowhide wingback chair. "I got the curtains and bedspread today and the furniture will be here next week. I got some wall decor for the chapel too." Her focus went to the coffee table.

Brock settled in the matching chair and followed her gaze to an architectural magazine with a picture of him on the cover. An article from long ago. The city girl reporter had flirted with him mercilessly, tagging him "the cowboy carpenter," and made a big deal about him wearing a Stetson instead of a hard hat. He'd built luxury cabins for wealthy clients all over Texas back then. A lifetime ago.

"Why did you stop building your cabins?" Chase gestured to the magazine. "The article's quite impressive."

His mouth went dry. He didn't want to get into the fiasco with Phoebe. And her father. "I went into partnership, tried to go on a grander scale, but it didn't work out."

"I wish we could afford your cabins here." Landry rolled onto her side. "I'm afraid ours probably seem beneath you."

"They're cozy and perfect for a vacation. Besides, I'm happy to be here. To help out a friend." He was. He just wished he wasn't constantly distracted by Devree and her pretty blue eyes. And his mother lurking about somewhere on the premises weighed heavy on his mind. He stood. "I appreciate y'all inviting me to supper, but I think I'll turn in."

"Glad you could make it. Eat in the dining room anytime you like. On the house."

"I don't mind paying."

"We know. But you're getting us out of a major bind. The least we can do is feed you."

"Good night, then." He headed for the exit. The night sounds—frog's croaks, cricket's chirps, horse's whinnies—tugged at him. He'd sat on the porch swing many a night with his dad. He knew he should get going, back to his room. But as housekeeper, his mom should be long gone by now. He could sit a spell.

Closing his eyes, he settled on the swing. Old spice cologne and tales of the day's handyman chores filled his memory. His dad's calloused hands gentle, his voice low. Brock leaning his cheek on his dad's arm. He'd often fallen asleep in the swing, then awoken in his bed the next morning.

The door opened and he became instantly alert. Surely, not his mom. He stiffened, then quickly relaxed as Devree stepped outside. Gasping when she spotted him.

"Sorry, I didn't know you were out here."

"I didn't mean to be."

"I love sitting on the porch swing at night."

He scooted to the end, patted the slats beside him. "Feel free."

She hesitated a moment, but headed his way in the end. The swing barely shifted with her slight weight.

"I don't know why I like it out here." She shuddered. "There's probably snakes lurking. Or bats. Or bears for that matter. Maybe even a man with wire cutters. But I feel safe so close to the house and I love the night sounds. You don't get that in the city."

"I imagine not."

"And the stars are so bright here. So many of them."

He scanned the horizon, ashamed he often took the

stars for granted. The black curtain sprinkled with sparkling flecks spread for miles. "So, why do you stay there?"

"It's where I belong. It's nice to visit the country—hear the sounds, experience the slowed-down lifestyle—but I could never live here. I'd be bored to tears."

Her statement was a good reminder. For a short time, they'd work together. Then they'd go their separate ways. "I could never live anywhere else."

"Do you think we put Landry's mind at ease? With my blurting out the mouse issue."

"She seemed relieved." The swing had almost stopped and he pushed off with his boot. "Just wish she wasn't right about someone trucking mice into the fishing cabin. Maybe I scared him off and the mice will be gone in the morning."

"Where do you even find so many mice?"

"Good question. Maybe the city dump."

"We should go there, ask around, see if anyone's been setting traps."

With the renewed swaying, a waft of apples caught his senses. "What are you, a detective?"

"I just want this craziness to end. If we don't get rid of the mice before the Brighton/Anderson wedding, it'll be a disaster."

"The cabin's caulked as tight as a storm shelter and the locks have been changed. I think the mice invasion is over."

"Maybe so. But if someone's trying to sabotage the dude ranch, they'll come up with another way. He broke into the cabin." The quiver in her voice tugged at him. "What if the ranch house is next?"

"The last thing we need is you playing amateur detective. We don't know what kind of person we're dealing with here. Leave it to Chase and me to ask questions or do any investigating. Understood?"

"Will you please talk Chase into calling the police?"

"I'll do my best." He pushed to his feet. "See you in the morning."

"First thing."

With all his worries over his friends and her reminder that she was a city girl through and through, why did he feel so pulled toward Devree? Despite the warm night, a chill settled in deep. He had absolutely nothing in common with her. He'd better tread carefully.

"Are they gone?" Devree peeked through the cracked door into the fishing cabin.

"There were five in the live trap and no extra traps." Brock scanned the living room. "I haven't seen any movement, so maybe."

Tentatively, she stepped inside, arms loaded with draperies.

"I told you I'd help with those." He grabbed the bundle from her with a grimace. "What is all this?"

His spicy cologne in her space. "Curtains."

"Men don't like curtains."

"Women do."

"Do they have to be flowered?"

"It's a honeymoon cottage."

"You're forgetting the cabin part. These timbers and caulking are rustic. You can't put flowered curtains up."

"This is shabby chic decor, which is considered rustic." She pulled up a picture on her tablet of floral wingback chairs paired with a cowhide rug against hardwood and log walls. "And you didn't complain about the ones in the bedroom."

"They're white and you can put as many cowhide rugs down as you want, but men don't like flowers." He wasn't being argumentative, just passionate.

"I can't do the whole place in white. It'll be—" she searched for the right word "—monotonous. Besides, Landry approved these curtains."

"Of course, she did. She's a woman. I bet Chase would balk if he saw them."

"You really think it's that important?"

"The wedding's all about the bride. The groom parades around in a penguin suit she picked out with a flower on his lapel and some girly-colored cockamamy vest." He covered his ears with both hands. "He's spent months hearing about bouquets, colors, cake flavors and designs. At least let him feel like a man in the honeymoon cottage."

Did his strong opinion on the subject come from experience? Had Brock been married? Whatever his story, his plea made sense. It really shouldn't be all about the bride.

"You know—you may have a point." She dug her phone out of her pocket, punched in Landry's number.

Her sister answered on the second ring. "Boredom 101 here."

"Hey, sis. Brock thinks the flowered curtains don't fit in the cottage and that I should try to incorporate male tastes too. What do you think?"

"That actually makes sense. But it can't be too manly. It's a honeymoon cottage."

"Agreed. But if we put our heads together, we could come up with a balance of feminine and masculine, so the bride and the groom will feel comfortable. Maybe Brock could go to Rustick's with me and give me some pointers."

He shook his head, held his palms toward her as if warding off a blow.

"I like that idea." Landry sounded entirely too pleased. Probably getting ideas about fixing her up with Brock. "Just don't go too masculine. No dead animals and such."

"I'll send you pictures of our choices, get your approval."

"I'll be here."

Devree ended the call.

"I don't shop."

"You're done caulking and Landry thought it was a great idea. And you'll love this store. It's all log furniture and deer antler chandeliers."

"And flowered curtains."

"We'll see what else she has. Landry's counting on you."

"You just had to throw that in there, didn't you?" He glanced down at the bundle of flowered curtains he held. "I reckon I'll go if it'll get these back where they came from."

"Come on, I'll drive."

"If it's all the same to you, I'd rather drive us in my truck."

"Whatever makes you feel manly."

With a chuckle, he followed her out, double-checked that the new lock clicked in place. Why had she suggested they ride together? They could have met at Rustick's in separate vehicles. Now she'd be stuck in his truck with him.

Him and his spicy cologne, enigmatic green eyes, cleft chin and dimples that came out of nowhere. What had she been thinking subjecting herself to all that in close quarters?

Chapter Five

❧

Saturday morning in town meant extra car and human traffic—vehicles whizzed by and pedestrians clogged the sidewalk. Faded logs notched together at the corners lined the exterior of the store, large windows flanking the glass doors—Rustick's seemed like Brock's kind of place.

An older gentleman sat on a long church pew in front of the store, carving a walking stick with a knife.

"Why, Jed Whitlow—" Devree plopped down beside him "—you're just the guy I need to see."

Jed shot her a wink. "Why's that, Ms. Devree?"

"Does your grandson still work at the landfill?"

Brock's hackles went up. He nudged her foot with his, a subtle reminder she shouldn't be doing the detective-thing.

"Sure does." Jed puffed his chest up. "He's a senior in college. Almost got 'er wrapped up."

"This is my friend, Brock McBride. He's thinking about getting a pet boa constrictor."

Clever. Not what he'd expected. Brock relaxed a bit.

"Sweet. I've always wanted one, but the missus would move out if I came home with one."

"Marilyn is a wise woman." She laughed. "I was thinking if Brock gets his snake, he might be able to get free food for it from the landfill while taking care of an environmental issue at the same time. Do you think they'd let him bring a live trap to catch mice for the snake's supper?"

"I can check with him. I reckon Steven would have to ask his boss, but he could probably fix you up with rats yea big." Jed spread his hands apart ten inches or so. "I don't think anybody would mind getting rid of them."

She closed her eyes, for just a second. "Ask Steven. But make sure Brock wouldn't be cutting into anyone else's territory. There might be someone else catching rodents at the landfill to feed a pet snake."

"I doubt anybody else would ask. They'd probably just sneak on the property at night and set their traps."

"Tell Steven not to say anything to his boss just yet." Brock gave Jed an eye roll. "My girlfriend's not sold on it. But thanks for your help."

Jed's knowing gaze pinged back and forth between them. "Anytime."

"See you around." Devree waved.

Brock opened the door to Rustick's and she stepped inside.

"What did you go and do that for?" she whispered, punching him in the shoulder. "Now he thinks I'm your girlfriend."

"I didn't say that. I was just coming up with a reason the kid shouldn't say anything to his boss." He shrugged. "If it gets around that we're asking about live traps, our culprit might hear we're trying to track him down. And besides—" he waggled his eyebrows at her "—would it be so horrible to be my girlfriend?"

"We barely know each other, we have nothing in common and we're both only here for a short time."

His chest deflated. Though he'd been convincing himself of the same thing, using those same reasons, hearing them come from her, hurt. And now that he'd put the question out there and been shot down, he had to play it off as a joke. He clutched his heart in dramatic fashion. "You wound me, fair lady."

She huffed out a sigh, and he tried to focus on their surroundings as opposed to her obvious lack of interest.

Man-cave paradise greeted him. A treasure trove of log furnishings. More than Brock could take in. But not enough to keep his mind off of Devree's words.

A slender woman stepped toward them with two little girls.

"Hi, Brock."

He looked down. Ruby. His gaze bounced up to the woman. Long light brown hair, kind gray eyes.

"I'm Scarlet Miller." She stuck her hand out and he clasped it. "I'm so glad you're here." Her smile was genuine. "I mean in Bandera."

"Thanks." He tried to keep it casual.

"This is my friend, Cheyenne." Ruby fought for his attention.

"Hi, Cheyenne." He glanced down at the dark-haired child with her.

"Come give me a hug before you go." A brunette woman scurried from the back of the store, knelt to Cheyenne's level. "You be good and use your best manners."

"We always enjoy having her." Scarlet took both girls

by the hand, but her interest returned to him. "Well, we won't keep you. But maybe you could come over for supper while you're here. I'd love for you to meet Drew, my husband."

"Thanks for asking. We'll see." Code for no. But a kinder way of putting it. "Nice meeting you." He opened the door for them.

"You too." Scarlet tugged the girls outside as Ruby waved goodbye.

"You brought the curtains back." The brunette sounded as if she'd expected it.

Devree introduced Brock and his position at the dude ranch. "He's helping get the fishing cabin ready for our honeymooners. He doesn't think the groom will like flowered curtains."

"I tried to tell you." The brunette propped her hands on her hips.

"You did. I should have listened." Devree turned to him. "This is Resa McCall, Landry's neighbor, friend, Rustick's owner and furniture designer."

"Your little girl looks just like you."

"Actually, she's my niece. But I just got engaged to her father." She winced. "It's not as weird as I just made it sound."

Sounded as complicated as his life. He'd just met his stepsister for the first time, though she'd been part of his family for twelve years.

"I'm behind." Devree grabbed Resa's left hand, inspected the sparkler gracing her ring finger. "When did this happen?"

"Just last weekend." Resa flashed a smile even brighter than the diamond. "Anyway, it's nice meeting you, Brock. What are we looking for?"

"Something not too feminine, not too masculine. A nice balance of both." Devree scanned the store.

"I've got the perfect thing. We just got a new line in from Dallas, the Burlap-and-Lace collection." Resa led them to the left side of the store where numerous draperies hung.

A few flowers, but mostly wildlife and horse designs. Devree must have worked hard to find the ones she'd bought.

"We have four different designs." Resa pulled curtains from the display rods, held one up for them to see.

Brock grimaced at the large burlap panel lined by a wide strip of lace. "Still too frilly. No offense."

"None taken." Resa held up the next choice.

"Too burlap." Devree shot down the panel with a thin band of lace.

"Next." Resa held up another.

"Not bad." Brock inspected the curtain, intermixed with broad strips of burlap and narrow lace. No flowers or ruffles.

"You could feel like a man with these?"

"They're tolerable."

"Good." Devree smiled. "I like them too."

"I didn't say I liked them. If it were up to me, I'd say no curtains."

"Good thing it's not up to you. Let's see the last choice."

Resa held up another curtain, glancing back and forth between them with a grin that said she knew something they didn't.

Burlap with a ruffle at the top and a band of white at the bottom with holes in it.

"Oh, I love the eyelet trim at the hem," Devree

gushed. "These would be great in the kitchen. And maybe the bathroom. Do they come in café style?"

"They do. And I have a shower curtain to match."

"What do you think?" Devree turned to him.

"Bearable." Though he felt his man card slipping a bit out of reach.

She rolled her eyes.

"What? I like them better than the flowery ones you brought back."

"Okay, I'll take the mix for the living room and the eyelet for the bathroom and kitchen."

For the next several minutes, the two women dug through the shelves to find the right size for each curtain, then stacked their finds in Brock's arms.

"So how's Landry?" Resa's brow furrowed.

"Bored to tears. But I think her stress level is down since Brock showed up and the cabins are coming along nicely."

"I wish I had more time to spend with her. But with the store and my designs, my hunky fiancé and now a wedding to plan…" Resa sighed. "There just isn't enough time in the day."

"She knows you've got a lot going on."

"But I shouldn't be too busy for my dearest friend. Hey, I know—we need to set up a meeting for wedding planning."

"Do you have a date in mind?"

"We're hoping for the third weekend in June."

"This June?"

"Please tell me you're available. Do not make me wait any longer to marry that man of mine."

Brock strolled through the store as the ladies hashed out their schedules. Why couldn't he have someone to love, someone who couldn't wait to marry him? Because he kept going after the wrong women.

Despite his mother's abandonment and Phoebe dumping him, he'd always longed for a family of his own. One like he'd had before his father's passing.

"Okay, got you on my calendar." But the smile Devree gave her friend wasn't real. She obviously, truly wasn't into weddings anymore. Why? He'd like to know what had soured her on her chosen profession. Though he couldn't dwell on why he cared.

"Let's do our wedding discussing at the dude ranch with Landry included. I mean, she is my maid of honor." Resa checked her phone. "What about May 18?"

"She'd love that." Devree grabbed Resa's hand, gave it a squeeze. "Let's surprise her. But wait. You want to meet on May 18 to plan a wedding for June 16?"

"We don't want all the hullabaloo. As long as I have my groom and a photographer, I'll be happy. And Landry's holding the great room at the dude ranch and the dining room for me on that date."

"Okay, lunch on the eighteenth."

"Sounds great." Resa added more packages to Brock's pile of burlap. "That should do it. Take these to the counter for me."

Brock did as he was told and Resa bagged the curtains. How had this become his life—shopping for curtains and wedding discussions? By hanging out with a city-girl wedding planner, that's how. He could suffer through it for Chase and Landry.

"These actually cost a little less than the floral draperies. I'll figure out the difference and send Chase the updated invoice."

"Thanks, Resa. See you on the eighteenth."

Brock grabbed both enormous bags, opened the door for Devree.

"I can take one of those."

"I've got them." He hurried to stash the bags in the back seat of his cab. By the time he climbed into the driver's seat, she was already in. "Getting hot." He started the engine, turned the air on full blast and maneuvered into the flow of traffic on Main Street.

"I'm glad we did this. The new curtains fit the cabin much better than the ones I originally chose. Thanks to you, hundreds of grooms will be happier." The last bit held a note of sarcasm.

"What do you have against grooms?"

"It's not so much the grooms." She closed her eyes. "It's the whole wedding thing."

"But you're a wedding planner."

"Event planner." Her gaze went past him, off into the distance. "It's more the marriage part that gets me. They don't seem to last."

"Some do." He stopped at the only red light. "So how'd you get into wedding planning, then?"

She huffed out a sigh. "Once upon a time, I was a romantic."

"But not anymore?"

"I went to my first wedding when I was twelve. My mom's cousin." A wistful lilt hung in her words. "Lace and flowers everywhere. I decided I wanted to spend my life creating stunning weddings. Making perfect days for brides without going overboard, without breaking the bank. Just a simple, beautiful day to remember and begin a marriage."

"What happened?"

"By the time I was putting together my fifth wedding, my second and third couples were filing for divorce." Her shoulders sagged. "After eight years, my divorce rate is at forty percent."

"That's not your fault. Focus on the sixty."

"I try." She lifted one shoulder. "But it's so discouraging. And I'm so jaded. Each wedding I plan now, I expect them to crash and burn in a few years. Or months. I just go through the motions."

"And never take the chance on love for yourself."

She met his gaze. "I don't see a ring on your finger."

"I haven't found the right girl." The right *country* girl.

"I hope it works out for you, but I wouldn't hold my breath."

"I know lots of happy couples. Look at Landry and Chase."

"Yes." She rolled her eyes. "But the first jerk she fell for dumped her at the altar. She had to get her heart broken before she met Chase."

"Still, she found him."

"Only after heartbreak." The dullness in her tone said she'd been there as well.

"Ever wonder if you're missing out?"

"No." She hugged herself. "I just want to get the Brighton/Anderson wedding done, see my niece or nephew born healthy and get back to my life. In Dallas." She sighed. "But now I'll have to come back for Resa's ceremony. At least it sounds simple and small."

The light turned green and he gassed it through the intersection.

"What about Resa's fella? Think they'll make it?"

"I've only met him in passing. I hope so."

Phoebe had left a bitter taste in his mouth for love.

But seeing Chase and Landry so happy gave him hope. And spending his days with the plucky wedding planner—turned decorator and aspiring event planner—had him thinking about a future he had no business entertaining. Especially not with her thoughts on love and her determination to get back to her beloved Dallas.

Devree peeked in the great room. Landry lay on the couch, flipping through a magazine with Chase nowhere in sight. She'd dreaded Sunday all week. For the first time since arriving in Bandera, she was on the rotation to go to church this morning. Maybe she could get out of it by offering to stay with Landry while Chase went.

"Hey, sis." She bustled into the room, sat in the wingback across from Landry's couch.

"Why aren't you getting ready?"

"For what?"

"Church. You're on the rotation this morning."

The Donovan family her sister had married into had been encouraging employees to take turns attending church services for years. "I thought I'd sit with you and let Chase go."

"No one needs to sit with me. It's only an hour. I'd love to go and I won't let you miss your chance."

"I really don't want to leave you here alone."

"I'm not alone. There are several of the staff here. And the chapel is a hop, skip and a jump away."

"I'd rather stay with you."

Landry's gaze narrowed. "Why don't you want to go?"

She'd have to spill. But Landry didn't need to stress

over her spiritual condition. Or a reminder of the reason. "It's been a while since I've been to church."

Landry looked at her quizzically. "Why?"

She couldn't let her sister know she hadn't been to church since seeing that tiny coffin.

A childhood hang up surfaced and she decided to go with that. "When we were teenagers, Mom and Dad planned all those wonderful family vacations and outings. But then some employee would get sick or quit, and we didn't get to go." A wave of guilt washed over her, but Landry didn't need to hear the truth.

"But you must realize that sick employees or unreliable ones aren't God's fault. That's just part of owning a business. And we got to spend plenty of time with Mom and Dad by tagging along to the store with them."

"I know. And as an adult, I realize how important the Christian bookstore is. They're getting to be almost extinct. But I figure after all this time of me being mad at Him and ignoring Him—" she ducked her head "—God must be done with me."

"Oh, Devree, how could you think that? God never gives up on anyone. He's just waiting for you to stop ignoring Him. All you have to do is ask for forgiveness. He's waiting right where you left Him."

Something inside her chest squeezed.

"When I moved here, after my first engagement ended so publicly, I was so mad and bitter I hadn't been to church in a while. But Chase's mom talked me into attending and all that anger began to melt."

"Last year, after our baby died, I thought I'd die too." Landry's chin trembled. "But God got me through it. Please don't try to wade through this world without Him."

Devree's vision blurred. What right did she have to be mad at God over Landry's tragedy, while her sister had chosen to lean on Him more fully?

"I won't. Not anymore." She swiped at a tear she hadn't even realized had fallen and stood. "I better go get ready."

Even though she hadn't told her sister the truth, she'd acknowledged it to God. And He'd heard her silent torment. She hurried up the stairs.

I'm sorry, God. I didn't have any right to get mad at You or ignore You. And it stops now. Peace replaced the pressure in her chest and suddenly she couldn't wait to get to church.

Brock was here at Chase's insistence. He wanted to be here. In the chapel on Sunday morning. But what if his mom was on this service's rotation schedule? He couldn't relax, and church should be the one place he could.

From his vantage point in the back pew, he could see that ranch employees and a smattering of guests made up the congregation. No sign of her. If he'd known she wasn't coming, he'd have chosen a closer pew.

Devree sat with Chase about halfway up. Looking way too pretty in her vivid purple dress.

Third row from the front, a child leaned over the back of the pew, staring at him. Ruby, with her hair done up in red ribbons. His gaze went to the woman beside her. Light brown hair, wavy. Slender shoulders. Scarlet. She whispered something to Ruby. The child promptly turned around and sat facing forward.

The man beside Ruby wore a typical western shirt, his arm across the back of the pew, hand on Scarlet's shoulder. Must be the husband, Drew. What were their supper conversations like these days? Did they discuss the black sheep stepbrother holding a grudge against dear sweet Becca? How had she managed to make him the bad guy when it had been all her?

At least she wasn't with them.

A thick, stocky man with a ruddy complexion stepped onto the stage behind the pulpit. "Good morning." Booming voice, perfect for preaching. "We're so glad you could be here with us. Turn to page fifty-four in your hymn book."

The piano started up—"I'll Fly Away." The old standard from his childhood brought a rush of good memories. Until he got that odd feeling. Someone was staring at him. He scanned the crowd.

Everyone seemed to be facing forward or looking at their hymn book and it wasn't the preacher. Brock's gaze went to the piano player.

His mom.

The words to the hymn stifled in his throat.

She gave him a tentative smile before her gaze went back to her music.

From adoring mom, to grief-stricken and neglectful, to drug addict, to remarried, stepmom, church pianist. His mom had certainly come full circle.

He didn't hear anything after that. None of the following hymns. None of the sermon. The man in front of him stood and he realized it was over. Down to the closing hymn and altar call. He rose to his feet as several people went up to the front, including Devree. The piano stopped, but the congregation kept singing. His mom descended the stage steps. He stiffened.

Would she approach him, make a scene? She knelt at the altar and he started breathing again.

The song wound down as people returned to their pews. Someone said a closing prayer. He was almost first out the door.

Heavy footfalls behind him. "Brock. Wait." The preacher.

Reluctantly, he stopped, turned around. "How do you know my name?"

The preacher's ruddy complexion was even redder with his exertion. "Ron Fletcher." He stuck his hand out and Brock clasped it. "I'm your, uh…your mama's husband."

Add preacher's wife to his mom's circle. He wanted to pull his hand away. But his manners wouldn't allow it.

"Look, son, I don't know what your relatives told you about your mama to turn you against her."

If this guy knew the truth, would he still be pleading her case?

"She's a good woman. Loves the Lord. Loves you like nobody's business. Cried many a night over you. Days too—like now. All worried you'll leave without talking to her."

"I'm staying until Chase finds someone else. Only because he's a friend and he needs me. But I don't think we have anything to discuss."

"Do me a favor?"

"Can't promise anything." Brock shoved his hands in his pockets.

"Give her a chance."

"Can't promise anything," he repeated and turned away.

"Just think about it."

How could he work here and continue to avoid his mother? Tell her to keep her distance or he'd bust her secret wide open? He wasn't into blackmail. But if he let her think he was, maybe that would keep her at bay.

He climbed in his truck, desperate for escape. But as he slowly maneuvered through the parking lot, past the church to the exit, he noticed Ruby standing at the glass door. Eyes locked on his, she waved.

Chapter Six

"Could you move it this way a bit?" Devree directed the Rustick's delivery guys on where to put the new couch. "Perfect. Thanks. And that's everything." She signed the work order, verifying she'd received each piece and the men left.

It was the last day of April, the week of the wedding. She was starting to feel the stress as the countdown to Saturday's nuptials began. Could they get everything ready in time? With some nut, trucking in mice?

"At least it's not flowery." Brock surveyed the furnishings.

"I thought the white fabric would brighten it up in here. I picked these up too." She placed a burlap-and-lace throw pillow at each end of the couch. "Can you help me hang the wall art?"

"At your service."

"This, centered above the fireplace." She held up the rustic window with four divided panes of glass to show him the right height, then stood back out of his way.

He used his drill to sink the screw and hung the window.

"What do you think?" She surveyed the piece. Curvy wooden letters painted pale aqua spelled out *Mr.* and *Mrs.* in catty-cornered panes of the window. A nice pop of color.

"The peeling paint of the frame balances the girly blue color. It's tolerable."

"This must be hard for you. From building designer cabins to seeing others doing the building while you end up playing interior decorator with me."

"I don't mind. Keeps me busy."

From the looks of that fancy magazine, he was quite talented. Not the country bumpkin she'd pegged him as at all. Humble and willing to put everything aside to help his friend. Appealing character traits. Not to mention the cute cowboy thing he had going.

"I'd like this over here." She picked up a galvanized windmill clock, held it where she wanted it. "Can you hold this and let me look from a distance?"

"Now, this I like. Nothing girly about it." He held it for her.

She took a few steps back. "A little lower and to the left. Right there."

Brock marked the spot, drove the screw into the wall.

"The great thing about logs, you don't have to worry about finding a stud."

"I saw you in church yesterday." He hung the windmill. "Guess we're on the same rotation."

"I think it swaps around." Should she broach the subject? It wasn't technically discussing his mother. "This was my first week to be on the rotation. I knew Ron was a military chaplain, but I missed the memo about him being the preacher here. If I'd known, I'd have warned you."

"He clued me in. I don't want to talk about it. What's next?"

Should have kept her mouth shut. "I thought this wreath would look nice here. It's made of vines from Grapevine, Texas and the cotton is grown locally too." She placed it on the wall where she wanted.

"Rustick's has some cool stuff." He took it from her.

She moved back. "To the right and lower. Perfect."

As he marked the spot, the door opened.

Devree turned around. Becca. Her breath stalled.

Brock glanced over, did a double take. "What are you doing here?"

"I was supposed to vacuum before the new furniture arrived." She looked around, bit her lip. "Guess I'm too late. But that's okay, I can move it and clean underneath."

"You know…" Devree tapped her chin with an index finger, as if she were thinking. "There was a clock made from a wooden electric spool at Rustick's. It would be perfect in the kitchen. I think I'll go back and get it. Maybe you can help Becca move the furniture?"

His mouth gaped, eyes begging her to stay.

"See you in a bit." Ignoring his silent plea, she backed out the door and shut it. She really had been thinking she should have gotten the other clock—but it could have waited. The conversation between mother and son, on the other hand, was a long time coming. Devree's legs shook as she got in her car. He'd be mad at her. But she cared about him—not in a romantic way, of course—about his well-being. Brock needed the only parent he had left, whether he realized it or not.

"How are you?"

"Busy." Brock bit the words out. "Five minutes and I'm out of here."

"Fair enough." She smiled sadly and said nothing more as she got the vacuum cleaner out of the closet.

Thoughts of bolting for the door tumbled in his gut, but the many questions he had running through his head prevailed. "Why are you here?" He splayed his hands. "I remember you badgering Dad—trying to get him to move. Before he was even cold in the ground, you dragged me to your beloved Dallas."

She jerked, as if he'd struck her. "I moved because I couldn't face the memories of your father here."

"But you obviously can now."

"I've learned a lot." Mom shrugged. "The city isn't all I thought it was and you can't run from problems. That's part of how I ended up—"

"On drugs. Abandoning your son."

"I didn't abandon you."

"You never picked me up from the babysitter."

"I was just so lost without your father. I wanted an escape." She covered her face with both hands.

"I guess I was a reminder of him you decided you could do without."

"No." She shook her head. "I never meant to leave you."

"But you did."

"No." She pressed her knuckles against trembling lips. "I'm ashamed to admit it." She closed her eyes. "I forgot where I left you."

"Forgot?" A twitch started up in his jaw muscle. "How could you forget where you left your kid?" he roared.

She jumped, tears streaming again. "Drugs." She lifted one shoulder. "I was so messed up and Mrs. Simons was a new sitter. I couldn't remember where her house was. And by the time I came down and could remember, I knew if I went to get you, they'd arrest me."

"So you just left me there?" He'd imagined she hadn't wanted him. That she'd have more money for drugs without him. Never that she'd forgotten where he was. People forgot where they left things. Their eyeglasses, their keys, their phone. Not kids. Not kids they loved, anyway.

"Mrs. Simons was a nice lady and I was such a mess. I figured you were better off with her." Her chin wobbled. "But I never forgot about you. I missed you so badly—as if I'd cut off a piece of myself."

"Not enough to come back for me."

"I wanted to. So much." Her voice broke. "You'll never understand unless you've been on drugs. I wanted my next fix more. And I knew if I went to jail, there wouldn't be another. I've been clean for fifteen years. You can ask my former parole officer if you don't believe me."

So in the end, she had chosen drugs over him. "Why didn't you try to find me?"

"You were a teenager by the time I got myself together, and I figured you hated me." Her chin trembled. "With just cause." Her cheeks reddened. "I got caught—ended up in jail—got parole by agreeing to enter a faith-based rehab program. I accepted Jesus as my Savior. Are you a Christian?"

"Yes." Thanks to Mama Simons. She was the one he should consider his mom. The best of his foster families—until Pop Simons's mother was diagnosed with Alzheimer's and Brock had to give up his room.

"Oh good." She let out a sigh.

"I'll move the couch and leave you to your cleaning."

"Please wait." She blocked his path. "Tell me about your life. I prayed so hard for you to have a good one. Hoped the Simons would adopt you."

He glared at her. "Didn't happen. She called child services the second day you didn't show and arranged to be my guardian, then went through the process to foster me. Until Grandma needed to move in. After that, I bounced from foster home to foster home. Some ditched me because I cried myself to sleep every night, some because they decided they wanted a dog instead of a kid. Eventually, I aged out of the system and I've been on my own since."

"I'm so sorry." Her voice took on a breathy quality. "But you built a successful business. Are you married?"

"No." He'd fallen for a girl in Austin once, almost married her, until she reminded him not to trust city girls. "How did you end up back here?"

"Once I got out of the program, no one would hire me. So I came back. Partly for a job, partly because I thought you might show up some day." She clasped the vacuum again. "Chase's grandmother was still alive then and let me have my old position back. I married Ron twelve years ago."

She nibbled her lip. "He's a wonderful man, as much in the dark about me as everyone else. I know I should have been truthful. But I was so ashamed and Granny said no one else needed to know. And once I started falling for Ron, I was so afraid he wouldn't love me if he knew everything. That he wouldn't want an ex-addict near his daughter."

"You better get back to work, so I can. Have Chase call me when you've finished." He moved the couch away from the wall, then bent to flip the vacuum she held on, effectively ending the conversation.

Her mouth opened, shut as the whine of the cleaner drowned out whatever she wanted to say.

He'd heard enough, anyway. It satisfied him immensely to walk out on her and slam the door.

Devree hesitated on the porch of the fishing cabin. Two hours had passed. Was Becca gone? Had she and Brock reconciled? Or had it out?

The door swung open. Brock stood there, grim-faced. "Don't ever do that to me again."

"I needed to get the clock. It's in the car. Kind of heavy. Can you—?"

"It could have waited." He stepped aside, ushered her in.

True. "But I wanted to get the kitchen done today. So how did it go? Did you and Becca talk?"

"Enough. If she ever shows up again, do not try to manipulate a reunion between us. If I ever decide I want to work things out with her, I'll do it. On my terms. And timing."

"Okay. I get it. I'm sorry. I was only trying to help." *Subject closed.*

"Just don't. I'll get the clock from your car, so we can get back to work." He hurried out the door.

She stared after him. How could she fix this? How were they supposed to work together if he was all mad and stiff?

The door opened and Brock strode in carrying the massive clock. Chase just a few steps behind him.

"Wow, this place is different." Chase looked around, a hint of sadness in his eyes.

"Don't worry." Devree hurried to reassure him. "All your grandfather's things are at the new house. What do you think?"

"I guess you had to girly it up some, but it's not too bad."

"So you approve?"

"Not too shabby. You've done a fine job."

"Brock was a big help. I initially picked floral curtains and throw pillows."

Brock gave no reaction to her praise. Still frowning, he focused on Chase.

"Nice save, Brock." Chase stepped into the kitchen, then the bedroom. "I just wanted to see the final result. And Landry wants me to take pictures."

"I think the mice are a thing of the past, thankfully." She rushed to cover Brock's silence. "While you're here, let me run an idea by you."

"What's that?" Chase took several pictures of the furnishings with his phone.

"I've been thinking of ways to promote my event planning when I get back to Dallas. I came up with a contest to bolster my services and then I thought of using the dude ranch as a venue. I could do a massive publicity campaign and have a drawing for a free company retreat here. With me as the event planner."

"After the baby?" Chase lowered his phone.

"Yes. You'd get publicity from the contest and retreat attendees would rent rooms. I can probably get florists and caterers I've worked with to donate services in exchange for exposure."

"Sounds feasible. I'll run it by Landry. And Mom and Dad might want to do the catering themselves."

"Great."

"My work is done here." Chase pocketed his phone. "I can't tell you what a load you've taken off Landry's mind, working together on this. She'll love what you did with the place."

"It's been kind of fun." Devree surveyed the room with pride. "I've never done anything like this, but we make a good team." She tried for eye contact with Brock, but he looked away.

Obviously, it wasn't fun for him. Not anymore, anyway.

Chase's gaze bounced from her to Brock. "You two getting along okay?"

"Well enough," Brock mumbled.

"Thanks for helping us out on this." Chase squeezed her shoulder, shook Brock's hand. "I know it's not really in either of your job descriptions."

"We've made it work," she promised.

Another curious glance between them and Chase left.

"Where do you want the clock?" All business. None of the warmth he'd shown Chase. Or the teasing connection they'd shared before she'd meddled in his mom situation.

"On the wall behind the kitchen table."

He stalked into the kitchen, obviously eager to wrap this up and escape her for the rest of the day.

Somehow, him being mad at her didn't sit well. As if she'd lost something...special.

Devree took the stairs two at a time down to the foyer, peeked in the great room. No Landry. She must be still asleep.

She had a meeting with the bride and groom at the bakery in town that shouldn't take long. Typical bride, considering a flavor change at the last minute. Miranda would probably end up sticking with her original choice.

After the cake consultation, she had a few finishing touches to make at the fishing cabin. And a tense cowboy to try to soothe. Maybe he'd be better today.

She slipped on her sunglasses and stepped outside. Cows. She gasped, clasped a hand to her chest. Half a dozen cows. Surrounding her car. Two of them licking her passenger windows.

Wearing a mustard yellow sundress and heels, she wasn't clad for herding cattle. Nor did she have time. And she wasn't a fan of getting up close and personal with cows. They were big and stinky, and she liked them a lot better when they were behind a fence.

But she couldn't bother Chase with this. And no one else was about. Yet, even if she could get them away from her car, she couldn't just leave them out.

At least they weren't longhorns. She drew in a deep breath, stepped purposely off the porch, waving her arms. "Shoo, shoo. Go back where you came from."

All six red-and-white faces turned her way. One bawled at her, but they didn't move. Two went back to licking her passenger side windows, leaving slimy tongue streaks from top to bottom.

"Shoo, shoo. Get back in your fence." She ran at them, but they paid her no mind. So she tried jumping up and down, waving her arms more frantically. "Come on, you stupid cows. I don't have time for this."

"Whoa. How'd they get out?" Brock rounded the ranch house.

"I don't know. They were just here when I came out."

"I'll get a feed bucket." He hurried toward the barn. Within minutes, he returned with a pail full of grains. One of the cows bawled, then headed in his direction. The others followed.

Brock backed to the gate, opened it, led the cows inside. Once all six were back in the fence, he fastened it.

"Thanks." She got in her car, started the engine. But the passenger windows were a streaky mess she couldn't see through. She jumped out, hurried toward the ranch house.

"Where are you going?" Brock jogged toward her. "I thought you had a meeting."

"I need something to wipe their slobber off with. I can't see out my passenger side."

"Get in your car. I'll take care of it." He rushed to his truck, came back with a spray bottle and blue paper towels. Quickly, he sprayed the window down and wiped it clear. "Go."

"Thanks. Again." She gave him her best smile, waved goodbye.

At least he wasn't so mad at her that he wouldn't come to her rescue. Maybe she'd offer to pay to have his cape dry-cleaned this time.

Five minutes later, she entered the bakery with time to spare.

"Devree." Miranda was as giddy as ever, with Joel's arm around her waist. If he couldn't care less about the wedding, he sure was putting on a good front.

"I hope you haven't been waiting long."

"Not at all. And you're early, anyway."

"Have a seat and I'll be with you in just a few." The owner waited on another customer.

"Thank you both for coming." Devree followed them to a table. "This is usually the most fun wedding prep meeting for the groom. Lots of cake flavors to taste. And you get to do it again."

"I've truly enjoyed all of it." Joel never took his eyes off Miranda. "It's meant I've gotten to spend time with the love of my life."

"Aww, isn't he sweet?" Miranda pressed her cheek against his. "Do you think we could see the honeymoon cottage since we're here? And maybe I could see those glass bell decorations you told me about."

"Sure." It was clean and ready minus a few wall decor items. And, hopefully, still mouse-free.

The couple stole a quick kiss.

And for some reason, this time, instead of gagging over their head-over-heels in love antics, Devree longed for what they had.

Brock reread the text from Devree.

Are you at the cabin? If so, is anything amiss? My bride and groom would like to see it while they're in town.

He'd replied that everything was fine. That didn't necessarily mean he had to stay. So, why was he still here? Because he didn't have anything else to do at the moment? He'd repaired the hole in the fence where the cows had gotten out. Reported the bad news to Chase— another fence cut. Adding to Chase's stress instead of detracting from it. He suggested it was time to call the police. His friend had promised to think about it.

In the meantime, one carpentry crew was hard at work completing the new house, another tackling the new honeymoon cottages and a demolition team was tearing down the old storm shelter by the chapel.

Sometimes he missed getting his hands dirty. This handyman gig wasn't enough to keep his mind busy. *Off of Devree.* Even with a fence-tampering vandal on the loose, he couldn't stop thinking about her. Despite their complete incompatibility and her interference with his mom yesterday, he was eager to spend the rest of his day with her. What was wrong with him?

He opened the door when he heard voices coming his way. Devree and the couple.

The sun set her hair on fire. The pretty mustard yellow sundress only accented her beauty.

"This is Brock, the handyman. And this is Miranda and Joel."

He forced his attention away from her and concentrated on the couple. He shook hands with Joel as they stepped up on the porch. "Nice to meet you."

"So is the cabin new?" Miranda frowned at the aged logs.

"It belonged to the owner's grandfather, but we recently updated the interior."

"Farmhouse decor." Miranda clapped her hands together. "I love it. It's so pretty."

"But still rustic. I like all the burlap." Joel looked around the living room.

Brock caught her gaze, gave her the tiniest smirk.

Her eyes narrowed. "You can thank Brock for that. I picked floral fabrics, but he gave me insight on the male perspective."

Nice. She gave credit where it was due. "I'll let you handle the rest of the tour. Good meeting y'all, and I'm glad you like what we've done here." He tipped his hat, headed out. He needed some air and to stop liking her so much.

"You like her, don't you?"

Brock stiffened at his mom's voice behind him. Definitely none of her business. He turned around, scowl firmly in place. "Who?"

"Devree. She's a sweet girl."

"Even if I did, she's too city."

"Opposites attract. Like your father and me. We made a great team."

"Our memories don't exactly line up. I remember you complaining about living on the ranch and causing arguments."

"All couples disagree sometimes." She leaned her elbows against the goat pen. "Your father and I loved each other. I was young and didn't appreciate this place then. But even with our issues, we were great together. You and Devree are too. I've watched you with her. You light up like a Texas sunrise when she's around."

"So, you're stalking me?"

"You make it sound so ominous. I can't help being drawn to my own flesh and blood."

He looked past her toward the barn. A cowhand turned away. Gossip traveled fast on a large ranch They were probably the hot topic at the moment.

"Please come to the chapel with me. Just to talk. Just for a minute."

He sighed. Might as well escape prying eyes. And besides, he had a feeling his mom wouldn't quit until he heard her out.

Chapter Seven

With the happy couple back on the road, Devree climbed up to the chapel loft carrying a box of glass bells.

The loft brimmed with lace, tulle and every other embellishment she'd accumulated over the years. She plopped down on the floor crisscross style. As she re-wrapped the fragile bells in packing paper, she heard the chapel door open, then two sets of footfalls before the door closed.

Her hands stilled. Maybe someone had come to pray. The sanctuary was open at all times and she'd been instructed that if she was decorating and guests arrived, she should leave them in peace.

But clambering down the ladder wouldn't be very peaceful. Staying put and quiet was best.

"We have nothing to talk about." Brock's words came out gruff.

Devree's jaw dropped.

"Please, Brock, I just want to spend time with you," Becca pleaded. "To get to know the man you've become."

"With no help from you."

Devree's face steamed. She shouldn't be hearing this. On the other side of the two rooms in the loft, a door led to an empty area with an open air window for pictures. Maybe she could bail without breaking a leg.

"I'm sorry I wasn't there when you were a child." Becca's voice broke. "When you needed me most. But I'm here now. Can't we build a relationship?"

"I'm not interested. As soon as Chase hires another handyman, I'm out of here."

He'd lost his father at the tender age of eight and had a falling out with his mother in the years since. His aloneness drew her to him. Made her hurt for him. The one thing she could always count on was family. How did people without that bond get through life's hard knocks?

Lord, help Brock and Becca repair their past hurts. Find their way back to each other. Thankfully, she'd repaired her relationship with God last Sunday. She knew for certain that He heard her now.

"I didn't come here to see you, and I'm not staying for you." Brock's angry tone jarred her from her prayer.

"Please, can't you forgive me?"

Silence echoed. Tension swirled. Devree looked at the door that led to the loft window. Maybe she could make it. A broken leg would be better than this.

"If you don't keep your distance," Brock growled, "I won't keep your secret."

"That will only work for so long." Becca sniffled. "I'm trying to work up the courage to tell Ron the truth. And eventually, I will. Until then, I'll respect your wishes."

"You do that."

The door closed.

Brock spewed out a sigh.

Okay, leave now. Stop this torment. Knowing there was a secret. Things she shouldn't know. And her right foot was going to sleep.

There was a movement near her knee. The glass bell rolled a slow circle, rustling the tissue paper. It got close to the edge of the stairwell. *Please stop!* If she reached for it, there would be more tissue rustling. In slow motion the bell reached the edge, teetered. And fell.

She closed her eyes in anticipation but there was no sound. No glass breaking. Impossible. She opened her eyes, leaned over to peer through the opening.

A large hand held the bell. "What are you doing up there?" Brock snarled.

"I'm sorry. I didn't mean to—Miranda asked to see the bells before they left. I was just putting them away when y'all came in." She scooted closer.

Stormy eyes as green as a prickly pear cactus met hers. "And decided to eavesdrop instead of letting us know you were there."

"I didn't know who came in. I thought it might be someone coming to pray, so I decided to be quiet and not disturb them." She stood, brushed the seat of her dress off. "I'll leave you alone. I can do this later." She descended the stairs, dreaded facing him.

At the bottom, she kept her gaze averted, started to sidestep him.

But he blocked her. Like a wall.

She slowly met his glower. "Before I forget to tell you, I saw Jed in town as I was leaving the bakery. His grandson doesn't know of anyone ever setting live traps at the landfill."

"For the record, I'm not blackmailing her." He closed his eyes. "I have no intention of telling anyone anything. I just want her to leave me alone."

"This is none of my business." She bit her lip. "But I've known Becca and Ron for a few years now. They're good people. Kind. And very happy. I'd hate to see them get hurt. She's your mother."

"A mother I haven't seen since I was ten years old."

Ten. Devree's eyes widened. What could sweet Becca have done to turn him against her?

"Haven't you ever needed a second chance?"

He looked past her, off in the distance. "I didn't know she was here." His tone dripped sarcasm. "I didn't come here to work through my mother-inflicted emotional baggage."

"Then what did you come for? And don't tell me the job. You could get a job anywhere."

Turbulent eyes zeroed in on her. "Every memory I have of my dad is here."

"He and your mom had a good relationship?"

"According to her. But I remember them arguing a lot about living here. My mom hated it—loved Dallas."

"Really?" She frowned. "Becca loves it here now. People change, you know."

"Sometimes for the worse."

"Sometimes for the better." She hesitated. Had probably said enough. "How do you think your dad would feel about it?"

He frowned. "About what?"

"Would he want you to give your mom another chance?"

His nostrils flared.

Definitely said enough. "Just think about it." She

scurried for the door, bolted for the ranch house. Away from his anger.

Two steps forward, five back where the brooding cowboy was concerned.

Something loomed just out of consciousness. It seared Brock's nose. Burnt rubber mixed with acrid sulfur. He woke to…the stench of skunk. Really close and inescapable. He threw his covers back. If only he didn't have to breathe. Was it in the barn?

Minutes later, fully dressed, he stepped out of his quarters. The cloying odor was closer to the ranch house. Great, just what guests wanted to wake up to. The reek worsened as he neared the fishing cabin.

Uptight voices sounded from the ranch house. Irate guests? Exactly what Chase and Landry didn't need. He headed that way.

"We can't possibly stay here." A snooty blonde aimed two children toward the drive.

"It'll die down by evening." Chase carried two suitcases. "You sure you don't want to stay? Spend the day in town and by the time you get back—"

"I don't think so." The woman shook her head.

"I'm sorry." An apologetic man, loaded with luggage, shrugged. "I grew up in the country, but the wife and kids, they're not used to waking up to skunk spray."

"Well, I hope you enjoyed your stay. Up until now, anyway."

"Don't worry, we'll be back."

The woman shot her husband a deadly look.

Poor guy.

Chase helped the man load the suitcases, still apologizing while the wife and children got in the car.

"It's not your fault." The man got in and drove away.

"Good news." A nasally voice came from the front porch. Devree, holding her nose. Pretty in a purple blouse and gray slacks. "The rest of the guests are staying. And your mom and dad are serving them a free breakfast for putting up with this rancid smell."

"The closer I got to the fishing cabin, the more it smelled," Brock reluctantly admitted.

Chase grimaced. "I hope it didn't have help finding its way in."

"I'll let you check it out." Devree went inside.

"Landry's upset." Chase rubbed the back of his neck. "She figures that woman will gripe to all her pretentious friends and we'll lose business."

"I think the lady failed to appreciate the charm of this place before the skunk ever sprayed. He just gave her a good excuse to get out of Dodge. I doubt she'd recommend the dude ranch to her friends, anyway."

"You're probably right."

"Go tend to Landry. I'll see if our offender is still around."

"Thanks." Chase headed inside.

Brock rushed to the fishing cabin, dug the key from his pocket. The stink was definitely worse here. The lock clicked and he opened the door, expecting to catch Pepé Le Pew in the act. But nothing seemed amiss. The smell was so potent that his eyes watered. Yet it wasn't inside. At least the striped suspect had moved on. Whoever their vandal was hadn't gotten past the new lock.

Devree had wanted to hang the final decor items today, and he still had two lighting fixtures to change out. But it would have to wait. If he couldn't stomach working here, she certainly couldn't. He'd report to

Chase, see if there was anything else to do for the day. He locked up, then hurried to the ranch house.

In the lobby, Devree paced, turned to face him when the door shut behind him. "The smell is nauseating Landry, and she's upset the Dawson family left. I think Chase is taking her to an inn in town until the stink dies down."

She may be a city girl with designer clothes and a persnickety attitude to prove it, sticking her nose in where it didn't belong, but she loved her sister. So, she couldn't be all bad.

"Chase will take good care of her. Don't worry."

"You're not mad at me anymore?"

"I figure Chase needs us to work together." He gave her a pointed look. "If you don't pressure me about *her* again, we'll be fine."

"Understood." She restarted her pacing. "The skunk wasn't in the fishing cabin, was it?"

"No. But it definitely sprayed outside there. No mice, either. I think we need to start calling it honeymoon cottage A."

"Agreed. For now. Eventually, Landry and Chase will come up with cutesy names for each like the guest rooms have."

"I'm assuming the finishing touches we planned for the day are out. Anything I can do around here to ease Chase's mind?"

"I need to put up a few permanent decor items in the chapel. You can help with that, if you want."

"At your service." He tipped his hat. Though he'd hoped the skunk would have allowed him to escape her for the day. He was better off mad at her. At least that way, she couldn't reel him in. But with a truce, all bets were off as far as his heart was concerned.

"The wall decor is in my car."

He followed her out and unloaded six stacked boxes from her back seat.

"I can carry some of them."

"I'm good." He bumped the car door shut with his hip.

"The wedding party arrives in two days for the rehearsal. Do you think this smell will be gone before then?" She opened the chapel door, held it for him. "What if he has friends. Or he likes it here and decides to stick around. Is there anything we can do to keep skunks away?"

"Maybe a dog. Or a cat."

"I'll google it." She swiped the screen on her phone, then tapped in her request. "Ugh. It says dog urine deters skunks. And orange peels. Interesting."

"Maybe we should check with Chase about a dog. And he already agreed to a cat to help with the mice. Initially, I think they were getting in on their own, so a cat would encourage them to hang out somewhere else."

"He's supposed to call later once he gets Landry settled in town. I'll mention it to him." She opened one of the boxes, pulled out a chapel-window-shaped frame with decorative metal scrollwork in the center. The finish looked chipped and weathered, yet the surface was smooth.

"There are three different designs. I want two matching ones at the front, framing the stage, one on each side in the center and two in the back, framing the door."

"Just tell me which ones where."

From building luxury cabins to interior decorating.

Whatever it took to help Chase. But Devree made the whole thing too pleasant. How had she gotten to him with her city-slicker ways? She was everything he'd sworn off, everything he didn't want.

As soon as Landry had the baby, Devree would be gone. Back to her beloved Dallas. He had no business getting used to having her around. Yet being near her set his heart to a different rhythm.

In the loft, Devree organized her decor items, so she could quickly whip the chapel into shape. The skunk had complicated things. They were supposed to finish the cottage today. Now, they'd be busy with it tomorrow, cutting into her wedding decor time.

Maybe she could put in some hours here after tonight's Bible study to get back on schedule. Besides, the smell wasn't as intense here as in the ranch house. Or was she getting used to it?

A loud thwack. She jumped, hurried down the ladder, scanned the expanse of green beside the chapel. Brock putting up a fence post. Right in the middle of where the outdoor reception needed to be held. Right where she planned to set up for photos for the wedding. Chase had never wanted to host weddings here, but she'd thought he was on board.

"What are you doing?" She stalked toward Brock, heels stabbing into the damp freshly sprinkled earth with each step.

He raised up, adjusted his cowboy hat. Eyes so intense she wanted to look away. "Building a fence for the petting zoo."

"No. No. No. Not right here. This is where I'll have outdoor receptions and photo sessions. I have an extremely important wedding in two days and I can't have smelly animals fouling up everything."

"I reckon you'll have to take it up with the boss man." A stubborn glint in his eyes.

At odds with the cowboy handyman. Again. "You don't understand how important this wedding is. If I ace this ceremony, it could secure my nuptial-free future."

"How's that?"

"The bride's father owns Brighton Electronics. If I impress him with a dream wedding for his daughter, he might hire me to plan his annual company retreat."

"So?"

"So. Something like that could put me on the event-planning map. And I wouldn't have to do weddings anymore. But not if Heidi the Heifer and Daisy the Donkey are stinking up everything."

Brock took off his hat, wiped his brow with the back of his gloved hand. "Chase's work order says to build it here so drive-by traffic can see it and kids will clamor to stop."

Hat head took nothing away from tall, dark and dimpled, even if he didn't get her dilemma.

"We need to postpone it. Until I can talk sense into Chase."

"So I reckon I need to pull this post up."

"Could you fill the hole too? And pack it hard enough, so no one breaks an ankle during the reception."

"Will do." He pulled the post up, threw it aside, then grabbed the shovel and went to work scooping the dirt back into the hole.

She hadn't meant to cause him extra work. But nothing and no one would stand between her and one perfect ceremony. Besides, such decisions needed to revolve around the newly constructed chapel and the dude ranch's future as a wedding venue. Even after she left.

"I'm sorry, Brock." She hoped he heard the sincerity in her tone. "Feel free to give me your best jab about women complicating everything."

"No worries. I'd rather it get built in the right place. And there's no rush. With the cottage on hold, I figured it was a good time to work on the pens. It doesn't even have to be done today."

Chase pulled his truck in the drive.

She vaulted toward him as he got out of the cab. "Is Landry all right?"

"The nausea stopped a few miles away. She's safety tucked in and sleeping at the inn with Mom."

"Why are you here?"

"I was in such a rush to get her away from the smell, I didn't pack a thing."

Devree's heart tugged. Sweet Chase—so tender, caring and totally in love with her sister. One of those rare marriages that would last.

If her sister could find lasting love, could she?

"What's going on by the chapel?"

She sucked in a deep breath, blew it out and explained the situation, careful to keep her tone unflustered.

"That can't possibly work. I thought the petting zoo was going near the goat pens."

The pressure in Devree's chest eased. "Good. I can assure you brides don't want stinky animals involved when their guests arrive."

"Valid point. Even at a dude ranch." Chase tunneled

his fingers through his short hair. "I guess I was distracted."

"We'll figure it out." Brock strode toward them. "I was just gonna work on it while I had time. But I'll find something else to do."

"Actually, it's a good time. The miniature horses need a pen instead of a stall in the barn."

"If you want it seen from the road, it could go on the other side of the drive." Brock pointed to a tree-lined spot. "We could use that less dense area. Maybe take out three trees. Four, tops."

"We had an oak wilt scare year before last, thought we might lose our trees. Neither of us can stand to think of cutting them down."

"What about back a ways, so no trees need to be cut? That would still make it visible, put it a good fifty yards from the chapel and downwind."

"I don't know how the work order got so messed up. I never wanted the petting zoo anywhere near the chapel. And I never said it had to be visible from the road." Chase frowned. "We can put a sign up for drive-by traffic. I thought it would be best if we put it near the barn."

"That's the logical location." Brock frowned. "I thought having it by the chapel was odd."

Devree had never known Chase to be that distracted. But with everything going on, she wouldn't be surprised if it hadn't been Chase at all who had filled out that work order. Had someone forged his signature?

"Sorry for the confusion, Brock." Chase blew out a heavy sigh. "I don't know what we'd have done if you hadn't shown up."

"Devree's the one who questioned it." His mouth twitched.

"Let me get some things packed, then I'll head to the barn and show you where I want it."

"Sure."

Chase strode to the ranch house.

"Poor guy." Devree hugged herself. "I've never seen him like this."

"I wish I could shoulder some of that stress for him. But I've got more bad news." He turned to face her, dug a sheet of paper from his pocket. "I don't think this is Chase's signature."

"I was thinking the same thing."

"Maybe we've been looking at this all wrong. Maybe it's you they want to sabotage."

"Me?" A chill moved over her heated skin.

"Do you have any enemies? Any ex-boyfriends with an ax to grind? Any wedding planners trying to steal your business?"

"No. Nothing like that. I dated a guy a while back, but he ended the relationship." All on his own when he'd almost married her client. "Dallas is big enough to support countless wedding planners quite well. And besides that, this was supposed to be my last wedding."

"Event planners, then? Maybe another planner doesn't want you in the field."

"I don't think so. Like I said, Dallas is big enough for all of us. I know Chase has faith in the other dude ranch owners, but I'm beginning to wonder." She vaguely remembered them being in a price war with another guest ranch when Landry had first come to Bandera. "He said others had underpriced him in the past."

"Maybe we need to check into that. Or ask around and see if any of the other ranches are struggling."

"I wish he'd call the police and let them figure this out."

"Part of me wants to keep this under our hats. Not stress him even more."

"He needs to know what's going on." And he'd be furious if he ever found out they tried to protect him by keeping things from him.

"I don't think it would hurt anything if I wait until tomorrow to tell him."

"Agreed. He's got enough on his plate today."

Brock was just as invested in Landry and Chase as she was. Softening the walls of her heart toward him.

And there was that extremely handsome thing he had going on. But that didn't mean she should let her guard down. He was still male. And she needed to run the other way.

Chapter Eight

The late afternoon sun beat down on Brock's back as he dug the last hole. Finished, he leaned on the diggers, wiped the sweat from his brow with the back of his gloved hand.

A little girl rushed his way from the ranch house with a woman lagging behind. As the child neared, he realized it was Ruby. And Scarlet.

"I can't wait for the petting zoo to open." Ruby darted right toward the hole he'd just dug.

"Easy." He grabbed her shoulders, gently stopping her in her tracks. "Watch for holes. They're as deep as you are."

Ruby looked down the hole, then up at him. "I'm not deep. I'm tall."

"I'm sorry." Scarlet stopped a few feet away. "Since Dad told her about the petting zoo, it's all she can think about."

"Well, it is exciting," he whispered conspiratorially. "I heard tell there'll be pygmy goats, sheep and miniature horses."

"Miniature horses?"

"They're about yea big, including their noggins." He held his hand less than three feet from the ground.

"Like a big dog?" Ruby's eyes grew wide.

"Exactly. Only they're horses."

"Do people ride them?"

"Kids can. And they can pull a small wagon. But they're mostly just for pets."

"When will they get here?"

"Don't tell anybody, but they're already in the barn."

Ruby whirled toward her mom. "Can we go see, Mommy?"

"We don't want to get Mr. McBride behind on his work."

"Pfft." Ruby giggled. "You mean Uncle Brock."

Scarlet's eyes grew huge. "Ruby!"

"It's okay. She broke the news the second day I was here." He was getting kind of used to the confusion in his world.

"She did? I'm so sorry."

"No worries. And as far as my work, the petting zoo isn't a priority. The cabin I was working on got skunked, so I couldn't work there today."

"Tell me about it. My client just had to pick today to see a house, so Ruby had to come to Stinky Ville after school." She pinched her nose.

"You're in real estate?"

"I am. When I have showings outside of school hours, Ruby ends up here."

"So what about seeing the mini horses?" Ruby begged.

"If you're sure you can spare the time."

"This way." He led them toward the barn.

Ruby dashed ahead.

"I'm really sorry. I shouldn't have told her who you were. I was just so excited when Dad and Becca told me you were here. I've wanted to meet you for a long time."

And he'd only learned she existed less than a week ago. "Why?"

"Becca talked about you a lot over the years." She settled her hand in the crook of his elbow, as if they were old friends. "My mom died when I was young and Becca came into our lives when I really needed her during those awkward teen years. I always wished I had a sibling, so when she told us about you, you became my fantasy brother." She let out a sheepish laugh. "It sounds silly now."

"Sorry to disappoint you."

"You haven't. I mean—I don't even know you. But I'd like to. Have you thought about that dinner I mentioned?"

"I'll have to check my schedule."

"Look, I know this whole step-kin thing is a lot for you to digest. But Becca has been such a blessing in our lives. Such a wonderful influence on me and my daughter. Drew's mom died a few years into our marriage. So if not for Becca, Ruby wouldn't have a grandma."

The sincerity in her tone tugged at him.

"I'll think about it." If Mom told them the truth. He couldn't stomach sitting through a family gathering and tiptoeing around the secrets of his childhood.

"Fair enough." Scarlet looked toward the barn. "Wait up, Ruby. Don't you dare open any of the pens."

"I won't, Mommy. But hurry."

They reached the barn and stepped inside the wide galley between the stalls.

"They're over here." He led the way to the fourth

stall where Sweetpea and Peanut were munching on hay, then helped Ruby climb up on the slatted wood gate so she could see.

The pint-size sisters looked up from beneath their pouf of bang-like manes resting across their foreheads. With pale golden coats and wooly cream-colored manes and tails, they were maybe two and half feet tall.

"They're so cute." Ruby's gaze fastened on the duo.

"Adorable." Scarlet leaned her elbows on the railing. "Thanks for letting us see. Come on, Ruby. Brock needs to get back to work."

"But I want to pet them."

"You'll get to another time. We need to get supper before Bible study tonight." She helped Ruby down, then turned to Brock. "Think about that supper. The invitation's open whenever you're ready."

"Thanks." He watched them go.

As far as stepsisters went, Scarlet wouldn't be a bad one. But his mom was another story. How could the same woman abandon her child, then end up being a great mom to someone else's teenager?

Sleeping with a dust mask on last night hadn't been fun for Devree, but at least the skunk smell was waning this morning. Landry and Chase were home and the guests were happy. The petting zoo was well underway and not anywhere near the chapel. It was late afternoon and honeymoon cottage A was almost complete.

Brock hung a shelf made from plantation shutters. "How's that?"

"Perfect. That's it. Can I help you with anything?"

"I just have the final chandelier in the bedroom to hang."

"I can hold tools or the flashlight for you."

"If you don't mind. And don't have anything else to do."

"After all the curtain rods and pictures you've hung for me, it's the least I can do." She headed to the bedroom with his booted footfalls behind her.

Brock handed her a flashlight, fiddled in the breaker box and the room went dark.

It took her eyes a minute to adjust as she moved to the curtain, tucked it in the tieback. The huge live oak outside the window shaded the area but allowed some sunlight in.

"Is it okay if we stand on the bed?" He sat on the king-size mattress and pulled one boot off, then the other.

"Sure." She sat beside him, kicked off her heels, then pulled her feet up.

He stood, offered his hand, helped her up.

This felt too close in the darkened room. She took a step back.

"The chandelier and tools are on the nightstand."

"Just tell me what you need me to do."

"I must say, I like this fixture." He dug a screwdriver out of his pocket, went to work loosening the cover plate on the antler chandelier with her shining the flashlight for him.

"I compromised on the curtains. And this one will go in Chase's office at the new house."

The cover plate came loose and Brock touched his rubber-handled pliers to the wires. Nothing. Next, he cut the wire in two and handed her the chandelier. "Got it?"

"Yep." She carried it to the empty nightstand, a bit wobbly, walking on a mattress with the heavy fixture.

But then she stepped too close to the edge, and almost lost her balance. "Whoa."

Strong arms came around her waist from behind. "Easy."

Goodness, he smelled good. And felt good. Muscled and sturdy. Protective.

"You okay?"

Not really. But all she did was nod.

His arms slipped away and he took the fixture from her. "Sorry about that. It is heavy."

He set it down on the nightstand, then walked across the width of the bed and picked up the new chandelier.

She forced herself to concentrate on the light fixture. Weathered white metal with blue mason jars surrounding each teardrop-shaped bulb and matching crystals underneath each light. The perfect accent for the room.

But she'd rather concentrate on the cowboy.

"Can you hold this one while I attach the wire? It's not as heavy." As she took it from him, their fingers grazed and her breath caught. Thankfully, he didn't seem to notice and went to work on the wiring as he held the flashlight.

Several turns with his pliers later, he dug orange connectors from his pocket and screwed them into place, then wrapped black tape around the wiring. He fished several screws and a driver from his pocket and reached for the chandelier.

She handed it to him, managing not to touch him this time.

He attached the cover plate and let the fixture hang, then helped her down and went to the switch box. Light flooded the room. "How's that?"

"Perfect."

"I believe honeymoon cottage A is ready for the happy couple."

"What a relief. Now just some fresh towels and we're set. Which reminds me, I meant to put the clean towels I brought over in the dryer." She hurried to the living room, grabbed the laundry basket full of wet terrycloth.

"Let me get that." His hands closed over hers and he whisked the basket away, leaving her struggling for air as she followed him to the utility closet by the bathroom.

He opened the dryer, dumped the towels in and started it.

"I meant to have them drying while I worked, then fold them before I left. Guess I'll come back later." She headed for the front door, eager to lose him. So she could breathe right. "Since the cabin is finished and it's Thursday, I'll be busy decorating the wedding chapel the rest of the day and preparing for the wedding party's arrival and rehearsal tomorrow."

"And I'll be busy finishing up Chase and Landry's house."

So they probably wouldn't see each other much until next week. Why did that bother her?

"Do you smell that?"

She sniffed the air. A hint of something…unpleasant. "What is it?"

"Dead animal."

"Oh, no. You didn't put any rat poison out, did you?"

"No." He walked around the room, sniffing, then down the hall, stopping at the dryer. "It's coming from here." He opened the door, interrupting the tumbling towels.

The odor permeated the room. She pinched her nose

between finger and thumb. "Oh, that's worse than the skunk. Is it the towels?"

"No. It's under the cabin. Probably coming up through the dryer vent. We may have found Pepé Le Pew."

"Oh, no."

"Relax. It's a good thing. If we get rid of him, he won't smell anymore. And the wedding is still two days away. I'll crawl under and see what I can find, but you'll probably have to rewash those towels."

"Want me to hold the light?" Though she really didn't want to. She longed to run to the ranch house where the air was breathable.

He chuckled. "You go on. This will get dirty. I'll set up a floodlight."

"Thank you. Thank you. Thank you." She laughed.

But why was walking away from him so hard? Even with a dead skunk in the mix.

The crawl space was wide open. Only human hands could unlatch it. Why hadn't he thought to check it before now? Brock shone his light under the cabin. Not his idea of fun—crawling in tight spaces where rattlesnakes might hole up to get away from the heat.

He hurried to the tool shed, grabbed a floodlight and thick work gloves, then returned to the cabin. With the floodlight set up just inside the crawl space, he could see the dryer vent, then scanned the area for any slithering reptiles. Nothing seemed amiss. He lay down on his belly, wiggled his shoulders through the opening and dragged himself along on his elbows, shining the flashlight in front of him.

A good fifteen feet later, he made it to the dryer vent, shone his light around. The stench was horrendous, but no body. Could it be in the vent? He touched the silver accordion tubing. Heavy, like there was something in it. He took in a deep breath, held it, and reached into the vent, grabbed whatever it was by the tail and tugged.

Pepé Le Pew was in his hand. Dead and stinky. He gagged, sucked in another breath, turned and crawled back to the opening fast. Less concerned about snakes with the stench flooding his airways. Near the hole, he threw the skunk out, then crawled out like a drowning man.

Outside, he grabbed the dead animal, obviously roadkill, bolted for the woods and threw it as far as he could. Well out of range of any guests.

"Not in my job description." He jerked the gloves off, dumped them in a trash bag and tied it up. With the air fresher, he retrieved the floodlight, latched the crawlspace and headed for his quarters. Never had he wanted a shower so badly.

Movement on the back porch of the ranch house drew his attention. Devree swaying on the swing, her hand clamped over her mouth, as if she were trying not to laugh.

"You thought that was funny?"

"I'm sorry. I've never seen you move so fast."

"Glad you enjoyed the show. But we have a problem." She sobered. "What?"

"The crawl space was open. Someone opened it."

"You think someone planted the skunk? You mean, like saw it and shooed it under the cabin."

"No, I think they saw it freshly dead on the road or maybe even hit it with their vehicle, then brought it here and shoved it in the dryer vent. So it would stink up the only honeymoon cottage we have ready on the week of your big wedding."

"That sounds pretty desperate." Maybe even unhinged. "But the skunk ran off guests. I still think that's what the guilty party wants." She tapped a finger against her chin. "But they may have gone too far this time. Whoever it is should be wearing the evidence. We initially smelled skunk. Whoever put it under there couldn't have gotten away unscathed."

"Exactly. Fill Chase in while I shower. We'll start with ranch employees, then move on to the other dude ranches in the area. Find out if anyone has been skunked lately."

"Without letting Landry know what's going on." Worry dwelled in the depths of her blue eyes.

"Of course. I think it's time to fill him in on the forged signature too." He jogged toward his quarters. Whoever was doing this was stooping to an all-time low. Attacking a pregnant lady's business. And not just any pregnant lady. His friend's wife. And Devree's sister. Whatever it took, he'd find the culprit and remove that worry from her eyes.

"Who would pull this?" Chase stalked toward the barn.

"Maybe we'll know soon." Devree had to practically run to keep up with him and Brock.

"You should have stayed at the house," he barked over his shoulder. "This might get ugly."

"I have a right to know who's trying to disrupt my sister's life."

They made it to the barn and the foreman met them under the shade of a live oak. "What's going on?"

"This may sound like a strange question, Troy." Chase adjusted his cowboy hat. "But have any of the hands smelled like skunk lately?"

"Not that I've noticed. What's this about?"

"We've had some vandalism lately. I know it sounds crazy." Chase filled him in on the mice, the rooster, the cows, the forged signature and the skunk. "We're just trying to figure out who."

"I'm sorry for the trouble and the lost guests, but I can't imagine any of my crew pulling such shenanigans. They're all hard workers. I'd vouch for every one of them."

"Has anybody called in sick in the last few days?" Brock shifted his weight from one foot to the other.

"Lee Jackson. He was out today and yesterday with that upper respiratory crud that's been going around. Sounded horrible on the phone. You don't think it's him? He's a go-getter and he's never missed a day's work before."

"We're just trying to get to the bottom of this." Devree tried to soften it. "And please don't tell Landry any of it. We have to shield her from the stress."

"Of course not. I'm praying for the baby and the missus."

Chase squeezed Troy's shoulder. "Thanks. It means a lot."

"I did hear something strange today though."

"What's that?"

"One of the hands was at a bar in town last weekend. He said Wilson Carter was in there bragging about how some guy paid him to quit his job here."

"That is strange." Chase frowned. "Let me know if you hear anything else."

"Will do, boss."

Chase headed back to the house. "If I get Lee's address, can you drive over with me and see if his place smells like skunk?"

"Yes," Devree and Brock answered in unison as they followed Chase.

"Not you." Chase stopped long enough to point a finger at her. "You stay out of this. I shouldn't have let you go to the barn. The vandal may have heard us and try something stupid. I've already got one woman to protect, and I don't need two."

"I'll go." Brock met her gaze. "Without you."

She stared him down, but he didn't give an inch. They climbed the steps of the ranch-house porch. "Who's Wilson Carter?" Brock asked.

"Our old handyman." Paid to leave Chase in the lurch. This definitely wasn't about her. She stopped as the two men went inside. They didn't seem to notice, and she bolted for Brock's truck.

Thankfully, it wasn't locked and she climbed in the back seat, hunkered down. The cab was hot as an oven.

Minutes later, the crunch of footsteps on gravel. Both front doors of the cab opened and she held her breath as the men climbed in.

"Where did Devree go?" Chase asked.

"I didn't see her. Maybe she went to the chapel to decorate some more for the wedding tomorrow."

"I should have told Dad to keep an eye on her too. I figured I'd have to physically block her from getting in the truck with us. She's too stubborn for her own good."

"She loves her sister to a fault though. When it comes down to it, you can't condemn her for that."

"I guess not."

She grinned. Several miles down the road, she raised up. "Hey, guys."

Brock's eyes widened, met hers in the rearview mirror. "Don't you have a wedding chapel to decorate?"

"Should have known. Turn the truck around, Brock," Chase growled.

"There's no time," she insisted. "Lee Jackson might be washing his truck down in tomato juice as we speak."

Brock's eyes narrowed.

She didn't flinch.

"You're not going. Turn around right here." Chase pointed out a wide driveway.

Brock slowed the truck.

She closed her eyes. "Think about it, Chase. What if it's not Lee? Maybe our thug was lurking in the barn listening. If I go with you, I'll be safe."

A sigh huffed out of him and Brock sped up again.

She should be decorating the chapel. But there was no way she'd be able to focus while some lunatic tried to put her sister out of business.

Chapter Nine

Brock had a bad feeling about this. They should have taken Devree back.

"According to the mailboxes, it should be the next drive on the right." She pointed up ahead.

"You stay in the truck," Chase ordered.

"I have a really good nose."

"In the truck, I said."

"Maybe I'll just roll down the windows."

Brock slowed, saw the house number on the box, and turned in. A white pickup in the drive. As he opened the door, a whiff of skunk assailed him.

"Smell that?" Devree announced from the back seat. "I think we've got him."

"And you're staying here."

"What about calling the police?"

"No. He's just a kid. I'm gonna try to figure out his angle and fire him. Maybe he just needs another chance."

"You're a good guy, Chase. For all your bluster, deep down, you're a softy."

"Grrr," he growled. "Don't tell anybody. Either one of you."

Brock and Chase got out of the truck. As they neared the farmhouse, Brock looked back a few times, expecting to see Devree. He was anticipating having to physically pick her up and stuff her back in the cab, then one of them sticking around to babysit her in order to make her stay put.

But she didn't get out. Maybe for all her bluster, this confrontation frightened her. Or she respected her brother-in-law enough not to cause him further stress. Either way, he was glad she'd surrendered.

Chase knocked on the door.

"I'm sick," hollered a voice from inside, followed by a round of coughing.

"It's Chase Donovan. I need to talk to you."

"I'm contagious."

"Come outside."

"I don't want you to get sick."

Chase turned the door knob. Unlocked. "Come out or I'm coming in."

"Okay, okay." The floor creaked from inside. The door opened a crack. A young cowboy, barely twenty, turned away and went into a fit of coughing.

Sounded fake. They waited for it to end.

"I smell skunk." Chase glared at the kid.

The kid's face went red. "I hit one with my truck on the way home from the doctor today."

"Or was that Tuesday night and you brought it back to the ranch and stuck it in the dryer vent of the old fishing cabin to go along with the mouse infestation you caused. You also cut the fence so Rusty got out, along with the hole in the cows' fence, and forged my signature on the work order for the petting zoo."

"I—I—I," the kid stammered. "I don't know what you're talking about."

"I think you do." Chase didn't back down. He looked as if he might tear into the kid.

"Okay, you're right. I did all those things. Are you gonna call the cops?"

"If you tell me why you vandalized my ranch, I might give you another chance."

"Nash Porter is my uncle." The kid swallowed hard. "He couldn't pay his bills, got drunk and ended up in jail. All because of you."

Chase's jaw clenched. "I fired him because he made the women at the ranch uncomfortable, he was disrespectful and insubordinate. You're fired too. I better not see you around my place again, and if I hear of you getting in any more trouble, I'll call the police. Are we clear?"

"Yes, sir."

"We'll mail your final check." Chase turned away.

"You're getting a second chance." Brock told the kid. "Use it for good and don't end up like your uncle."

"Yes, sir."

Brock followed Chase to his truck, opened the door.

"What happened?" Devree asked from the back seat.

"He admitted everything." Brock met her gaze in the rearview mirror as he started the engine, backed out of the drive.

"Why?"

"His uncle is the troublemaker I told you about. I didn't know they were related." Chase sighed. "Lee blamed me for his uncle ending up in jail."

"What about Wilson Carter? Did Lee's uncle pay him off?"

"I doubt it since he couldn't pay his bills."

"Why don't we go ask Wilson who paid him? He lives around here, right?"

"I'm sure part of his job was to keep quiet about it. He probably doesn't even remember spouting off in the bar."

"Did you call the police? Sounds like Lee's on the same track as his uncle."

"No. I gave him a chance to turn it around."

"I sure hope he takes advantage of it."

"Me too."

"Well, at least we got to the bottom of it." Brock turned onto the highway. "Maybe things will settle down now."

"Once Landry has the baby, I'll tell her about all this and how you gave that boy a second chance." Devree patted Chase's shoulder.

"You'll ruin my reputation."

"You're gonna be a great dad."

Her gaze met Brock's in the mirror. Mutual respect for Chase passing between them without words. Maybe they did have something in common.

Devree was cutting it close with her wedding party arriving today and the rehearsal tonight. She wound tulle around the pillars on each side of the stage, draping it just so. She'd done it so many times, she could almost do it in her sleep. Next, the ivy-and-pearl garland.

The door to the chapel opened. "Heard you could use a hand." Brock strode up the aisle.

"I thought you were busy with Chase and Landry's house."

"I did too. But Landry doesn't want you climbing the ladder in here alone."

"Well, you're too late, I've already been up there and I'm none the worse for wear. She's a worrier, but I'm fine." Finished with the pillars, she started to move the ladder to the lattice archway behind where the preacher would stand.

His hands landed on hers. "I'll get that."

Warmth moved up her arms. Reluctantly, she pulled away. "Over here, then. Underneath the archway."

He placed the ladder for her as she grabbed more tulle from a plastic bin and started up the rungs.

"I can do the climbing if you'll tell me what to do."

"I'm fine. And you don't seem like a decorating guru."

"I'll take that as a compliment. Guess I'll stand here and make sure you don't fall, then."

She climbed the ladder, wound the tulle through the lattice. "Can you hand me the ivy-and-pearl garland."

"This?" He held up the greenery.

She took it from him, wound it among the tulle, then started down the ladder to do the sides. But her foot slipped. "Oh!" She teetered, lost her balance. Strong arms caught her, lowered her safely to her feet but didn't let go.

"What are you thinking climbing a ladder barefoot?"

"It was either that or my heels."

"Why do you always wear those ridiculous stilts?"

"The wedding party is arriving today. I wanted to look the part."

His gaze held hers prisoner, then lowered to her mouth as he dipped his head.

Her breath hitched as his lips neared hers.

The chapel door opened and they sprang apart.

"Devree. It's lovely." Millicent Brighton stepped inside. "Miranda will be so happy."

"Thanks for putting so much into our little girl's special day." Phillip Brighton followed her as they continued down the aisle.

"Every bride should have the perfect wedding. This is Brock McBride." She managed to keep her voice steady. "He's the handyman here. My sister was worried about me being on the ladder, so she sent Brock to help. I'm finished with the high stuff now, if you need to go."

"If you do any more ladder climbing, call me."

"I will."

He turned away, strolled down the aisle and out the door.

As the bride's parents chattered on about the quaint chapel, the decorations and the wedding, one thought crowded everything else out.

Brock had almost kissed her.

And even more than that—she'd wanted him to.

The wedding rehearsal and dinner kept Devree busy for the rest of the day and evening. Brock hadn't seen her since he'd almost tested the sweetness of her lips. Something he hadn't planned on. Not at all. The attraction between them was getting out of hand.

Yet, it was more than attraction. She was empathetic, loyal and family meant everything to her. The kind of woman who, once she committed her heart to someone, wouldn't leave. The kind of woman he'd looked for his whole adult life. But, there was the Dallas-thing. And that created a big hurdle.

He tucked the kennel under his arm, grabbed the bag of food and supplies, then hurried to the cabin. The light was on inside. *Huh?* He hesitated. Maybe the bride and groom? No, the bride had a room in the ranch house and the groom was in one of the hunting cabins. They weren't scheduled to be here until after the ceremony tomorrow night.

Had Lee Jackson come back to cause more trouble? Brock set his load down, opened the door, ready for battle.

Devree whirled around, her mouth open, obviously ready to scream. Instead, she clamped a hand to her heart. "What are you doing here?"

"I could ask the same thing?"

"Making sure there are no stray mice."

"I told you I didn't want you coming here alone."

"Lee Jackson doesn't work here anymore."

"But he might be mad he got fired and he doesn't live far enough away for my comfort. And don't forget, someone is willing to pay people to disrupt things around here."

"But we're onto them both. Surely they won't pull anything else. So why are you here?"

"Same as you."

A meow sounded from the porch.

"What was that?"

"My solution. Come on, I'll show you." He stepped out, waited for her to follow, then opened the kennel. The orange-and-white cat tumbled out. He filled the bowl with food as the cat checked out his new territory.

"He's so cute."

"I got him from the lady at the coffee shop. She said he's a great mouser. There are two more in the barn."

"Will they stay here?" Devree squatted, reached her hand palm up toward the cat, but he ignored her, rubbed against Brock's leg and then went to the food bowl.

"He'll warm up to you. The barn will be safe and they'll stick around as long as we feed them and there aren't any dogs to pester them."

"But Chase is considering getting a dog."

"We'll find one that doesn't mind cats."

The cat finished eating, slinked over and rubbed against Devree's leg. She stooped and he let her pick him up. "Oh, you're just a little sweetie." She rubbed her cheek against the cat, scratched his jaw until he purred. "I've always wanted a cat, but Mom is allergic, and my apartment doesn't allow pets."

"I think he likes you and wants to be yours."

"But I'm not staying here. And I wouldn't be able to take him home when I leave."

She still thought of Dallas as home. How could he even think about getting involved with her? But as she set the cat down, he was drawn to her once more.

"Maybe Morris can be my cat while I'm here. And after I leave, he can be yours."

"I'm not planning on staying, either." Especially, if she didn't. "But I guess that'll work. For now. Why Morris?"

"Remember those old cat food commercials with the orange cat?"

He did. But she intrigued him more. Intent on finishing what he'd started yesterday, he stepped close. "I was hoping you might decide to stay. I mean—Landry will need you even after the baby comes."

Her gaze locked on his. "Is that the only reason?"

"No." He dipped his head and she stood on tiptoe as he slipped his arms around her waist. Their lips met, soft and sweet as her hands inched up his shoulders.

But she stiffened, pulled away. "We can't do this. I'm only here to relieve my sister's stress and ace a wedding. I have a business to revamp back in Dallas. A relationship with you won't fit into the plan."

"I'm sorry." Regret spread warm and heavy in his chest. "I shouldn't have done that and it won't happen again." His arms dropped to his sides and he walked away. He didn't stop until he slipped inside his quarters.

What had he been thinking? He hadn't. She was intent on leaving him behind for her beloved city, just like his mother had.

Chapter Ten

The wedding rehearsal and dinner had gone off without a hitch last night. Now, if the ceremony would just come together glitch-free, maybe Devree would be on her way to planning Brighton Electronics' company retreat. She lay in bed a few minutes longer, reveling in the rooster-less morning, reliving Brock's kiss despite her need to forget it.

Hoofbeats nearby and cattle bawling interrupted the peaceful moment. What was going on down there? She got up, went to the window and peered out. Hooping cowboys on horseback herding cows. A cattle drive? On the very day of her most important wedding ever.

Five minutes later, she was dressed and dashing down the stairs, out the door. Troy, the foreman, made a loop around a stray cow, got it back in line.

"Troy!" she cupped her hands around her mouth to be heard.

"Morning, Miss Devree." He tipped his hat.

"What's going on here?"

"A cattle drive."

"But I have a wedding today." Her tone was on the

verge of panic. "The cattle drives aren't supposed to happen on the same weekends as weddings."

"Apparently, Lee set it up before he left and got our guests all excited about it."

She looked past him. Three city slickers having the time of their lives. "You have to cancel it."

"What's going on?" Brock asked behind her.

"We can't have a cattle drive the day of the wedding." She was near tears and seeing him after last night didn't help her nerves.

"Can you move the cattle to the back of the property?" Brock shouted.

"Sure." Troy called orders to his hands. Within minutes, the herd was headed away from the ranch. Dust swirled in their wake, then began to settle.

"Problem solved." Brock's posture was stiff as he strode away.

Except the problem stirring in her heart.

She hurried inside to apologize and calm the bride. In the foyer, the father-of-the-bride—the man she really needed to impress, descended the stairs. A grim frown on his face.

"I'm so sorry, Mr. Brighton. We had a scheduling issue, but they've moved the cattle drive to the back pasture and you won't even know it's going on."

He opened his mouth.

"Daddy, wasn't that fun?" Miranda hurried down the steps, slid her arm into the crook of her father's elbow. "I've never seen a real cattle drive before. What a great way to begin my wedding day."

"I'm glad you enjoyed it." Apparently her bride wasn't as metropolitan as she'd thought. "Maybe you can come back sometime and go on a drive."

Miranda laughed. "I don't want to get that close. But I just had the best idea. Maybe Daddy could have the company retreat here. And the men could go on a cattle drive."

Great idea. "The dude ranch is open for events and I'd be happy to plan it for you, if you decide to go that route." Devree smiled, as if she hadn't been conspiring since she'd agreed to plan the wedding.

"Something to think on. But right now, I'd like to take my daughter to breakfast while she still has my last name."

"Of course. Just let me know if you need anything."

They strolled across to the dining room. As the doors closed behind them, Devree pumped her fist in a victory gesture.

The front door opened and Brock stepped inside. "Guess everything's good in here." He barely looked at her.

She told him about her conversation with the bride's father. "That's what this whole wedding has been about for me."

"I'm glad you're getting what you want." He strode toward the dining room.

Except, she wasn't. Deep down—she wanted him in her life. But he'd never move to Dallas and she could never stay here. How had she let herself get so attached to him?

From the porch of the ranch house, Brock watched the newlyweds flee the chapel as guests threw birdseed and stopped them for last-minute hugs. Reception over, the couple climbed into the waiting horse-drawn carriage and were whisked away to the cottage. The crowd dispersed to their cars. Once he saw the parents of the bride leave, he stood and headed that way. Though he'd rather do anything else. But he couldn't turn down a pregnant lady's request.

Inside the chapel, Devree was already on the ladder, unwinding poufy white netting from the pillars. Barefoot.

She stopped, turned to see who'd come in. "What are you doing here?"

"Landry sent me to help you clean up."

"Surely, wedding cleanup isn't in your job description."

"Neither is digging a skunk out of a dryer vent. But I'll do whatever Chase and Landry need for as long as I'm here."

"Suit yourself." She shrugged. "I'll go move my trailer around front, so we can load this stuff up."

"You have your own trailer?"

"It's small, but all this stuff is mine. I need somewhere to store it and it makes it easy to transport with a trailer."

"Why have I not seen it?"

"It's in the garage at the new house." She grabbed her purse, slipped on her shoes. "Be right back."

The one place he hadn't been on the property. "What can I do while you're gone?"

"Move the pillars and those totes I've already packed on the front pew to the door."

Left alone, he moved the items she'd requested. None of them were heavy, but they were bulky and awkward. Just as he moved the last tub, she stepped back inside.

"Want me to take these on out?"

"No. The arbor needs to go in first, then the pillars, then the totes." She started to move the ladder.

"I've got it." He manhandled it from her, grazing her hands along the way, stirring his pulse. "Where do you want it?"

"Under the arbor so I can take the ivy and tulle off."

He moved the ladder. "Do you use the greenery and netting for every wedding?"

"Most of them. Sometimes a bride will get picky and want something else."

"Why don't you just leave it on until you get a picky bride?"

"It doesn't keep as well. It gets dingy and frayed and I don't always use the same fabric. Besides, it doesn't take long to put it on or take it off. I've done it so many times, I could do it with my eyes closed if I had to." She loosened the last bit of netting and stepped down from the ladder. But didn't stumble this time. The air crackled between them as her gaze caught his.

He stepped aside as she unwound the decorations from one side of the archway and he tackled the other. He moved underneath the arbor, now stripped free of trappings, and lifted it. "This thing's heavy."

"I didn't mean for you to do it alone." She grabbed one side. "Let me help."

"I've got it. Just get the door."

She let go and hurried for the exit, held it open for him, then unlocked the trailer and stood out of the way as he walked his load inside.

"How do you handle this stuff on your own?"

"I don't. I have a guy."

Of course, she did. His breath caught. If she was involved with someone else, what was she doing kissing him? Technically, he'd kissed her, but she'd definitely kissed him back.

"His mother is a florist I use often. He's sixteen and a fullback on his football team. I hire him to do my heavy lifting."

Oh. That kind of guy. "So what's on your agenda, now that the wedding is over?"

"I'll be decorating the new honeymoon cottages. And I'll help get the new house move-in ready for Chase and Landry. They approved my contest idea, so I'll be doing publicity for that along with finding vendors to volunteer services for the winning retreat. What's next for you?"

"Getting Chase and Landry moved into the new house, fixing whatever needs fixing around here and helping with the new cabins." Which meant, they'd still be working together much of the time. With this attraction sizzling between them. But it was more than that. She'd gotten past all his defenses. Yet Dallas was too big of a gulf for them to span.

"So when can they move?"

"Technically—Friday. Once the painters finish, we'll do the flooring and finish work. The furniture is arriving Thursday, so everything will be ready. But Chase wants to wait until the next week to make certain the paint fumes are gone."

"He won't take any chances with the baby." The corners of her mouth kicked up, a dreamy expression softened her eyes. "Not many men like him in the world. And I'm so glad Landry found him after everything she went through before."

"Yet their happiness—even after losing their first child—hasn't restored your faith in love?"

"Most of the time, it doesn't work out so well." She rolled her eyes, slipped her shoes off, hurried back up the ladder.

Silly woman. Must she wear those excuses for shoes even when cleaning up after the wedding?

But deep down, he hoped she'd lose her balance again. So he could catch her.

No Devree at morning service. They must be on a different schedule now. The closing prayer ended with an echo of amens. Brock shot from his seat, headed for the door. Ron or his mom wouldn't get the chance to pull him aside today. He was out of here.

"Hello, I'm Ella Jones." A salt-and-pepper-haired woman headed him off. "I'm on housekeeping detail here at the dude ranch."

"Brock McBride." At least his last name wouldn't tip her off since it was different than his mom's. "Handyman." He clasped her outstretched hand.

"Oh, yes. I heard they hired someone. Do you sing, young man?"

"I'm afraid not."

"I'm trying to put a choir together. Do you know of anyone employed here who does?"

"Brock has a wonderful voice," his mom said appearing on his left.

"Really? Are you trying to hold out on me, Mr. Mc-Bride?"

"Not at all. She hasn't heard me sing since I was a child." He spared her a glance.

Color suffused her face. "That's true. But he had a wonderful voice the last time I heard him at ten years old. Usually if a person can sing as a child, they don't lose the ability as an adult."

"That's true. You knew Becca when you were little?"

"It was a long time ago." Brock worked at keeping his tone pleasant for Ella's sake.

"Listen, the chapel is mainly for dude ranch employees and guests." Ella looped her arm through the crook of his elbow, leaned close as if they were conspiring. "It'll be difficult since we attend on separate shifts. But all congregations need a choir. How can I convince you to join?"

"Let me try." Mom smiled up at him. "Since we go way back."

"Excellent idea." Ella patted his shoulder. "I'll be expecting you in the choir, Mr. McBride. Nice meeting you." She moved on, leaving them alone.

Brock looked around. They were alone. Even Ron was gone. As if the entire congregation had conspired to get them together.

"I'll pretend you tried to talk me into it." He started past her.

But she touched his arm. "Ella's watching and if you go scowling off, she'll ask questions. Besides, I never got the chance to ask you how you like the ranch?"

"It's all right." Except she was here. He pulled away from her.

Her hand dropped to her side. "You've relieved a lot of Chase's stress."

"That's why I'm sticking around." Not to reunite with her.

"What's next on your to-do list?"

"Get Chase and Landry moved into the new house. Finishing touches and paint. Trim work and flooring."

Get through Dad's birthday on Tuesday. Did she even remember the significance of the date? "Setting up the nursery and furniture."

"My crew is all set to clean. Just let me know when."

He'd be sure to make himself scarce, then. "Your crew?"

"I'm head of housekeeping."

If the Donovans knew the truth, would they trust her with that position?

"Look, why don't you come to the house for lunch? Ron would love to visit with you. And I would too."

He wanted to bite her head off. Tell her all the reasons he'd never step foot in her house. But standing inside a church wasn't the proper place and the manners Mama Simons had instilled in him came to the surface. "No, thank you."

"Because I haven't told Ron everything?"

"The subject will come up. Where was I as a kid? What did Dad's family supposedly tell me to turn me against you? I won't go through that."

"I just want to spend time with you."

"Then tell him the truth," Brock growled.

"He's such a good man." Mom's eyes begged for mercy. "I don't want to lose him."

"If he's the kind of man who'll leave over past mistakes, maybe he's not worth having."

"It's not that. Ron is a stickler for the truth. He'll be deeply hurt that I withheld my past from him."

"Maybe you should have thought of that before you married him. Until then, I think we've said all we need to say."

Eyes glossy, she nodded her head as if she'd expected

him to decline. "Will you at least consider singing in the choir? God wants us to use the talents He's given us."

"God expects us to keep our word when we say we'll leave someone alone too." His jaw clenched.

"Grandma." Ruby ran up and hugged his mom. "Grandpa said the petting zoo is set up. When can I come, Uncle Brock?" She lowered her voice to a whisper on the last bit.

"Let me know next time you're at the ranch after school and I'll give you a private tour."

"I can't wait." She looked up at his mom. "Is Uncle Brock coming to lunch with us?"

"Sorry. Not today, kiddo." He twirled her curly ponytail around his finger, then strode away. Actually, never—if Grandma was invited too.

Who was his mom to tell him what God wanted? God wanted parents to stay off drugs. To remember where they left their children. To pick them up from the babysitter. To love them. Not to abandon them. To do everything opposite of what she'd done.

The chatter and song of various birds serenaded the morning sun as Brock stepped out on his porch. His cell rang. He swiped his hand down his work shirt and dug in his pocket. The contractor. "Brock here. What can I do for you?"

"Can you retrieve the redhead?"

"You mean Devree? What's she doing?"

"She's here at the new house, second-guessing everything we do. Can you call her off?"

"I can't promise anything." He tucked his phone back in his pocket, jumped in his truck and headed that way. Minutes later, he killed his engine. No power tools sounded. Had she managed to single-handedly bring construction to a standstill?

The buzz of a compressor started up, followed by the thunk of a nail gun, along with the whine of a circular saw echoing from inside. Okay, maybe not even Devree Malone could stop progress.

He opened the door, stepped inside. There was sawdust everywhere. A thick fog hung in the air, what with the doorways to the rest of the house closed off with heavy plastic sheeting. Exposed insulation and multicolored slats of wood lined the walls.

Devree's mouth was moving, but the compressor drowned her out. "Excuse me!"

The compressor silenced just as she shouted. All eyes turned on her.

"Ahem." Her face turned four shades of red. "As I said, I'm Devree Malone—I'll be overseeing interior design. Is there any way y'all could do the sawing outside, so there's not dust everywhere?"

Snickers.

The gray-haired construction foreman, Ben Myers, stepped toward her. "Like I said, sawing inside saves time and we're on a tight schedule here."

"But cleaning up all this sawdust will take time."

"Not as much time as carrying our lumber in and out. It's a construction site. Things get messy. But we'll clean up when we're done." He propped his hands on his tool belt. "Anything else?"

Not easily intimidated, she straightened her spine, raised her chin. "The lumber is all willy-nilly, mismatched with no pattern."

"That's the way it's supposed to be, according to the work order. It's a focal point." The compressor started up again. Ben held his hands palm up, then turned away and went back to work with his men.

She scanned the walls once more, dug her phone from her pocket, took pictures from different angles as the sawdust swirled. Noticing him, she turned to give him a mouthful, only he couldn't hear a thing she said.

He grabbed her elbow, pointed her toward the exit. Thankfully, she complied. Outside, the noise faded as he shut the door behind them.

"If I'm going to oversee the design, you have to make them listen to me."

"He's right on the sawing. It would be time-consuming to do it outside. And they need to get the wall done, so the painters can tackle the rest of the room. I told the contractor I'd help with the finish work after that to speed things along."

"Let me know when I can set up the nursery. I want to do that for Landry."

"Will Wednesday work?"

"Perfect. But do you really think the house will be dust-free enough by then?"

"I've seen thousands of construction sites. Trust me, when it's over, you won't know there was ever sawdust involved." Especially with his mom on the job. They might have their issues, but she excelled when it came to cleaning.

"I thought that wall was all supposed to be barn wood." She scrolled on her tablet, turned it to show him. A picture of a reclaimed lumber wall with little variety in color.

"Barn wood is usually all different colors from sun and weather. As long as they're putting it on the right wall, I don't see a problem."

"But there has to be some sort of pattern."

"Huh?"

All animated, she drew in the air with her hands. "A pattern—light, dark, medium."

"You mean like stripes?"

"Something. Right now, it's a mismatched mess."

"Can I see your tablet?"

Her right eyebrow lifted, but she handed him the tablet and he googled *rustic wood interior.* Several walls popped up with a mix of wood shades. She stepped beside him to see. Apple shampoo tickled his senses.

"See, it's a new trend." He tried to ignore her nearness, her cinnamon hair against his arm. "You blend different shades. There's no pattern and it turns out great."

"If you say so." Her nose crinkled. "It seems like the wood should at least go from wall to wall. With them layering it in short pieces, it looks like a mess. Apparently, the mix of shades couldn't be helped. But shouldn't there be some sort of order instead of chaos?"

"You're not into rustic design, huh?"

"Not really. Rustic weddings are always a challenge for me."

"Then I reckon you'll just have to trust me. I'll admit it looks like a mess right now, but wait until you see the big picture."

Her blue eyes met his. And he had to fight the pull he felt toward her. She'd made her intentions about her future clear. "If I send the pictures to Chase, he probably wouldn't see the problem. Should I bother Landry with it? Would it stress her out?"

"From what I understood, Landry made the call. The wood came from an old outbuilding on the property that collapsed."

"I think I will show her the pictures to make sure she knows what it looks like."

"Go for it."

The backup generator whirred to life and she jumped right into him. He steadied her, his hands on her shoulders.

"What's that?" Her eyes wide.

"The generator, so we don't blow a fuse when they use all the tools at once."

She stayed there, too close, for a few seconds longer. His cell started up and she stepped back.

Tugging his gaze away from hers, he dug his phone from his pocket, scanned the screen. Wallace Montgomery. The architect he and Tuckerman once worked with. He jogged away from the generator before answering.

"Brock McBride here. Good to hear from you, sir."

Wallace chuckled. "You still have me in your phone after all these years. I'll take that as a compliment."

"You're one of the best I ever worked with."

"Same here, which is why I called. I've got an opportunity to design luxury cabins for an upscale resort in Fredericksburg. Wondered if you might be on board to work with me."

"I'm surprised you'd want to work with me again." Brock focused on the wildflowers dancing in the slight breeze. "After the way things went down before."

"The problem in that partnership was Tuckerman. You're the most skilled builder I've ever worked with. Honest and reliable to boot."

"I appreciate that, sir." Relief washed over him. Maybe his reputation wasn't completely in shreds. "I'm afraid I might be tied up for the next few months, but after that…"

"It'll be August at least. I'll call again when we get a definite timeline."

"Thank you, sir. It'll be a privilege to work with you again." Brock hung up, turned around.

Devree stood right in front of him.

"Sorry. I wasn't trying to listen in. Just frantic to escape the racket before it drives me completely buggy." But there was a dullness in her eyes. "You've got a job opportunity?"

"Yeah. I thought I'd blown it the last time we worked together, but apparently not."

"Thanks for putting it off for Chase and Landry." She slipped her hands in her back pockets. "Is there anything I can do to help speed completion along here at the house?"

"The ceiling will be old rusty tin. It all has to get several coats of polyurethane to meet code. You can help me with that." He expected her to decline. She wanted the work done, but did she want to get her hands dirty?

No answer. She headed to her car.

"Guess I'll take that as a no."

"Actually, I'm going to change clothes. Be right back." She glanced over her shoulder at him.

And his heart did a funny thing in his chest. This could easily get out of hand. Who was he trying to kid? It was already out of hand.

Chapter Eleven

Devree parked her car in the lot and hurried to the ranch house, mentally cataloguing her supply of work clothes. Definitely lacking in that area. But she and Landry were the same size—at least until the pregnancy. Maybe she could borrow something.

As the door shut behind her, she stopped. In the foyer, she found Becca pacing.

"What's wrong?"

"There's a man in the office applying for the handyman position."

Her heart sank to the pointy toes of her high heels. "Maybe Chase won't hire him."

"He will if this guy is qualified at all. Brock has made it abundantly clear he's only here as a favor." Becca wrung her hands. "I thought this was my chance to get reacquainted with my son. If he leaves now, I'll probably never see him again."

"I can't believe that. Surely God put you both here at the same time for a reason." Devree slipped an arm around Becca's thin shoulders. "Say this guy gets hired. Chase and Brock have rediscovered their friendship. I bet if Brock ends up leaving, he'll come back to visit. Especially when the baby's born."

"I just need time. To chip away at his armor. Soften his heart. And find my place in it again."

"We'll have to hope the applicant is underqualified. Or overqualified for that matter."

"But then that makes me feel bad." Becca went back to pacing. "What if this man really needs the job?"

"You're so sweet. Always putting others before yourself."

Becca scoffed. "I try. But believe me, it used to be all about me."

The conversation she'd overheard in the chapel popped into her brain unbidden. What was Becca's secret? None of her business. Something for Brock and his mom to work out among themselves.

"You go on about what you need to do. Don't let me hold you up."

"I just came to borrow some work clothes from Landry, so I can polyurethane rusty tin."

"Not exactly in your event planner job description."

"No, but it'll speed completion on the new house, so I'm up for it. Tell you what, I'll go change and then I'll wait here with you."

"You don't have to do that."

"How long can an interview take? Not long enough to make a big difference in my schedule. Be right back." She headed to the great room.

No Landry. She crossed to her sister's suite, silently turned the knob, pushed the door open. Dark inside. Her eyes adjusted to the dimness enough to make out the form of her sister in the bed. Lying on her side, the heaviness of her abdomen propped on a pillow.

Devree tiptoed across to the closet, stepped inside, shut the door.

With the small light flipped on, she felt like an interloper sifting through Landry's clothes. She found the jeans all hung together. She grabbed a paint-splotched pair with a pink T-shirt in the same condition and pulled both from the rack.

Minutes later, she stepped from the closet dressed in Landry's clothes. Though they were practically the same size, the jeans were a bit loose in the waist. Should have thought to grab a belt, but she was halfway to the door when Landry mumbled something in her sleep. She'd have to make do.

She stopped in her tracks until Landry quieted. Looking for a belt wasn't worth waking her sister over. She'd find hay twine or something and pull an Elly May Clampett. Tiptoeing, she made it to the door and out without disturbing her sister.

A whimper came from the couch. Becca sat there, shoulders slumped, face in her hands.

Oh, no. Chase had hired the new handyman. Brock would be leaving. Emotion clogged in her throat. Why did she care? Empathy for Becca? Yes. But mostly because, despite her best efforts, she'd developed feelings for him.

"I'm so sorry, Becca." She sat down beside his distraught mom.

Becca raised her head, dabbed under her eyes with her thumbs. "Sorry. I just needed a moment to pull myself together."

"Are you sure Chase hired the guy?"

"I was in the foyer when they came out of the office.

Chase took him out to show him around, said he could start first thing in the morning."

Her eyes stung. More than anything, she wanted to cry with Becca. "Maybe you can get Brock's number before he leaves. And I'm working with him most days. I'll try to convince him to talk to you before he leaves."

"No, don't." Becca grabbed Devree's wrist. "That will only make him angry at you. He'll probably have to give notice. I'll try to meet with him before he leaves. See if I can't make some headway to repair our relationship."

"Becca." Ron hurried to her side. "What's wrong?"

"Oh, Ron." Becca dissolved into tears.

Devree quickly explained the situation to Ron, then left them alone. Back to spread polyurethane on rusty tin. Side by side with Brock. Would Chase tell him the news with her there? Would she have to pretend she was pleased? While all she wanted to do was beg him to stay. Not for Becca's sake. But for her own.

Cup of coffee to his lips, Brock stood in the doorway of the wide galley between the barn stalls. He needed to get to the new house for day two of poly on tin. Devree was probably already there. Maybe it would be tolerable if she clammed up today the way she had yesterday.

But today was different than any other day of the year and he always felt closest to his dad here. Memories of him repairing the stalls, the roof, the slatted flooring in the loft. Letting Brock *help*. Dad's birthday had driven him here this morning.

"You always loved coming to the barn with him." Mom behind him. "Happy birthday, Wesley."

The quiver in her voice forced him to face her. So she did remember.

Chin trembling, she clamped a hand over her mouth, sank to a hay bale. "I loved him so much. So much, I couldn't function when I lost him. Even though you needed me. I just wasn't strong enough. Especially after I lost our apartment and we had to move in with your grandfather."

Her obvious pain drew him to her. The only person on earth who missed his dad as much as he did. He settled beside her on the hay bale, could feel the racking sobs she held back in his heart.

"I'm so sorry." She leaned into him. "Your grandfather was always in his alcoholic stupor, feeling no pain. I wanted to feel that way, just once. Just for a little while until I could get a handle on things." Her words ended on a sob, followed by a long pause.

He put his arm around her, absorbed her shudder.

"I didn't want to end up like my dad. So there was this guy at the motel where I cleaned. I knew he dealt drugs." She shrugged. "I thought I could handle it. Just once. But I was hooked before I knew what hit me. Isn't that the stupidest thing? I didn't want to end up an alcoholic, so I tried drugs instead."

Words failed him.

"I let you down. And you're right, I did abandon you. But I didn't mean to. I loved you. I still do." She raised up, looked at him. "I'm so proud of the man you've become. With absolutely no help from me." She scoffed.

"You got the wind knocked out of you. We both did."

"But we survived. I have Ron and a chance to make things right with you. I hope."

And he had memories of his dad. No woman to love. No family. Except this woman he'd spent so many years hating.

"If I'd had God back then, things would have been so very different."

"Maybe He's giving us a fresh start."

"I'd like to make the most of it." She sniffled. "How much longer will you be here?"

He frowned. They'd taken a step forward together this morning. But he wasn't sure he'd stay permanently. "I'll stick with the original plan. Until Chase hires a new handyman or the baby's born. Whichever comes first."

"But I thought he hired someone yesterday."

"Oh, yeah. I heard about that. He wasn't qualified. But he had experience as a hunting guide and a ranch hand, so Chase hired him for that."

Mom pressed her face into his shoulder, blubbered unintelligibly.

"Even if Chase found someone to replace me, I'd give two weeks' notice." His arm tightened around her. "I'd be here for that length of time no matter what."

"So, do I still have to stay away from you?"

"No. You stink at it, anyway." He eased her away from him and stood. "I'll see you around, but right now I gotta get to work."

"Please give me a second chance. I won't blow it this time."

"We'll see." He strode away, a mix of emotions roiling in his gut.

His dad's death hurt her as much as it did Brock, and she loved him with a mother's love. But the abyss of their years apart still yawned between them.

* * *

Devree rolled thick gooey polyurethane on a piece of tin that looked like it needed to be condemned. But Landry loved all things rustic, even the mismatched wood in the den. And Devree would do whatever it took to keep her sister happy and stress-free.

Which meant continuing to work side by side with Brock. Every day she felt closer to him as every day brought them closer to going their separate ways.

But where was he this morning? He was usually here by now. Was he consulting with the new guy? Would the new handyman be as agreeable to work with as Brock had been? Or would he think helping her hang curtains and wall art was beneath him?

But more pressing was that when Brock left…she'd miss him. Only days ago, he'd kissed her. And she'd shot him down. He'd been all business since then.

It wouldn't have worked, anyway. Her heart was in Dallas. And Brock's could never survive there. It was best that it ended. She just needed to get through however long of a notice he'd given Chase and maybe her heart would one day go back to normal.

With her long extension pole, she dipped back into the goo, rolled off the excess.

"Sorry I'm late."

She chanced a glance up.

His face looked drawn, haggard.

Maybe, deep down, he really didn't want to leave. "Are you okay?"

"Today would have been my dad's fiftieth birthday."

"I'm sorry." Pushing her topsy-turvy emotions aside, she set down the extension pole and placed her hand on his arm.

"I was in the barn." His shoulders sagged. "He made lots of repairs there when I was a kid and let me hang out with him. It was our place."

"I'm glad you're here. Where you can feel close to him."

"My mom showed up."

"How did that go?"

"I've been angry with her for so long." He picked up his roller, sank it in the poly. "But we talked. It was nice."

"I'm so glad. Everyone needs family."

"Can you keep a secret? Even from Landry and Chase."

"As long as it won't hurt them, I won't tell anyone. I promise."

"It won't. It's ancient history." He sighed, long and hard. "My mom got hooked on drugs after we left here. I was raised, and not raised, by a series of foster parents from the time I was ten. Some good, some bad." He grimaced. "Some really bad."

"I'm so sorry. I had no idea." Devree tried to hold in her shock. Act like the bomb he'd just dropped was no big deal.

"She told everyone here, after she got out of drug rehab, that I was with my dad's family. That they turned me against her. Covering her tracks."

"I can see why you've been so angry with her." She leaned on her paint-roller rod. "And I'm honored that you trust me enough to talk about it."

"She told Chase's grandmother her secret, but that truth died with Granny—that's what everybody called her. Not even Ron knows about the drugs. But today, I got a glimpse of how much Dad's death truly devastated her." He swallowed hard. "And it hit me, we were both dealt a really bad blow when he died. My bitterness toward her is hurting me as much as her. And we've both had enough pain."

"It's really good that y'all are talking things out. For both of you. You need each other."

"I can't stay here and keep her secret though. When I first came, she promised to work up the courage to tell Ron the truth." He let out a harsh laugh. "I mean, imagine family dinners. Say, Ron asks me if I played basketball in school and I have to tell him that I was never with one family long enough to be under one coach and learn the rules of the game."

"Just give her time." With all his ambivalence toward his mother, he wore his hurt like a cloak. And she longed to comfort him. But her words came out sounding like platitudes. "I'm sure she's scared of how he'll take the news and what he'll think of her."

"Does it change your opinion of her?"

She thought for a moment. Of how kind and supportive Becca had always been. "No. Your mother is very sweet. I won't pretend everything you've told me isn't a shock. But her past is her past. And if anyone else had told me about it, I probably wouldn't have believed them. That's a reflection on the person she is now."

He gave a curt nod at her statement. "I'm holding up production," he said, obviously wanting to change the subject. He rolled his dripping paint rod, sloughed off the excess and spread the coating on the tin.

All she wanted to do was hug him. The parentless child he'd been. And the hurting man he was now. Instead, she rolled the sealant on her piece of tin and said a prayer of comfort for him.

"So since you made progress with your mom, are you still planning to leave?"

"Guess you heard about the new hire too. The guy didn't know a pipe wrench from a crescent."

"A common mistake. They both have those adjusty things." She tried to keep it cool, as if the new hire had no effect on her. That it didn't matter one iota if Brock stayed or left.

"Adjusty things, huh?" He grinned. "Anyway, turns out he had experience in other areas Chase was looking to hire for."

The combo of his knee-jolting smile and her own relief clogged her brain. She didn't hear exactly what the new hire's job description entailed. Didn't care. "So, you're staying?"

"For the time being."

The most beautiful words she'd heard. In weeks. A reprieve. Their time together would still come to an end. But not yet at least.

Surrounded by freshly painted sage green walls and crib parts, Devree peered at the directions.

"Need some help?" Brock leaned in the doorway.

"Why does it have to be so confusing?"

"It makes it a challenge." He settled beside her, his knee almost touching hers, took the instructions from her and focused on them.

After a few minutes, he sorted the pieces into neat stacks. A bit more reading and he picked up two pieces, fit them together, then screwed them in place. "What about kids?" He looked up at her.

"What about them?"

"Ever picture yourself having any?"

"I've always wanted a couple." Her heart sank a little at the admission as she'd pretty much given up on that dream.

"How do you reckon that can happen if a relationship isn't in your plan?"

"So are you a relationship expert?"

"Hardly." He assembled two more pieces. "After my dad died—my family was splintered. Since then, I've always wanted a family of my own. A do-over—the chance to get it right."

"Any progress on that?"

"Not so far." A harsh laugh escaped him. "I fell hard once, even got engaged."

So he did have experience in the prospective groom department. Was he still hung up on his ex-fiancée? "What happened?"

He joined another piece of the crib in place. "I worked with her father. He and I didn't agree on some of his business practices, so I got out. She took his side in the matter. Chose her dad and to live in Austin over me."

"I'm sorry."

"I'm over it. For the most part. What about you?"

She blew out a big breath.

"I'm not buying that it's all because of the country's divorce rate. You mentioned there was a guy who broke things off with you."

Her gaze settled on the floor. "That's not exactly accurate."

"Care to share?"

"I've never talked about it with anyone."

"Not even Landry?"

"It was too fresh at first and by the time I wanted to

dump on her, her doctor couldn't detect her first baby's heartbeat and she was rushed to delivery. But it was too late." She swallowed the knot in her throat. "After that, my disastrous dating saga was trivial."

"But it still hurt you. Come on, I told you my tale of woe. See if you can top me."

"Oh, but I can." Her tone turned bitter, as she fiddled with a pack of screws. "I had a phone consultation with a bride-to-be. She hired me and we met to talk about the wedding. When I walked in, she was sitting with... with my boyfriend. He was the groom."

Brock let out a long, slow whistle, set down the pieces of the crib he'd assembled.

"I was so stupid."

"No. He was a jerk. Did you tell the bride?"

She scoffed. "I didn't have to. He took one look at me and got all weird. She knew something was up and asked me if I knew him."

"It sounds like one of those soap operas my eighth foster mom used to watch when I was a kid."

How many foster families had he had? "I apologized and told her that after rechecking my schedule, I'd overbooked myself and couldn't do their wedding. Before I could escape, she got in his face, demanded to know what was going on between him and the wedding planner. I hightailed it out of there before it got any more heated. Needless to say, they never made it to the altar."

Why had she just dumped all that on him? A guy she'd known only a matter of weeks.

"I don't understand. Why would he do such a thing?"

She shrugged, tried to keep her tone matter-of-fact. "Apparently, he really liked me, but she was from a wealthy family. He thought he could have his cake and eat it too. Didn't work out for him at all."

The whole thing with Randall had been embarrassing, but she hadn't loved him. Her boyfriend drama paled in comparison to his trauma with his mother.

"You win."

Laughter bubbled up and escaped from her in a high-pitched giggle. And she couldn't seem to stop. It was such a relief to talk about it after all this time. Especially since Brock hadn't judged her for being naive and too trusting. Finally, she got a reign on her hilarity, clamped her mouth shut.

"I'm sorry." His hand covered hers. "You deserve better."

"Thanks. You do too."

"At least I'm willing to keep trying." Green eyes pulled at her. He picked up two large constructed pieces of the crib, fit them together and screwed them in place.

She scooted over a bit, put some space between them. Even though they'd bonded over their hurts, they had nothing in common. He was as country as she was city. There was no other way for it to go. They'd end up parting ways.

In the meantime, they needed to remain on separate paths.

No matter how appealing Brock McBride was. No matter how perfect his kiss. No matter how the neglected child inside him tugged at her.

Chapter Twelve

"I promise, there are absolutely no fumes," Devree whispered to Chase, even though Landry was sound asleep in the back seat. Her sister had had to go into the hospital after experiencing some contractions, but it had been a false alarm.

Still, Devree and Brock had picked up the pace on finishing up Landry and Chase's home. Which they would move into soon if Chase could just trust her.

"I had Becca come smell and you know what a good nose she has."

"I don't want to drive her over there, get her hopes up and the smell still be strong—affect her in some negative way. Let's just wait until Monday like we planned."

"It's been four days since the painters were here. Trust me, the house is ready and don't you think she'll rest and relax better here?" Devree glanced back at her sister. "She's sound asleep. I'll stay in the car with her while you go look around. If she wakes up, I'll tell her you had to check on something. If you're not convinced, we'll go back to Granny's old room at the ranch lickety-split and wait it out a few more days."

"All right." Chase turned into the drive, continued past the ranch house, down the winding road to his and Landry's dream home.

It really was lovely, she thought as they neared the grove of live oaks where the driveway disappeared. A few more yards of woods, shaded with a clearing around the house. Log on the outside, drywall on the interior walls. Farmhouse and rustic decor. A perfect mixture of her sister and the man she loved.

Devree glanced back at Landry as Chase parked, quietly opened his truck door, got out and pushed it to. Landry didn't stir.

Chase disappeared inside. Minutes ticked past. And she started to worry. It wasn't imperative that Landry move in right away. But it sure would help her outlook. She'd rest better without dude ranch guests around and Chase had relinquished his duties until the baby was born. However, he was so overcautious. If he detected the slightest hint of paint fumes, he'd nix the whole idea.

The front door opened and Chase came out. As Devree held her breath, he gave her a thumbs-up. Her smile spread from ear to ear.

He opened the back door, tried to rouse Landry. "Sweetheart, we're home."

Landry opened her eyes for a second as Devree got out.

"It's time to move into the new house." Chase kissed Landry's cheek. "Want to sleep in our new bedroom tonight?"

Landry's eyes opened again. She looked around and her mouth formed a small *o*.

"All ready to move in."

"Really?"

"Yep, scoot over here so I can carry you across the threshold."

Landry sat up, gingerly moved over to the edge of the seat and Chase scooped her up.

"Get a picture, Devree." Landry beamed over her husband's shoulder.

Devree dug her phone out, snapped several pictures.

"You did this, didn't you?" Landry wiped a tear.

"Along with Brock, a whole carpentry crew and every ranch hand on the place. Every stick of furniture, every picture, every doodad should be right where you wanted it."

"You're the best sister ever."

"Right back at ya."

Chase opened the door and Devree snapped one final shot. "I'll text them to you."

"Aren't you coming in?" Chase turned back to face her.

"She needs to rest and y'all don't need me hanging around. I'll stop in tomorrow."

Landry blew her a kiss and the door closed.

Oh, to have a love like that. A man so tender and caring. So completely devoted.

"Psst."

With a confused frown, Devree turned around.

Brock leaned out from behind a tree. "I wanted to see her face."

"She was thrilled."

"I noticed." He held his hand up for a high five.

Sparks flew at the impact of her palm against his.

"Want a ride back to the ranch house? I parked on the other side of the grove there." His gaze dropped to her feet. "I figured you'd have your usual footwear on. Not good for a trek that far."

Thoughtful and caring. "Sure."

She didn't need a man *like* Chase. She needed Brock. But from all indications, he'd never leave his beloved countryside…not even for her.

Brock rang the bell of the new house, hoping not to disturb Landry. But his boss had summoned him here.

The door swung open revealing a tired-looking Chase. "Just the guy I needed to see. It's Saturday, May 12."

Brock frowned, searching for the significance. The day before… "Do you need me to pick up a Mother's Day gift for your mom or Landry?"

"No. I'm on top of that." Chase waved him inside. "But Mom called and reminded me the annual Medina River cleanup is today. With everything going on, I forgot all about it. She and Dad volunteered to provide the fixings and sides for the barbecue. Can you help them set up and serve?"

"Sure. What time?"

"They serve from five to seven. Probably set up at four."

"Can I get in on the cleanup too?"

"That would be great. Landry and I usually volunteer, so you and Devree can fill our spot. She's already here. I'd arranged for her to stay with Landry, while I went. But the other day's contractions convinced me to bail."

Brock almost swallowed his tongue. A tug-of-war raged inside him. The longing lodged in his heart to spend the day with her while his brain said to run while he still could. He needed to avoid her. Keep his heart safe from her charms.

Chase rushed into the living room. "Devree, I don't mean to *chase* you off, but the cleanup starts soon."

"I'm going, I'm going." She stood, noticed Brock, went still.

"I'll load the canoe."

"Wait! Canoe?" Devree trailed after Chase. "I don't know how to canoe. Can't I just walk along the shore and clean?"

"Other people are doing that. Devree and I always take the canoe. But no worries, Brock is going with you. He knows how."

Her eyes went wide. Then met his. Obviously wishing she hadn't agreed. Welcome to the club. The rational part of him didn't want to spend the day with her any more than she wanted to hang with him.

"You good with getting wet in what you're wearing?" Chase asked.

Brock considered his shorts, T-shirt and tennis shoes. Work clothes that could use a good dunking. "I'm good. I'll help with the canoe." He followed Chase into the garage where Devree's storage trailer was parked inside.

They tugged a long boat hauler to Brock's truck and hitched it in place, then trekked back to the garage. Each of them grabbed an end of the canoe, lowered it off the wooden brackets on the wall. Brock backed his end out toward his truck.

By the time it was loaded, sweat trickled down Brock's back. Splashing around in the river would be welcomed. Just not with Devree.

"Thanks for helping with this." Chase turned back to the house.

"No problem." He headed for his truck just as Devree exited the front door.

She scurried his way, climbed up in his cab. "Maybe I can catch a canoe with someone else."

He'd love to take her up on that. But… "I think since you're inexperienced, we should stick together." He started the engine, backed out of the drive, headed for the road. "You need to know a bit about canoeing before you hop in one."

"Like?"

"The bow is the front end. The stern is the back."

"Why not just say front and back then?"

Good question. "The person in the stern steers, so you'll need to be in the bow. That way, all you'll have to do is paddle. To keep the canoe straight and steady, each person will paddle on opposite sides of the boat. If you get tired, say *switch* and we'll change sides."

"Sounds easy enough."

"If we come to a turn in the river or we drift too close to the shore, we'll need to paddle on the same side for a little while." He wouldn't go into what to do if they turned sideways or hit the shore. No need to overload her. If he schooled her on the important stuff, the what-ifs wouldn't happen.

"Anything else?"

"Don't stand up once we're out in the water. You'll tip us over if you do. Can you swim?"

"Yes."

"We'll wear life vests, anyway."

"Got it."

They reached the river and he turned into the gravel lot and found a parking spot.

Should be a fun day. Spending it with the one woman he could imagine spending the rest of his life with—but never would.

The canoe swayed beneath her feet as Devree stepped into it.

"Crouch low, keep your weight centered and hold on to both sides until you get to the seat," Brock instructed.

"It keeps moving."

"I've got the canoe, it's not going anywhere until I get in. You don't have motion sickness, do you?"

"No." She inched to the front of the canoe—the bow, that is.

"Good job, you're almost there."

Finally, she settled on the seat, but kept her grip on the sides just in case.

"Perfect. Now just sit still while I get in and push off. Remember what I told you about paddling?"

"I start on the left." She glanced around. A few other canoers gave her reassuring smiles. Was she the only newbie?

The canoe shifted with his weight and suddenly she was propelled forward. She held on white knuckled.

"Paddle, Devree."

Oh, yeah, that. She stuck her oar in the water, pushed back with it, then up and repeat.

"Lengthen your stroke a bit. Don't pull up so quick."

She pushed back, kept her oar in the water longer.

"That's it. You look like a pro. Now, we're clearing out trash and debris from last year's flooding. Use your pinchers while I steer. Don't worry about getting the big stuff. Someone with a bigger boat will handle that part. I may tell you to lean right or left to keep us steady."

This was getting more complicated as they went. Why had she agreed to do this again? There were plenty of people here—a convoy of canoes in front of them. Chase and Landry wouldn't have been missed. There'd been no need for Brock and Devree to take their places. Unless it was a setup. Was Landry trying to matchmake again? Why, oh, why hadn't Devree figured it out before she'd agreed to come?

"See that bottle floating there? Can you get it? Don't lean too much."

She eased her grabber into the water, nabbed the bottle, then pulled it in and dropped it into one of their trash bags.

"Good job. Switch."

She moved her oar to the other side. Much easier since she was right-handed.

She grabbed an aluminum can and several plastic utensils.

"Lean right."

A big piece of something glistened to her right up ahead. They neared it and she jabbed her oar at it. Heavy. The boat dipped sideways a bit.

"Leave it. I think it's part of a car or something. One of the bigger boats will get it."

But the canoe was turning sideways.

"Switch," Brock instructed.

The canoe righted itself into a straight line, but nearer the shore than they'd been.

"Switch," he shouted.

She scrambled to follow his command, but move-

ment in a branch too close to the boat caught her attention. Snake. She screamed, jumped up.

"Devree, sit down!"

The boat flipped, tossed her in the water, but her life
vest kept her from going under. She swiped at her eyes,
searched for the limb where she'd seen the snake and
realized she was too close.

She swam away from it. If there were snakes in the
trees, they were probably in the river too. And the only
kind of snake she knew of that hung around rivers were
extremely venomous water moccasins. Her hands hit
something solid. She screamed, swatted at the water.
But it was Brock.

"Calm down." He grabbed her by the shoulders.
"What are you doing?"

"There was a snake on the limb and they're probably in the water."

"They're not poisonous, just water snakes."

"Water moccasins?"

"No. Stop freaking out, so I can swim the canoe to
shore and we can get back in it."

She nodded. But something touched her thigh. She
kicked and flailed, screamed again.

"I can't get the canoe if I have to hold on to you."

"Something touched my leg. That may have been a
water snake in the tree—" she shuddered, though the
water was a nice temperature "—but there probably are
water moccasins in the river. Right?"

"I've never heard of anyone getting bit by one in
the water. Here, hold on to me while I get the canoe."

She reluctantly slipped her arms around his neck.
Her fears forcing her to do his bidding.

"No flailing around, okay? You're fine. I'll get you back in the canoe if you'll work with me."

She held on tight, bit her lip until she tasted blood, as he swam the canoe to shore. As they neared the tree line, he was walking. She should get down, but she held on like the big scared ninny that she was.

"You can walk now. I can see the bottom. There aren't any snakes. None on the shore, either."

She put her feet down, let go of him. "Sorry. I can't tell you how much I hate snakes."

"Would have been nice to know before I got in a canoe with you on a river where snakes have been known to hang around." He grinned, dragged the boat ashore, tilted it on its side. Once the water drained out, he turned it upright.

"Ready to get back in?"

"Are there any alternatives?"

"Walking back to the truck."

Thick overgrowth lined most of the shore on each side.

"I'll hold it steady while you get in like before."

A whimper escaped at the prospect, but she climbed in, hunkered low, held on and made her way to the seat in the bow.

"I'll get you down the river in one piece. I promise. You're doing great. I'm getting in now." The canoe shifted with his weight and they propelled forward. "Paddle on the left until we get her straightened out."

The boat glided to the middle of the river, then turned to go with the flow.

"Switch."

"We lost all the trash we picked up."

"Someone else will get it. I have a feeling we'll do good just to get to the other end intact."

"How will we get back to your truck?"

"Volunteers are waiting. They'll take us back."

This debacle certainly hadn't endeared her to him. "I'm really sorry."

"It's okay. We'll do our part when it comes time to dole out the food."

Just get across the river without flipping them again. Another few hours and this torture of being with him would be over. Then maybe they could work in separate cottages. Until her niece or nephew, Sprint, was born and she found the courage to leave him behind.

Brock helped carry the portable buffet warmers to the long line of tables set up. Tray after tray of baked beans and corn on the cob. Iced down coolers held vats of coleslaw and potato salad.

"What do we charge?" he heard Devree ask. "Since I'm at the end of the line, am I responsible for the money?"

"It's free." Chase's mom said as she handed out dippers and tongs.

"Free? I guess it brings in customers."

"I hadn't really thought about that." Janice shrugged. "We just do it because it's a good thing for the community."

Devree really had a lot to learn about country life. But he knew she wouldn't stick around long enough for that.

"What about drinks?"

"Someone else is providing those. I can't remember who." Janice bustled around, stirring the hot dishes.

"This part's much easier than canoeing." Elliot patted Devree's shoulder. "You got this." Chase's dad always had a great sense of humor about everything.

She chuckled. "Hey, I managed to fill a trash bag."

She was always a good sport about getting ribbed. At ease with everyone but him it seemed. Yet, when she'd overturned their canoe and was so scared, all he wanted to do was protect her. Tell her that he'd keep her safe forever…if she'd let him.

But they couldn't build a relationship, not with her longing to return home and reinvent her business in Dallas. And even if she stayed, she'd never fit in around here, never be happy. He knew from experience with his mom and dad that if he asked her to stay she would probably end up resenting him.

"You're on slaw duty." Janice handed him a slotted spoon.

Right next to Devree and the potato salad. "Let's pray," the cleanup coordinator shouted. Everyone bowed their heads. He couldn't make out most of the words, but after a few minutes, a round of amens moved through the crowd.

The line started up and he plopped coleslaw on countless plates, bumped elbows with Devree a few times. As usual, the slightest touch sent a shock through him.

Eventually, the end of the line came and they served the last volunteer.

"Maybe we'll have time to eat before the volunteers from the other routes get here." Janice jabbed a dish at him, then Devree.

They filled their plates in silence.

Brock glanced around. A boy scout troop played a

rousing game of touch football in the distance. Volunteers lined long tables that had been set up with folding chairs, along with picnic blankets and canvas seating. Tents lined the parking lot since many had camped last night.

"Where do we sit?" She looked around. "Were we supposed to bring chairs?"

"I brought a blanket for us." Elliot spread a bright quilt on the ground. "There's plenty of room."

He and Janice settled on one side, leaving him and Devree the other. As if they were a couple. Was all of Bandera out to drive him to distraction, intent on keeping her near him?

Since things were easier with his mom, he wasn't itching to go like he'd been before. Maybe he could stick around, repair things further between them. But having Devree near kept him off-kilter. Even if he stayed, she definitely wouldn't.

"Here, I'll hold your food while you sit." He took the dish from her.

"Thanks." She settled on the quilt, then took both plates from him.

His knee grazed hers as he joined her. "Sorry."

"Oh, look." Janice set her hand on Elliot's calf. "More volunteers from one of the other routes. We better get back to the buffet line."

Elliot helped her up. "Y'all stay and eat. There aren't many. We can handle them."

And here they were, alone again. Like a date. But it wasn't and never could be. He searched for something to say. A band started up from a flatbed trailer at the edge of the river.

"So, since you and Becca are getting along better, do you think you'll stay in Bandera?" She'd beat him to it.

"Maybe so. I like it here."

"No offense to your dad's line of work, and handyman is an honorable and much-needed profession, but I saw the magazine Becca had. You're way overqualified and over-talented."

Another lifetime ago. It seemed like it, anyway. "I'll admit, working in the cabins has made me itch to build them again. Once Chase no longer needs me, I have an opportunity to get back into cabin design."

"And still stay here?"

"I'm willing to travel, but my home base could be Bandera."

"I'm glad. I mean—that you're sticking around—for your mom's sake. And yours."

"What about you? Are you planning to leave as soon as Landry has the baby?"

"I may stay a few days after until they get settled."

Hadn't anticipated that. He'd expected her to be gone ASAP. But she did love her sister.

An elderly couple strolled over. "Are you Devree Malone?"

"Yes." She set her plate aside and stood.

"Wonderful. A lady told us you're an event planner in Dallas."

"That's right."

"Oh, good." The woman patted her husband's arm. "I'm Gladys Hewitt and this is my husband. Stanley and I live there and our sixtieth anniversary is in August. Our kids are planning a big party on the twelfth, but we'd like to remove the burden from them, so they can enjoy it too."

Brock stood. "I'll find some chairs for y'all."

"We have some—the two red ones by that big cy-press tree." The man pointed, and Brock went to fetch the them. "Thank you, young man."

Minutes later, Brock set the chairs up for them. "I'll let y'all talk planning."

"You don't have to leave," Devree protested.

"Might as well get used to going in different directions."

She blinked. "Thanks for the chairs."

He strolled away, wishing he could leave right now and drive back to the ranch. But he'd brought her here and even though she could ride back with Janice and Elliot, he'd never been the type to shuck his duties off on someone else, and he wouldn't start now.

Dallas was already calling her home. Maybe once she left, his chest would stop with the constant ache.

Chapter Thirteen

Devree scrolled through her calendar on her phone, but she was too distracted to focus. Was Brock eager for her to leave? It sure seemed like it. From the moment she'd agreed to stay at the dude ranch and help out until Sprint was born, she'd counted down the days until she could go home. But now, that meant leaving Brock behind.

Obviously, Brock didn't feel the same way. Something jabbed deep in her chest.

"Do you have the date open, dear?" Mrs. Hewitt pressed.

"Let me just check something." She scrolled to August. "I have the twelfth."

"Perfect." Mrs. Hewitt clapped her hands.

"Do you have a venue?"

"We already booked the Empire Room in Dallas for that day."

"Nice. I'll put you on my calendar. What do you say we meet there toward the end of next month and talk specifics?"

"That sounds great. I'm so glad we happened upon you."

They settled on a time.

Devree wrote the details on the back of her business card then handed it to Mrs. Hewitt. "What brings y'all to Bandera?"

"Both our families are from here. This is where we met and fell in love." Mrs. Hewitt looked at her husband, obviously as love-struck as she'd been when they were young. "Our jobs took us to the city. We always planned to return to Bandera, but then the kids settled in Dallas. So we come back every year for the cleanup."

"We help supply drinks." Stanley winked at his wife. "And Gladys brings a cobbler. She makes a mean cobbler."

Their affection for one another was so strong and vibrant that Devree could feel it. The kind of love she'd longed for. If she could have acclimated to living in Bandera, could she have had that with Brock? She'd never know since he obviously wasn't interested. Her throat constricted as a painful knot settled in.

"Sorry we ran your young man off." Gladys stood. "Let's leave the happy couple alone, Stanley."

"We're not—" Her words stalled. They weren't together, but she wanted to be.

As soon as Brock saw the Hewitts getting up, he headed back over. "Leaving already? Not on my account, I hope."

"Not at all." Stanley folded his chair, picked it up. "It's past our bedtime."

"I'll get the chairs. Just show me where your car is."

"Such a nice young man." Gladys patted his cheek,

then waved at Devree. "We'll see you in Dallas next month."

"See you then."

Brock followed them to the parking lot. A few minutes later, she spotted him returning. More volunteers streamed in from another river route. She and Brock were destined to have their short time left together interrupted. Probably for the best.

She headed to the buffet line to help.

"Janice, y'all never got to eat." Brock claimed his spot beside her. "We'll take this round. You and Elliot get a fresh plate and get some grub."

"I guess we should have eaten in shifts. Now we've wasted food." Elliot filled new helpings for them.

"I think there's plenty." From what she understood, there was only one more river route of volunteers who hadn't arrived yet.

Janice and Elliot left and the line of hungry volunteers trickled to an end.

Scarlet, Ruby and Drew brought up the rear.

"I'm so glad you're here." Scarlet looked like she wanted to hug Brock. "This is my husband, Drew. I've been wanting y'all to meet."

Brock offered his hand. "Nice meeting you."

"You too. Did you eat plenty?"

"Too much." He patted his stomach. "But I'm still planning to dig into that cobbler." He shot Ruby a wink. "When are you coming for your private tour of the petting zoo?"

"I've been wanting to. Maybe this week."

He grinned at Scarlet. "Bring her anytime."

"Thanks."

The family moved on. Definite camaraderie there.

Maybe someday, they'd all sit around a big table and share a holiday celebration together. Brock needed that. And Scarlet obviously longed for it.

"I'm diving into this cobbler while I can." Brock grabbed a bowl. "Want some?"

"Yes. The lady I was talking to earlier, Gladys Hewitt, made it. They grew up here and come back every year for the cleanup."

"They seemed really nice. Did you take the job?"

"I did. I'm meeting with them next month at the Empire. It's an event venue in Dallas."

"Believe it or not, I've been there. That's where my wedding was supposed to be."

"I'm sorry." Her heart pinged at the thought of him loving someone else that much.

"I'm not. She was the wrong woman, and it definitely wasn't my kind of place." He closed his eyes. Savoring a bite of cobbler? Or remembering his heartache?

The Empire Room drove home their differences once again. She loved it. He hated it.

"Looks like you'll have plenty to do once you get back to Dallas."

Apparently, that's where he wanted her. And not a moment too soon. She'd had her chance with him and she'd blown it. No do overs.

She'd just have to put on her big girl heels, wait for baby Sprint's arrival and then hightail it back to her life in Dallas. Whether she wanted to or not. She could not stay here and pine over him.

Exhausted, Devree stifled a yawn as she drove to her sister's house. Between all that rowing and the tension with Brock yesterday, she was toast. At least she'd slept well last night. She checked her watch.

Thirty minutes before Sunday school class. Not long to visit with Landry, but her sister had called and begged her to stop by. And she couldn't say no. As she neared the house, she noticed movement on the porch. Someone swinging in a hammock over to the right. Landry.

With a grin, she parked and got out.

"See what Chase got me for Mother's Day?" Landry's head popped up. "Isn't it wonderful? Now, I can at least come outside to lay around."

"I wish it would stay cool enough all day."

"You know me. Heat doesn't bother me like it does you."

The front door whipped open as Mama and Daddy spilled out of the house. "Surprise!"

Devree gasped, then hugged them both. "When did y'all get here?"

"Late last night, after both you girls were already in bed."

"I couldn't be away from y'all on Mother's Day." Mama gave Devree another hug. "Especially since Landry's about to be a mom again." Mama gasped as she apparently realized the implication of her words. "But not like last time. Not at all."

A reverent silence crackled with heaviness. None of them would ever forget little Landon Charles.

Landry scooted over, patted the hammock. "Get in with me."

"What? I'll flip you."

"No, you won't. It's like the one Mama and Daddy have on their porch in Aubrey. We used to lay in it all the time when we were kids."

"The emphasis being on the word *kids*." Daddy chuckled.

"Come on, Chase got in with me last night. It's quite sturdy."

"Hold it steady for them, Owen," Mama instructed.

Devree eyed the contraption. It was anchored in four places instead of two. She grabbed the side, pushed down on it. Nothing. She'd muss her hair and her dress. But she'd do anything for Landry.

"I've got you." Daddy steadied the side for her.

She slipped off her heels, settled on the side of it, then wiggled over and lay down beside her sister. Giggling ensued at her jerky movements, just like when they were kids.

"It was definitely easier to maneuver around in one of these things when we were younger."

"But I think it's even more fun now." Landry giggled.

"Shhh." Mama pressed a finger to her lips. "Listen."

Horses whinnying, the hooting of an owl, the low murmur of ranch hands, the chatter of birds.

"It sounds like home," Devree admitted.

"I knew it." Landry jabbed a finger at her.

"What?"

"You don't think of Dallas as home anymore."

Hmm. She used to. What had happened to her?

The door swung open. Chase eyed them, holding a tray loaded with glasses of lemonade, each with a bendy straw. "Looks like a passel of trouble to me." He handed the glasses to them. "How did you ever get these two raised, Tina?"

Mama laughed. "With lots of love and giggling."

"We used to lay in Daddy's hammock together when

were kids. Even tried to sleep there a few times. But Devree always chickened out and ended up inside."

"Landry was always our nature girl." Mama sipped her lemonade.

"Just don't flip my precious cargo when you leave." Chase set down the tray, settled in a chair.

"You look tired, Dev." Landry leaned up to sip the lemonade then sat it down on a side table.

"Flipping a canoe is hard work." She tasted the lemonade. Just the right amount of sweet and tart. She almost drained the glass before placing it next to her sister's.

Daddy guffawed. "We heard all about it."

"Janice thought she saw some sparks between you and Brock." Landry elbowed her.

"Who's this Brock?" Daddy barked.

Devree's face steamed. There'd been definite sparks—for her, anyway.

"The new handyman," Chase volunteered. "An old friend of mine."

"He was just trying to keep me calm and get me back in the canoe. I don't know what you and Chase were thinking, setting me up in a floating ski."

"You do look tired." Mama leaned over them, giving Devree a good inspection. "Did you sleep okay?"

"I bet you haven't slept since you got here." Daddy winked at her. "Too quiet for you."

"The first few nights were rough. But since then, I've slept like a log the entire time I've been here. Except for the rooster waking me up a few mornings. But he's gone now."

"I knew it. You're a country girl at heart." Mama grinned.

"It's so peaceful here." Landry yawned. "I love the slowed-down lifestyle. Where you get to know your neighbors and people care. A lot like Aubrey. Are you sure country life hasn't grown on you again, Devree?"

These days, she wasn't sure about much.

"Ooh." Landry grabbed Devree's hand, pressed it to the mound of her stomach.

Devree felt a jab from inside and teared up. "Does that hurt?"

"Not really. It's just kind of startling sometimes."

"Let me feel." Mama set her hand next to Devree's.

"I can't wait until he or she gets out here." Landry stretched her back.

"You and me both." Breathing and healthy this time. "Trust me." The movement stopped and Devree checked her watch. "I'd love to hang out with you and Sprint all morning, but I better get to church." She sat up, got her toe hung in the netting. Daddy held the hammock steady, but by the time she was safely on her feet, they were both giggling again.

"We're going with you." Mama grabbed her purse from the porch rail.

Devree's heart squeezed. She hadn't been to church with her parents since she'd lived at home.

"Come back after church."

"We will." She blew her sister a kiss and headed for her car with a troubled mind.

Did she really want to go back to Dallas? It was so peaceful here. And she loved being with her sister. It was so much fun with Mama and Daddy here to see them both instead of one at a time. When her niece or nephew was born, could she really just walk away?

* * *

The service ended and Brock headed for the door. He should have sat Mother's Day out. It was torture sitting through the sermon with his stepdad singing the praises of his mom while she withheld a big whopping secret from him.

It brought all his anger toward her freshly to the surface. Undermining the steps toward reconciliation they'd made on his dad's birthday.

At least Ron hadn't exposed him as her son.

"Brock? Is that right?" An older man stopped him, offered his calloused hand. "Jed Whitlow. We met at Rustick's a few weeks back. The missus and I have our own church, but our son works as a hand for the Donovans, so we came here today. Can you help us set up some more tables in the fellowship hall? We've got a bigger crowd than Chase expected."

"Sure. You ended up with Rusty the rooster, didn't you?"

"We did." Jed ambled through the side door toward the fellowship hall as he spoke. "He's beautiful and quite happy in his new home."

"Just watch him if he gets out. He's got an attitude."

"So I hear. How's the construction going here at the Donovans'?"

"Coming along. We have three out of a dozen cabins complete."

They made it to the fellowship hall. Women, including his mother, scurried about the kitchen while the men moved the seating around and grabbed more. He helped carry three tables, set them up with chairs.

"I think that's it." Jed swiped his hands back and forth

against each other. "You're gonna stay and eat, aren't you? Chase's dad catered it, so the mothers wouldn't have to work so hard. I can vouch for the cook and it sure smells good."

"Thanks, but my recliner's calling me."

"Well, if I'd known you weren't staying, I wouldn't have made you work."

"I didn't mind. Nice seeing you again, Jed."

"Same here."

He headed for the foyer, then toward the exit. The rushed click of heels sounded behind him.

"Brock, I wish you'd stay," Mom begged.

"I can't." He kept his back to her.

"But I haven't had a Mother's Day lunch with you since you were ten."

He turned on her then. "Wonder why that is?"

"I thought we were okay."

"I can't have a family meal with you and Ron the way you want. Not without him knowing the truth. He might ask me something mundane like how Dad's relatives are. And I have no clue." Because he'd never laid eyes on them in his entire life. At least, that he remembered, anyway.

"Oh, Brock, I'm so sorry."

"You being sorry doesn't fix anything. You need to tell your new little family unit the truth."

"What truth is that?" Ron stepped through the doorway from the sanctuary, his gaze bouncing back and forth between them. Scarlet stood behind him.

Mom sucked in a big breath, nodded. "You're right. It's time. Let's go to your office, Ron. You too, Scarlet.

There's something I need to tell you both. Something I should have told y'all years ago."

"You coming?" Ron asked. "Sounds like you're part of all of this?"

"No. I'll let y'all hash it out." He exited, leaving her to clean up her own mess.

At his truck, he hesitated. She was finally doing the right thing. Even though she was being forced into coming clean since Ron overheard their argument, she was finally doing it.

Maybe he should stick around, help her with the fallout. He strode back inside, settled on the back pew and did something he hadn't done since he was ten—said a prayer for his mom.

Even though Devree had a good reason for leaving earlier—taking her sister and Chase a plate, visiting with her parents—she felt bad for not helping with the cleanup in the fellowship hall. As she stepped inside the foyer, Ron rushed from his office and out the exit with Scarlet on his heels. Neither said a word. Odd. Brock came barreling from the sanctuary, stopped when he saw her.

"Is Ron okay?"

"No. I'll see to him. My mom's in the office. Can you stay with her until I get back?"

"Of course." She hurried to the office at the side of the foyer.

Inside, Becca sat hunched, her face in her hands.

"Becca, Brock asked me to stay with you. He went after Ron."

"Oh, Devree. I've made such a mess of things."

"You don't have to tell me anything. I'm just here for support."

"But I need to tell it. I should have fessed up when I came back here fifteen years ago." The story tumbled out of Becca, interrupted only by hiccupped sobs. The grief over Brock's dad, the move to Dallas, losing her apartment, her alcoholic father, the drug use, forgetting where she'd left Brock and child services.

"I'm so sorry, Becca." She'd known some of it, but not the gory details like she did now.

"No one knew. Except Granny Donovan. She hired me when I came back here. Said my story was between me and God. But people knew me here and asked about Brock. So I made up a story about his father's family taking him from me, turning him against me."

Devree patted her shoulder.

"I don't think Granny's advice applied to keeping it from my husband. When Ron and I first started seeing each other, I was afraid my past would scare him off. Once we started getting serious, I didn't want to lose him."

"I'm sure he's shocked, but he loves you."

"He said it's not the drugs or my losing Brock that upset him. It's that I didn't trust him enough to tell him. And he's a big stickler on truth. I don't know if he can ever forgive me. Poor Scarlet was shell-shocked."

"I'm sure Brock and Scarlet will calm Ron down."

"Unless none of them can forgive me."

"They're all Christians. Forgiveness is part of the package." Devree took Becca's hand. "Let's pray about it."

Becca sniffled, nodded.

"Dear Lord, ease this situation. Give Ron, Becca,

Scarlet and Brock peace and comfort only You can provide. Help them forgive each other. To love each other. To leave the past behind and embrace the future together. In Jesus's precious name, amen."

"Thank you, Devree." Becca squeezed her hand. "I'm sorry you got tangled up in my drama."

"That's what friends are for."

But only God could fix this.

Chapter Fourteen

Brock caught up with Ron and Scarlet at his truck, the door already open.

"Great, she sent you to plead her case?" Ron stood between his pickup and the open driver's door, leaned his elbows through the window, fists clenched.

"No. I came on my own. I'm the one who challenged her to tell you the truth, so I should be around to support her."

"Why didn't she tell me?" Barely controlled anger writhed in Ron's eyes.

"Dad, listen to him." Scarlet touched Ron's arm. "Becca's been so good to us. Let's just leave her past in the past and move forward. She must be distraught. I'll go see about her." She started toward the church.

"I asked Devree to stay with her."

"Then maybe I'll just go inside and pray."

"It's gonna take a lot of praying," Ron closed his eyes. "She would have kept her secret if I hadn't overheard your conversation."

"She would have told you eventually. It was eating at her." Brock kicked at the gravel with the toe of his boot. "You gotta know she's a different person now. As upset as she is at this moment, I seriously doubt she'd go back to drugs."

"It's not the drug abuse or the parental neglect that gets me. She didn't trust me enough to tell me the truth."

"She probably thought you'd figure she was a bad influence if you knew and wouldn't let her near your teenage daughter." Why was it so easy to defend her?

"I wouldn't have broken things off. I loved her."

"And you still do."

"Of course, I do. I'm just…hurt."

"Then don't run out on her. She needs you to love her. To accept her truth. To forgive her for not telling you sooner." Was he forgiving her too?

"How'd you wind up so smart?"

"I had a Christian foster family." For a while. No need to tell Ron about the difficult years his mother's drug abuse had caused him.

"I'm glad. I'm glad you ended up back here." Ron shut his truck door, strode toward the church.

Brock matched his stride. "Me too." And he actually meant it. Despite the turmoil with Devree.

"My first wife passed away when Scarlet was nine. She always wanted a brother and I always wanted a son. I mean, I could never take the place of your dad, but I'm hoping you'll stick around, build a relationship with your mama. And with me and Scarlet."

"I'd like that."

"Wanna take her out to dinner after evening service?"

"Sure." As he'd counseled Ron to forgive his mom, the words had resonated in his heart. It was time he forgave her too. They couldn't retrieve the past, get back what they'd lost, but they could make up for lost time now.

He opened the glass entry door and Ron went inside, straight to his office.

Mom and Devree sat in front of his desk. Both turned to face them. Ron stepped in, pulled Mom to her feet, wrapped her up in his arms.

"We'll leave you alone." Brock gestured Devree out. "But I'll see you later, Mom. How about we go to the Old Spanish Trail for a Mother's Day supper after evening service?"

"I'd like that. A lot." Tears streamed down Mom's face, but they were obviously happy tears now.

Devree exited and Brock followed.

"Sorry you got mixed up in that."

"It's okay. I'm glad it all worked out. I like happy endings."

"You had guests with you this morning. I didn't mean to keep you away from them."

"My parents."

"Mother's Day. I should have figured that out. Scarlet's in the sanctuary. She got caught up in the vortex too. I should check on her." He wouldn't look at her. Couldn't.

"I returned to help clean the fellowship hall." She stopped. "I better get back there or they'll have it done."

"Go, spend time with your folks. There's plenty of cleanup help. How long has it been since you were with your whole family?" He risked a glance her way.

"A while." Her eyes turned sad. "I think I will go."

He found Scarlet on the front pew. Head bowed. Her head whipped up, as she heard his approach.

"Are they okay?"

"They're hugging it out in the office as we speak."

She blew out a big sigh. "Good."

He strolled up the aisle, sat down beside her. "How about you? You okay?"

"It's a lot to take in. But I think I know why she didn't tell us in the beginning."

"Why's that?" He relaxed his shoulders, stretched his legs out, crossed his ankles in an effort to release some of his pent up tension.

"We needed her so bad. And we put her on a pedestal from the start. It must have been a lot of pressure for her. To measure up to how we saw her." She reached for his hand.

He clasped hers. "I shouldn't have forced her. It was selfish. I refused to lie about my childhood, that's why I wouldn't ever agree to that dinner you kept insisting on. I figured the subject would have come up."

"Since they're okay, I think it's good that we know everything she went through. Makes me love her even more."

"You're a good woman." He squeezed her hand. "We're taking Mom to OST for Mother's Day tonight. Hope y'all can come."

"I wouldn't miss it." She laid her head against his shoulder for a few seconds. "I've been trying to arrange a family dinner since I first laid eyes on you. Are you bringing Devree?"

"No." *Absolutely not.*

"You should. Y'all make a cute couple."

"But we're not. Her life is in Dallas and it turns out, mine's here."

"I thought my life was in San Antonio. Until I met Drew. I can't wait for you to get to know him tonight.

He's heard so much about my fantasy brother." She giggled as her cheeks turned pink.

"Careful now. I'd topple right off some pedestal." He shot her a wink. "Didn't you grow up here?"

"I couldn't wait to get away—to live in the city." Her gaze grew distant. "As soon as I graduated high school, I went to San Antonio to get my real estate license. I was happy there. Or I thought I was. Until I came to visit Dad and Becca and met the new ranch hand next door."

"And you're happy in Bandera now?"

"Blissfully. The right man changes everything. Maybe you could be Devree's right man."

"I don't think so." But, oh, how he wished he could.

"Mama." Turning around, they saw Ruby. "You're missing Mother's Day."

"You're right, sweetheart. I am." She stood, caught the little girl's hand. "You coming?"

"Hurry, Uncle Brock. They have yummy pie."

"Right behind you. I've never said no to pie." He followed them to the fellowship hall.

Now that things were fully reconciled with Mom, he'd definitely stay here. It could even be his home base if he got back into building luxury cabins again.

During his partnership, Tuckerman had bullied landowners into selling too low and Brock's reputation had gotten tarnished by association. But apparently enough time had passed, and their old architect was willing to take a chance on him. Could he start over?

Maybe he could—but not with Devree. With jobs stacking up for her in Dallas, she'd never stay here. Never be content in Bandera. There would be no happy ending for them.

* * *

Monday morning, back to work. On his hands and knees, Brock locked the tongue and groove hardwood flooring together in the completed cottage. Whoever invented kneepads rocked. His hands were busy, his mind was occupied, so why did Devree keep distracting him as she hung curtains and wall decor?

Because he'd gone and done it. Fallen for another city girl. Though she wasn't as selfish as his mom had been in her youth, or calculating like his ex-fiancée, there was just no getting around Devree's obvious need to start her new business in Dallas.

Why did he always fall for the wrong woman? He was twenty-eight years old. At this rate, he'd never have that do-over he always wanted. His chance of having the perfect family was quickly fading.

"Oh, good. I found you." Mom's voice was panicked. "We need your help."

Devree's cordless screwdriver stopped. "Is Landry okay?"

"She's fine. But the pregnant goat, Polly, is missing. She was tucked away in the most secure stall in the barn. I don't know how she got out, but Troy came to the house looking for you. He said you have a way with goats."

"He has a way with the feed bucket." Devree chuckled, her gaze catching his for a brief moment.

Making his heart take a dive for her all over again. "But that won't work since I don't know where she is."

"The hands have searched the entire place. If they don't find her, they're afraid coyotes will get her and the kid."

"Sounds like it's time for a picnic."

"Why didn't I think of that?" Mom smiled, her eyes going warm at the memories.

Shared memories. Good ones.

Devree scrutinized them. "What am I missing?"

"When Brock was little, I took him on a picnic. Six goats were out that afternoon, but we didn't even know it until they all showed up at our picnic."

"Because they were hungry?"

"They were curious." Brock locked another hardwood plank in place, then stood, brushed off the knees of his jeans. "Goats will investigate anything out of the ordinary. They can't seem to help themselves." He turned to his mom, offering an olive branch. "Got time for a picnic?"

Regret filled her expressive eyes. "Oh, how I wish. But we have a full house of guests and this is my cleaning time while the majority of them are out to lunch. But I'd love a rain check on my day off."

"I can probably manage that."

Her chin quivered like she might burst into tears, but she gathered herself. "In the meantime, I'll send one of the kitchen staff over with a basket and you can take Devree."

His heart kicked into overtime. Did Mom know he had a thing for her? Was this really about the goat?

"I do love a picnic, but I have work to do," Devree sighed, as if she truly longed to go. Obviously for Mom's benefit. "But does it really take two people?"

"Goats are very social." Mom peeked out the window. "Conversation seems to draw them out. Please don't make Brock go on a picnic all alone and talk to himself too. It won't take long," she insisted. "And this is Landry's favorite doe. If anything happens to Polly, she'll be crushed."

The trump card. He could almost literally see Devree caving.

"All right."

"Great. I'll send a basket over ASAP." Mom's gaze pinged back and forth between them. A satisfied smile settled in place and she scurried out.

Was the goat even missing? Or was she onto him and trying to spur things along between him and Devree? Was she trying to help him with his happily-ever-after? If so, she was on the wrong track.

Surrounded by the perfect picnic, Devree tried not to look at the captivating cowboy sitting on the bright tablecloth in the middle of the field with her. A basket filled with yummy food fresh from the buffet. No goat in sight.

"We need to talk about something to draw her attention."

Devree searched her brain. They had nothing in common. While she worried about spiders or snakes finding their picnic, he was perfectly content experiencing nature. She loved the hustle and bustle of the city, he treasured the sound of crickets and frogs.

"So what do you plan on doing once you get back to Dallas?"

That again? Why was he so hung up on her leaving? His enthusiasm for her departure might just convince her heart to settle down. "The contest has gotten me several family and high school reunions, along with a couple of company retreats and conferences."

"Good. So you got what you wanted."

Not really. "How was the family dinner last night?"

"It was nice." He scanned the field surrounding them. "This place always felt like home to me, so it's great to be back. For good."

"I'm so glad. I mean—that you and Becca are working things out. She's a very sweet lady." If only they could overcome Dallas. A pang lodged in her chest. "The Fletchers and Millers are awesome people. You landed in a pretty cool family."

"Don't look now. But we have a pregnant goat at ten o'clock."

"Really? Where did she come from?"

"That thicket of oaks behind the barn. I didn't figure she'd gone far."

"How do you think she got out?"

"That's the thing. I don't think she did. Someone had to have let her out."

Please, no. "But Lee's not here, anymore."

"No. But he doesn't live far. Whoever paid the last handyman off could have found someone else to do his dirty work."

"Chase really needs to call the police. Is the goat still coming toward us?"

"Sure is."

"How do you plan on catching her?"

"She'll probably come all the way over, let us feed and pet her. I have a rope. You distract her and I'll slip it around her neck."

Which would bring their time together to an abrupt halt. Yes, they'd be back at the honeymoon cottage with him doing flooring and her working on decor. But their forced conversation would end. She hated this strain between them. Wished the kiss had never happened. But then, she wouldn't have the memory to savor.

Her cheeks heated. Dry grass crunched behind her as the goat approached. At least, she hoped it was Polly.

"Right behind you. No sudden moves." He set a container of watermelon between them. "Hey, Miss Polly. Fancy meeting you here," Brock crooned as if speaking to a child. "Want some of my melon?"

The goat nuzzled the container, stole a slice.

"Can I pet you, Polly?" Devree reached toward her, palm up, non-threatening. "You're a pretty goat. As far as goats go." Her hand made contact on the side of Polly's neck. She didn't flinch, just crunched on her watermelon rind. She had thick wiry gray hair with patches of black and white on her face, ears and feet. For some reason, Devree had expected it to be soft. "You still stink though."

Polly raised up to chew, nuzzled Devree's shoulder, probably leaving a pink streak on her favorite white blouse.

"You haven't smelled stink until you get a whiff of a buck." Brock smoothed his hand along Polly's back. In one swift motion, he slid a rope over her head. "Gotcha."

The goat didn't seem to mind. Just kept chewing as Devree patted her shoulder. "You're a good girl, aren't you?"

"I reckon I'll get her back to the barn and we can continue our work." Brock stood. "Leave this. I'll come and clean it up later."

"I'll take care of it." She wiped her hands down with sanitizer. "We can take it back to the cottage. Nibble while we work."

"I'll track Chase down, tell him somebody's up to no

good again, then meet you there." He led the tethered goat toward the barn.

Her heart slid even farther down the slippery slope, landing at Brock's booted feet. Landry's due date couldn't come fast enough. Devree needed to escape the handsome cowboy's magnetic pull. While she still could.

Brock sent a text to Chase.

Is Landry asleep?

No.

Brock dialed the number.

"Your mom suggested I bring plates for y'all. I'm calling to take your order."

"I can come get food." Chase chuckled. "Trust me, I won't go hungry."

"But if I bring it, then you can stay with her." And give him a reprieve from working with Devree for a bit longer. No more picnic lunches with her.

"Good idea. Thanks."

Brock strolled down the buffet, naming off its contents.

"I'll text you our orders. You sure you don't mind?"

"Not at all. Any last minute tasks need done at the house?"

"Not a thing. I think Landry has slept better the last few nights than she has in months. You'll never know how much I appreciate you. Bring your lunch and visit with us."

"Glad to be here. I'll have our food over in two

shakes of a goat's tail." He went to the kitchen, asked for to-go boxes.

"Better send four." Janice, Chase's mom handed him the Styrofoam containers.

"Why so many?"

"It'll take two for Chase's order, trust me. And one's for salad. Landry always likes salad."

"What kind of dressing?"

"Ranch."

"How much?"

The kitchen door opened and his mom stepped in, gave him a warm smile. "Just checking on the lunch crowd to see when I can start cleaning the dining room."

"Becca, could you help Brock with portions?" Janice grabbed the salad box back from him, handed it to his mom. "He's taking plates over to Chase and Landry."

"Sure." Mom's eyes lit up as if this task was the highlight of her day.

"But remember, she's eating for two."

A few weeks ago, he'd have been livid over this turn of events. "Thanks, Janice." He strolled to the door, held it open for Mom, then followed her into the dining room. There were a few stray guests, but it was mostly empty.

"How about you hold the boxes and I fill them up? Just tell me what she wants."

"Sounds like a plan." He dug his phone from his pocket, read off the text from Chase.

"I was thinking maybe you could join Ron and I for supper tonight." She put lettuce, tomatoes and cucumbers in the box. "Just the three of us this time."

Could he have another nice evening with his mom, without Scarlet and Ruby there as buffers? Or would it get awkward? Her preacher husband was a fine man. Loved the Lord. Spent years working at a dude ranch. They had a lot in common.

And Ron knew the truth now, so he wouldn't have to worry about watching his every word.

Maybe Devree could go with him this time. No. He couldn't get any more attached to her than he already was. His heart couldn't take her nearness, anyway.

"That sounds nice."

The dressing spoon Mom held stopped drizzling. Her hand trembled slightly. "Thank you."

A large lump lodged in his throat. He swallowed. "You're welcome."

Mom set the container filled with salad aside and went to work on the meat and veggies. With a second box finished for Landry, she handed it to him, patted his cheek. "See you tonight." Her eyes closed, voice quivered. "I never thought I'd say that."

"I'll be there." He squeezed her hand.

"Oh, Devree—" Mom looked past him, cleared her throat "—can you help Brock deliver lunch?"

"Sure."

"Thanks." Mom squeezed her arm, hurried to the kitchen.

Devree's questioning gaze met his. "Is she okay?"

"She's emotional. Since the moment I showed up, she's wanted me to come to their house for supper with her and Ron. I finally agreed."

"Want me to go with you?"

Yes. No. Maybe. "I thought about asking you. But sooner or later, we're gonna have to communicate without a referee. Eighteen years doesn't just magically melt away." He picked up four containers. "Ready to go?"

"When did we start delivering lunch?"

"They're for Chase and Landry."

"So this is why they didn't want me to bring anything over for them."

"You checked too?"

"I did. Landry said they were taken care of, but to bring my lunch over and eat with them."

"Chase invited me. Guess we'll be sharing a meal together again." *Great.*

But healing his relationship with his mother, getting to know her, Ron, Scarlet and his niece was worth sticking around for.

He'd just have to grow a tough hide around his heart. At least where Devree was concerned. And as soon as her niece or nephew was born, she'd be out of the picture, anyway. Why did his heart always give a painful tilt at that knowledge?

Chapter Fifteen

W hy did she keep getting stuck with Brock? As if the entire dude ranch was conspiring to constantly shove them together.

She stepped up on the new house porch and pressed the bell while holding four food containers. Brock held the other four.

The door swung open and Chase grabbed her load. "Thanks, guys. She's in her fancy living room."

"I heard that," Landry called.

Devree's shoulder brushed Brock's arm. Gooseflesh swept over her, as she hurried through the foyer to the living room. The smile on her sister's face was worth all the hard work.

"It's just feminine." She scanned the floral fabrics, the shabby chic painted furniture and decor in shades of pale green and aqua, with splashes of lilac.

"I think I lost my man card when I walked in." Brock looked around as if really seeing it for the first time. "Can we even eat in here?"

"Oh, shush. Of course not." Landry sat up. "We're going to my new kitchen."

"I'll carry you." Chase started to pick her up.

"If you don't let me walk, I'm going to lose the ability to. And the doctor said I can get up to eat and shower." She stood, waddled toward the kitchen.

Devree grinned. It was sweet and odd to see her normally slender sister so cumbersome.

Landry and Chase settled at the table as Devree and Brock doled out the containers.

"So you like the house?" Devree looked around at the white cabinets, lace curtains and chicken wire accents.

"I love it. You did such a great job. It's just the way I'd have done it."

"Well, you basically coached me through it. I was your hands and feet."

"Ooh." Landry patted her stomach. "Speaking of hands and feet. This little one is really active today."

"Maybe Sprint is hungry." Devree clasped her sister's hand. "Say a prayer, Chase."

"Would you do the honors?" Chase turned to Brock.

He bowed his head and they followed suit. "Dear Lord, thank you for keeping Landry and the baby healthy. Please continue to keep your hedge of protection around them. The Donovans are such a blessing to so many, along with this ranch. Keep everyone here safe and in your will. Thank you for this food and the new friends I've made here. Thank you for repairing my family and helping me decide to make Bandera my home. Amen."

"You're staying?" Landry smiled.

"You still need to hire a new handyman. If that doesn't happen, I'll wait until after the baby comes."

"But I thought you liked it here. You seem so at home

and Becca said y'all talked. If you're staying in Bandera, why do we need a new handyman?"

"The ranch will always be close to my heart. But I don't belong here anymore."

"Then where do you belong?" Chase asked.

"In Bandera. Just not in your bunkhouse doing odds and ends. I'm thinking of going back to building cabins. But I won't leave you high and dry."

"I'll admit your talents have been badly underused during your stay." Chase gave him a sheepish grin.

"Thanks to the publicity for Devree's contest, we've gotten several new reservations." Landry dug into her meatloaf. "Maybe eventually, we'll need more cabins built, and we know just the guy to call."

"I hope so."

"Devree's gotten several jobs from the contest too. In Dallas?" A hint of sadness tinged Landry's tone.

"Yes. But not until after the baby is born. And you know I'll be around to visit."

"I just wish you weren't so intent on leaving. Chase and I hoped you'd end up staying too."

"You know my life is in Dallas." Her gaze clashed with Brock's.

Small talk resumed, but Devree kept quiet through the remainder of the meal.

"I better get my princess back to her throne." Chase scooped Landry up.

"I'd love to walk."

"You already did. Only one-way walking, if at all." Chase carried Landry into the living room as Devree and Brock trailed him. As he settled her on the couch, a knock sounded at the door.

"Want me to get that?" Brock offered.

"Please." Chase sat next to Landry with her feet in his lap.

Brock stepped into the foyer, opened the door. "What are you doing here?"

With a wall between them, Devree cringed at the bitterness in his tone.

"I need to see the Donovans." A man's voice.

Chase shot to his feet, strode to the foyer. "How dare you come to my home. Get out."

The door shut. Voices outside. Brock must have gone outside with Chase.

"Who was that?" Devree tried not to sound as worried as she was.

"Judson Tuckerman, a land developer." Landry rolled her eyes. "He's been hassling us to sell. Keeps upping his offer. He ought to catch on by now that this ranch is Chase's family heritage. We'll never sell. And besides that, the property is worth a lot more than he's offering."

"Why does he want it?"

"Who knows. Probably for some housing development or a high-end resort."

The front door opened. "And don't come back," Chase snarled, as he slammed it shut once more.

She'd heard him upset, frustrated, worried, but never like this. Tuckerman must really push Chase's buttons.

"Sorry about that." Chase stalked back into the room.

"What's the big deal?" Devree spread her hands, palm up.

"He had my grandfather's friend almost signing his property over to him for a fraction of what it's worth. Thankfully, his son got wind of it and put a stop to the transaction."

That put Chase's anger in perspective.

"Did Brock leave?" Landry asked.

"He's still trying to talk sense into Tuckerman. Apparently, they were partners a few years back. Probably until Brock figured out what he was about."

Brock worked with Tuckerman? Devree's brain whirled.

"I think we could all use some sweet tea." Chase turned toward the back of the house. "Can you help me with that, Devree?"

"Sure." She followed Chase to the kitchen. Why would Brock work with a land developer who tried to swindle owners into underselling to him? Why would he come to work here as a handyman when he used to build upscale cabins?

Chase grabbed the phone.

"Who are you calling?"

"The sheriff. Get the sweet tea for my cover, will you?"

She filled the glasses while he made the call. As soon as he hung up, he grabbed two teas and started back to the living room.

"Hold up," she whispered. "Brock used to work with the Tuckerman guy."

"Yeah. So?"

"I overheard a phone call a while back. It was someone he'd worked with before and it sounded like they'd ended up on bad terms. After he hung up, he said he had an opportunity for him to get back into building cabins at an upscale resort in a few months."

"That's great. We both know we're wasting his talents here."

"But what if it was Tuckerman? What if he's the one that paid the old handyman to leave? And put Brock up to taking over where Lee Jackson left off? Maybe Brock is scoping out the ranch, trying to figure out a way to get you to sell?"

"No, he's not like that." Chase leaned on the counter.

"Do we really know what he's like? You knew him when you were both kids. He's had a rough life since then."

"He has?"

"Just think about it. He came to work here, way over-qualified. Why?"

Chase looked past her, out the window. "All his memories of his dad are here."

"Or he's still working with Tuckerman and he thinks he has pull with you. Maybe they need this property for their high end resort."

"Come on, Devree, can't you just trust?"

"I've learned there are very few men who can be trusted."

"Well, trust me." Chase held her gaze. "Brock is one of them." He headed back to the living room.

She started to follow, but her cell phone started up and she slid it from her pocket, planning to turn it off. Until she saw the name on the screen. Brighton Electronics.

Had pulling off the perfect dude ranch wedding paid off for her? "Devree Malone speaking."

"Devree. It's Phillip Brighton. How's that daughter and new son-in-law of mine?"

"Week two of living their happily-ever-after, sir. I saw them in the dining room last night, still blissful."

"Good. I've been thinking and I've come to the conclusion that Chasing Eden Dude Ranch is the perfect place for Brighton Electronics' annual company retreat. And you're just the gal to put it all together for me."

"I'd love to work with you again, Mr. Brighton." She tried to keep the exhilaration from her voice, to remain businesslike.

"Can you meet with me tomorrow in Dallas to discuss what I have in mind?"

Tomorrow? Landry had been in the hospital only last week. "Let me check my schedule and see if I can move some things around."

"You do that and call me back."

"You'll hear from me tonight, sir. Thank you."

The line went dead and she pressed her phone to her mouth. How could she leave her sister? They'd always been close and if anything bad happened, she wanted to be here. But Mr. Brighton wasn't known for his patience. If she left him hanging, he might just find another event planner.

By the time she got back to the living room, Chase was back in his usual spot at Landry's feet.

"Devree, you okay?" Her sister's brows scrunched together.

She set the tea glasses on the coffee table, relayed the conversation with Mr. Brighton.

"That's awesome. But why don't you look happy?"

"I can't go to Dallas tomorrow."

"Why not?"

"I can't leave you alone. You were in the hospital last week."

"Look around, I'm not alone with Mr. Hovercraft here."

Chase frowned at the description but didn't argue.

"But I want to stay until Sprint is born."

"Does Mr. Brighton want you to go back to Dallas for good?"

"No. Just to meet with him. An hour. Maybe two, tops." Long enough for Sprint to be born. Or complications to arise.

"I'm fine. You can leave me for a day."

"Mr. Hovercraft is firmly on Landry duty." Chase patted her leg. "I told the staff not to schedule me for anything around here. Go to Dallas if you need to."

"But what if you go into labor?" *Or something goes wrong?*

"I'll call you if I feel the slightest twinge. Dallas is only five hours away and I bet if it was an emergency, Mr. Brighton would fly you on his fancy plane."

"I don't know." She'd never forgive herself if anything happened and she wasn't here for Landry.

"You can't let this opportunity pass you by. It's what you've wanted for months. It'll put your name on the event-planning map and I don't want you to let it slip through your fingers on my account. I'd never forgive myself."

"Are you sure?"

"Positive," Chase interrupted. "You've been slaving on our behalf for weeks. You helped get the honeymoon cottage finished in time for our newlyweds. You pulled off the wedding of the year. And you made this place just the home Landry wanted. She's completely stress-free thanks to you. It's time to do something for yourself for a change."

Her insides warmed. She'd never really known if her brother-in-law liked her. Respected her—yes. Put up with her as part of Landry's package—yes. But she'd always suspected he rolled his eyes over her dirt, insects, reptiles and rodents issues.

"I'll be back tomorrow night."

"You most certainly will not." Landry tsk-tsked. "You can't drive five hours, have a two-hour meeting, then drive five hours back home. You're staying in your apartment tomorrow night. I'll see you Thursday evening."

"I believe that's an order from the honorable Lady Landry." Chase bowed his head.

"I'll be fine. Go make your dream come true. And when you come back, I want to hear all about it."

"Okay. I'll do it. But I mean it, the slightest twinge and you call me. I won't miss Sprint's entrance into the world."

"Promise."

And despite her worries over her sister, an excitement started to build. Dallas. Her apartment. The hustle and bustle of her normal life. The chance to taste it again and build her business.

Lord, keep Landry and the baby safe.

And then it hit her: she'd be leaving Brock behind too. A good thing. Especially if he was in cahoots with this Tuckerman creep. But if Brock stayed, could she leave, knowing he might be conspiring against her sister? Or would she be forced to stay and keep an eye on him? Especially if Chase was wrong about his childhood friend's loyalty.

"Stay away from them, Tuckerman." Brock's jaw clenched. "Chase meant what he said. He's probably called the sheriff by now."

"It's a free country."

"You can't just wander about on private property, especially if the owner wants you to leave and has a *no solicitation* sign up." He jabbed his finger toward the warning in the drive.

"What are you doing working as a handyman here, McBride? With your talent, this is beneath you."

"It's a good place to avoid unscrupulous men like you. I sleep much better at night, knowing I haven't helped swindle any land from befuddled owners."

"You can't tell me you're content with this."

Not entirely, but that was none of Tuckerman's concern. "It was good enough for my dad. It's good enough for me."

"You're happy wrangling goats, cattle and roosters? Not to mention skunks."

Now, it all made sense. "You paid Lee Jackson off to cause trouble around here. Didn't you? To convince the Donovans to throw up their hands and sell to you."

"Lee who? What are you talking about?"

"How else could you know about the hijinks around here?" Heat crawled up his neck.

"I was at that restaurant in town the other day, heard one of your ranch hands talking about it all."

"Uh-huh. If I find out Jackson's on your payroll, you'll be in jail so fast your head will spin."

"I don't know any Jackson. You're barking up the wrong fence post. And you've got no proof."

"If you're involved, I'll find proof, if it's the last thing I do."

A police car pulled into the drive, parked behind Chase's truck and the sheriff got out. "Mr. Tuckerman, how many times do I have to tell you to stay off Mr. Donovan's property unless you're invited?"

"I'm leaving." Tuckerman put his hands up in surrender, hurried to his car, leaving Brock alone with the sheriff.

Should he mention Lee Jackson and his possible connection with Tuckerman? Or just fill Chase in? Knowing Chase, he'd probably want to handle it himself.

"Thanks for coming out." He shook the sheriff's hand.

"Just let me know if he comes back." The sheriff asked Brock a few questions, took some notes, asked him to have Chase call him. He got back into his cruiser, backed out with a wave.

Brock punched Chase's number up. It rang twice.

"Did you get rid of him?"

"The sheriff did. Can you come out for a minute? I have new information."

"Be right there." Chase hung up. Minutes later, he stepped out. "What's going on?"

Brock filled him in on his conversation with Tuckerman.

"Sounds like I need to pay Lee Jackson a visit. Did you mention any of this to the sheriff?"

"No. I figured that was your call."

"Want to go talk to Jackson with me?"

"I have a better idea. You stay here with your wife and let me handle it."

"This isn't your problem."

"No. But you've got enough to deal with. If I can convince Jackson to talk to the sheriff, you'll probably have to come to the station to give a statement. Let me get things rolling for you."

"Make sure Lee knows if he'll tell the sheriff everything, I won't press charges against him." Chase clasped his hand, pulled him into a back slapping hug. "I owe you. A lot." He let go, headed back inside.

Brock hurried to his truck, made the short drive to Jackson's place.

At the door, Brock knocked, waited. No answer. "It's Brock McBride. I know you're in there, Lee. Your truck's here. And I know Judson Tuckerman paid you to disrupt Chase Donovan's ranch. If I can't talk to you about it, I'll talk to the sheriff."

The door opened and a shame-faced Jackson stepped outside. "It wasn't my idea. He sought me out."

"If you're willing to tell the sheriff everything, Chase won't press charges against you."

Jackson blew out a big breath, looked toward the sky. "You promise?"

"He's a man of his word. But if he hears of you getting in any trouble in the future, he will have a talk with the sheriff."

"I'll do it."

"I'll give you a ride."

Brock trailed Jackson back to the truck. Hopefully, this would end Tuckerman's career.

Dressed in her pajamas, Devree threw herself back onto her bed. Home. She dialed Landry.

"How's it going in the Big D?"

"Busy and noisy and wonderful."

"To each his own. Or *her* own, rather."

"You feeling okay?"

"Other than boredom, I'm fine."

"Is Chase with you?"

"No. The supper rush is over, so his mom is babysitting me. Him and Brock are acting weird. I think something's going on with Tuckerman and Chase is trying to shield me. Have you talked to Brock?"

"Um, no. It's not like we're friends or anything." And he might be conspiring against them. But she wouldn't dump that on Landry. Learning of Brock's history with Tuckerman put everything in a new light. It made no sense to her for Brock to apply at the dude ranch as a handyman when he was famous in Texas for building high-end cabins.

"So how'd the meeting go?"

"I aced it. Mr. Brighton hired me to plan his company retreat, and he wants to have it at the dude ranch. We're supposed to get back to him on dates once I get home."

"That's wonderful. If you keep us booked like this, we'll have to hire you as our full-time event planner." Suddenly, Landry gasped.

"What? Is Sprint okay?"

"We're fine. I just realized you called the dude ranch *home*."

"No, I didn't."

"You most certainly did." Landry repeated her words back to her.

"A mere slip of the tongue. Anyway, I'll plan anything you like as long as I can do it from here." She plumped her pillow.

"You still love it there?"

"As much as you loved Aubrey when we were kids. As much as you love Bandera now. Dallas is where I belong. Here, everything's so filled with purpose and in a rush."

"And that's a good thing?"

"For me, it is. It energizes me. Give baby Sprint a hug for me and I'll see you tomorrow afternoon."

"Drive careful." The call ended.

She snuggled into her pillows, her sheets, turned off the lamp. A siren sounded, grew louder as it neared, then faded away. The buzz and rumble of constant traffic. No crickets. No frogs. She turned on her side, put a pillow over her exposed ear.

Another siren, someone yelling in the street. A boom box with thumping bass from down the hall. She put another pillow over her head, clamped them both to her ear.

In Bandera, when she'd first arrived, she couldn't fall asleep because it was so quiet. But once she'd gotten used to the silence, the peaceful night sounds had lulled her to sleep. There was nothing peaceful about her apartment.

Loneliness swept over her. No one in Dallas loved her. They only wanted her to plan their events.

In the last three weeks, she'd gotten used to having her sister near. And even bonded with her brother-in-law. When Landry had the baby, Devree would miss out on his or her life.

Could it be possible that Dallas wasn't home anymore?

Chapter Sixteen

Piles of planking surrounded Brock as he methodically covered the floor in honeymoon cottage C. Devree had been gone all day yesterday—and she'd left without saying goodbye. But she was supposed to return this afternoon. She might even be here by now. Why was that the thing most prevalent on his mind?

The door opened and she strutted inside. Didn't even spare him a glance. Went straight to the pile of curtains Rustick's had sent over.

"Well, hello to you too. Did you have a nice trip?"

"Yes." Monotone.

"Did you get the job?"

"Yes."

He was sick of the strain between them. So, they'd end up going their separate ways, but it would be nice if the remainder of their ranch days could be stress free.

"You're not gonna make this easy, are you? Can't we get rid of this tension? We still have to work together for a while longer."

She ripped the cellophane package open, jerked out the curtains.

"Are you mad about something?"

She dropped the curtains, turned on him. "Are you in cahoots with Tuckerman?"

"What? No. Of course not."

"It doesn't make much sense for you to go from designing and building luxury cabins to dude ranch handyman."

"Just what are you suggesting?" He pushed to his feet.

"That maybe you're on your former partner's payroll, the way Lee Jackson was. Maybe you've been behind the mishaps around here lately."

"First of all, I was once in a partnership with Judson Tuckerman." Heat moved up his neck. How could she accuse him of being so devious? "But when I realized he was dishonest, I put an end to our affiliation. And second of all, why would I cause mishaps for myself to fix?"

"So you and Tuckerman can get your hands on the dude ranch property no matter the cost."

"You really believe I'd pull something like that?"

"If I find out you've done anything to hurt my sister, you'll regret it. And I think it's best if we work in different areas from now on. I'll do the decor in cottage D while you finish here, then come back and finish up here once you move on." She stalked out, slammed the door behind her.

His stomach sank—he couldn't believe that she'd think him capable of such betrayal. He had to get out of here. Away from the Tuckerman ordeal and now this new source of friction with Devree. He could live somewhere else and still build a relationship with his mother. If only he could cut and run. Leave town, start over somewhere else. Immerse himself in building upscale cabins again.

But he couldn't. He couldn't leave Chase in the lurch. Couldn't let him down. He had to stay—at least until the baby was born.

The afternoon echoed with bird chatter and song as Devree strode from her car to her sister's porch. Landry swung in the hammock, raised her hand in a wave.

"Did you sleep there?"

"No. But I probably will soon." Landry patted the netting beside her.

"I'll sit in the swing. If I lay down, I might go back to sleep with all this peacefulness." Devree sat in the middle of the porch swing, pushed off with her pointy-toed heel.

"You got the job. I would've thought you'd slept like a baby in your apartment the other night."

"For the first time since I initially moved to Dallas, I heard all the traffic, the sirens, the arguments."

"I knew it. This place has grown on you." Landry wiggled and turned until she faced Devree. "Chase finally filled me in on what's been going on. I can't believe you didn't tell me about all the mice, live traps and cut fences."

"He's the one who said not to tell you. We were trying to keep your stress level at zero. Why did he cave?"

Landry shrugged. "I guess it'll be in the paper since there's been an arrest."

Devree's heart sank. Had Brock been arrested? She hadn't wanted to be right about him. If she was, it would kill Becca.

"I can't believe Tuckerman was behind it all. If Brock

hadn't been here and figured it all out, we'd still be in chaos and losing guests."

"Brock figured it out?"

"He convinced Lee Jackson to turn Judson Tuckerman in."

Relief relaxed her tense shoulders. "So Brock wasn't involved."

"Of course not. He and Tuckerman parted ways years ago because Brock realized he was corrupt."

He was innocent. And Devree hadn't believed him. Firmly driving a wedge between them. Even if she decided not to return to Dallas, to stay near her sister and baby Sprint, there was definitely no hope for them now.

A black car pulled in the drive and parked. Resa popped out, hurried to join them as Devree scooted over on the swing.

"Cool hammock." The swing jerked as Resa sat down.

"Chase got it for me for Mother's Day." Landry patted her stomach. "How are you, my long lost friend?"

"I'm absolutely blissful. But I'm a terrible friend."

"Stop. You're busy. With the store, your designing, planning a wedding. You don't have time to babysit me and baby Sprint."

"Sprint?" Resa's eyebrow rose.

Landry laughed, shot Devree a chagrined glare. "You've got me calling him or her that now."

"Chase is the father, so Sprint is the baby." Devree clarified.

"Cute." Resa dug her phone out of her bag. "So I'm dying to marry that man of mine. And I love all the choices you sent me. I found the flowers, colors and decorations I'm going for."

"Let's see what you've got." So much for getting away from weddings. But she couldn't let her friend down. No matter how bad she wanted to.

They compared notes and pictures.

"Can you make it happen?" Resa scrolled through more pictures.

"Of course. But why the great room instead of the chapel?" Devree looked up from the phone.

"My parents were married in the great room. I want to follow their tradition."

"I can't wait." Landry readjusted her weight in the hammock.

"Me neither." Resa clapped her hands. "I was worried. I can't believe you had an opening in June. I assumed it would be your busiest."

"Devree's moving away from weddings into events."

"You can't do that. You're the best wedding planner in Texas."

"Thanks. But I haven't been inspired by my work for a while."

"Some guy broke her heart." Landry's tone echoed certainty.

"Why would you say that?"

"Because I can tell when my sister is hurting. I've been waiting for you to tell me about it."

Landry was right of course. Devree took in a big breath, then filled them in on Randall. How embarrassed she'd been.

"Oh, Devree, I'm so sorry." Landry blew her a kiss from where she lay. "Why didn't you come to me?"

"You were having a difficult time back then. I thought you had enough to deal with."

"I'm never too heartbroken to hear your heartache.

But you can't give up on weddings, or men for that matter, because of one jerk."

"Well, I don't think she's given up on men, at least." Resa chuckled. "I saw some pretty impressive voltage between this one and Brock that day in the store."

Devree's face went hot. "Trust me, there was no voltage. We were only working together—trying to turn the fishing cabin into a honeymoon cottage."

"I thought I detected something there also." Landry waggled her eyebrows. "Something I think you should stick around for."

The front door opened and Chase stepped out. "Lunch is ready."

Devree wanted to hug his neck for saving her from the inquisition. But truth be known, she missed Brock. And it had only been yesterday that they'd decided to work apart.

She'd never been so happy to be mistaken about someone. Now, she had an apology to make. Would he accept it?

She'd pegged Brock completely wrong. She should have known the man determined to smooth the hurt between his mom and stepfather wasn't a man who'd conspire with Tuckerman to attain Landry and Chase's ranch. If she admitted her error, would he forgive her for making the accusation?

Brock stepped out on the back porch of honeymoon cottage E to cut a half inch off the flooring plank. With four cottages complete, Chase had told him to start taking Saturdays off. But that would give him too much time to think.

He looked up when he heard footfalls coming up fast.

Devree darting toward him. Face panic-stricken. Something was wrong.

He rushed to meet her. "What's wrong?"

"Landry's in labor." She held up her keys. "I can't find my key fob and I'm shaking so much I can't get my car unlocked with my spare."

"Give them to me." He grabbed the keys. "You're a mess. Let me drive you."

She nodded, ran to the passenger side as he unlocked the door, flipped the button to let her in.

"They have to be okay. Both of them." She fastened her seat belt.

"Her due date is next week, so everything should be fine."

"This is week thirty-nine. Her stillbirth came at thirty-five weeks. The baby's lungs weren't developed enough." She took a deep breath. "And Landry's had similar complications with this baby."

He grasped her hands. "Dear God, put Your hedge of protection around Landry and the baby. Keep them both safe and healthy. Ease Landry and Chase's fears. Give Devree peace. Hold them all in the palm of Your mighty hand. Amen."

"Thank you." Her voice quivered.

"Where are we going?"

"Fredericksburg. Chase took her for a checkup this morning and the doctor didn't like the baby's oxygen level, so he induced. He said it shouldn't be long now." She sucked in a deep breath, as if ready to do battle. "Landry told me Tuckerman alone was behind all the problems at the dude ranch."

The abrupt subject change caught him off guard.

"And you believed her but not me when I told you the same thing?"

"It's hard not to believe since you convinced Lee Jackson to turn him in. But I overheard the conversation you had with a former coworker and assumed…"

"Wallace Montgomery. He's an architect."

"I'm sorry I accused you of still working with him."

"Apology accepted." But the words came out icy.

With her on the edge of her seat, Brock turned the almost one-hour drive into forty minutes, tension propelling him. At the hospital, he let her out at the front door, went to park, then made the trek across the lot, and stepped inside the cool building.

A nurse sat at the desk just inside.

"Landry Donovan?" His nerves were about to jump through his skin.

She pointed to the elevators, gave him the floor.

"Thanks." He strode over, pushed the button. The elevator seemed to move in slow motion.

When it finally opened, he saw Devree sitting in the waiting room, her face in her hands, with Chase's mom patting her arm, his dad pacing.

Bad news? Please, no. "Devree? You okay?"

Her hands dropped away. "Just worried."

"What did they say?"

"That she's progressing nicely and the baby's vitals are strong. I'm sure everything will be fine." Devree's smile quivered. "Chase is in with her."

"What about your folks? Are they coming?"

"Get this." Her chuckle came out high-pitched. "Resa's dad owns a small jet. He sent it to get them."

"That comes in handy."

"They should be here any minute."

As if on cue, the couple he'd seen at church with her hurried toward the waiting room. The man's face was florid, clashing with his red hair. The woman's curly graying brown hair was wild. Her blue eyes—so much like Devree's in color, shape—were filled with worry.

"How is she?" Devree's mom asked.

Devree stood, hugged her mom, shared the latest news.

"No complications?" Her dad waited his turn, then embraced his daughter.

"So far, so good." Elliot shook hands with her dad. "This is Brock McBride, a friend of Chase's. Meet Landry and Devree's parents, Tina and Owen."

They exchanged greetings though obviously distracted. Was it his imagination or did her dad's gaze linger on him a bit long? Had she said something about him to them?

The doctor stepped in the doorway. "Donovan family?"

"Yes," several voices answered in unison.

The doctor smiled. "We have a healthy girl."

"Thank you, God." Devree whispered as relieved and excited words from others blended together.

"What about Landry?" Owen asked.

"She's fine. The baby is seven pounds, six ounces. All her organs are fully formed. You can come back and see her if you like."

All the new grandparents, along with Devree hurried after the doctor.

Brock leaned back in his chair, let the stress ebb away.

"Are they okay?" He opened his eyes to find Resa standing there with a cowboy.

"They're both fine. It's a girl. Their families just went back to see them."

"Oh, what a relief. Her parents got here in time." Resa sank into a chair across from him.

"Thanks to you, I hear."

"Just glad I could help. This is my fiancé, Colson Kincaid. Colson, this is Brock McBride, a friend of Chase's and the dude ranch handyman."

The two men exchanged pleasantries as Colson took his seat beside his bride-to-be.

More people showed up, crowded the waiting room. Some employees along with a few faces he recognized from church, including Mom and Ron.

"Wow, where did y'all come from?" Devree stopped in the doorway.

"Everybody okay back there?" Jed Whitlow asked.

"Just fine, Jed. Landry wants Resa and Chase wants Brock to come see little Eden. You can come too, Colson. After that, they'll take the baby to the nursery and everyone will be able to see her."

Aww's echoed. They'd named the baby after Chase's deceased sister. A lump formed in Brock's throat.

He followed Resa and Colson, trailing behind Devree down a long hall with rooms on each side. Pink or blue bows donned most of the doors. She stopped and opened one with a pink bow. Inside, Janice held a tiny bundle.

"Stop hogging her." Devree plopped down by Chase's mom. "It's my turn since I'm back."

Janice handed the baby over and Devree pushed the blanket back so everyone could see the tiny face framed by dark hair. She looked good cradling the baby in her arms. Natural and content. Like she'd be a great mom someday.

But not to his children. She'd return to Dallas now. And find some businessman in a three-piece suit to give her the happy ending Brock could never provide for her.

Chapter Seventeen

She could leave. So why didn't she want to? Enchanted with the tiny baby in her arms, Devree couldn't take her eyes off her little niece. She'd barely torn herself away long enough to go to church this morning.

"I may never sit down again." Landry strolled around the living room. "Much less lay down. I may sleep standing up, propped against a wall."

Devree chuckled. "Or like a horse, free-standing. I'm glad you're enjoying your mobility."

"I am." Landry eased down on the arm of the couch beside her. "But little Eden was worth it. I'd do it all again—for her."

"She's a doll baby."

"Not enough to keep you here though." Landry sighed. "When are you leaving?"

"I'll stay a few days." Why? Her niece? Yes. The country life? Yes. Brock? Yes. Though there was no hope for them. Not after the way she'd treated him. "I want to get to know little Sprint here."

Landry giggled. "I hope she likes your nickname for her." Landry's phone rang. She stood and dug it from her pocket. "Hey, Becca, everything okay there?" A pause. "Really? She's right here. What a small world." Another pause. "Sure, I'll send her over."

"You'll never believe who's here."

"Who?"

"The very first couple you married." Landry's eyes sparkled. "They just happen to be here celebrating their eighth anniversary. They were sharing wedding memories with Becca and mentioned what an awesome planner they had in Dallas. Becca realized it was you and told them you're here. They invited you over for lunch at the ranch house."

"They're still married?" Her heart warmed to the point of almost making her teary. "Wow."

"And apparently, happily. Go on over, they're waiting."

She kissed Eden on the forehead, reluctantly handed her over to Landry. "I'll be back, Sprint. Don't you do anything fun without me."

Landry cradled the baby closely as Devree hurried out to her car.

Minutes later, she parked in the dude ranch lot, dashed inside.

Ava and Tyrone Webber waited for her in the foyer. "Devree, it's so good to see you."

"It's good to see y'all." Especially together. She hugged Ava, then Tyrone. Her throat clogged with emotion.

"You've got time for lunch?"

"I do, if you'll let me buy."

"Absolutely not." Tyrone opened the door to the dining room for them.

"I insist. Y'all are just what I needed."

"Why's that?" Ava sat down at a round table.

"I hate to depress you." Devree settled across from her, relayed her post-wedding statistics. "Seeing y'all still living happily-ever-after is a balm to my insecurities."

"You can't blame yourself. What are you doing here? Planning another of your awesome weddings?"

"I did, a few weeks ago. But mainly, I've been here helping my sister out. She was in the last legs of a high-risk pregnancy. But she had my niece yesterday, and they're both fine."

"Wonderful." Ava scanned her menu. "We have two kids. A boy and a girl."

"Really? How old?"

"Six and four."

Tyrone reached for Ava's hand, squeezed it. "And we have Devree to thank."

"I can't take all the credit. God brought you together, and you were smart enough to propose to this beautiful lady."

"He did. And I was. But you made our dream day come true."

Devree stared unseeingly at her menu, even though she knew it by heart. Maybe if she could find a preacher willing to counsel her prospective couples as part of her planning package—focus on the long-term marriage instead of the wedding alone—that would give couples a firmer foundation to start with. Maybe Ron? Probably not, if she returned to Dallas.

If? She didn't even want to anymore. Somehow, Bandera and life in the country had grown on her. It had everything she wanted to stay for. Her sister. Her niece. Brock. But she'd blown her chance with him. She couldn't possibly stay here and see him on a daily basis after the wedge she'd driven between them.

Brock had promised to meet Mom and Ron for lunch, but when he stepped inside the ranch house foyer, Devree was there.

"Hey." She seemed almost shy.

"Hey yourself. I'm meeting Mom and Ron for lunch."

"I was hoping to talk to Ron. Let me run something by you first." Her cell rang and she dug it from her pocket, looking a bit confused when she glanced at the screen. "Unknown number, but it might be a potential client, so I better take it." She swiped the screen. "Devree Malone, at your service. How may I help you?"

Why was he still standing here, watching her, hanging on her every word? He could wait for Mom and Ron in the dining room. Or in the great room. But his feet stayed rooted in place.

"Let me put you on speaker phone, so I can check my calendar." She pushed the button. "What day?"

"October 21. I know it's short notice, but we want to get married on the anniversary of the day we met." The hopeful bride-to-be sounded apologetic.

Barely past mid-May, with October still months away. How long did these shindigs take to set up? And didn't she hate weddings?

"I'm open for that date. Where are you located and where will the ceremony be held?"

"Dallas for both."

"Could we meet next week?"

"Yes, please."

They settled on a day, place and time. Devree put

notes in her phone. "You're on my calendar. I'll see you next week." She ended the call.

"I thought you were trying to get out of weddings."

"I know, isn't it crazy?" Genuine excitement lit her eyes. "The thought of another wedding used to make me cringe. But meeting the Hewitts at the river cleanup helped me remember my parents and Landry and Chase are still living happily-ever-after. And I just now had lunch with the first couple I ever planned a wedding for. They're still blissfully happy and have two kids."

"I'm glad you got a glimpse of the sixty percent." He was happy she'd seen the value in weddings. But it was just another reason for her to return to the city.

"Me too. Anyway, it made me rethink some things. I may stick with weddings, but help my couples focus on the marriage more than the ceremony. Do you think Ron would counsel couples for me?"

"You can ask him. But surely there are preachers in Dallas."

"Yes, but I don't know any of them." She ducked her head. "I sort of stopped going to church when I moved there."

"It sounds like you need to find a church home. I mean—if you're staying in Dallas."

Her gaze caught his, sadness looming in their depths. "I'm not cert—"

"Brock, there you are." Mom rushed to embrace him. Since they'd worked things out, she couldn't seem to hug him enough. Trying to make up for a lot of years, he supposed.

"Are you joining us for lunch, Devree?" Ron's gaze bounced back and forth between them.

"I appreciate the offer, but I already ate. I was going

to talk to you about something, but it can wait. Enjoy your lunch."

"Let's go in the great room, lunch will keep." Mom locked arms with Devree.

Brock stayed in the foyer.

"Join us, Brock." Mom waved him on. "Unless, it's something private."

"No. I already told Brock about it." Devree glanced back at him.

Mom and Ron took their seats on the couch with Devree and Brock facing them in matching wingbacks.

She quickly summed up her lunch with former clients and the impression the Hewitts had made on her at the cleanup. "It hit me that the thing most of the long-term couples I know have in common is that they're Christians. Some of my couples who've ended up divorced were also, but the majority weren't."

"I don't know how people do marriage without Jesus." Ron shot Mom a loving glance. "Love is a powerful emotion. But you're still dealing with humans, with different backgrounds, needs and annoying habits, then expecting them to live together peacefully."

And secrets that pop up twelve years in. But apparently, Ron had recovered from Mom's dose of reality.

"Exactly." Devree explained her idea. "You could set up a fee and I'd include it in my services package, so you'd be paid for your time. All couples might not take me up on it, but I figure it's worth a shot."

"I'm honored for you to think of me. But can't you find a preacher in Dallas?"

"Honestly and regretfully, I don't know any." She hung her head. "I am planning to change that. But in the meantime, I was thinking we could do phone consultations."

Or maybe she could bring her couples here. Give him a chance to see her every once in a while. *Stop it.* He needed to put her firmly in his past. And when she was forced to return to Bandera, he needed to avoid her like oak wilt. In the same way the disease squeezed the life out of trees, she smothered his heart.

"Tell you what, I'll do it. Until you find someone in Dallas. And if any of your couples need face-to-face in the meantime, I'll commute."

"Thank you. So much."

"My pleasure."

"I'm sure you'll do a great job." Mom squeezed Ron's hand.

"I've held up your lunch long enough." Devree stood. "I'll call you to set up the specifics on counseling."

"We hate to lose you around here." Mom hugged Devree. "I heard you're leaving soon."

"I'm all packed. I plan to spend the rest of the day cuddling my niece and then I'll leave first thing in the morning."

Brock's heart took a nosedive.

"We've enjoyed having you here." Ron followed up with a bear hug.

"Y'all made me feel at home. Even when I didn't." She chuckled. "It's like a great big family around here."

"I know you'll visit with the new baby and all." Mom patted her arm.

"I will. And I'll be back for Resa's wedding next month. Along with a few other events to be held here."

"You be careful, in case I don't see you in the morning."

"I will. See y'all later." Her gaze landed on him, mouth moved, as if she wanted to say something. But she didn't, just turned and then hurried to the foyer.

"Go after her." Mom gave his shoulder a nudge.

"Why?"

"Because you're crazy about her. And she's crazy about you."

"I think the only crazy one around here is you if you believe that."

Mom rolled her eyes. "Ron, talk sense into him. Tell him what a gift love is and that he shouldn't let it slip away."

"Sorry, I gotta sit this one out." Ron checked his watch. "New guests should arrive any minute and I'm on luggage duty. But she's right, I will say that." He strode toward the foyer.

"Why won't you go after her?"

"She accused me of working with Tuckerman, causing all the mishaps around here, so he and I could get the land from Chase and Landry."

"That's all?" Mom splayed her hands, palms upward. "It wasn't a crazy assumption since you used to be partners with Tuckerman."

"Maybe not. But she loves the city. I love the country. She can't wait to get back to her business in Dallas and I can't stand in the way of her dreams."

"Are you certain about that? I think this place grew on her. She almost sounded like she didn't want to leave."

He couldn't listen anymore. "I've got flooring to lay."

He stalked out, but his mom's words echoed through his head. And in his heart. Did Devree really want to leave? Could he stand by and watch her go?

* * *

"Don't you dare cry, Landry Ann Malone Donovan." Devree hugged her sister and niece cradled in her arms. "You'll get me started."

"I can't help it." Landry's voice broke. "It's been wonderful having you here. And we didn't really get to enjoy it with me being stuck in a prone position almost the entire time."

"You know I'll be back to visit."

"No, you won't," Landry pouted. "You'll get busy and have an event every weekend, and we won't see you for months at a time."

"Even if that happens, I have to come back next month for Resa's wedding, in July for the Brighton Electronics retreat, and I'll probably get to plan more events here in the future. It'll be the first venue I mention to couples."

"Just don't get too busy for us."

"I won't." She pulled away, kissed Eden's forehead. "You be a good little girl, Sprint."

Landry laughed as Chase carried Devree's suitcases to the foyer. She opened the door for him. With a final wave to her sister, she hurried out to her car, opened the trunk.

"Thanks for coming, Devree." Chase gave her a warm hug. "I don't know what I'd have done without you around here."

"Glad I could help. Take care of them."

"You know I will." He waved, headed back to the house as she got in her car.

She drove into the thicket that separated their home from the dude ranch, then neared the barn. Movement in the goat pen caught her eye. A tiny goat. It seemed Polly had her baby. She parked, got out.

"What a cutie. Polly, you did such a good job."

"Wanna hold her?"

She jumped, clamped a hand to her heart as Brock stepped out from behind the play station. Was it beating out of her chest because he'd scared her? Or because… he was Brock?

"Sorry. I was making sure she gets along with everybody. I just put them back in the pen. Polly was sick of her stall. Do you want to hold little Molly?"

"Can I?"

"Sure."

"How do I hold her?"

"Just like a dog or cat pretty much." He picked up the kid, handed her to Devree.

As his hands briefly touched hers, tingling swept over her skin. "She's so cute." She snuggled the little body close, trying to ignore the effect Brock had on her.

"You off to Dallas?"

She nodded, not trusting herself to speak as her vision clouded. She blinked several times, swallowed hard. "You know when Chase asked me to come, I dreaded staying here. Even though I love my sister. But now, I don't really want to leave."

"Why? I thought you loved Dallas."

"I thought I did. But when I went there last week, it was so noisy I couldn't sleep. And lonely. I guess this place grew on me. I hate leaving Landry, Eden, even little Molly here." But most of all, she hated leaving him.

"Then don't go."

Her breath stalled. Was he just being nice? Or did he care whether she left or not?

"I mean—you shouldn't leave a place if you don't want to."

"But I can't stay here if you hate me."

"I don't hate you, Devree. Far from it."

"I'm so sorry for misjudging you. You didn't deserve it. You're nothing like Tuckerman. Nothing like Randall." She ducked her head. "I'm hoping you'll give me another chance."

Laying her heart bare here. *Please don't crush it.* "See, I'm thinking about staying in Bandera. Since I decided to continue weddings, if I stay here, Ron could easily counsel my couples. And I can base my business anywhere as long as I'm willing to commute."

"I really like that idea."

"You do?"

"I want you to stay, Devree. Not for Landry or Eden. But for me."

Her gaze met his. "You mean to help with the cottages?"

"No. I want you to stay because somewhere between your screaming hysterics over a mouse and you flipping our canoe, I fell in love with you."

Her insides went to mush. "Really?"

"I tried not to. I thought you were city through and through, that you'd leave me behind. But you're not. Not at all. You're loving, caring and tenderhearted."

"I love you too."

"You love me?"

"You had me back when I realized how fully invested you were in protecting Chase and Landry's ranch. No matter the cost to you."

"Does that mean you'll stay?" He pulled her close, with little Molly nestled between them.

"For as long as you want me to."

"How about forever?" His lips met hers.

It was everything she'd ever dreamed of in a kiss.

"Baaaaa." Polly nuzzled Devree's knee.

She giggled, rested her face against Brock's chest, as he kissed the top of her head.

"I think mama goat wants her kid back." He gently took Molly from her, set her down in the pen. "So what's your answer?"

"For some reason, my head is all fuzzy. What was the question?"

"Will you stay with me forever?" He cradled her face in his calloused hands.

"Definitely." She closed the gap between them.

Epilogue

Six months later...

Brock had been so mysterious. Refusing to let Devree decorate the chapel for their wedding. Instead, Landry had acted as her planner, giving her all the choices she usually gave her brides. She could only imagine what it must look like.

"You can open your eyes now, sweetheart." Daddy patted her hand.

She opened her eyes, expecting to be at the chapel doors. Instead, they stood in front of a curtained wall by the river behind Landry and Resa. "What's going on?"

"You'll soon see. Brock wanted to surprise you."

The music began. Landry slipped through the curtain, carrying Eden. Seconds passed before Resa disappeared through the drapery. The music swelled and transitioned into the traditional "Wedding March." The curtains were swept aside to reveal a long white walkway with a gazebo at the end. And Brock grinning at her. Dressed in jeans and a blazer with a white rose on his lapel. No girly-colored vest required.

"We don't have a gazebo," she mumbled.

"He built it for you. Ready to do this?"

Her heart fluttered. "I was ready six months ago."

They walked slowly down the aisle, like she'd shown all her brides. Tulle and twinkle lights draped in the trees over their heads, with satin bows on the back of each white chair. Beautiful. But none of it mattered in comparison to her groom and the future stretching before them.

She'd come here to help her sister and plan a wedding. She hadn't counted on falling in love. But now, she was definitely counting on the cowboy. Forever.

* * * * *

HER TEXAS COWBOY

Jill Lynn

To the God who makes all things possible—
even books that feel impossible—
all glory and honor to You.

T, S & L—
I'm so thankful home is wherever we are together.
There's nowhere I'd rather be
than with the three of you.

To my editor, Shana Asaro—
thank you for your hard work and dedication.
Your wisdom and guidance is priceless to me.

Being confident of this very thing,
that he which hath begun a good work in you
will perform it until the day of Jesus Christ.
—*Philippians* 1:6

Chapter One

Time to make a break for it.

Rachel Maddox beelined for the back of the church and the sanctuary of the outdoors.

In the last five minutes, since the service had ended, she'd been cornered by three well-meaning women. Each had wanted to know every detail of her life since she'd left town six years ago. The first had wrinkled her nose with confusion when Rachel mentioned her future plans, instead—moving to Houston for a high school guidance counselor position she hoped to get. As though she hadn't understood Rachel's desire to hightail it out of Fredericksburg as quickly as possible.

The second had been hard of hearing, and she'd asked what perfume Rachel was wearing. Since the answer was none, she'd tried to change the topic, but after numerous requests, she'd finally piped up and said, "It must be my deodorant," at a volume high enough to have several confused glances swing in her direction. *Sigh.*

Number three had questioned why she wasn't married yet—as if twenty-four equaled old maid status—

all while giving her a pointed look that said she knew exactly why. Rachel had been reduced to a teenager in that moment—as though her old mistakes, attitude and poor decisions were strapped to her back for the world to see.

Ouch.

The nosiness was just another reason she wanted out of this small Texas town she'd grown up in. Rachel had this strange desire not to live in a place where she'd been a mess. It was time to start somewhere new, and just as soon as she got the job in Houston, that's exactly what she planned to do.

She dodged around two older gentlemen, the need to escape causing her throat to constrict.

Rachel had grown used to anonymity over the last few years. She attended big churches where nobody knew her name and lived in a city where people didn't stop her at the grocery store to chat about the weather or to ask how her sweet nephews were doing. This town was suffocating her, and she'd only been home a few days.

How was she going to survive a month or two?

People parted before her, and she clicked along in her sleeveless blue pencil dress and strappy brown wedges, the taste of victory and freedom spurring her forward.

When a little girl darted out in front of her, Rachel screeched to a stop. Tiny strawberry-blond pigtails bounced on the top of the girl's head like small antennae. Based on the fact that she roamed the sanctuary without a parent in tow, Rachel assumed she must be escaping, too. They were kindred spirits.

She only looked to be around two years old. Too small to continue her romp of freedom alone. So much for her escape plan. Rachel knelt down, gently touching the child's arm. "Where's your mama, sweetie?"

"Mama." The girl's face broke into a smile. Adorable. Not exactly helpful, but definitely cute.

"Should we go find her?"

The tot's head bobbled. Rachel attempted to take her hand, but the little girl didn't budge. When Rachel opened her arms, the girl came right to her. No stranger danger with this one. Rachel scooped her up and stood, a sweet orange scent reminiscent of the push-up treats she used to eat as a kid tickling her senses as she scanned the space for a harried mom. None appeared. Hmm. She couldn't exactly drop the toddler in the lost and found.

And then, instead of a worried mom, she saw a man steaming toward her. One she knew well. Hunter McDermott. Never fun to run smack-dab into a past mistake. And to think, she'd been so close to making a getaway.

He stopped in front of her, and to her surprise, the little girl lunged into his arms. Hunter…had a daughter? Rachel hadn't heard that he'd married. But then, when her sister-in-law, Olivia, started telling her about local news, Rachel often tuned out.

"Rach, I didn't realize you were home." Surprise laced his voice, joining the quirk of his eyebrows. The fact that he'd used her nickname seemed lost on him. "Sorry about that. Kinsley's a bit of an escape artist."

"It's okay. I completely understand." But, then again, he should know that. Hadn't he been upset with her for making a break for it six years ago?

Time had barely aged him. Hunter had never lacked in the spine-tingling looks department, yet he managed to pull it off without any effort. Of course he'd wear a casual, short-sleeved plaid shirt and jeans to church along with cowboy boots. His cropped, dark-blond hair looked as though he'd shoved a hand through it, glanced in the mirror and shrugged. He somehow managed to look laid-back and dangerous all at the same time. Two good words to describe the man who'd trampled all over her heart before she'd left for college. Though he would probably claim she'd been the wrecking ball.

"You home to see your family?"

"I just finished grad school and now I'm staying here while waiting to hear about a high school guidance counselor position I'm hoping—" *planning* "—to get in Houston." Rachel had already filled out tons of paperwork and done one interview over Skype.

His jaw hardened, brow pinched. "Sounds like you plan to escape as fast as you can."

She strived for polite, resisting the temptation to roll her eyes at the jab. She'd matured over the years, hadn't she? She could handle an adult conversation with Hunter. "Is this your daughter?"

"Kinsley?" Hunter lifted the girl higher, grinning at her. The softening of his face caused a tightening in her chest. Once upon a time she'd craved that smile of his as much as oxygen. "No. She's my niece. Autumn's oldest. She's pregnant with their second. I'm not married."

The words dug like a knife and twisted. He could have added *because of you* to the end, just to make the torture more complete. It was true he'd asked her to marry him once. But they'd been young—way too young. And she'd wanted out. A chance to start over where she hadn't been an immature teenager. Time to pursue her dreams. Was that so wrong?

Rachel still had hopes and aspirations that didn't involve this town. After high school, she'd gone to Colorado for college and concentrated on her studies. Now she planned to focus on her career.

Houston was four hours away. Close enough that she could see her nephews whenever she made the drive and yet far enough that she could start fresh. Rachel wanted to be in Texas and somewhat close to her brother, his wife and their kids—they were her only immediate family, since their parents had passed away when she'd been thirteen. But she didn't want to live in Fredericksburg. She enjoyed bigger cities. Liked everyone not knowing what she was up to and then gossiping about it.

For instance, just the fact that she was conversing with Hunter would cause a ripple that would echo across the smooth surface of this town.

"Hunter. Rachel."

Their heads both snapped in the direction of the voice. The associate pastor, Greg Tendra, approached, sporting a grin that wasn't mirrored on Hunter's face or hers. He wore a green dress shirt tucked into black pants and no tie. The man was an inch or two shorter than Rachel, with raven curly hair, and the smell of spicy aftershave wafted with him.

"I'm glad to see you two have met."

A laugh almost escaped from her throat, but she managed to stem it before it burst out. Being new to town, Greg obviously didn't know any of the history between Hunter and Rachel. Fine by her. What had happened between them would stay in the past, as far as she was concerned. She didn't need to confess to the pastor that they'd once had a vibrant relationship that had turned toxic. That when she did come home, she and Hunter couldn't manage more than a few minutes—seconds, really—of stifled surface-level conversation.

But why would Greg care if she and Hunter had met? Unless…

Her stomach plummeted to her cherry-red-painted toenails. No. It couldn't be. Dread crawled across her skin even as she tried to talk herself out of the idea.

"You're my leaders for building the float with the youth group this summer. The brawn and the brains." Greg's face wreathed in a teasing smile as he glanced from Hunter to Rachel, and her world crumbled around her. She'd agreed to do one thing while home—help the youth build a float for the Independence Day parade. She'd said yes for a number of reasons. It would give her something to do while home. It would even look good on her résumé, and she needed all the help she could get to land this job. But mostly, she loved teens. All the snarky sides of them. Just like she'd been, way back when.

But she hadn't realized the opportunity would come with Hunter attached.

She was supposed to work with him? Rachel wasn't sure how to handle that. She only knew her plans remained the same: get the job she wanted and break out of this town. And just like the last time, she couldn't let Hunter McDermott stand in her way.

Hunter's ears were ringing. They felt like Kinsley had taken a pot and a pan and banged his head between them. His niece squirmed in his arms, and he realized that during Greg's revelation, he'd been squeezing her pretty tight. When he spotted his sister, Autumn, talking to someone about ten feet away, Hunter placed Kinsley on the ground. A soft pat on her diapered bum had her scooting off toward her mom. When he was satisfied she'd been captured by his sister, Hunter turned his attention back to the strange turn of events happening in front of him.

By the look of pure shock on Rachel's face, Hunter imagined Greg hadn't informed her of who the other leader would be, either. He must have assumed they didn't know each other. He couldn't be more wrong on that account.

Would Rachel run now? She was certainly good at it.

Hunter winced. When had he turned so bitter? He was morphing into his father, and he didn't like it.

He could be a gentleman and back out of helping. Rachel was the teen whisperer, not him. He was pretty much the brawn, like Greg had joked. Hunter had been asked to help with the float because he had a truck and a flatbed trailer. Two things that were needed. He'd agreed to help because he loved the youth group. He'd spent plenty of time there as a kid. It had become a safe place for him after his mom left, and he wanted to give back to that. He still did, but how could this ever work?

"We're thankful to have the two of you helping. I honestly wasn't sure what we were going to do. But now that we have you both, crisis averted." Greg's sigh of relief told Hunter even more than his words. Hunter only knew Greg a little, but the man had been thrown into numerous roles at the church, even having to cover for the youth pastor who'd left unexpectedly.

So much for Hunter's idea of quietly disappearing. He wouldn't leave the church or the kids abandoned like that. Building the float had been the highlight of a few of his summers, too. It was tradition, and he remembered how much he'd looked forward to it.

Hunter sought Rachel's eyes, wishing he could read her like he used to be able to. Back when they'd been inseparable. When she hadn't looked at him as if her dog had just died and he was to blame. What was she thinking? "Didn't you say you were here waiting on a job?" How would she have time for something like this? How long would she actually be home?

"I am." She toyed with a gold R pendant that hung on a slim chain around her neck, her fingers a stark white. "The school is doing more interviews and then waiting for a decision from the board. It might take a month or two."

"We'll take you as long as we can have you," Greg chimed in.

That made one of them. Been there. Done that.

Greg's hand momentarily rested on Rachel's arm after his comment, and Hunter fought annoyance at the man and at himself for caring. What Rachel did or didn't do wasn't any of his business and hadn't been for a long time. But Greg was young—maybe just a few years older than Hunter—and not blind. Rachel was beautiful. Tall, with straight, light-blond hair that landed inches past her shoulders and mesmerizing green eyes. He'd always been partial to the subtle smattering of freckles on her face that he knew she despised.

Her beauty hadn't been the reason Hunter had once wanted to hold on to her, but it had been a perk to look at her pretty face every day and see her smiling at him as though he made the stars shine at night. Only he hadn't been enough to keep her here.

A quick glance at the ring finger on her left hand

told him she wasn't engaged or married. He assumed he would have heard if she was. Lucy Redmond—Olivia's sister—used to feed him tidbits of information about Rachel. But even Lucy's optimism couldn't overpower the messy past between Hunter and Rachel or the fact that they wanted completely opposite things.

Rachel had always had one foot out the door of this town, and his life was here. Hunter should have known to leave well enough alone when they were younger and not pursue a relationship with her, but she'd been hard to resist.

Greg had continued talking, and Hunter forced himself to concentrate on the conversation. "The search for a youth pastor probably won't wrap up until the end of July. But with you two handling the float, we only have the lock-in to cover, which I'm heading up, and then we'll hopefully have a new youth pastor starting in August or September."

The man looked pleased as punch. Hunter didn't know what to feel. For so many years, he and Rachel had avoided each other. They'd never dealt with what had happened between them. It had just been easier to sweep their past under the rug. He blamed her for so much, and he was just as sure she held him responsible for what went wrong.

And now he sounded like his father—stuck. Unable to move on.

If there was one thing Hunter wanted more than a quiet, content life of ranching, it was to not turn into his dad. He would do just about anything to avoid following in his old man's footsteps.

The three of them talked for another minute about when the float building was scheduled to start—this

Wednesday. And what time—seven o'clock. Then Greg split off to catch up with someone else.

"I—" Rachel looked as though she'd witnessed a terrible car accident, a bit of green dusting her face. "I should go find my nephews and Cash and Liv. They're probably waiting for me."

She didn't leave him any time to respond before she headed for the front doors of the church. Should he follow her? Make sure she was okay?

Nah. She wouldn't welcome his intrusion.

Hunter watched her burst out into the sunlight, angst churning in his gut. The memories with Rachel flooded back, fast and furious. Before their relationship had gone so wrong, it had been good.

But what had stood between them six years ago still stretched between them now. That and a lot of hurt.

Hunter refused to turn into his father and grow resentful, holding on to the past. Which, if Rachel and Hunter were going to be working together with the youth, meant one thing. The two of them were just going to have to learn to be friends again.

Whether she wanted to be or not.

Chapter Two

*O*uch. Rachel jolted awake when her elbow met the wooden side of her nephew's fire truck bedframe. She rubbed the spot and stared up at the ceiling.

The house Rachel had grown up in—where her brother, his wife and their two boys now lived—only had three bedrooms upstairs and a small office downstairs. Her four-year-old nephew, Grayson, occupied one bedroom, and Ryder, who was just a year old, had a slightly smaller one. Cash and Olivia were in the master. There was no guest room, which meant that, with her added into the mix, Gray was sleeping on Ryder's floor so she could have his room. He currently considered the situation "very cool" and liked "camping" every night, but that wouldn't last forever. Certainly not for the month or two she'd be home. And while she didn't mind sleeping in a twin bed the shape of a fire truck, she was willing to live somewhere else and give Cash, Olivia and the boys their own space back. Except that, with her limited amount of time in town plus the fact that she should be saving money, she wasn't sure how to solve the space dilemma.

"Auntie Rach, watch out, the stampede is coming!" Grayson tore into the bedroom and jumped onto the bed with her, causing air to rush from her lungs.

"Grayson Warren Maddox, I told you not to wake her." Olivia paused in the doorway to Rachel's temporary room. She blew a wayward hair from her forehead, looking a little frazzled for eight o'clock in the morning.

Rachel's sister-in-law had aged well in the years since she'd met and married Cash. She wore khaki shorts and a navy blue T-shirt, her long mocha hair pulled into a ponytail. Even without makeup, she was striking. But more than her outside beauty, she was tender and compassionate with enough snark to make her likeable. The sister Rachel had never had. When Rachel had been in high school, Olivia had been her volleyball coach. She'd made a huge impact on Rachel and mentored her at a time when she'd been missing her parents and floundering.

"Sorry, Rach. Gray needs to get dressed and I had planned to sneak in and grab a few things without waking you. But it seems our boy had a different idea."

Rachel captured Grayson and tugged him close, holding him in a tight grip that made him squirm and giggle. "It's okay. I was up and hungry, and I love to eat little boys for breakfast."

He squealed and tried to get away while she smacked a kiss to his chocolate hair that still carried the sweet, fruity smell of kiddo shampoo from last night's bath.

"Auntie Rachel, will you take me riding?" When those hazel eyes peered up at her, Rachel didn't stand a chance of saying no. Not that she wanted to. Part of her plan for the summer was to help Liv with the kids. If she was home waiting on a job, she could at least lend a hand. She'd already finished all of the requirements needed by the State of Texas in order to be ready for the new opportunity. Which meant now she needed to occupy herself while playing the waiting game.

"Yep. Just let me get dressed. Can't ride in our pajamas."

Grayson's eyes lit up. "But that would be cool."

Within a half hour Rachel had eaten a bowl of cereal and downed a cup of coffee. Now she and Grayson were saddled up and headed out. He looked so happy, sitting in front of her in the saddle, mini cowboy hat on his head. Her heart just about gushed out all the love it held. She really, really adored her nephews. They were one plus in being home this summer.

The two of them meandered out on the ranch, stopping to visit with Cash and a few of the ranch hands before riding to the east edge of the property.

Rachel had forgotten about the old house that popped into view. It had been part of a ranch that had gone under decades before, and her parents had bought the land as an addition to the Circle M. She remembered a story about a skirmish between her dad and Hunter's, as they'd both wanted the property flanked by their two spreads. Her father had won the tussle, and she and Hunter had grown up on neighboring ranches.

Not that the McDermotts cared about this small slip of ranchland anymore. They were like land barons. They'd snatched up a number of smaller ranches over the years and now had a massive operation.

She directed Bonnie, the sweet mare they were riding, toward the house. A grayish hue tinted the white paint, as though the siding had given up fighting against the Texas sun years before. It looked deserted. No recent tire tracks. The grass around it was unruly and long.

Strange. Before she'd left for college, various ranch hands had rented the small house or negotiated living there as part of their pay. She didn't know what Cash did with it now.

Movement to the east caught her eye. A man on a horse crested a hill on the McDermott ranch. Too far away to tell for sure who it was, especially with the cowboy hat, but the build could definitely be Hunter's.

"Can we get down and look around?" Grayson questioned.

"Sure!"

Gray looked at her a little funny, and why wouldn't he? She'd just shown a lot of excitement for poking around an empty house. But if it would help her avoid a run-in with Hunter—if that was him—she couldn't resist.

Rachel still couldn't believe the two of them were in charge of building the float with the youth. That would have been useful information to have when Greg had asked Rachel to help. Since their conversation at church yesterday, she'd gone over and over the situation, and she couldn't see an escape route. She'd committed, and she wasn't going to back out and leave the church strapped. Besides, she wanted to work with the teens. This would be a great opportunity to show the town she'd changed—that she wasn't the same immature girl she'd once been.

Rachel wanted people to see her as who she'd become. Not the queen of bad decisions. A crown she'd once had the monopoly on.

She and Hunter would just have to function around

each other. If they limited their interactions to Wednesday nights and the occasional sighting at church, Rachel would be out of here and on to her new life in no time.

Bonnie meandered to a stop on the west side of the house, and Rachel and Grayson slipped down from the saddle. Her nephew was more at home riding than most adults she knew. Definitely her brother's child. When they'd been kids, Cash had always been out working with the horses, doing anything mechanical, helping move cattle and bumming around the ranch with Dad, even at a young age. The memory coaxed a smile. She was thankful the ache of missing her parents had lessened over the years, though it always remained with her.

What she wouldn't give to be able to go back for one day and tell them how much she loved them.

Gray had already taken off around the front of the house, so Rachel secured Bonnie to the hitching post and trotted after him. The kid only had one speed—fast.

"Can we go inside? Maybe we'll find a snake!" He'd already climbed the front steps and now stood on the small wooden porch. He tossed his hat on the stair railing, leaving a thick head of mussed brown hair visible. "Or a black widow spider. Or a tarantula." His excitement increased with each suggestion, while Rachel's mind screamed, *Turn around. Fast*.

She peeked through the front window. Papers, a turned-over chair, clothes and some other random items littered the floor. On the front porch, an abandoned wooden swing hung by only one chain. The other side scraped eerily against the floorboards in the slight breeze.

No one lived here. Not at the moment.

"We can try, bud, but I would assume it's locked."

Rachel attempted to turn the knob, but it didn't twist. Mostly to prove to Grayson that she'd tried, she shoved on the door with the palm of her hand. Amazingly, it eased open. The latch must have been broken. She pushed the door open wider, and it creaked and groaned as though arthritis crippled its hinges.

Before going inside, she gave the porch a good hard stomp, just in case any critters did live inside. Ignoring the creepy feeling that a spider was about to descend on her head, she took a tentative step inside. It smelled… musty. But daylight streamed in through the windows, illuminating a basic, but surprisingly roomy space. A small bedroom was visible through an open door to the right, and the kitchen area held a few cabinets and an avocado-green stove. An older fridge—the kind that would probably go for megabucks as vintage on eBay—had the doors propped open. Thankfully the contents had been cleaned out before it had been left unplugged.

"Whoa." Grayson had followed her inside and now stood next to her, thumbs hooked through his belt loops as he studied the room. "This could be my fort. I'd pretend the bad guys were coming." His fingers formed guns as he faced the door. "I'd have everything ready. They wouldn't stand a chance against me."

Just like Grayson to see the possibilities instead of the obstacles. At four years old—soon to be five—he had the sweetest optimism about life. Rachel would like to take a scoop of it with her wherever she went. She ran a hand through his soft hair. "Totally, buddy. You'd have the fastest guns, for sure."

Grayson walked the open stretch of floor, boots echoing against the wood. He stopped at the end of the room, head tilted in concentration. "Think Dad would let me move out here?"

She managed to stem the laughter bubbling in her throat. "I don't know about that, Gray."

Though she could understand his interest. The place did have a certain charm—if she looked past the mess that had been left behind. For a family, it would be tiny. But for one or two people? Cozy. Quiet.

If she could get this place cleaned up, maybe *she* could move out here for the next month or two. She could give Olivia, Cash and the boys their house back while still being around to help and spend time with them. Rachel pressed the pause button on her rampant thoughts. The idea was crazy. The house might not be falling to pieces, but it would take too long if she attempted it on her own. Rachel could admit it was as tempting to her as Grayson's fort was to him, though.

"Auntie Rachel, can I go outside?" Grayson had already zipped through the small bathroom and bedroom and must have gotten bored with the space.

Liv let Grayson play outdoors by himself for little bits of time, so Rachel thought the same rule could apply here. "If you stay within five steps of the house."

"Five giant steps?"

With his little legs? "Deal."

"Front and back?"

"Just front. That way I can keep an eye on you through the windows."

His nose wrinkled as if to say he didn't need that kind of supervision, but then he scampered outside.

She moved into the bedroom, watching through the old, white-wood-framed glass window as Grayson scooted down the porch steps, and then, true to form, counted out five long strides from the house. When he reached the limit, he bent down, grabbed a stick and began drawing in the dirt.

Rachel wandered to the east bedroom window and scanned the horizon. No more sign of the rider who had been there minutes before.

If it had been Hunter, he was gone now. Relief rushed in, cool and sweet.

Sometimes she looked back on what had happened with Hunter and wondered how it had all gone so wrong. How they'd switched from best friends to not speaking at all.

Most people didn't know that Hunter had gotten it into his head to propose to her back then. She hadn't even told her brother, simply because Rachel had known it couldn't happen. Getting married at such a young age might have worked out for Hunter. He'd known what he wanted and that it was here. He was a rancher. It had always been this town, this life, for him.

But Cash had given up a lot for her, and she'd been working on maturing at the time. That hadn't included eloping and throwing away a volleyball scholarship. Even for Hunter.

To say the least, he hadn't understood.

Their relationship—even their friendship—had been crushed.

Something skittered across the wood floor and Rachel screamed. An old brown chair had been left behind in the corner of the room, and she ran for it, jumping up. It wobbled under her weight but thankfully held. Screeches continued to slip out of her as the mouse paused to stare her down, then ran for the edge of the room.

She shivered as it disappeared beneath some warped trim. *Eek*, that thing had freaked her out. Her heart stampeded, and she sucked in a calming breath, thankful no one was around to see her silly antics over such a tiny creature.

"What are you doing?" Hunter leaned against the bedroom doorframe, arms crossed. Looking casual. Amused.

Her eyes momentarily closed. So it had been him she'd seen. He must have left his hat somewhere, because his hair looked as though a hand had scrubbed through the short, dark blond locks only seconds before.

Stinky, stink, stink. How long had he been standing there? She looked down at the chair under her boots, then back to him, contemplating asking, *God, why? Why Hunter? Why now?*

"Nothing."

"Just standing on a chair in the corner of a deserted house?"

"Yep." Rachel didn't have to explain anything to Hunter. For all he knew, she'd been looking at something on the ceiling. Or examining a crack in the wall. Or checking out her ability to fly if she jumped from the chair.

The real question was, what was he doing here?

He motioned to the floor. "Tell me that wasn't a reaction to the cute baby mouse that just went through here."

Rats. He'd witnessed her dramatics.

"What happened to the country girl I knew? The one who could ride as fast as the boys. Wasn't afraid of snakes. Got dirtier faster than anyone else."

"Most of that was true, but I faked the part about

snakes. I was afraid of them. Just didn't want to admit it. If I had, you would have tormented me with them."

He laughed, the lines on his face softening. "Well played." He nodded toward her strange standing place. "Don't suppose you want any help getting out of here." His dimples flashed. "You know, so that mean, scary mouse doesn't get you."

"I'm fine." The mouse was long gone. Wasn't it? Either way, Rachel wasn't going to do anything to prolong being in Hunter's presence. Even if that creature came back out. Ran across her boot. Gave her the heebie-jeebies again.

She could handle a little rodent. Just not the man looking at her with far too much amusement.

Besides, with all of the noise they were making, the mouse would be miles away.

Rachel only wished Hunter would follow suit.

"Don't you have a ranch to run?" Rachel huffed loudly enough to blow the walls of the house down like the big bad wolf in the three little pigs story.

Hunter tried to stem the curve of his mouth, but it wasn't working. He'd forgotten how much fun it was to rile up Rachel. "Trying to get rid of me?"

Her head tilted, ponytail bouncing with the movement. "Am I that obvious? Because I'm trying to be."

Despite claiming she didn't want help, she was still standing on the chair. He might be enjoying her predicament and annoyance with him just a bit too much. It had been a few years since he'd gotten any emotional response from her, and he kind of liked knowing he still affected her, even if it meant she wanted to smack him.

"All right, princess." The name earned a scowl as

he approached her chair/throne and offered her a hand. "Let's get you out of here."

Her body language screamed *get lost* and *don't touch* in one easy-to-read display. "What are you doing?"

"Helping you."

"I told you, I'm fine." She made a shooing motion. "Just go."

"Now, Rach. I'm not so much of a jerk that I'm going to let you get mauled by a mouse." Her squeak of indignation and the fire in her eyes told him how she felt about that comment. "Come on." He grew serious and dropped the teasing act, re-offering his hand. "Let's go."

"No, thank you."

He'd also forgotten just how stubborn she was. When they'd been younger and first started hanging out, it had taken Hunter some time to prove she could trust him. Rachel'd been the queen of building walls and defending them. Eventually he'd gotten through. And once he had, it had been worth it.

But she'd had years to rebuild. Which meant they could be here all day. And, honestly, he just didn't have time for that. Despite what she thought of him, he'd heard her scream when the mouse had spooked her, and he wasn't going to just leave her stranded.

Before he could analyze how mad she'd be, Hunter bent and scooped her over his right shoulder.

She screeched and whacked him on the back, where the upper half of her body hung. Wiggled trying to break free. He strode through the bedroom and living room, one arm looped around her legs so she didn't fall to the floor with all of her squirming.

"What are you doing? Put me down, you big ogre."

His chest shook with quiet laughter as he exited

through the front door. Rachel's nephew Grayson played nearby, destroying an anthill with a stick. He only glanced up for a second—not the least bit concerned about the racket his aunt was making or the fact that she was slung over Hunter's shoulder—and quickly went back to his digging and investigating.

Hunter deposited Rachel on the front porch. "This far enough or do you need me to go farther?" He adopted a serious face and nodded toward the field. "But who knows what-all is out there. Could be a spider or, even worse, a crow—they make scary noises. I've heard stories about them swooping down and snatching up small children. You're a skinny thing. Can't be too careful."

This time her hit landed on his arm. He chuckled, which, judging by the way her face had turned as menacing as a thunderstorm, was only making her more upset.

"Are you done making fun of me yet? I don't appreciate you taking the liberty to cart me around like a sack of feed." She growled the last bit, crossing her arms over a simple white T-shirt that made renewed laughter catch in his throat. He'd been too amused and distracted by her antics inside to notice what she was wearing. Most often when she came home to visit and he caught a glimpse of her, she was dressed up for church. Always looking so put together. Usually in heels, too. Not cowboy boots and faded jeans and a fitted white T-shirt. The simple outfit almost knocked him over.

Though, right now he'd better concentrate on her not kicking him in the shin. She looked mad enough.

"I think I'm done, though I reserve the right to make fun of you about this again in the future. What are you two doing out here, anyway?"

He'd been out checking for signs of coyotes when he'd spotted Rachel and her nephew. He'd stopped to talk to her because he thought they needed to get some things worked out. Like, was she still planning to help the youth build the float? If not, he'd need to find someone else. Hunter was happy to help with the float building, but he didn't feel qualified to be the only one in charge of a group of teens.

"Grayson wanted to explore." Rachel stared straight forward after answering him, her jaw set in that stubborn look she did so well.

"Did you back out of helping with the youth?"

Her cheeks pinkened, highlighting her freckles. "No. I didn't."

"So you're committing?"

Her gaze snapped to him. Oops. Bad choice of words.

When she finally nodded, his worry decreased. "That's good. They need someone like you in their lives."

At that, her demeanor softened a bit. "Did you back out?"

"Nope. Wouldn't want you to lose out on the delight of working with me."

That earned him an eye roll and a shaking head. Just like the old Rachel.

He nodded over to Grayson, who was now inspecting under the front porch as though he might find a treasure. "Ran into Grayson on my way in and he told me he was planning to move out here."

Cute kid. Always dressed like a miniature cowboy, that one. Boots. Jeans. T-shirt. Coupled with scrawny arms, a mop of brown hair and eyes that brimmed with curiosity.

"I wish."

"What's that mean?"

Rachel peered through the front window before releasing an audible sigh. "Cash's house is so crowded with me added in. Grayson was asking if this could be his fort, and I was thinking the same thing. That I want to move out here."

"With the mouse?"

Was that a halfway smile claiming her mouth? Hunter should call the *Fredericksburg Standard*. News like that could make the front page.

A visible shudder followed. "Definitely not with the mouse."

"You know, you can get rid of mice. The place didn't look too bad when I was in there. Seemed mostly cosmetic. Cleaning. Paint. Looked like someone had the law on their tail and left half their belongings. Granted, you were screaming like someone was after you, so I didn't get a great look."

"I could never do it on my own, and I'm not asking Cash. He has enough to do."

"I would help you." The words were out of his mouth before he had time to think, but once they registered, he decided the idea wasn't so crazy. If he was going to follow through with the two of them getting along and putting the past behind them, he might as well jump in with both feet.

Curiosity and concern mingled in the depths of her distractingly beautiful green eyes. Maybe even a bit of fear. "Why?"

"Why not?"

It was easier to answer that way than to tell her the truth. *I don't want to turn into my father* seemed like a strange answer. There was one thing he'd never seen his dad and mom do—make amends. Forgive. Move on. Therefore, that's exactly what Hunter planned to accomplish.

And this way, when Rachel did her next disappearing act for the job she wanted and came back to visit her family, she and Hunter would be able to get along. Wish each other well.

She studied the toes of her camel-colored boots as though they held the answer to all of the world's problems. "It was nice of you to offer, but I can't accept."

Couldn't? Or wouldn't? He could pretty easily guess the answer to that. Her response didn't surprise him. She wasn't the type to welcome his offer—or anyone's for that matter—with open arms. Nope. Rachel had always had a bit of an edge to her, and that was putting it nicely. The woman had more spunk in her pinkie finger than most people had in their whole body. It had been one of the things he'd liked about her back then. Still did.

"We need to get back." Rachel shut the front door of the house. She grabbed the small cowboy hat propped on the stair railing and tromped down the steps, heading for their horse and calling Grayson at the same time.

After a few seconds of complaining from the boy, Rachel and Grayson mounted up. They took off with quick waves in his direction.

She was sure in an all-fired hurry to get out of here. Away from him. Not that he blamed her. He'd been a jerk when they were younger. He'd asked her to stay when he shouldn't have.

Some people just weren't built for this life.

Hunter had learned that lesson too well. A painful

brand had been burned into him because of his mother's unhappiness. She'd detested ranching and small-town living. Yet Dad had convinced her it would grow on her one day. He'd pursued her until she'd agreed to marry him and live on the ranch. Hunter had heard the beginning of their story many times.

But the middle and end had never improved. In all of his childhood memories, his mom had been sad. Lethargic. Broken. When he was nine, she'd given up pretending and left them. Moved to Dallas.

After, Dad had sunk further and further out of reach. It wasn't that they didn't see each other. It was that they didn't really talk about anything besides ranchTing. His sister, Autumn, had been his saving grace. Three years older, she'd taken to mothering him.

Hunter wouldn't copy his father's mistakes again. He'd been selfish asking Rachel to stay and marry him. She'd only been eighteen. He'd been twenty. Hunter had watched his mom live a life she didn't want. He'd witnessed her unhappiness. He'd known better than to ask Rachel to do the same, yet he'd been grasping at straws to keep her in his life.

And, in the process, he'd lost her completely.

Suggesting they get married had been impetuous of him, and when Rachel had said she loved him but she couldn't, he'd reacted so badly. Out of hurt, he'd pushed her away.

Not a shining moment for him.

But it was time to turn all of that around. Hunter had been at a loss about how to prove to Rachel that they could get along again. She'd built so many walls between them over time—and he'd only been too happy to help her hold them steady—that he wasn't sure where to begin.

But now that he knew about the house, she'd given him the perfect way to start.

He only hoped it wouldn't backfire on him.

Chapter Three

Rachel surveyed the small ranch house from the doorway, frustration zinging along her spine. It was Wednesday, and she and Grayson had gone out for another ride. He'd been antsy after it rained all day Tuesday, and he'd wanted to visit the house again—which he'd started referring to as his fort. But since they'd been out on Monday, someone had been here. Supplies were sitting just inside the door, paint cans included. The mountain of trash was gone.

All fingers pointed to Hunter, since no one else even knew what she'd been thinking. What part of *no* didn't he understand? She did not appreciate his intruding in her life like this.

Rachel slipped her cell phone from her pocket, hoped the reception would work and called her friend Val. The two of them had been best friends since junior high, and the fact that Val still lived in Fredericksburg was, for Rachel, a definite plus in being home. They'd kept up their friendship over the years—one of the only people Rachel could claim that about. Val had always been levelheaded back when Rachel had been anything but.

Now she hoped the two of them were on a more similar plane. Except, at the moment, *level* was not a feeling Rachel was experiencing.

"Hey," Val's voice sounded in her ear. "Connor is eating mac and cheese, which means I'll probably have to go in a sec when he puts a piece of it up his nose even though I've tried to teach him not to do that a million times."

"Okay." Not for the first time, Rachel thought what a strange thing motherhood was. "You are never going to believe what Hunter did."

"Ooh, what?"

She explained about finding the deserted old ranch house, running into Hunter and the conversation that had ensued. "And now he's started fixing it up after I told him no. I didn't even know he'd been out here and a bunch of stuff got done."

"Huh." Prolonged silence came from Val's side of the conversation. "That's…horrible?"

"It is horrible! I don't want him involved in my life."

"Technically he's not involved. You weren't even there when he did anything."

"Whose side are you on, anyway?"

A stifled cough-laugh combination answered her. "I mean, how could he just help you like that when you didn't even give him permission?"

"Your sarcasm is impressive."

"Thank you. I learned it from you. So, do you want my old-married-lady advice?"

"You've been married two years, so I don't think that qualifies you as headed out for pasture yet, but sure." Rachel's mouth curved despite her annoyance with Hunter. "Hit me with it."

"Let him help. You're out of space at the house. I'd offer to let you stay here—"

"You guys don't have room for me, either."

"That's why I'm telling you to accept his offer. At some point, you need to let go of what happened between the two of you. This is the perfect opportunity."

"No."

"Just…no? That's all you've got?"

"Yep." Rachel might be using toddler logic right now, but she didn't care to adjust her maturity level. She didn't have to explain her feelings, did she? How could she, when she didn't even understand them herself? "Why would he do this?"

"Maybe he likes you." Val stretched out the phrase, sounding as though she was imitating one of the second-grade students she taught.

"Ha." Rachel swallowed, mouth suddenly devoid of moisture. "That's not funny."

Laughter floated into her ear, then stopped abruptly. "Oh, no." Resignation laced Val's tone. "There went the mac and cheese. Gotta go."

They disconnected and Rachel glanced at the pile of supplies. What was Hunter thinking? Could Val's joking insinuation be true? Was Hunter trying to…? No way. He couldn't have feelings for her. Could he? He had talked to her more in the last few days than he had in years. *Was* he trying to rekindle things? It made no sense, especially since he always seemed annoyed or offended by her presence. At least, he had before this visit home.

Rachel didn't know what to think. It couldn't be. But why else would he do something like this?

It wasn't like he hadn't gotten a crazy idea regarding them before. His suggestion they get married had been completely unexpected.

Back in high school, Rachel had made some stupid decisions about guys. She'd dated one she would rather forget and had done a number of things she regretted during her teenage years.

In the last part of her senior year of school, when she and Hunter had first started hanging out, she'd been wary of making another mistake. Another stupid decision about another guy. But she'd quickly noticed the differences in Hunter. He'd been genuine. Always respectful. He'd made her laugh. He was one of the few people she'd talked to about her parents and he'd talked to her about his mom.

They'd hung out a long time before they'd even so much as held hands. Their first kiss had been…heart pounding. They'd been on a walk. He'd been teasing her about something, and the next thing she knew, he'd stopped, buried his hands in her hair and kissed her. Kissed her as though she was oxygen and he needed to breathe. After, he'd backed away. His grin slow. Easy. "I knew it." Then he'd grabbed her hand and kept walking while she stumbled to find coherent thought again.

She'd fallen for him. Hard.

Falling for him had been the easy part. But even back then, they'd known she was moving for school. The knowledge had hung over them like a storm cloud that followed their every step. At first it hadn't been menacing—just something to deal with in the future. But as the time for her to leave had neared, the cloud had changed from might-rain-sometime into a dark, severe-weather thunderstorm.

They'd avoided talking much about her looming departure for college, neither of them knowing what to do about it.

The week before she'd been set to move, they'd been sitting on the porch swing at his dad's house, concern over the future stealing their words, when Hunter had squeezed her hand. "Don't go," he'd said. Her head had snapped in his direction. "Stay. I know people will say we're young, but I don't want to do life without you. Marry me." At first, his eyes had flashed with surprise at his words, but then he'd leaned toward her as if the idea had gained momentum. "We should get married. We could elope."

Rachel remembered precisely how she'd felt. Like a car had rammed into her. She'd loved Hunter, but had known instantly that she couldn't. As much as the thought of leaving him had hurt and refusing him had felt like the hardest thing she'd ever do, she'd been certain she had to follow through with her plans.

Her stomach had tied itself into thousands of knots. She'd tried to tell him how much she cared about him… but that she couldn't stay. Couldn't marry him. Not at eighteen.

In the middle of her explanation, he'd shut down. His eyes had hardened. And then he'd told her to go. That if she didn't feel the same way about him as he did about her, she might as well leave immediately. In the next week, before she'd left, they hadn't even seen each other. It had been so painful.

She couldn't do that again. Rachel didn't know what Hunter was thinking, but she had to talk to him. They were going to be working together with the youth. They'd be seeing enough of each other that she had to make sure she was clear with him about her future plans and that nothing could happen between them. They couldn't go back down the road they'd once traveled.

It was Wednesday. Tonight was the first night of working on the float with the teens. She'd head over early and have a conversation with him.

She had to. Because, despite having moved on from their younger years, she knew she couldn't survive that experience twice.

"Are you sure you know what you're doing?"

Autumn was perched on the desk in the barn office/storage area while Hunter rummaged through the bins the church had given him for float decorating.

When he glanced up, her pointed look told him she expected an answer. His sister packed a lot of punch for five foot two. But despite her petite size, she'd always played and fought just as hard as the boys.

"Yes, I know what I'm doing." He set aside two bins. "Just because you're older than me doesn't mean you're wiser."

"You are correct." She twisted her light-brown hair over one shoulder. "Age doesn't matter, but I am wiser."

He didn't bother answering that sassy comment.

"You do remember what happened the last time? I mean, I think Rachel's great and all, but you were a mess when she left."

He didn't need the reminder. "I wasn't a mess." He might have been a small version of that word. "But that's not going to happen again. This is about being a friend. What I should have been to her in the first place before I let stupidity cloud my judgment. She needed someone to be there for her, and back then I made it about me and what I wanted. She deserves to be treated well, and while I didn't accomplish that the last time, I am going to this time."

"So, you're just going to help her with this house whether she wants it or not?"

"Pretty much."

"And you're trying to prove…"

"That I'm not Dad." The words slipped out, and Hunter almost rolled his eyes. How did Autumn always pull information out of him he didn't plan to give?

Her eyebrows stitched together. "Hunter, you're nothing like Dad. You work hard, so I guess you have that in common, but that's about it."

Except for the part where he'd asked Rachel to stay and he shouldn't have. And the next part, where he'd been a jerk and reacted badly when she'd said no. Autumn didn't understand because she and her husband Calvin had met when they were older. Dating…marriage…it had all just fallen into place for them without any stupid decisions to atone for.

"Think about it this way. If you knew you couldn't have Calvin as anything more than a friend, wouldn't you want that? And if you'd hurt him, wouldn't you want to rectify that?"

Autumn studied him. Finally, she nodded, but her brow remained pinched. "I just don't want to see you get hurt."

He tapped a fist on his chest. "I'm practically a superhero with all of these muscles."

She groaned in response, then stood and rubbed a hand over her growing belly. His nephew was coming in about three months, and Hunter was more than ready. It had been a rough pregnancy, and Autumn had been sick for much of it.

She might be his older sister, but he still felt protective of her. Which meant he understood her concern about him. But she was just going to have to trust him. Hunter had prayed over this decision, and he felt peace about it. Moving on and regaining a friendship with Rachel was the right thing to do.

Autumn stretched her arms over her head, accompanying that with a huge yawn. "I'm hungry."

"What's new? It's been an hour since you last ate."

"Jerk." Humor puckered the skin around her eyes. "I'll see you later."

She let herself out through the office door, and a few seconds later he heard her car start. Hunter grabbed the extralarge gray tote filled with float-building supplies and strode toward the open end of the barn where the flatbed trailer waited.

Rachel stood just inside the large sliding doors. She looked fighting mad. Gorgeous—no surprise there— but not happy. He changed course, walking in her direction.

Was she just here early for the first night with the youth? Or had she found out he'd been at the house? Based on her expression, he'd say the latter. Hunter had hoped helping make the place livable for her would work in his favor, but he was starting to doubt his plan.

Rachel wore a green sleeveless shirt with pressed flowered shorts. Coupled with sandals that daintily looped around her ankles, she looked perfectly put together, yet she still had that edge. The one that said, *I don't belong in this Podunk town. I'm meant for more and don't you forget it.*

Though he read her message loud and clear, it didn't stop him from appreciating the sight. He'd thought jeans, a T-shirt and boots might do him in the other day, but as it turned out, it didn't matter what she wore.

Caused a bit of trouble, that. He wasn't supposed to be noticing how she looked—though, really, it would be impossible for him not to. He was supposed to be renewing their friendship. And he wasn't off to a great start by the look of it.

He set the large tote on the ground by their feet. "Hey, you're here early."

"I need to talk to you before the kids arrive."

"About the float?" He could only hope.

"No."

Ah. So she'd found the stuff.

"I assume it was you who started working on the house?"

He didn't have anything to hide. "I did."

"I wasn't even serious about it. It was just a passing thought. Why would you do something like that?" Her breath hissed out. "It doesn't even make sense. I'm only going to be here for a month or two."

"What's Cash planning to do with the house?"

"I don't know. I asked Olivia what happened with it. She said the last renter trashed it, and Cash hasn't had time to deal with it since."

"So after you live there for the summer, he can rent it out again. If none of his ranch hands want to lease it, one of ours might. We're not talking about remodeling the place. Just cleaning it up and making it livable so you can stay there while you're home."

Silence reigned. Rachel opened her mouth, then closed it. Finally, she lifted one freckled shoulder. "I guess that makes sense." Just that movement made his mouth go dry. Pesky attraction. At least he'd had a lot of practice shoving it down and ignoring it over the years.

"But why are you helping me?" Her forehead crinkled. "Why would you do that? I don't know if you've forgotten, but you and I aren't on the best of terms. It makes no sense. Unless…" She might as well spit it out since he didn't have any idea what she was trying to say. "Hunter…" Her voice lowered as though someone was hiding around the corner and might overhear them. "You're not trying to restart anything between us, are you?"

What? She thought he was…oh, man. He hadn't even considered that working on the house would make it look like he wanted something more with Rachel. Partly because the idea hadn't even crossed his mind. But, of course, she couldn't read his thoughts.

"We can't." Her lips pressed together. "I can't."

He agreed with her. He couldn't, either. "I'm not trying to start anything between us. I was just sick of—" he raised his hands "—fighting. Not being able to be around each other. Figured it was time to move on. I knew you could use a hand, and this is what friends do."

"So you're not…"

"Nope."

"Oh, good." Distress dropped from her frame, her sigh audible. And a little bit offensive. Did she have to be *so* relieved about it?

Whatever. It didn't matter. Hunter wasn't on the hunt for a wife, anyway. What had happened with his mom and then Rachel had tainted that idea for him. He just wanted a quiet life on the ranch. No drama. No women who didn't want to be there. If he found someone, that would be great, but he wasn't going to do backflips to make it happen. He could be content on his own.

"I'm not trying to pursue anything more than friendship with you, so you can relax. I wouldn't do that to you." Or to himself. "I would never ask you to stay again, Rach. I know you don't belong here." Silence swirled between them, the past rearing up with ugly memories. "Promise. You can trust me."

Her pained glance told him she wasn't so sure about that.

"Will it put you at ease if I'm not the only one working on the house? Because Brennon called and said he and Val want to pitch in. They're planning to come out Saturday."

"What?" Exasperation laced the word. "When did you talk to them?"

"Just a bit ago. Why?"

Sounded like she muttered *traitor*. "What is up with all of you? I didn't even ask for help. This is crazy."

"Are you really surprised? Don't you remember what it's like living in a small town? This is how it is. When someone needs something, everyone pitches in. That's the deal. You'll just have to adjust to the idea."

"And what if I don't want to?"

Hunter knew the answer to this question. His life had taught him this truth numerous times. "You can't always get what you want."

Chapter Four

Somewhere along the way, her plan had backfired. Go over there and tell Hunter to back off. Rachel pictured herself doing that "go to the mattresses" punching move like Meg Ryan in *You've Got Mail*, fists jabbing into thin air. And then failing miserably—also just like the character in the movie.

Of course she wasn't going to let her friends work on the house without pulling her own weight, which meant she'd be spending even more time with Hunter. Rachel had definitely lost the battle to avoid him while home. He'd said he didn't want anything more than friendship with her—and she believed him—but she still didn't relish being in his presence. Even the friendship he wanted felt too far out of reach for them. Their bridge had washed out years before, and it was too late to rebuild.

Get used to having people intrude in your life, he'd told her.

Well, she didn't plan to. Rachel wasn't about to let her guard down and have him and a whole town rushing in.

Was. Not.

Liv had agreed that Rachel staying at the house was a great idea. Which meant now she just needed to broach the subject with her brother.

They'd just finished dinner, and Grayson had run off to play.

Olivia collected Ryder from his high chair. "I'm going to change his diaper." She shot Rachel a look, as if to say, *do it, already*, then headed up the stairs.

Fine. "Cash, what are you planning to do with the little ranch house?"

Her brother finished a long swig of milk. "Not sure. T.J. took off about three months ago. He quit without notice and made a mess of the place. I haven't had the time or energy to deal with it." His back pressed into his chair. "I might just let it sit there. Not a real fan of being a landlord, anyway."

"What if someone got it back in functioning order for you? And then lived there for a little bit and then you could rent it out again?"

His forehead creased. And why wouldn't it? She was talking in circles.

"I want to live there while I'm home. It will give you guys your house back—"

"This is your house, too, you know."

"Technically it's yours." When they'd settled things with their parents' will, Cash had bought out her portion of the house. She hadn't wanted it.

"This will always be your home. You are always welcome."

The strangest prick of emotion touched her eyes. "Okay." She heard him. But no matter how many times he said it, she would always feel like a leaf scraping along the pavement in a gust of wind. Rachel didn't really belong anywhere.

When she moved to Houston, maybe she'd settle in. Put down roots.

"If I can stay at the house, I'll be close by. My friends are going to help me get it cleaned up and functioning, and then when I leave, you can rent it out again. If you want to. Hunter even mentioned that one of his ranch hands might want to rent it if you'd rather not deal with knowing the tenant personally."

"I don't know." Cash pushed his plate forward and propped his arms on the table. "I just don't know how safe that would be for you."

She laughed.

He scowled.

"Oh, you were serious? I thought you were kidding around, because it's in the middle of two ranches where I know both families. The only visitors would be crickets and frogs." And hopefully not mice.

Her brother did remember she'd been living on her own for the last six years, right? In a city much bigger than this one. A bit of that old friction radiated between them. Rachel had been excellent at pushing Cash's buttons in high school. Admittedly, she'd enjoyed every minute far more than she should have. But she really didn't want to fight with him now. She wasn't that girl anymore. Or, at least, she made a serious effort not to be.

Liv came back downstairs with Ryder on her hip and paused at the edge of the table, glancing between Cash and Rachel. "It's weird how Rachel rarely comes home to visit. Here she has all of this tension waiting right here for her and she doesn't even take advantage."

Rachel couldn't help it. She laughed, earning another frown from her brother.

Ryder bounced in Olivia's arms and Rachel reached for him. He came right to her, and she lifted him in the air, earning a flash of baby teeth, a sloppy grin and a bit of drool. When she settled him on her lap, he grabbed the R pendant she wore on a simple gold necklace and gave it a firm tug. Thankfully the chain withstood his efforts.

Grayson might be her favorite nephew for adventuring, but Ryder was the best at snuggles. His hair was a few shades lighter than Gray's. Almost had an auburn shade to it. No one knew where that had come from. His cheeks were squishable, and the boy was as solid as a summer day was long. Liv talked about percentiles and other momish mumbo-jumbo, but Rachel just knew her nephew was built like a one-year-old linebacker.

Oliva dropped into the chair next to Cash. "Rachel and I talked about the house earlier today, and I think it's not such a crazy idea. In fact, I think it's a good one. How many times have we said we need to get it cleaned up, even if we don't decide to rent it out again? You don't have the time. Rachel and her friends will have it done in a few days. We could even use it as a guesthouse if you don't want to rent it. My parents could stay there when they visit. And Rachel would have a place to crash when she comes back to see us."

Every time Rachel thought she couldn't love Olivia more, she was proven wrong.

"Rachel staying there makes perfect sense," Liv continued. "I'm surprised we didn't think of it earlier."

Cash looked part contemplative, part concerned. "I don't know why she'd want to live in that hunk of a house, anyway. It's as big as a cracker. And old." And Rachel didn't know why her brother was talking about her as if she wasn't in the room.

"And quiet. And quaint." Liv sat up straighter in her chair. "Maybe I want to move out there."

"Ha." Cash's eyes narrowed. "Not funny."

She stacked their empty dinner dishes. "Who says I'm joking?"

A shaking head–grin combination came from Cash. "You'd miss me, city girl."

Before Liv could retort—and Rachel had the utmost confidence her sister-in-law would have had a good one—Cash turned serious again. "I don't know that it's a good idea for you to be out there by yourself, Rach. Something could happen."

"And now this sounds like when Rachel was in high school." Liv jumped in, compassion evident despite the disagreement. "She's twenty-four. Not seventeen. Besides that, by the end of the summer she'll likely be living in Houston by herself." If anyone could talk her stubborn brother into something, it would be Liv. "Ryder cries at night, and even though he's going back to sleep, he's waking up Grayson who's crawling into bed with us. I, for one, am exhausted. I'd like to sleep without a foot in my mouth." Olivia scooted closer to Cash, placed her elbows on the table and propped her head in her hands. "Do you see this face? This is a tired face."

In answer, Cash leaned forward and pressed a kiss to her lips. "It's a beautiful face."

"Flattery will get you everywhere."

While Rachel appreciated Liv having her back, she wasn't sure how much PDA she could handle. The house might not be worth it. "I like to think I've evolved into a mature version of myself, but you two are kind of grossing me out right now. Somehow you are just as annoyingly sappy as you were when you first got married."

They laughed.

Rachel glanced at the time on her cell, which was lying on the table. She'd told Hunter she would meet him at the house tonight so they could start working, assuming her brother wouldn't have any issue with it. She should have known better. The two of them had always been like rams, crashing into the other until one of them won. Though they had gotten better over the years since she'd been gone. Rachel appreciated her brother far more now than she had when she'd been a teen. She'd pushed and clawed at him in high school, but he'd never backed away from her. Even at her snarky teenage best.

She could do the house without his agreement; she knew that. He'd come around eventually. But it wasn't about permission. It was about getting along. She liked the idea a whole lot better without her brother being upset. They'd been down that road one too many times before, and she had no desire to repeat history.

Which was why, if he really didn't want her to live in the little house, she wouldn't.

"Well?" The toe of Rachel's flip-flop tapped under the table, her gaze steady on Cash. "What are you thinking?"

His hands rubbed his eyes as he leaned back in the chair. "Are you actually waiting to hear my opinion?"

Ryder shifted on Rachel's lap, as though he wanted to get down. "I'm a docile version of my old self. Sweet. Compliant."

Cash snorted as she deposited Ryder on the floor,

and he toddled toward the couches and toy bin. He'd only recently started walking, and every few steps he'd tumble to the floor and crawl a little before pulling himself back up on a piece of furniture.

An accusing look flashed from Cash to Rachel and Liv, though it was tempered with amusement. "If I even attempt to say no, the two of you will conspire and do it, anyway."

Liv's hand landed on her sternum. "Rachel and me, scheme? That would never happen." She shot a grin in Rachel's direction. "Plus, you heard Rach. She's the picture of innocence these days."

In the past, her name and *scheme* in the same sentence would have offended her, even though it likely would have been true. But now Rachel could embrace the humor instead of the embarrassment.

"I'd never forgive myself if something happened to you," Cash continued. "I know you can make your own decisions and take care of yourself. It's just having you here makes me think you're my responsibility again."

"We've been over this." He'd struggled so much with protecting her after their parents passed away. Over feeling responsible for things that weren't in his control. "God's got me covered. I've always been in His hands." And it was true. Rachel didn't always understand the way God answered prayers, but she did know what-ifs got a person nowhere. "Something could just as easily happen to me in Houston as it could here. There are no guarantees."

"Well, that's not helping anything." A reluctant tilt claimed one side of his mouth. "At least promise me you're going to fix the broken latch and put the best lock known to man on there. In fact, I'll get the replacement lock. I'll spring for whatever supplies are needed to get it functioning again. Only makes sense if we're going to benefit from your work."

She whooped and ran over, hugging him.

"Who did you say was going to help you?"

The feeling of excitement plummeted as she straightened. "Val and Brennon on Saturday, and… Hunter."

"He's a good kid."

The *kid* part made her mouth lift. Hunter was eight years younger than Cash.

Her brother's head cocked to the side. "Didn't the two of you—"

"Yep. We did. But that was then. Nothing to do with now."

Cash raised palms in defense. "Okay. Just…be careful." He began to drone on about safety with power tools and being sure to ask Hunter about the sink, because it was leaking. And how they should wear masks when they painted. But Rachel was already light-years ahead of him.

They might have slightly different takes on his warning, but Cash didn't have to tell her to be careful twice. Because that's exactly what she planned to do.

Hunter left the door of the house open while he worked. The summer heat clung to him, and the light breeze brought in much-needed relief. He swiped the back of his arm across his forehead. Sweat changed places and he winced. Good thing he wasn't trying to impress Rachel this time around. He was pretty sure he looked a mess. He'd come straight from the ranch, only stopping to nuke two of those sorry excuses for frozen burritos for dinner. He'd wolfed them down in his truck on the drive over, then wished he'd have made three.

He heard Rachel's vehicle approach and turn off. A few seconds later, her footsteps sounded on the porch.

"Hey." She paused inside the doorframe as though waiting for an invitation to come in.

"Hey."

Hunter grabbed the water he'd brought along from the counter and took a long swig while Rachel stepped inside.

She wore a yellow T-shirt, cut off jean shorts and flip-flops. Her toenails were painted with bright blue polish, the color of one of those slushy drinks kids loved.

She walked over to the bedroom and peered in before facing him.

"You got a lot done."

"Mostly just removed all the trash. It's not so bad without the junk."

"Sorry I'm late. Cash threw a hissy fit about me living out here alone. Like I'm not old enough to take care of myself or something."

Eye roll. Hair toss. Hunter bit down on his amusement since Rachel wouldn't take kindly to it. He might doubt his fair share of things, but he was certain of that.

"You're fine. I just got here. Did you work it out?"

She'd bent down and started looking through the paint cans he'd brought over. "Yep. Where'd you get all of this paint? I should pay you for this. Cash said he'd cover supplies since he's the one benefiting. Said to tell you thanks for helping out." She paused. Let out an audible breath. "And that anyone who puts up with me should get a medal for it."

Quiet laughter shook his chest. "He did not say that."

She met his eyes, a smile tracing her lips. "He was joking. He did say thank-you, though."

Hunter nodded toward the supplies. "There's no need to pay for any of that. I had some stuff left over from my house. Didn't buy a thing."

"Your house?" Her tone carried surprise.

"Yeah, I built a few years back."

"Don't you live with your dad?"

"Nope. My house is on the west side of our property. Not too far from here." Hunter knelt to look through the tool bag he'd brought. "You know my dad. He had his fists wound so tight he would never have let me have any ownership of the ranch until he left this earth. I threatened to work somewhere else if he didn't let me buy in. I wouldn't have, but he didn't call my bluff."

Rachel's mouth swung open as if on a hinge. What had she thought? That he'd just sat around pining for her all of these years? Hunter grabbed an adjustable wrench, dropped to the floor and scooted the upper half of his body under the sink, wincing at his thoughts. Those old hurts always seemed to pop up with her when he least expected it. Friendship didn't hold grudges.

"Cash said that's leaking." Her voice sounded hollow from his perch inside the cabinet.

"I can tell. That's what I'm working on."

"Oh. Okay." He heard Rachel shuffling things around while he tightened the retention nut on the supply valve. After she'd left for Colorado, he'd gone through varying stages. Hope that she'd change her mind. The knowledge that she shouldn't. Moping. He'd been great at that. And then anger. He'd stayed there for a good long while. At himself. At her.

Now that he was working on letting those responses go, the load on his back was starting to feel a bit lighter.

Starting.

Not that he expected her to let him in easily. He hoped by the time they got this house back to rights, he and Rachel would have a functioning friendship again. Maybe even a bit of trust. Or, at least, he would have gotten past one of her walls. Hunter didn't want to spend the rest of the time she was home dealing with her still halfway despising him.

"How's your sister?"

Hunter loosened the water line then scooted out from under the sink to grab the joint compound. "Bossy. She still does the books for the ranch, and she's about to have a boy. Kinsley's beside herself to have a little brother."

"Tell her congratulations from me."

"I will." He went back under the sink to apply the compound. He wasn't sure exactly what was causing the leak, but hopefully if he hit most of the reasons it could be happening, he'd get it stopped.

Once he'd finished, he wrenched himself out of the cabinet. Not so roomy in there. Rachel had started sweeping the floor, and now she was going at cobwebs that hung from the ceiling with the broom. One must have dropped on her, because she released the broom and started swiping her arm as if whatever had landed there might do her in.

He stifled a laugh. She'd definitely gone city over the last few years.

Her phone dinged as Hunter pushed up from the floor, body aching from being in the cramped space. When had he gotten old?

Rachel's fingers flew over the keys as she answered whoever it was. She might not have a ring on her finger, but that didn't mean she wasn't attached to someone. He swallowed the heat that rose at the thought. Nothing for him to get upset about. Though he was curious.

"Boyfriend?"

She jumped and fumbled the phone, dropping it, then catching it again before it hit the floor. Slid it into her back pocket. "No boyfriend."

Hunter pulled out one of the kitchen drawers and placed it on the countertop. He grabbed his drill from the tool bag. "Did I ruin it for you for life?"

His teasing earned a forced smile. Didn't look like she was ready to call him her best friend just yet. "No. I just didn't really have time to date in college. I was too focused on school. Unlike high school, where I focused on the opposite."

He tightened the screws holding the drawer together and the *zzzz-zzzz* of the drill filled in the silence.

"You weren't so bad in high school."

She snorted in answer then swept the mess she'd collected into the dust pan and deposited it in the black garbage bag he was using.

Sure, Rachel had made some interesting choices before they'd dated. Had a boyfriend Hunter would have liked to punch in the jaw. But she'd come around. Hunter had known she would. By the time they'd started hanging out, she'd already begun changing. Didn't she know that? Still, the years had made a difference. On Wednesday, she'd been amazing with the kids.

"You were great with the teens last night." He slid the drawer back in and started on the next.

"Thanks. I feel like I barely got to know anyone."

The night had gone quickly. Mostly spent dealing with suggestions for the float. After a bit of fighting among the kids, Rachel had suggested they draw their ideas and put them up for a vote at church this Sunday. A good way to make peace. The teens had spent the rest of the night brainstorming in groups, so Rachel hadn't had much opportunity to talk with them yet. Hunter knew a few from church, but some were new to him, too.

"It will come with time." Not that she had a lot of that.

"I guess."

"So, if by some strange chance you don't get this job in Houston, what's your plan?"

"There's a teen rehab program that my friend works at in Dallas. I'll apply there if this doesn't pan out. It sounds like they're looking to hire." She didn't have to fill in the rest. Hunter could read between the lines. Her options were anywhere but here.

There wasn't even a minute chance of her staying. That was good for him to know and remember. Rachel had a *Do Not Touch* sign flashing on her forehead, and Hunter planned to obey the directive this time around. Besides, after one night of seeing her with the teens, he could tell the job she wanted was exactly what she was meant to do.

Hunter faced the countertop again and replaced the drawer. "You seem…content with the career you've chosen. It fits you. You did the right thing leaving when you did."

He felt her gaze heat the back of his neck and turned. Her jaw had slacked. She blinked once. Twice. "Leaving you or this town?"

Emotion rushed across his skin. "Both." If she hadn't

gone, she wouldn't have this new opportunity that was obviously right for her. She'd be stuck. Unhappy, just like his mom.

"Going to school was the right choice. It would never have worked between us." He couldn't believe he'd just said those words out loud. What was he doing, bringing this up? But she should know the truth. "You wouldn't be able to do what you do with the kids if you hadn't. After one night, I can tell you were made for it."

It almost looked as though a sheen of moisture had glazed her eyes. "Thanks." She opened her mouth as if to say more, and then her demeanor changed as fast as a flash of lightning. She shuttered, attention dropping to the floor. "I should start on the bedroom." She snapped up the broom like it was her saving grace and took off as though another mouse was on her heels.

That was odd. What just happened? Hunter had thought they were actually getting somewhere by talking openly. But, then again, he was dealing with Rachel. What had he expected? The woman warmed at the slowest possible pace. She'd stopped letting him in emotionally a long time ago. One confession, one moment of baring his soul regarding what he should have told her years before wasn't going to instantly mend what had happened between them.

Twenty might not do the trick, either.

Chapter Five

The metal bed frame pressed into Hunter's palms as he stood just inside the door to Rachel's new hideaway on Saturday morning. "The room ready for me to set up the bed?"

"Yep." Rachel paused from wiping down the kitchen cabinets. "The paint is probably still a little damp, so maybe set it up in the middle of the room and I'll just slide it over later when the wall is dry."

"Sounds good. Smells like a pool in here." One Hunter wouldn't mind taking a dip in.

"Bleach." She tossed the rag into the bucket by her feet. After rolling her neck, she swiped the back of her arm across her forehead. "It's hotter than a june bug in July."

His cheeks creased at her declaration and returning accent. About time her southern roots showed up. "Did Olivia take off?"

They'd had a slew of helpers show up. Cash last evening. Olivia this morning to help paint, but she'd had the boys with her, so she'd spent most of the time corralling Ryder. And Val and Brennon had been working most of the day, painting, cleaning, moving stuff in. They'd cut the workload in half and had been a Godsend. Currently they were out grabbing the last load of Rachel's stuff from Cash's barn where she'd been storing it.

"Yeah. She wanted to get the boys down for naps since we're heading over to Lucy and Graham's for dinner." Rachel cracked open a bottle of spring water and took a long drink.

"Nice."

She smiled, head shaking. "Chaotic."

"Lot of kids between the two families."

"Five. Though Mattie is like an adult."

True. Any time Hunter saw Graham and Lucy's oldest at church, she was never loud or crazy. She always had a shy smile, but she observed more than she destroyed.

Rachel turned back to her cleaning, and Hunter accepted his dismissal without complaint. He'd gotten used to Rachel's behavior on Thursday and Friday evening while they'd worked on the house, and then again today. The second she realized she was opening up to him—like even that simple conversation right there—she shut down and poured herself back into a task. Hunter felt like a kid on a teeter-totter, but he wasn't sure how to get off the equipment and find any stationary ground with Rachel.

Moving into the bedroom, he began piecing together the simple bed frame he was letting Rachel borrow along with the mattress set. It had been sitting in his guest bedroom, unused, since he'd replaced his a year ago.

Once Hunter finished, he strode back into the kitchen. No Rachel.

He found her standing on the front porch, fanning herself with a small towel. He stepped around to face her.

"What's up?"

"Val texted that they were on the way, so I was checking for them. And trying to cool off. Why did I think moving back to Texas was a good idea?"

"Just think about the winter. You'll love it."

Her eyes narrowed. "You might be right."

With Rachel, that much of an admission was a victory. "I got the bed frame set up. I need to carry the box spring and mattress in. Want to help me?"

"Sure. You got the frame set up that fast?"

"Yep. It's just a simple metal frame. No fancy headboard or anything. Hope it's up to your citified standards—"

"One of these days you really need to learn when to stop talking."

Hiding a grin, Hunter took off for his truck. People might call him crazy, but this was the Rachel he preferred. Because when she was sassy and sarcastic with him, he knew he was getting the real deal. And he liked that truthful version.

When he reached the truck's tailgate, he glanced back to see Rachel had followed him.

"I'll pull and you catch the other end when it slides off." He lugged the box spring halfway off the truck bed, then slowly slid it the final few feet while she grabbed hold. She must have lost her grip, because the other end crashed to the ground, a puff of dirt rising up.

"Oh, no!" She slapped a hand over her mouth. "Thought I had it. Sorry! Ah, man. Now it's all dirty. You let me use it and I'm already ruining your stuff."

She thought he'd be upset about a little dust? Did she not remember what he might be covered in at the end of the day? "It's fine. No problem." He motioned with his head toward the box spring. "Though I'm still holding this if you hadn't noticed."

Rachel tugged on her ear, adopted a casual stance and made no move to help him. "Did you say something? Sounded like a fly was buzzing around my head."

Mouth quirking, he scooted the box spring up until it stood tall and rested against the tailgate. "I'll have Brennon help me when they get back. Wasn't sure what I was thinking, asking you to haul it in, anyway. You're only half as big as a minute."

She squeaked with indignation. "I'm a mammoth."

"You?" A laugh burst out of him. "Are you joking?" Rachel might be tall—around five feet ten inches—but nothing else about her even remotely represented that word. "You're not embarrassed about your height, are you?" He didn't remember any conversations about that in the past.

"No. At least I can use it to intimidate people." Her chin jutted to the side with playfulness.

"You don't intimidate me one bit." An internal buzzer sounded, calling Hunter's bluff, and it had nothing to do with height. Because underneath all of Rachel's bravado, she was sweet and smart and funny. And gorgeous. What guy wouldn't get a little tongue-tied around her? She even smelled good despite the oppressive heat—something girly and tempting that he couldn't name.

Although he believed he was doing the right thing, moving on from the past and mending things with Rachel, he still doubted at times. Some moments, it was downright painful to be around her. When he caught glimpses of her sassy side. That smile. The way she teased him. Those reminders of what they'd once had were hard to stomach. But he knew better than to gallop down a treacherous hill. They were friends, and friends was all they'd be.

If she even let him have that.

Rachel's arm had a smudge of white paint on it, and Hunter reached out without thinking, sliding his thumb along her skin. He'd thought the paint would be wet and wipe off, but it had already dried. And then, like an idiot, he didn't let go. Suddenly he was twenty again, driving in his truck with his girl, a hand on her arm, the warm sun—

"What are you doing?" Rachel snapped her arm against her chest as though he'd scalded her. If he had to pick a word to describe the way her eyes flashed, he'd settle on *displeasure*.

"I just…you had some paint there."

Brennon's truck rumbled down the drive.

"Oh." Her look changed to curiosity, as if to say, *Why did you touch me? Touching is off-limits*. He wanted to answer her silent query with *I don't know* and *I agree*.

Brennon backed his truck up to the house while Rachel gave a forced, tight-lipped smile. "One last load and we'll be done."

The doors on the truck opened and closed. She backed a step in that direction, then paused. Held his gaze. "Hunter, thank you for your help on the house." No edge remained. Only softness. Sincerity. "I couldn't have done it without you."

She took off to catch up with Val and Brennon, leaving Hunter reeling. The woman switched from teasing to upset to earnest in a matter of minutes. This was exactly how she'd messed with him in the past. She built walls to keep everyone out—she even had with him, at first. But when she let them down—when her sweet, sincere side showed like just now—it could take a man's legs straight out from under him.

He'd done this for the right reasons, hadn't he? It wasn't about restarting anything with Rachel, was it?

No. It couldn't be. He was at the point where he really did want to regain their friendship—no ulterior motives.

It was just…being with her reminded him of all the reasons he'd liked her in the first place, and that was trouble.

Their futures were headed in different directions. Staying wasn't an option Rachel was considering—she even had a second job opportunity lined up—and his life was here. He owned part of a ranch. He couldn't walk away from that. Plus, he didn't want to. Hunter loved his work.

So he needed to remember why he'd started all of this and stick to that plan. No veering off course.

He had a feeling the safety of his heart depended on it.

"Okay, kids. It's time to let Auntie Rachel go free." Lucy Redmond, Olivia's sister, approached the couch where her daughter Lola and Rachel's nephews had fake tied Rachel up.

Lucy had moved to Texas years ago. She'd met and married Graham Redmond, a local doctor, and adopted his daughter, Mattie. Since then, the two of them had added two little girls to the mix. Graham was very much outnumbered, though he didn't seem bothered by the abundance of females in his house.

Dinner had ended a while ago, and since then, a game of cops and robbers—with a cowboy flair—had been in full swing. Two-year-old Lola was dressed in a princess costume. She'd spent the evening running around the house, Ryder toddling after her, while Grayson "saved" her from Rachel, who'd agreed to be the robber.

Rachel had pretended to have her hands tied together when she actually had three-month-old baby Senna— Lucy and Graham's newest addition—sleeping in her arms. The soft, sweet bundle had done the same for much of the evening despite the decibels of noise surrounding them. Occasionally she yawned in a perfect little O.

"Wait!" Grayson approached, hands on his hips. "The prisoner has to eat a worm to gain her freedom."

Rachel's nose wrinkled. She assumed the request was fake, but with Grayson's infatuation with all things slimy, slithery and of the insect family, she didn't know for sure.

She tossed her hair back dramatically as best as she could with her hands occupied. "I refuse to eat your detestable worm. I'd rather spend the rest of my life in captivity."

The haughtiness in her voice caused Lola to go into a fit of giggles, but Grayson kept a straight face, as though truly contemplating her refusal.

His small chest deflated. "Okay, I'll let you go this time, but next time…" His head shook. Rachel somehow resisted a smile. He was so stinking cute she wanted to eat him up. But she definitely had no plans to eat a worm, no matter how much she adored her nephew.

Lucy transferred Senna from Rachel's arms to her own. With her free hand, she directed the children until they stood in front of Cash and Graham, who were still sitting at the dinner table talking. "You guys should ask your dads to take you outside." The enthusiasm in Lucy's voice transferred to the kids, and they were soon jumping in front of their dads, their requests loud.

The two men shared an amused look but stood without argument, as if knowing their fates were sealed.

"All cowboy cops and damsels in distress to the backyard." At Graham's call, Grayson and Lola raced for the back door. Ryder followed but fell behind, so Cash scooped him up on his way outside, giving him a lift.

Once the whole lot of them had exited out the back door, a strange silence descended on the house.

Being at Lucy and Graham's was a bit like being smack-dab in the middle of a circus, but it was a homey sort of chaos.

These were Rachel's people. Olivia and Lucy had adopted her too, in a way. Starting back when Cash first met Liv. And then Rachel had gotten to know Lucy well when the two of them had both lived in Colorado. Now, they included her in anything sisterly.

Nights like this tugged on Rachel's heartstrings a bit too much. Maybe Lucy was right. It was time to stop being an auntie. Time to go. Rachel was afraid if she did too many more of these dinners, they'd begin to chip away at her resolve not to live in this town.

"I should probably get going."

Lucy propped her one free hand on her hip. "Oh, no,

you don't. We haven't even had a chance to catch up. You've been too busy wrangling children all night."

Olivia had been wiping the kitchen countertops but now came over and sat next to Rachel on the couch. Lucy placed Senna in a brightly colored infant seat and buckled her in. Her eyes opened. She observed her surroundings, but didn't make a peep. Weren't babies usually more demanding? Connor had been so fussy that Val hadn't sat down for months after his birth.

Lucy popped the pacifier into Senna's mouth and then dramatically dropped into the chair across from them. The back of her hand landed on her forehead. "Raising children is not for the faint of heart."

Rachel's mouth curved. "Speaking of kids, where is Mattie tonight?"

"She's at a friend's house. She already had plans, so we didn't want to make her cancel. So…" Lucy's eyebrows waggled, face alight. "Tell me everything. How's it going? Liv says Hunter's been so helpful with the little ranch house."

Funny that Lucy didn't mention anyone else who'd pitched in. And so it began. "He has been. We just finished up today." Rachel couldn't help tacking on a clarification to address Lucy's insinuation. "And he's just being neighborly."

"Neighborly." Loose blond curls cascaded over the other woman's shoulder as her head tilted. "Is that the new name for it?" Despite the teasing, Rachel couldn't find it in herself to get upset. Lucy managed to do pretty much everything in life without offending. Most everyone who knew her instantly loved her.

Though Rachel should still set things straight. "Honestly, there really isn't anything between us. We're just attempting to get along at this point."

And they were doing okay.

Now that they were done with the house, Rachel could relax. Take a full, deep breath again without the masculine smell and presence of Hunter interrupting her every thought.

Somehow, she'd survived working with him unscathed.

The man had a way of sneaking past her defenses, but she'd managed to spend countless hours with him in the last three days and not…what? Get hurt? Let him in too much?

All of the above.

"Hunter and I are just friends." Sort of friends.

Lucy's nose wrinkled. "But that's so boring. He's adorable."

"I'm right here!" Graham's voice carried from the kitchen into the living room. "I had to grab some bottles of water. Do I need to stay and police the rest of this conversation?"

"Hollywood, you know you're the only one for me."

Graham chuckled, looking equal parts besotted, amused and mistrusting. "Don't let her push you, Rachel. She always has something up her sleeve."

"What?" Lucy let out a squeak, fingertips landing against the neck of her casual electric-blue cotton sundress. "I would never." She grinned at Rachel and Olivia as the back door shut and Graham returned to the kids. "I have always liked Hunter. He was one of the first people I met in town." She toyed with her outrageously gorgeous wedding ring. "I found out later that it drove Graham crazy, even though Hunter was too young for me. And of course I fell for the first guy I beaned in the head when I moved here."

Olivia and Rachel laughed. Only Lucy.

"Seriously, though," Lucy continued. "You don't feel a thing for Hunter?"

Rachel shook her head.

"Not even an iota?"

"Nope." Her conscience screamed *liar*, but she ignored it.

Her feelings for Hunter had been buried years ago. Except for that moment today when he'd touched her arm. Every nerve in her body had sprung to life. She'd immediately shoved down her reaction, hoping Hunter wouldn't notice. Her response to his touch had only made her more determined to stay at least one foot away from Hunter at all times. Maybe two. How was it she could know he wasn't right for her and be attracted to him at the same time? His looks were easy to swallow, like the first sip of hot coffee on a frigid morning. And those dimples—they were overkill. Shouldn't God have spread out some of that attractiveness instead of depositing it all in one man?

On top of that, Hunter walked through life with a laid-back vibe that instantly put people at ease. To Rachel, that only made him more troublesome.

The whole time they'd been working together, she'd had to remind herself to focus on the house. Keep her head down and do the work. Not let Hunter get past her defenses. Her thoughts had sounded like Olivia back in the days she'd coached Rachel in volleyball. *Do this! Don't do that! You can do it!*

If only her heart took direction so easily. It had always had a soft spot for Hunter. Foolish organ. It needed to remember she was moving. That she wasn't ready for anything more than a surface-level friendship with him.

"Well, boohoo." Lucy's disappointment only lasted for a few seconds before she perked up. "So, any chance you want me to set you up while you're in town? I'm a great matchmaker."

"She's a horrible matchmaker," Olivia chimed in, humor lacing her voice. "Her record is zero for three." She patted Rachel's capri-clad leg. "Not that I don't want you to find someone who would tempt you to stay, Rach. Of course I do. But I also understand the need to make your own life. Sometimes starting over means finding home."

If Rachel had learned anything while being stuck in this town, she'd confirmed that she really, really loved her sister-in-law.

Olivia asked Lucy about her plans at the dance school she owned and somehow managed to run along with mothering three children, and Lucy filled them in on who she'd found to help out with the kids once classes started back up in September.

Minutes later, their chat was interrupted by screams coming from the back door. Cash held Ryder, whose cheeks were dripping with plump tears, while the rest of the group tromped in behind him. "Injury. Nothing serious. Just bonked his head and needs his mama." Cash deposited Ryder into Olivia's outstretched arms. "I think he's tired."

"I'm sure you're right." Olivia swept a hand over Ryder's forehead, and his cries turned to whimpers. "We should go."

Despite complaints from the kids following that comment, the next few minutes were spent rounding up toys and getting everyone out the door.

Rachel followed Cash and Olivia home in her Jeep—they'd driven separately since she'd been late getting over to Lucy and Graham's. When she reached the turn for the house, she waved and split off while they kept going.

She pulled up to her new place and got out, quiet greeting her. Contentment zipped along her spine at the knowledge that Cash and Liv had their house back and she had this little haven.

Her furnishing were sparse since she'd sold a lot before leaving Colorado. Besides the bed from Hunter, she had a comfortable chair and side table in the living room. A small kitchen table and two chairs, plus a dresser she'd found for ten dollars at a garage sale in town. Cash had donated an old microwave he'd had stored out in the barn. For how long she planned to stay, she didn't need anything more.

Rachel popped up the steps, stopping on the porch when a strange humming noise disrupted the otherwise peaceful night. She walked back down and around the side of the house to find the source.

Her feet froze a few yards from her east window, where an air-conditioning unit now perched. She knew it hadn't been there before, because she'd wondered more than once while they were working on the house how she was going to sleep in the stifling summer heat.

Cash had been with her tonight, so he couldn't have installed it. And Val and Brennon didn't have any extra money to be throwing at this hunk-of-junk house.

That left Hunter.

Pushing himself into her life. Without permission.

Again. She was never going to forgive him. She stomped up the front steps, marched inside and slammed the door behind her. Her head fell back as ice-cold air washed over her.

Okay, maybe she could be persuaded to extend some grace.

Rachel changed into pajamas and made the bed, then propped her pillows against the wall, grabbed her cell and climbed in. Peace. Quiet. And air-conditioning.

Hunter was wearing her down. "What am I supposed to do with him in my life again?"

The empty house didn't answer her. But the southern politeness ingrained in Rachel dictated that she thank him. She swiped her phone screen, and then her fingers flew across the keys. Thank you for the air-conditioning. It's amazing.

She had almost given up on hearing back from him when her phone notified her of a text.

What's this about an air conditioner?

I know it was you. Don't even try to pretend.

That knowledge sank into her bones. No one noticed her quite like Hunter did. At that scary thought, she texted him again.

Just accept my gratitude. Once he did, she could put the phone down and move away from how he made her feel.

His text came back quickly.

Actually, your brother got the air conditioner. He asked me to install it as a surprise for you.

Cash. She glanced at the time. He'd be getting the boys into bed, then crashing himself. Rachel would thank him in the morning. It was sweet of him. She should have known he wouldn't be able to *not* take care of her while she was home. But instead of making her irritable, like it would have when she was younger, she was thankful. She really did have the best brother in the world—it had just taken her a few years to realize it.

And Hunter… Her pulse galloped. He'd spent his Saturday night installing an air conditioner in this old house simply because her brother had asked him for a favor. It sounded exactly like something Hunter would do.

Earlier, when she and Hunter had been talking about her going to dinner at Lucy and Graham's, Rachel had thought about asking him if he wanted to come. But something had held her back—fear, she supposed. If he was really a friend, she would have invited him, knowing full well Lucy would welcome another person. Especially Hunter. Rachel should have included him. But, instead, she'd taken the opportunity to put more space between them. And what had he done? Something for her.

She'd been keeping him at arm's length so that he couldn't worm back into her life. But who was she kidding? He'd already made his way in. She was simply denying it. Punishing him. Holding on to all of that old hurt.

She texted him.

You still want to be friends, huh? Even after spending the last few days with me? I would have thought you'd be running by now.

A small part of Rachel had assumed if she held out, Hunter would give up. Go away. Leave her alone. But he hadn't. Just like the last go-round, when he'd pursued her despite her initial attempts to resist him.

Nah. I still want to bless you with the precious gift of my friendship. I can put up with you if I have to.

Humor creased her cheeks.

You mean I can put up with YOU if I have to.

His text dinged back quickly. Who is this again?
She laughed. Hunter got her in ways other people didn't. He knew when to tease her and when to be serious. She liked that about him. She liked him. Spending time with him had reminded her of that fact.
Not that she planned to admit that to him yet.

You're a dork.

I don't accept abusive texts. I think you have the wrong number.

Rachel snuggled lower into the sheets, amusement threading through her.
She couldn't believe how effortlessly he'd eased back into her life. More than one night over the last six years, she'd lain awake wondering how it had gone so wrong between them, fighting the temptation to call or text him.
But this wasn't about the past. It was a chance for something different for the future.

In the last three days of working together, Hunter had broken down a bit of the barrier that had stood between them. Rachel didn't have a clue how to stop him. Or if she wanted to. She only knew she couldn't let herself go beyond friendship. But maybe, just maybe, she could allow that.

It would be safe, wouldn't it? They both knew everything that stood between them and how much they would lose again if they messed this up. Her fingers hovered over the keys. Had he already moved on from their conversation? She couldn't resist checking.

Go to sleep, Hunter.

I will when you stop texting me.

Her laugh echoed off the walls that were void of decoration, reminding her just how little time she planned to spend here. But she'd deal with that thought another day. Because, at the moment, she felt content. Almost peaceful.

Ever since she'd started college, she'd been driven. Like she had something to prove. Busy chasing the next goal. But tonight she could sleep soundly without her future to-do list tightening like a vice around her chest. And while she might pretend it had nothing to do with the man on the other end of the phone, once again she'd be lying to herself.

Rachel turned her phone on silent, clicked off the lamp and burrowed beneath the blankets. If she fell asleep with a smile on her face, no one needed to know about it.

Chapter Six

"I still can't believe the church chose this design for the float." Rachel held up the paper that boasted a sketch of a goalpost with a large sign hanging from it that read *All things through Him*. Someone had drawn football players in uniform and a gaggle of cheerleaders littered across the float, faux green grass beneath their feet.

Hunter had bent to look through one of the bins next to the flatbed trailer, and she had to nudge him with her knee to get his attention. "Hello?" She shook the paper near his head.

"Huh?" He looked up. "Oh." A half grin made his dimples sprout. "It's Texas. Have you forgotten that football is almost a religion here?"

"No, I haven't." Her nose wrinkled. "But it's a football float, not a church float."

"Of course it's a church float." He pointed to the drawing. "Right here along the skirt at the bottom, the church's name is big and bold."

She laughed. Resisted slapping a hand against her forehead. "Okay, I get the concept of everything, even sports, as honoring to God. After all, volleyball made a huge impact on me. If I hadn't met Olivia when I did…" She shrugged.

Hunter had gone back to sorting supplies, but Rachel was having a hard time letting go of the float concept. "It doesn't have anything to do with the Fourth of July." Though there were a number of flags and handmade red, white and blue decorations drawn in along the sides. "Did you see the other sketches on Sunday?"

No answer. Hunter just kept digging in the bin for something. Rachel felt pesky—like the moths that would descend on Colorado in the summer, invading every nook and cranny and driving everyone crazy.

Just when she was starting to doubt he'd even heard her, he glanced up and answered. "Yeah, I did."

"So you know there was one that actually had an Independence Day theme? With an immigrant family arriving in the United States. And the Statue of Liberty. And a small church replica with a Welcome sign hung across the door."

"I saw the same thing as you."

"That should be the float we build."

"I agree." Hunter shot her a pointed look. "But *someone* told the kids that whichever float got the most votes at church would be the winner. No arguing."

A sigh escaped. "I did say that, didn't I?"

"Yep. You're kind of bossy, in case you didn't know it."

"That's because I know more than you when it comes to dealing with teenagers. If the kids hadn't agreed to that, they'd be fighting about it right now."

"Like you are?" He stood. "Aaand, good to know you're humble."

Laughter bubbled from her throat. Strangely enough,

being teased by Hunter felt good. Only it didn't last. His smile fell quickly, much like it had been doing since she arrived. Her counselor instinct told her something was off, but she couldn't put her finger on what.

Hunter nodded toward the growing group of kids. "We should probably get started."

"Okay." Rachel wasn't used to an all-business Hunter. Was he upset about something? Did it have to do with her? He'd fought for a friendship between them, but now she couldn't help wondering if he regretted that.

He walked toward the kids and she followed. There were more teens than last week. A good thing, since they had a lot to do. Maybe Hunter just wanted to get things rolling. She could understand that.

"Hey, guys, listen up." Conversations slowly trickled to a stop, and the teens faced them. "We're going to form teams to work on different sections of the float." Hunter pointed to the right side of the group. "The netting to go under the trailer…" Then he pointed to the middle. "The goalposts and grass…" Finally, he motioned to the left. "And red, white and blue decorations and flags. Rachel found directions online for most everything and they're posted by each station. Some things we'll have to improvise, so let us know if you have questions."

Most of the kids split off. Hunter called out to two girls standing a few yards away who were talking and hadn't moved toward a project yet. They glanced in his direction, looking as though walking over to Hunter—and Rachel, since she was right next to him—equaled cleaning up manure. After a moment's hesitation, the girls approached.

"This is Rachel Maddox." Hunter motioned to her,

then to each girl. "Bree." Strawberry blonde, Rachel noted, committing her name to memory. "And Hannah." Dark hair. Equally pretty. Rachel didn't remember seeing either of them the week before.

"I've known these two since they were up to here." His hand sank to around hip level. "Bree's dad and I were in a men's Bible study together."

Bree folded her arms, stance somewhere between wary and downright irritated, and Rachel recognized a bit of herself from high school. She pressed her lips together to keep from smiling at the girl's obvious annoyance.

"So, what part of the float are you girls thinking about doing?"

"We're going to work on the red, white and blue decorations." Bree raised one perfectly manicured eyebrow toward her expertly highlighted hairline. She probably meant to come off strong and aloof, but the hurt radiating from her overpowered her attempt. Rachel tucked away that knowledge to dissect later. Bree's partner in crime had remained quiet, but both sported looks that shouted *bored*. *Old people alert.*

Had Rachel really acted this way when she was younger? Sigh. Double sigh. She'd *so* been these girls. And she'd had the same snarky attitude toward Olivia when she'd first moved to Texas.

Rachel would have to apologize to her—again—when she saw her tomorrow.

She asked a few questions in an attempt to get to know them. Hannah answered, but Bree only gave stilted responses. After the third one-syllable reply from Bree, Rachel gave up.

"It was nice to meet you girls." They took her comment as the dismissal they'd been waiting for, turned in unison and bent their heads together as they crossed the barn.

"They were…sweet." Actually, Hannah had been fine. Just on the quiet side.

Hunter watched their departure, concern pulling on his mouth. "Bree's parents are getting divorced, and she's been a mess lately. I'm sorry for her rudeness."

Now the hurt/brave act made sense. "I'm not offended. I was her in high school."

His warm caramel-brown eyes crinkled at the corners. "You were never that bad."

Rachel simply raised an eyebrow in response, then laughed when she realized she'd just imitated Bree's facial expression. But Hunter didn't join in her amusement or say anything further. His gaze had already drifted over her shoulder, unfocused, lost in some thought she wasn't privy to. Something was going on with him, but flipping through options of what it could be wasn't getting her anywhere.

"I'll go check on the guys doing the goalposts." Hunter nodded toward the group. "They look confused."

"Okay, I'll just—"

He was already gone, long strides taking him across the barn. He wore a heather-brown T-shirt tonight, the fabric worn yet still intact. Jeans that looked as though they'd lightened with washing and sun and time. Boots, of course. It was like a uniform with him, and she didn't have any complaints. It fit his normally casual, laid-back vibe, which had been squashed by something tonight.

"Check on these kids." Rachel spoke to herself and wandered over to a group, only realizing at the last minute it was where Bree and Hannah had migrated to. Oy. Well, she knew how to speak teenager, didn't she?

"Do you guys have any questions?"

Bree barely glanced in her direction. "Nope." The word crackled with tension. "We've got it."

Rachel decided not to push. To give the girl some space. She backed up a step. "I'll be over here if you need anything." Good thing the school she wanted to work at couldn't see her now. Leadership skills with teens? Absolutely none. Ability to communicate with students? Nope.

The kids would accept her eventually, she assumed. Once they warmed up to her. And that's about when she would be leaving.

"Hey, Rachel, how's it going?"

At the sound of a woman's voice, she turned. Hunter's sister, Autumn, approached, wearing jeans, cowboy boots and a yellow V-neck maternity T-shirt that had ample room for her round tummy. Her light-brown hair was twisted into a no-nonsense braid.

"It's going." Rachel waved a hand in the direction of the kids closest to her. "They love me, obviously." She added some Bree sass to her voice, and Autumn's face wreathed with humor.

"They'll come around."

"That's what I'm hoping." She asked Autumn about her pregnancy and her daughter Kinsley, then finally voiced the question weighing on her mind. "Is Hunter… okay? He's not acting like himself today."

"You noticed that, did you?"

Rachel nodded.

Autumn seemed to contemplate her words, studying her brother across the space with a pinched brow.

"This was the week our mom left."

The quiet words detonated like a bomb, and Rachel's throat constricted.

"He always gets this way. Quiet. Not himself. Hunkers down for the week, and then he comes back. I guess I'd be more concerned if he didn't turn into himself again after, but he always does. I've tried to help him process before, but nothing I do makes any difference. I just have to let him work through it."

"I'm sorry." Rachel hated this for them. "Are you okay?" It wasn't just Hunter whose mom had scrammed. Rachel's stomach twisted at what they'd both been through.

"No." A sad smile accompanied the answer. "Yes and no." Her hand etched over her pregnant belly. "I just can't imagine leaving them. Being a mom makes it seem all the more impossible."

"You guys ever hear from her anymore?"

"Sometimes. But it's few and far between. She sends birthday cards some years. Very occasionally there's a phone call." She gave a disgruntled laugh. "I'm actually amazed she remembers the dates."

A rendition of "My Girl" blared to life, and Autumn snagged her phone from her back pocket, glancing at the screen. "I need to take this. I was going to ask Hunter something but I'll just do it later." She swiped to answer and waved goodbye to Rachel as she walked toward the barn doors.

Rachel scanned the room, finding Hunter still stationed across the barn. He was working on the goalposts with a small group, but he didn't seem to be conversing much. Definitely not joking around like he normally would. It physically pained her to think of how much he'd been hurt when his mother left. She wanted to hunt the woman down and confront her.

Rachel might not be able to do that, but she could be there for Hunter. He'd been good to her. A true friend.

Now it was time for her to do the same thing for him.

On Thursday evening, Hunter wrenched off his boots in the mudroom located at the front of his house, tossing them with more force than necessary toward the spot they usually sat.

He headed straight for the shower, intent on washing off the long day. It was almost eight o'clock, and he hadn't eaten dinner. A recipe for disaster with him. Not that he'd needed anything to push him into a bad mood. He'd handled that all by himself, and he'd been nursing it all week.

When he'd popped into the main house to grab something for lunch today, Autumn had called him crabtastic. But her bark was way worse than her bite. She was just concerned about him. He'd told her he was fine, but his sister had a habit of not listening to anything he said.

After showering, he threw on a clean pair of jeans, fresh socks and a green T-shirt emblazoned with the name of Kinsley's preschool—Kid Kapers—along with the name of the orphanage they'd sold the T-shirts to help support. Which explained why Hunter had another two just like it in his drawer. He'd just walked into the kitchen, planning to scrounge for some dinner, when someone knocked.

Autumn. She seriously could not leave well enough alone. What did he have to do to convince her that, yes, he was okay, and no, he did not need a pint of ice cream and a chick flick to make him feel better? That was Autumn's comfort cure, not his.

He twisted the knob and wrenched the door open. "Autumn, you're driving me—"

Rachel stood on the landing, wearing a simple white top, a casual navy skirt that landed above the knee and yellow sandals. "Crazy?"

"I was going to say nuts. But that works."

"Siblings will do that to you." No explanation followed for why she was at his house, but something brewed in her striking green eyes.

Did he even want to know? "Come in." Maybe he could eat while she spilled whatever was on her mind.

She didn't budge. "Actually, I need you to put your shoes on."

His head cocked to the side. "Something wrong?"

"No."

He stood stock-still. Somehow he was missing something.

"What's going on?"

"I need you to put your boots on." She stretched out every word as though talking to a mischievous two-year-old. What in the world? The temper that rarely ignited in him turned up a notch.

"Listen, Rach, I'm not sure—"

She grabbed his arm and yanked him over to the mudroom bench, then shoved him down. The combination of surprise and curiosity took the fight out of him, and he sank to the seat. She pointed to his clean boots, and after one long breath, he obliged.

Women. Would he ever understand them?

"Did my sister send you over here?" He slid on one then the other, adjusting his jeans over the tops.

"No." She tugged him off the bench, then out the front door. "Your sister has no idea I'm here." After shutting the door behind them, she paused. "Do we need to lock it?"

"Nah."

Rachel still had hold of his hand, sending an electrical current up his arm. She pulled him across the gravel drive to where her Jeep was parked.

"Is this the same Jeep you had in high school?"

"Yep." She opened the passenger door and motioned for him to get in. "Still runs, so no reason to give it up."

She went around to the driver's side as he got in, climbed inside and started it up.

"It smells good." He sniffed toward the backseat. "Like Italian."

"If you're a good boy, you might get some of that."

His stomach rumbled in agreement, and she took off down the drive, the tires kicking up dust. She'd left the top off the Jeep, and the wind toyed with pieces of her hair that had come loose. She paused at the end of the drive to redo it, twisting the light locks into a low bun that whispered against her neck before turning for town.

"Did you cook?"

"Puh-lease. You really think I've changed that much? I can only handle meals with four ingredients or less."

If she wanted to feed him, she could have just dropped off food. Wasn't that what most people did? And why in the world did she want to feed him?

They reached town, and Rachel parked the Jeep near Marktplatz. Hunter could hear the twang of a country band performing, and the memories of the two of them doing this very thing flooded him. Back when they'd dated, they used to park near whoever had live music playing, sometimes grabbing food or ice cream, and listen to the band play in the background while they sat in her Jeep or his truck and talked.

She dug into a bag in the backseat and handed him a Styrofoam to-go box and a set of plastic utensils while the warm summer air surrounded them, heavy with traces of humidity and the simplicity of the past.

"I assume you haven't eaten, or if you have, that you'll eat again."

Both true statements. He wasn't one to turn down food. Especially Italian.

She pulled out the same-sized container for herself. His held lasagna and a piece of warm bread, hers manicotti. The tantalizing scent of baked garlic and cheese made his taste buds kick into high gear. Hunter was so hungry, he didn't even bother asking what was going on. He just dug in. They ate in silence as the day edged into night and music drifted toward them.

Using the last bit of bread to sop up the remaining sauce, Hunter popped the morsel into his mouth. He gave a contented sigh and closed the box. That had almost been worth it. But he'd still rather be home than here.

"You going to tell me what's going on now?" He tossed the container and trash back into the paper bag still in the backseat, then shifted forward again, eyes up and taking in the first twinkling lights appearing against the gray sky.

How many nights had he and Rachel done this very thing? Stared up at the stars and talked. He'd wished on the shooting ones with everything in him.

Those hopes and prayers hadn't come true, though.

Rachel tossed her container into the bag, too. It took

her a minute to meet his gaze and speak. "Autumn told me this week is the anniversary of your mom leaving. I don't think I ever knew the exact timing of—"

"Her disappearance?"

She nodded.

"Gotta love my sister."

"It wasn't her fault. I couldn't figure out what was wrong with you. You were acting so strange. She was just answering my question."

"Which she didn't have to answer." Wasn't Autumn supposed to be on his side? Hadn't she been worried about Rachel hurting him again? So much for the brother-sister bond.

"True. She didn't. But I'm glad she did." Rachel looked up through the open roof. "You don't have to talk about it. I just didn't want you to be alone with the memories."

He covertly studied her profile while she stared at the sky. This was why he'd missed her. Why he'd been so mad at her for leaving. Rachel had an incredibly soft side that so many people never got to see. Not that she wasn't nice and kind and all of that—she was, whether she thought so or not. But this…this was why it had been so easy to love her.

But his mom's unhappiness and discontentment were the very things that reminded Hunter not to want Rachel to stay when she didn't desire to be here.

"The week before my mom left, she was happy."

Concern wrinkled the skin around Rachel's eyes, the usually bright green fading to evergreen in the darkness. She reached out and squeezed his arm. He knew she was being there for him purely as a friend, but he still gave himself a quick mental warning before continuing.

"It was the most peaceful I'd ever seen her." Unwanted emotion pricked behind his eyes, but Hunter fought against it. Cleared his throat. "She was up early instead of sleeping late, the sadness and dark circles gone from her face. Everything about her was different. Even the way she made eye contact. I remember coming home to find cookies baked one night. I thought…" The disappointment of that week choked him, and he had to swallow before continuing. "I thought she'd finally come around. That she was feeling better, or something good had happened. That she was actually going to be happy with us. I felt so hopeful. I thought my prayers had been answered."

And wasn't that the worst of it? To have faith as a kid and then not have it answered in the way he'd known God could answer? It had taken Hunter years to work through that knowledge. To wrestle with God about it. Eventually they'd tussled to the point where God had won. Hunter trusted Him now, almost *because* of that hurt. He'd had to realize the world was fallen and not what God created it to be. He'd had to trust that what the Bible said was true—that God loved him and had good plans for him. Hunter had chosen faith instead of doubt. But it had taken him a long while to get there.

Rachel had stayed silent. Waiting. Listening.

"Turns out she was at peace because she'd decided to leave. When Dad told me she was taking off…that's when I figured out what had been going on." He'd been nine, but felt as though he'd grown into an adult in that moment. In the realization that she hadn't been getting better. Hadn't wanted to stay for them. She'd been relieved to be running away, even knowing she was going to break her kids' hearts. Or maybe she'd just never really thought beyond her own escape.

Never realized what it would do to them.

Tears were silently slipping down Rachel's cheeks. He wanted to reach over and gently wipe them away but the move would be too intimate. Too much like something he'd once had the right to do. Hunter searched the backseat, grabbed a box of tissues and handed it to her.

She snagged one and swiped under each eye. "You never told me that."

"I put it out of my mind most of the time. But for whatever reason, the week of… It always gets to me. I'm sorry I made you cry." He'd always hated to see her in tears. With Rachel, those occasions were few and far between, but when she did cry, it made his chest feel like it was being run over by a tractor.

"I'm sorry your mom stinks."

His mouth curved. "So eloquent."

"What? It's true." The sound of her laughter reached in, filling the canyon-sized cracks in his heart.

She'd redeemed this no-good day for him. Did she know that? This friendship business was going to be harder than he'd originally thought.

"You were pretty crabby when I forced you out of the house tonight."

He stayed facing her instead of the stars. One view he could have forever. The other would likely only last a few more weeks. "I don't really like you. You totally ruined my night." His grin stretched far too wide to make his words even remotely believable.

She answered his smile with a gorgeous one of her

own. The kind that stole all coherent thought. That had made him suggest they get married even though he'd known better.

"That works out well, then, McDermott, because I don't really like you, either."

Chapter Seven

"I need to leave at five."

Hunter knew his dad had heard him by the way a scowl creased his weathered cheeks.

His father's gray hair was thick under the rim of his hat. The gray had come in slowly over the last decade, reminding Hunter that his dad was getting older. Probably too old to continue ranching for another twenty or thirty years as he'd like to do. Not that Hunter would have a say in any of his father's decisions. Dad had always done things his own way. Rachel might have a touch of stubborn, but his father dug his feet in hard then poured cement around them.

Dad branded while Hunter held the calf's head still and their vet, Willie—who looked about as old as the sun itself—administered shots. Hunter couldn't remember a time when Willie hadn't sported bright white hair. It was as if he'd always existed and never aged. In a simultaneous movement born from years of working together, they let go while one of the hands ushered the next calf down the chute.

"What's that supposed to mean? Think you've got

a nine-to-five job, all of a sudden, and you clock out on Friday?"

A parade of calves had already gone through today, and they weren't done yet. Normally Hunter would never leave something half finished. He worked as long and hard as any of the hands—longer most days. Just like his father. Dad could have quit showing up years ago. Holed up in the office and let everyone else handle the dirty work. But he still worked the ranch every day.

"Nope. I've just got something I need to do."

His dad grunted. "You leave early, we lose money."

So what if they lost a few dollars? Some things in life were more important than making a buck.

It was the youth group lock-in tonight, and Greg had asked Hunter to help. They were going all-out with games and fun activities. Lots of kids were inviting friends, and the RSVP list had grown bigger in the last week, causing Greg to call for reinforcements.

Hunter had been happy to help.

Growing up, his family had always gone to church. Even after Mom left, Dad continued going. But it had felt more like the thing to do and not like a relationship with God. Hunter had learned about God and grace when he'd started attending youth group. That's when he'd grown close to Him. So, was it such a shock he wanted to help provide that opportunity for other kids?

Dad didn't talk about God much, but every so often Hunter would see his Bible out as if he'd been reading it. His father was a confusing man. A mix of hard business and quiet expectations. Hunter had never wanted to let him down or disappoint him. But he'd grown up in the last few years and started standing up for himself. Surprisingly, Dad had given in on Hunter buying into the ranch and building his own place. Maybe because he'd realized he would lose his son if he didn't budge. Hunter would gladly attempt to mend the stilted years between them and move forward like he was doing with Rachel, but he didn't know where to start.

"Yep. You're right. We are spending extra money when I leave." They let the calf go. Waited for the next and repeated the same motions with it. "But I don't want to make the ranch my whole life." *Like you did after Mom left.*

If the words made an impact, his father didn't show it. Hunter motioned for one of the hands to switch places with him and then took off for his truck.

It was a waste to do any more explaining. Dad would never understand. He'd made horrible mistakes with Mom, and Hunter didn't plan to repeat any of them. Especially not with Rachel. They were getting somewhere, and he was feeling freer with each day that passed. The anger and hurt he'd held on to for so many years had been like a weight strapped to his back. But each day, more of that disappeared. He was starting to believe he and Rachel really could move on and have a friendship.

That he might not turn into his father, like he'd feared he would. Dad didn't know how to forgive or let go or move on. He'd let the past turn him gruff and bitter. Hunter was well on his way to avoiding those same blunders.

He'd realized something the other night when Rachel had shown up at his house and forced him out. When she'd saved him from his own sorrows. Or, at least, shared them with him.

She was changing.

Opening up, bit by bit—and not just with him. When

she'd first come home, all the walls had been up and operational. But time seemed to be softening her.

And he was starting to think God might be using him to help with that. This whole journey of letting go and healing what had happened between them might have nothing to do with him. It might have everything to do with her and what God was doing in her life.

And he was okay with that. Willing to be a part in whatever way God wanted him to be. Hunter had given up his own plans years ago. And now he trusted that whatever God had in store would likely surprise him, most often push him and always be better than what he'd expected.

Rachel checked the time on her phone, which was perched on the kitchen table. She and Olivia were having a cup of coffee after dinner at five thirty on a Friday evening—totally something her parents would have done—because she hoped it would help her stay up while wrangling teens at the lock-in tonight. Olivia didn't have the same excuse. Her need for caffeine was based purely on addiction.

Cash was still out working, and the boys were now playing in the living room.

When Pastor Greg had called Rachel yesterday morning, she'd had no idea why his name had popped up on her phone screen. Admittedly her first thought had been panic. Fear that she'd done something wrong with the float or the teens. Visions of high school had flooded back, and it had taken a few seconds of conversation to realize that he wasn't contacting her about a problem—he'd been calling to ask her to help chaperone the lock-in.

That realization had felt like dipping her feet into a pool on an achingly hot summer day. Refreshing to be asked to help instead of being asked to change her behavior.

She'd said yes.

Rachel welcomed another opportunity to show the town she'd changed. That she wasn't the same messed-up kid anymore. She liked people looking up to her. Respecting her. Not headed in her direction to reprimand her for another bad decision.

"Have you heard anything about the job?"

An ache flashed beneath her ribs at Olivia's question.

"Nope." Nothing in the few weeks she'd been home. Rachel had been told it would take time, but she was anxious to find out something. Anything.

"I texted my friend Dana. She works in human resources and she's the one who told me about the job in the first place. She's going to sniff around and see what she can find out."

Rachel was trying to be patient, but it wasn't her strong suit. She'd been stalking the campus online. It was gorgeous, with beautiful old buildings and a grassy outdoor space. She'd be close to the coast. Shops and restaurants at her fingertips. She missed living in the city. Not that this life wasn't good. It just wasn't what she wanted.

But until she heard more, Rachel would just have to keep doing what she was doing. Now that she and Hunter were in a good place and he'd returned to himself after dealing with the emotions of his mom leaving, she could turn her concentration elsewhere.

Which for her, meant Bree. The girl was never far

from her mind, and Rachel assumed God was putting that pressure there for a reason.

She'd heard Bree talking on Wednesday night about going to the lock-in, and it had given Rachel another reason to agree to chaperone. She wanted to get to know Bree better, and tonight would hopefully provide more opportunity to do that.

"I'd better get going. I need to be at the lock-in early for an instructional meeting. I'm sure it takes more than a few rules to keep the kids out of trouble." She shuddered. "Can you imagine what I would have done at something like this?"

Olivia laughed. "You would have caused Cash more than a few gray hairs." She twisted her coffee cup. "But, then again, you know every teenager does stuff—every adult, for that matter, does stuff they regret. That's why there's forgiveness and grace. God doesn't keep a list of mistakes, Rach. And neither does your brother."

She wasn't so sure. Sometimes Rachel felt like people were watching her. Waiting for her to screw up. She'd never been able to shake the thought that her next disgrace was right around the corner. Probably why she worked so hard to make sure that didn't happen.

In school, she'd been so focused on gaining her degrees and succeeding that at times she'd forgotten the social side. Sure, she had friends. But when it came down to it, very few people knew her inside and out.

Olivia did, and her sister-in-law still loved her. That had to count for something.

"You have everything you need for tonight?"

"I packed a small bag and I took a nap earlier. Hopefully it's enough to tide me through."

"They really don't sleep?"

"I don't know. I think they bring sleeping bags. I know there's a girl's quarters and a guy's quarters, and I'm hoping that some of them will want to sleep, which will allow me to do the same."

They both stood, and Olivia gave Rachel a hug. "Don't forget to have some fun."

"I'll do my best." Rachel headed for church. When she arrived, she pulled into the far side of the lot—the portion not covered in jousting stands, a huge blow-up slide, a batting cage and a Velcro wall. A misting tent was set up to help combat the summer heat. The kids would love this. Rachel might even be willing to try something out herself—for the sake of the teens, of course. Just to make sure everything was safe and functioning properly.

She had a bit of a competitive streak in her. Nothing compared to Liv, but perhaps a close second. She'd known there would be games, so she'd worn casual clothes. Capri jeans with a few textured tears and holes, a dark blue V-neck T-shirt and strappy flat sandals that tied around her ankles. She'd thrown her running shoes in her bag just in case she needed them.

She tugged her backpack out of the backseat but left her sleeping bag to retrieve later. Then she strode across the parking lot, not wanting to be late for the meeting in the church library.

When she stepped inside the room, Greg was already attempting to gain the group's attention. Oops. She slid in along the right wall of the filled room and spied a window ledge to perch on in the back. She dropped her backpack on the floor and braced herself on the make-shift seat, stretching her legs out.

The chair in front of her, one of the wheeled seats

that surrounded the huge oblong table in the middle
of the room, scooted back until it almost bumped into
her sandals. She inched her feet away from its path. No
reason to ruin a perfectly gorgeous pair of shoes over
someone who obviously lacked personal space boundaries. And…there came that snarky side she tried to
tamp down. Rachel glanced up, hoping whoever it was
couldn't decipher her true musings, when her mouth
filled with dust.

She recognized those shoulders in a charcoal-gray
T-shirt, his cropped, disheveled hair and, as he turned
slightly to face her, the light layer of scruff covering
his cheeks.

Hunter leaned against the back of his chair, stretching its mechanical limits.

"Hey." He grinned at her.

Her traitorous mouth curved in response before she
could even decide if she wanted to smile back. The sight
of him had her stomach tumbling like a child rolling
down a grassy hill. She hadn't known Hunter was helping, hadn't expected to see him. She would have prepared if she'd known. Shored up any off-limits, giddy,
girly excitement that might ignite at his presence.

Thoughts about being happy to see him had no business sprouting when she hadn't given them permission.

"I didn't know you were going to be here." She kept
her voice to a whisper. "Are you stalking me?"

The faint echo of dimples etched his cheeks before
his eyes narrowed. "I didn't know you were helping,
either. Maybe you're stalking me."

Greg's instructions continued to drone on: *No boys
and girls left together without a chaperone in any part*

*of the church. Roped-off areas are off-limits. Kids found
going into them will be sent home without any warning.*

"Don't you have a ranch to run?"

"Yep."

"Don't you have other things you should be doing?
How do you have time for this?"

He met her gaze with heat. "I have time for this. It's
important."

Sweet man. He certainly had his priorities in order.
One day—likely soon—he'd find a woman who
wouldn't let him get away like she had. Hunter would be
a great husband. Attentive. Fun, yet steady as the Rocky
Mountains she'd recently left behind. Why hadn't he
ever gotten married? Had she messed that up for him?
Or had he just not found the right one?

And why, oh, why, was she thinking about marriage
right now? In the same thought as Hunter?

"And that's about it." Greg announced. "Other than
that, we just want everyone to have fun. This is an out-
reach night, so a lot of the kids have invited friends.
We're hoping that once they feel at home here, they'll
be willing to come back again on Sunday nights for
youth group. And if anyone is interested in helping
with the float for the Independence Day parade, Hunter
and Rachel are heading that up on Wednesdays." Greg
motioned in their direction, and Rachel jolted back to
her windowsill perch, face warm, while Hunter lazily
turned around to face the group. Why had she stayed
that close to Hunter after they'd stopped talking? Embarrassing.

Just because Hunter was here and she hadn't expected him to be didn't change anything. Just because

her heart had pitter-pattered at the sight of him didn't mean she had to worry. They were friends. That's why she was happy to see him.

Rachel had a plan for tonight that had nothing to do with the distracting shoulders in front of her. And, like Yoda, stick to it she would.

Chapter Eight

They were winning.

And so was Rachel. Behind the church was a sand volleyball court. And in the midst of a match, the teens had begun referring to her as *coach*. The word made her smile on so many levels, including deep in the part of her that secretly wondered if she was ever going to amount to anything. To be whoever God wanted her to be.

Rachel had thought of Olivia as her coach for years, because that's the role she'd played in Rachel's life in the beginning—on and off the court. It had taken Rachel a long time to call her Olivia or Liv. The fact that the kids were now referring to her with the same endearment and respect had Rachel feeling rather giddy.

Plus, there was Bree. She'd been on Rachel's team for the last hour, and they'd been taking down one competitor at a time. With each play, game and subsequent win, her face had lost another inch of scowl. She'd even smiled at Rachel a few times. Nothing raised a person's mood like winning.

They only had to score two more points to be named

lock-in volleyball champions. And when the ball hit the sand for the second time, the girls screeched and cheered. Rachel received a number of hugs, her hope soaring. Leave it to sports to be the glue that melted any concern over her.

Bree gave her a fist bump. No physical display from her. Which Rachel totally understood.

"Do you want to joust?"

Bree's question momentarily stole Rachel's words. She went with a casual "Sure," as an answer, attempting to keep her grin at an acceptable level. Anything more and the girl would be rolling her eyes.

The padded base and pedestals were set up in the middle of the parking lot. After waiting for a turn and donning the protective gear, they climbed up on the pedestals, each with a padded jousting pole in hand. The goal was to knock one's opponent down to the mat. Rachel took it easy on Bree while they jousted. They spent much of the time laughing. Both wore soft helmets, but she could still see Bree's eyes. They held a spark of competitiveness, but none of the malice she'd previously harbored.

Each of them knocked the other down once, and then, in the third round, Rachel gave some effort, but not enough to win. Bree sent her flying to the mat below. She stood, still laughing, and congratulated Bree.

A bunch of the teens had gathered around, and Hunter grinned at her from where he stood with a group of boys. She would have thought maybe, just maybe, he'd wear tennis shoes tonight in order to participate in the games. But no, his typical boots, jeans and faded T-shirt dress code was still intact.

The kids were yelling about something, and Rachel

glanced around, trying to figure out what had their excitement level increasing so quickly.

"Coach…" Bree took off the padded jousting helmet and tossed it onto the mat, and Rachel did the same with hers. "Are you going to do it?"

"Do what?"

"Joust with Hunter." A smile flashed. "I think you could take him down."

Ah. Rachel melted. The girl looked like whatever problems usually weighing her down had been put on hold for the evening.

Hunter had an eyebrow raised in challenge. "What do you say?"

"If you want to lose, I'm happy to joust with you."

The kids burst into laughter at her smack talk. Hunter grabbed the other jousting stick and inched close to her, lowering his voice. "Maybe you could give an actual effort this time?"

Oh, no, he didn't. "She's a kid." She matched her volume to his. "I was playing nice."

"I assume you won't have that same concern with me."

"You know what, McDermott? For once in your life, you're right."

Hunter had planned to go easy on Rachel, but she was pummeling him. He'd spent the last few minutes defending himself against her attacks. The hits were coming in fast and furious. They didn't hurt, just jostled him.

Had he wakened a beast?

One caught him on the left side. He lost his balance but managed to regain his footing.

Hunter took a swing at Rachel, planning to whack the jousting stick from her grip, but just as he was about to make contact, she wobbled and her body shifted forward. It was too late to change the point of impact. His stick connected with her noggin. Hard. Her head rocked to the side, and she flew off the pedestal. He was down beside her faster than he could count to two.

"Rach." Her eyes were open but dazed. She blinked numerous times. Even with their padded helmets on, that hit had rattled her. He removed her helmet and gently ran fingertips along her scalp, checking for a bump. "Are you okay?"

Her eyes filled with moisture that didn't spill. "I'm fine."

Tough girl. His sigh came out ragged—half relief, half exasperation. "You're not fine. I struck your head pretty hard."

Hunter removed his helmet, and she shifted as though she was trying to get up. He helped her to a sitting position.

"The world's a little spinny, but I'm fine."

Spinny wasn't a word. So *not* fine.

"I'll get some ice."

"No. I'll come."

Arguing with her—head injury or not—would be pointless.

Hunter supported her as she stood, keeping his arm around her. She wasn't completely herself because she didn't shove him away. Until they stepped down from the mat and their feet met the pavement. Then she pushed his arm off. "I'm fine."

Three "fines" didn't make it true.

He wasn't taking any chances of her crashing to the

parking lot and injuring herself more. Despite her protests, Hunter kept her tucked against him and leaned
down until his mouth met her ear. "Every kid and leader
here is watching you right now."

She peeked out from his T-shirt while he continued.
"And if you don't let me help you inside, I will pick you
up and carry you. And despite how strong you think
you are, I will win that tussle."

A gush of warm, frustrated air leaked out against
his chest.

"Fine."

Number four.

Greg jogged over, concern splitting his brow. "Is
she okay?" He touched Rachel's arm, and something
in Hunter flamed to life. Jealousy. Outrage. Protective-
ness. Any option worked. "How do you feel? Bree said
you took a blow to your head. She came flying over to
tell me."

A soft grin lifted Rachel's mouth. "She's a good kid."

Greg let out a relieved laugh. "She is, but right now
I need to make sure you're okay. Should we call an am-
bulance?"

"Absolutely not."

"Do you want someone to take you in to the clinic?"

"No," Rachel answered, head shaking, then she
winced and stopped the movement. "I think ice will
work. It's not that big of a deal. Better me than one of
the kids."

Hunter tightened his grip around Rachel's shoulder.
He might not like the circumstances that got them here,
but he sure didn't mind her being snug against him. And
when she actually stayed there? Without kicking? Better than a Cowboys win.

"I'll help her." At Greg's nod of acceptance, Hunter walked toward the church, prompting Rachel to move with him. Once inside, he dropped her off in the back of the sanctuary, and—in spite of her grumbling—had her lie in the last row of chairs. "I'll be right back."

He trucked down to the kitchen, bagged some ice, grabbed a cloth to wrap around it and then headed back upstairs. Amazingly, she'd stayed put. She must be more messed up than he'd thought.

He sat on the chair next to her head, and she opened her eyes while he tucked the ice on the side where he'd made impact.

"Thanks." Her eyes closed again.

With the lightest touch, he swept a strand of hair from her forehead. "You're welcome. I'm sorry I almost killed you."

She shook with laughter, and the gold R pendant on her necklace slipped behind her neck. "You're not *that* strong, cowboy."

That sounded like an endearment to him. His heart was a jumping bean while he was this close to her. Touching her as though he had the right to. He should back away. Give them both some space. His attraction to her right now was nowhere near the friendship level he'd committed to.

"It was an accident, you know. I was aiming for your jousting stick, but then you lost your balance and moved, and I nailed your head instead."

"So you're telling me you weren't even trying to knock me down. Thanks a lot. That makes it even worse."

Amusement tugged at his mouth. She was still his Rachel.

"Did you see Bree tonight? She's softening. Letting me in."

His fingers slid along her hairline again, and when she didn't complain or fight, he continued the soothing motion.

Do you see yourself? Talking to me like it used to be? "Yeah, I saw. You're good for her. For all of them."

"Thanks."

"That's three thanks in a row." Though one had been sarcastic. "I think we'd better take you in to the clinic."

"Ha."

"Seriously, Rach. I do need to know you're okay." He cupped a hand over her mouth, forcing himself to ignore the fact that he was *touching her lips*. "And, no, you're not *fine*." Begrudgingly, he let go.

After an audible sigh, she slid her phone out of her back pocket and held it up. "We can text Lucy and she can ask Graham. Does that work for you?"

"Sure."

Hunter got his phone from his pocket. Rachel rattled off Lucy's number and he sent a text explaining what had happened and asking Lucy to check with Graham about what they should do.

Rachel shifted to sit up in the chair next to him as Lucy's reply came back quickly. Is she okay???

She seems to be. She's talking and sitting up now, but I want to make sure.

First off, stare longingly into her eyes. Do that for at least five minutes and then get back to me.

He laughed. Leave it to Lucy to use this as an opportunity to make this about him and Rachel.

"What?" Rachel questioned.

"Nothing."

When Lucy had first moved to town, she'd figured out pretty quickly that he harbored feelings for Rachel—though they'd been masked under layers of upset and hurt. She'd often thrown him tidbits of information about Rachel over the years that he hadn't asked for, but had secretly appreciated. Though lately, thankfully, she'd quieted down on any matchmaking attempts.

Another text from Lucy came through.

Hang on, I'm checking.

"She's going to ask Graham."

"Okay." Rachel's head tipped his way, then landed on his shoulder. He froze. Something must seriously be wrong with her.

She smelled so good. He imagined it was her shampoo teasing his senses, but he didn't know for sure.

He inhaled. He wouldn't be this close to her again, maybe ever, so he might as well take advantage.

It's Graham. Did she lose consciousness?

"Did you black out at all, Rach?"

"Nope."

Is she disoriented? Stumbling? Slurred speech? Dazed?

Doesn't seem like it.

Anything abnormal you're noticing?

Huh. How to answer that question? Well, she's being unusually grateful and nice. Not her typical behavior.

Ha! Is she related to Lucy by blood??

Hunter chuckled.

"What? What is he saying?" At Rachel's exasperated tone, he glanced in her direction. Her eyes were open, and she shifted her head against his shoulder as though she might move. He held his breath, only starting up again when she didn't scoot away from him.

"He's just asking about you."

His phone beeped, and Hunter read Graham's questions aloud as they came through.

"Do you feel dizzy?"

"No."

"Ringing in your ears?"

"Nope."

After a few more questions with the same answer, Hunter started to relax.

I need you to look at her pupils. Check if they look bigger than normal (if you can tell) or if they're unequal sizes.

Again, laughter rumbled in his chest. So Lucy had been right. He did get to stare longingly into Rachel's eyes. He was torn. Part of him wanted the opportunity to be that close to her, but he also didn't want to leave his current position.

"Enough, McDermott. I don't know why me being injured is so amusing to you."

"It's not. Doc Redmond's just making me laugh." He set the phone on the chair to his right, then scooted her away from his shoulder so that they were face-to-face. "I'd never be okay with anything happening to you, Rach." Their close proximity made him pause and swallow. "It would kill me to know I'd seriously hurt you."

He'd done exactly that in the past. It had been emotional hurt that time around, but that was almost worse, in Hunter's opinion. Who was he kidding? Both options were unacceptable.

His hand had involuntarily moved to her arm, and she didn't move away from his touch. The warmth of her skin made his pulse skip like a scratched CD.

"What are you doing?" Her voice didn't hold her usual bite. Just curiosity.

"Checking your pupils."

He forced himself to ignore the fact that for the first time in six years, his lips were seconds away from hers. Made himself focus on her gorgeous eyes. He studied one, then the other. Compared. They seemed fine to him, but then again, he wasn't a doctor. But the pupil sizes matched, at least.

"I think they look okay." Although that wasn't a term he'd use to describe himself at the moment. He was not "fine" or "okay" or anything anywhere near that. He was a mess. He hadn't thought it was possible to want Rachel more than he had the day she'd left for college and taken his heart with her.

But he'd been wrong.

Chapter Nine

If she was okay, then why was Hunter's face still inches from hers? One of those instances where if either of them leaned forward their lips would be reintroduced.

Rachel's breathing shallowed out. His eyes were the color of maple syrup and, by the way they held her attention, just as sticky sweet. The usual scruff covered his cheeks—as if he'd shave when he got around to it—though she'd never witnessed him with an actual beard. He always hovered somewhere in between.

"Why don't you shave every day?"

"I don't know. Just easier, I guess." His voice was low, amused and wreaking havoc on her. "Are you telling me I should shave every day?"

"I don't care what you do. I'm just curious." She was prolonging their close proximity with stupid conversation. She couldn't actually want to be near him, could she? Maybe the blow to her head was making her crazy. After all, she'd just been tucked against Hunter's shoulder like she owned it. Like it was her personal spot to rest on. And, honestly, it had felt like a perfect fit. He was muscular, yet his shoulder had felt just right.

She was stinking Goldilocks.

"Rach?"

"Yeah?"

He leaned forward and everything stood still. His lips pressed against her forehead and held before he eased back. Disappointment and relief tangoed in her gut.

"I'm really sorry I hurt you."

Tears surfaced but thankfully didn't fall. Was he referring to today or six years ago? Maybe all of the above.

"Hunter…about what you said a minute ago—I hope you know I wouldn't be okay if anything happened to you, either." And it was true. He might have scarred her way back when, but she would never wish him harm. He was a part of her past. And that made up the pieces of who she was now. Those months with him at the end of high school had been some of the softest of her life. She rarely opened up like that and probably hadn't since.

His fingers slid into the hair at the nape of her neck, and his lips trailed down from where they'd touched her forehead, landing on one cheekbone, then the other. Her lungs flat-out quit functioning. Amazing how her body could stay alive without oxygen.

What was he doing? He pressed a kiss lightly to her nose. She should tell him to stop. But in the last few seconds her body had turned to undercooked brownie batter. Soft. Warm. Compliant.

Surely he'd pull back now. Surely her eyes weren't refilling with tears at his gentleness. This was just about the fact that he'd injured her, wasn't it?

Rachel didn't even realize her eyes had closed until she thought to open them. His mouth was a whisper away from hers. Now's when she would end this. She'd already let things go too far. But when he'd brushed her hair from her forehead earlier and then continued the soothing motion, she'd melted. And she was having a hard time forming a backbone again. That thing that told her to retreat. To remember what had happened between them in the past. The gut-wrenching way he'd responded to her and shut her out. How it had hurt with a pain that had radiated through her body. How it had taken everything in her to walk away from him.

It didn't work the last time and it won't work this time. Nothing has changed for either of us. Plus, YOU'RE MOVING.

Her conscience might be screaming directives at her, but her stupid heart wasn't listening. Which was why, when Hunter's lips met hers with the slightest touch, she let it happen.

His hands were warm, gentle, as he eased her closer. She didn't fight it. How could she? She'd never been able to resist Hunter. That was part of the problem.

Rachel gave in to the kiss, and those symptoms he'd asked her about started happening in rapid succession. Dazed. Dizzy.

Somehow she'd gone from wanting to run to being a willing participant.

"Rachel, are you—" Greg's voice came from the back of the sanctuary. She wrenched back, managing to put a foot between herself and Hunter in one giant lurch.

Both of their heads snapped to Greg, and by the stunned look on his face, he'd witnessed their lip-lock. And why wouldn't he have? It wasn't like she'd been worrying about someone walking in on them. Nope. She'd just let herself go straight back to the land of immaturity. No thinking. Just feeling. And for a split second, it had almost felt worth it.

Greg didn't exactly look upset—though he had the right to be. She and Hunter were chaperones at a youth group lock-in, and they were the ones caught kissing. Her face flamed. What had she done? What was she thinking? And, seriously, how much brain damage had that jousting stick caused?

"You okay?"

She managed one nod to Greg's question, and then Hunter took over.

"We checked with Dr. Redmond. She doesn't have any of the symptoms he asked about." His voice didn't hold the same panic she felt coursing through her. Did anything ever upset him? The man was as calm as a lazy river or a hammock in the summer sun. She, on the other hand, felt more like the frayed edges of an old flag that had endured stormy weather for too long. "And if anything pops up, she'll be contacting him." Hunter's statement left no room for arguing. Rachel had no choice but to agree. Pretend she hadn't just thrown away all of the strides she'd made in the last six years in one idiotic moment.

Disappointment roared through Rachel as Greg walked toward them.

He was going to reprimand them. Rachel detested that feeling. Hated the knowledge that she'd let herself get here. And for what? It wasn't as though a relationship could happen between Hunter and her. They'd already had this conversation. Set the boundaries that she'd just flown right by without even blinking.

"I realize you guys are adults, but just…" Greg looked away, his face mirroring Rachel's discomfort.

"Not here, okay? If I'd been one of the kids walking in, that wouldn't have been good."

"You're right. I'm so sorry." Rachel stood. She wanted nothing more than to flee. "I'm going to go check on my girls." Because she was the best chaperone and should get back to it. Obviously. She reached the doors of the sanctuary and ran out before either Hunter or Greg could continue the most uncomfortable conversation *ever*.

Her head ached, but it wasn't from connecting with a jousting stick. It was from the certainty that she'd messed up. Big time.

This was why she hadn't wanted to be around Hunter in the first place. Why she avoided him whenever she came home. Because she couldn't make a mature decision when it came to him. Show the town how much she'd changed. Keep focused on the teens. Get to know Bree.

How'd that plan work out for her?

Rachel had taken a giant leap backward. She'd basically proved the opposite—that she was still the same girl. That scene with Hunter had been eerily similar to something she would have done in high school.

It had also landed her a warning from Greg and a heart dangerously close to losing its protective shell.

Hunter scrubbed a hand across the back of his neck. That hadn't gone well. It had for a few seconds, but then…back to reality. To possibly leaving things worse than when he'd first walked in here with Rachel.

"I'm sorry." He stood to face Greg. "That was completely inappropriate." Seriously. Who kissed someone while acting as a youth chaperone? Him, apparently.

He just hadn't been able to resist. Once his lips had touched Rachel's skin, he'd been as gone as a fly ball over left field.

They'd finally been in a good place—had managed a friendship after all of this time—and now he'd ruined it all with one impetuous kiss. And until he could talk to her and apologize, he'd just have to live with the question of how much he'd messed things up. Would it take another six years to make up for this?

And it didn't bode well for him, either, that she'd just been whacked in the head—by him—and he'd taken advantage of the situation. Yes, she'd seemed okay. Hadn't had any of the problems Doc Redmond had questioned them about, but that didn't make what he'd done right.

"Apology accepted," Greg responded. "I'm not one to hold a grudge. I'm actually quite a fan of grace."

"Makes sense, you being a pastor and all. It won't happen again." Unfortunately, ever. Hunter headed out of the row and met Greg as they walked to the back of the sanctuary.

"I'm guessing you wish I would have waited a few more minutes before barging in here to check on Rachel, aren't you?"

Amusement rose up. "In the spirit of honesty, that would have been helpful." Hunter pushed open the door, holding it for both of them. "You're a pastor. Are you even allowed to say something like that?"

Greg laughed. "Since I'm also human, yes, I am."

After heading back to the kids, they split up, leaving Hunter to deal with the repercussions of what had just happened. He knew better than to seek Rachel out right then. If he went anywhere near her anytime soon, he had no doubt she'd find one of the jousting sticks and take it to him. At this point, he needed to leave her alone until after the lock-in, at least. Maybe longer.

But the persistent thought running through his mind—the one he'd really like to dismiss—was, why hadn't Rachel flinched from his kiss? Backed away? Slapped him? Instead, she'd been with him every step of the way. After the slightest hesitation, she'd been all-in.

That plagued him the most. Because that was the Rachel he used to love. She was high and low, and sweet and snarky, and everything about her surprised him in the best way. She used to kiss him like that. Like she needed him as much as he needed her.

If Hunter let himself dream, he could picture Rachel staying in this town. The two of them married. They'd have the occasional fight, and she'd win. No doubt. And he'd be fine with that—as long as he got to keep her. But eventually she would question if she'd chosen the wrong fork in the road. Just like his mom. Even his imagination didn't provide a happy ending to that tale.

On his tenth birthday, Hunter had been missing his mother. She might have been half a mom, she might not have been the most present, but she'd been his. He'd sneaked into his dad's bedroom, tucked into his mom's side of the bed and allowed himself some tears. Then he'd opened the drawer of her bedside table, hoping to find—what, he didn't know. Something to remind him of her. To comfort. He'd come across a letter in his father's handwriting. Worn, as though it had been reread numerous times. He'd put it back in the drawer and tried to ignore it. But after a minute, he'd caved. Pieces of it would forever be ingrained in his memory.

Please don't leave us. I love you. We need you. Stay with us.

That was when Hunter understood why his father had turned so bitter. He'd begged his wife to stay, and she hadn't. That knowledge had hurt on so many levels. More than Hunter had been able to comprehend at that age.

His mom had never been happy on the ranch. And when his father had asked her to stay and she'd still left, it had shattered his dad. But instead of becoming sad and broken, Dad had turned hard. He'd shut down.

Hunter had never admitted to his father that he'd gone snooping that day—and that really hadn't been his intent. But the words, the pain of that letter and his mom's reaction had stayed with him all of this time. The roots of that discovery had grown deep in him. Hunter had come to the conclusion that his dad should never have convinced his mom to marry him in the first place. To live a life she didn't want.

He believed his mom had tried to be there for them. That more than a few of the tears she'd cried had been over the fact that she'd wanted to connect with him and Autumn, but could never quite cross the chasm. He'd gone to his friends' houses. He remembered gathering around supper tables, the way parents would tease each other, laugh and hug their children. Those things had happened sparingly in his home. There had been days Mom hadn't gotten out of bed. Some snapping and moments she'd lose her temper. Apologies and more tears after. By the time she left, he'd forgotten what it meant to hope.

Hunter refused to repeat any of that scenario with Rachel.

She'd been very clear with him about what she wanted, and it wasn't this town. Or to live on a ranch. Or even with him. Which was why he would never again ask her to stay.

Even if it took everything in him not to.

Chapter Ten

On Tuesday evening, Rachel sat on her front porch swing, waiting for Bree. She had a book to pass the time, but so far she hadn't made it through one page. Bree's text had come in about fifteen minutes ago.

Are you busy? I need to talk to someone.

I'm at home. Want to stop by? Rachel had included directions in the text and Bree had responded that she'd be over shortly.

Rachel was over the moon that Bree had reached out to her, but worried about what could be wrong. Was it her parents? Or an issue with a friend?

She prayed for wisdom to know how to best be there for Bree.

It had been an interesting last few days since the lock-in. Not a lot of contact from Hunter, which Rachel was just fine with. She felt absolutely no need to revisit their foolish kiss. Though she had beaten herself up over the infraction. Hunter had texted on Saturday to check on how she was feeling. She'd replied that her head was fine. No concussion symptoms. And then she'd told him that he should stop worrying and feeling guilty. His retort of *I'm just glad you're not going to file a lawsuit* had made her laugh.

And then, to add to the eventful weekend, Rachel had come home after church on Sunday to find an unexpected guest on her porch. A speckled Great Dane. No sign of where the animal had come from. No collar or tags. Rachel had given him some water to drink and then fed him. She'd tried to get him to come inside that night, but he'd balked. On Monday morning, she'd opened her front door to find him asleep on her porch. When the shelter had opened, she'd called, but they hadn't had a record of anyone searching for a lost dog matching his description.

They'd also been out of space. So she'd done something stupid. She'd said she would keep him for a bit. Until they had room. Rachel had started calling him Moose because his long legs reminded her of that animal, and every dog needed a name, even if it was only temporary.

Moose rose from his resting spot to her right, gave a squeaky yawn and stretched, then came to sit in front of the swing.

Rachel scrubbed behind his ears. "You're such a good boy. I think somebody is missing you." She hadn't used a leash to keep him at her place, but in the last three days, he'd stuck close by. Perhaps the dog food she'd bought for him had something to do with it. For such a large animal, Rachel would expect him to be rambunctious. Knock things around and cause a ruckus. But he was more partial to snoozing. She'd rinsed him down this morning—he'd been dirty as all get-out—but he'd need a real bath one day soon.

Once he found new owners. Or his current ones. "You can crash here for a little bit, big guy, but don't get too comfortable because I'm not staying much longer." She gazed into his mournful eyes, hopefully communicating dog speak, wondering who she was reminding—herself or Moose.

Dust rose up from a vehicle coming down her drive. Bree.

The girl parked and walked up the steps. She wore denim boyfriend capris and a striped short-sleeved shirt, her strawberry blond hair down in loose, beachy curls. Moose greeted her with some sniffing, a few licks and one *roo-roo*—as if saying hello. His intrusion broke through the gloomy fog surrounding Bree, and she fleetingly brightened.

"Did you get a dog?"

"No." Rachel shook her head with a vengeance.

Bree eyed the stainless steel water and food bowls that were stationed at the shady end of the porch—also necessary purchases.

"Are you dog sitting?" She sat next to Rachel on the swing, and Moose followed. Bree rubbed her fingertips along his head and back, giving in to his obvious plea for attention. After a few seconds, he settled on the strip of porch in front of them.

"Something like that. He's a stray. I'm just keeping him until the shelter finds his owners or has room for him."

Moose looked up at her with hurt in those big dark eyes.

What? I told you I'm leaving. You should have lis-

tened and not started getting attached. Advice Rachel could also give to herself regarding so many things. Hunter, for one. The girl next to her on the swing. Even this town was growing on her.

"So, tell me what's going on."

"My dad is moving to Austin." Bree's words came out in a rush, like water bubbling over the edge of a boiling pot. "I know it's not that far away, but…" Her voice dipped. Wobbled. For a second, Rachel thought the tears pooling in her eyes would spill, but Bree blinked them back. "He didn't even ask me or my younger sister our opinions. Just told us he got a new job. We get to visit him on weekends." Sarcasm spewed from every pore. "Because that's what I want to do on the weekend— leave my friends to stay in another town with my jerk of a dad in some apartment."

"That really stinks. I'm sorry." Rachel let the words rest for a second, wishing she could find a way to make it better. But sometimes life just wasn't easy.

She contemplated what to say before speaking. "I don't know your dad, obviously, but maybe he's just looking for a new start. Maybe he has no idea how upsetting this is to you. Do you think he would listen if you talked to him about it?"

Bree's shoulders inched up, then drooped as though carrying a massive weight. The faint creak of the swing's chain filled the otherwise tranquil evening. "Maybe." Her answer came out softly. Filled with very little hope. "I guess it's worth a shot."

"What about your mom? Have you talked to her about it?"

The girl's head shook.

"I understand that speaking to your parents about

all of this is hard and probably uncomfortable. I get it. But I know from experience that it's better to say something now than to wish you had after the fact." Rachel had learned that lesson at a young age. On the morning of her parents' deaths, she'd fought with her mom over something so stupid—when she could have a cell phone. How all of the other kids had them, except for her. She'd screamed and raged and slammed her bedroom door. She'd been a typical teenager—so she'd been told. But the rest of the story wasn't normal.

Before they'd left for the cattle auction, her dad had come into her room. He'd always been so good to her. Calm and loving and patient. He'd hugged her. Told her everything was going to be okay, and that once she calmed down, she should apologize to her mother.

They'd left, and Rachel had known immediately that she should make amends. But instead of calling, she'd waited. Let her anger continue a little longer.

She would apologize later, she'd decided.

But not everyone got a later.

Her parents had never come home again. The car accident that had taken their lives had seen to that.

"Before my mom died, we fought. It was an unnecessary argument. Totally my fault. I had the opportunity to call her and say I was sorry, and I didn't."

Sympathy moisture pooled in Bree's eyes.

"I've worked through it now. Someone—" *Olivia* "—helped me back in high school." Rachel had come to understand that her mom had loved her. That a disagreement and Rachel's immature behavior wouldn't change that. And knowing her mother, she could accept that truth—the kind of limitless love her mom had had for her. "But if I could go back and do it differently, I would. Not that your situation is the same as mine, but I think it applies. Your parents don't have any idea how you're feeling, and they won't unless you talk to them. You still may not end up with some perfect scenario, but it might give you some peace."

Bree nodded contemplatively. She pressed the toes of her simple green sandals against the porch, sending the swing into motion. "Thank you for sharing that about your mom. It helps that you're not just telling me what to do without backing it up."

Rachel's mouth curved. "I was the same way as a teenager. I needed the real deal. No canned advice for me."

"Right?" Bree laughed. "Adults should realize that we can sniff out the fake stuff."

"I couldn't agree with you more."

They stayed on the swing for a while after that. Talking some. Sitting in silence for part of it.

Before Bree left, Rachel prayed for her.

The girl's walk down the steps was less dejected than her way up. She even waved right before she got into her car and gave a relatively cheerful, "Thanks, Coach."

In the land of teenagers, Rachel would call that a victory.

The next night, Rachel drove to Hunter's thirty minutes before the youth would show up to work on the float so she could help set up. She wore an old, long volleyball T-shirt that had her name and number scrawled across the back over capri leggings. Last week her cute ruffled shirt had gotten a hole in it, and Rachel wasn't about to sacrifice another piece of her favorite clothing.

She'd been tempted to arrive right at seven to avoid

alone time with Hunter, but she was determined to do everything as she typically did.

She hoped if she ignored that their kiss had occurred, it would blow over and they could go back to the good place they'd been in. Hopefully Hunter wouldn't bring it up. But what was there to even say?

The two of them had been done a long time ago. They wanted different things, and one rogue kiss wasn't going to change that.

Hunter had only asked about her supposed injury since the lock-in. He hadn't brought up anything else. Which meant maybe he wanted the same thing as her—to just move forward as friends per their original conversation.

Which would be perfect, because then Rachel wouldn't have to delve into why she'd let the kiss happen in the first place.

When she entered the barn, Hunter was dragging out the large plastic totes. Tonight the group would adhere the fake grass to the trailer and then mount the other props they'd crafted. The youth would be excited to see the float finally take shape.

"Cowboy." She greeted him when she reached his side.

Hunter's dimples flashed as he nodded hello. "Teen whisperer."

They fell into a rhythm as they set up. No talking. No awkwardness. Relief skipped along Rachel's spine. Maybe they really were going to just let the kiss slide into the past. They could add it to the pile of their history together.

Hunter wore a simple white T-shirt tonight. The kind that came out of a three-pack and shouldn't look so good on someone. If Rachel tried to wear something like that, she'd resemble a box. Hunter could star in their ad. He even smelled good—something yummy and masculine.

This whole being friends gig would be a lot easier if he wasn't so stinking attractive.

At least, that's what she told herself.

When Rachel ran out of things to prep, she panicked. There was still fifteen minutes left before the kids would start trickling in. Far too much time for an unapproved conversation to sprout.

"What else do we need to do?" *Please, please keep me occupied. Give me a job.* Something. Anything. Perhaps she could volunteer to go check on the cattle.

"Think that's it." Hunter placed the last of the staple guns on the trailer.

"Did I tell you I found a dog camped out on my porch?" Of course the answer was no. Rachel caught him up on the appearance of Moose. "He even slept inside last night, which he wouldn't do at first. I put a rug by the front door for him, but in the middle of the night, he curled up on the floor by my bed." Relaying that story to Hunter ate up all of two minutes. *Moose, why couldn't you have caused some kind of trouble?* Then she would have been able to fill more time.

"That's crazy no one has reported him as missing yet. Though it's not a bad idea for you to have a dog for protection since you're living by yourself." And now Hunter sounded like her brother. His eyes narrowed slightly. "I'm actually a little shocked that you're here tonight."

"Why?"

"I just wasn't sure if you were ever going to talk to me again."

What? It wasn't as if he'd been knocking down her door. "I haven't heard from you except for the texts on Saturday, so maybe you're avoiding me, McDermott."

"Not avoiding." Hunter clarified. "Giving you space. There's a difference."

"Is there?"

"Yes, Your Sassiness."

Rachel planned to stick with humor. If she kept replying with sarcasm, she'd exasperate Hunter, and then maybe he'd give up on having this little chat.

"As to your earlier comment and whether I *want* to talk to you again, I'd have to go with maybe." Rachel tapped a finger to her lips as though contemplating. "Probably." She stretched the word out.

"Are you ever not going to be snarky when I ask you a question?"

"It's unlikely."

A sigh leaked from him. "That's the answer I expected. I don't suppose you're ready to talk about what happened at the lock-in yet."

"I already told you my head is absolutely fine."

"That's not what I mean and you know it."

Why did Hunter have to push? Why couldn't he let it go? Ever since she'd been home, people—including Hunter—had been infiltrating her life.

The other day, Val had pulled out of Rachel that Hunter had kissed her. It had been like extracting a tooth, but still. And then her friend had responded with a sympathetic, "What are we going to do about this?"

Rachel had almost burst into tears at the "we." While she'd been away, she'd forgotten what that felt like. Ever since she'd been back in Fredericksburg, *we* was exactly what she'd experienced. Hunter and everyone helping on the house. The church needing her. The boys and Cash and Liv thankful to have her home. Drawing her in like a toasty blanket on a cold, dreary day.

That *we* was exactly what scared her, though. She remembered the *we* of being a family. A real one. With a mom and dad who loved her. A brother who both tormented, annoyed and delighted her. One who wasn't her guardian but just a sibling.

But she knew *we* didn't last.

Rachel broke it. She always wrecked things. Relationships. That last fight with her mom—no matter how many times she forgave herself, it haunted her. Hearts, like she had with Hunter.

That's why Rachel was careful. Kept people at a distance, sometimes without even realizing what she was doing. Only her family and Val had slipped in through the cracks. And now Hunter, once again.

Hadn't he learned well enough the last time? Why did he even want to be around a broken piece of glass like her? Didn't he know her jagged edges would cut him? If he'd started hoping for something between them after their kiss, he'd be disappointed. Again. She was still planning to move. That hadn't changed.

"Listen, Hunter, there's nothing that needs to be said. We're adults. It happened. It shouldn't have. End of story."

After Rachel delivered her verdict on their relationship—unwilling to discuss anything deeper than surface level, of course—she had the audacity to pick up a staple gun as if she planned to get to work.

But Hunter wasn't done. Whether Rachel wanted to

or not, they were going to hash this out. He took the staple gun from her hand and set it back on the trailer.

"We're talking about this."

A scowl cut through her forehead. "We already did."

"That wasn't a conversation, Rach. That was a one-woman conclusion. I was part of what happened too, you know."

Wide eyes greeted him. "Trust me, I know." Her arms crossed. "You want to discuss it here?" She glanced around the empty barn.

The kids wouldn't show up for another ten minutes, so, yes. Here. Now. Those were Hunter's choices.

Based on Rachel's deflection since she'd arrived, Hunter would guess she'd prefer never.

The woman was good at steering clear when something made her uncomfortable. Five days had passed since the lock-in. He'd given her plenty of room, and he was done waiting.

"Why? Do you need a fancier place to hold a conversation?"

"No. Of course not. But there's nothing that needs to be said. We'll just put it aside. Pretend it didn't happen."

"Rach." His voice was low, gravelly. Hurt, confusion and remorse all swirled between them.

Her demeanor softened. She lost a bit of the act. "We're okay, Hunter."

Were they? He didn't think so. But he'd been praying awfully hard over the last few days that they would be.

"I have something I need to say to you."

She didn't speak. Just waited.

"I promised you could trust me, and then I broke that with the kiss. I'm sorry."

She twisted the toe of one flip-flop into the dirt,

her bright orange polish gaining a layer of dust with the movement. Rachel memorized the ground for what felt like years. Finally she looked up. "I *do* still trust you. Besides, it wasn't just you. We both participated."

The temptation to let that thought warm him was strong, but he shook it off. Hunter didn't need the reminder. He'd thought about that fact plenty in the last few days. "I know. I just… I don't want to lose you over this. I don't want us to go back to fighting or not talking or avoiding. I like being friends with you."

"You're not going to lose me." The way she held eye contact with him gave him hope she was telling the truth. "You're not." And the secondary declaration helped, too. "Believe it or not, McDermott, you're actually starting to grow on me."

The tension that had been thrumming through him for days began to ebb.

"I am hard to shake."

"Exactly." Contemplation furrowed her brow. "Like a leech. Or a wasp that won't stop buzzing around my head."

She was back to joking around, but he was okay with that now that he'd said what he needed to. "Promise we're good?"

"Promise."

Pent-up air leaked from his lungs. "I feel better. Aren't you relieved I made you talk about this?"

Her mouth curved. "No."

"Stubborn. You can't just admit it, can you? You could give our bull a run for his money."

"Did you just compare me to a bull?" Her nose wrinkled, and the humor dropped from her face as her gaze flitted past him like butterfly wings. "I don't know why it matters so much to you, anyway." The words were so quiet, he almost didn't catch them.

Felt like she was really asking why *she* mattered so much to him.

A question he was tempted to answer. To tell her he'd always cared about her. Always would. But Hunter couldn't go there. Couldn't unravel all of that. His original thought in pursuing a friendship with Rachel was not to turn out like his father. Not to repeat those mistakes. And he was light-years ahead of his old man in that regard. Hunter clung to that right now, unwilling to let it be about anything more with Rachel. She was still planning to move, so it couldn't be. "It just does."

There. He'd just have to leave it at that. But he couldn't resist at least attempting to erase her look of sadness.

"Besides, if I didn't have you in my life, who would torment me?"

She rolled her eyes and whacked him on the arm, making his chest shake with amusement. He wasn't sure he'd truly relaxed since their kiss. The fear that he'd ruined it all had been ruling him. But they were okay again. He wasn't going to lose her over one impetuous decision.

By the light in her eyes, his teasing seemed to be working, so he kept it up. "I'm not sure what I was thinking, trying to keep our relationship intact. I mean, you call me names. You don't even make any home-cooked meals for me, which I'm pretty sure would be a sign of a true friendship. And you're always hitting me." He rubbed the spot where she'd just done that very thing, acting as though she'd wounded him.

"You're a dork." Her tone was as dry as sawdust.

"See! This is what I'm talking about."

Her laughter stitched him back together, and peace rushed in. She might have been worried at first that he'd wanted more than the platonic relationship they'd agreed upon, but he'd talked her down. He—and God— had fixed it. Got them back to the good place they'd been in before he'd kissed her.

Hunter wasn't about to analyze why he was so concerned about losing Rachel when he knew that very thing was going to happen one day soon.

Tonight he was just going to rest in the knowledge that she was still in his life, even if he felt the limited time with her slipping like sand through his fingers.

Chapter Eleven

The sun hung low in the sky as Rachel drove home, and she flipped her visor down as she made the final turn. The last two days had passed in a blur.

After her talk with Hunter on Wednesday night, she'd gotten a phone call from Dana, calling about an interview. The board had narrowed the candidates down to Rachel and one other person. So on Thursday she'd driven to Houston, and this morning she'd had the interview.

Rachel thought—or hoped—it had gone well. Tough questions had been lobbed at her, but she'd never felt as though she was drowning without an answer to hold on to. The conversation had given her confidence that the school board would have her back if she landed the job, and the whole experience had only made her more confident it was the right opportunity for her.

Which conflicted with the rest of her emotions. Because she'd missed home. Had she really started to think of Fredericksburg as that again? Despite her attempts not to, she'd felt the absence of her friends and family in the short time she'd been gone. Her nephews' sweet dispositions. Hunter.

That last name made her stomach twist with concern. She couldn't miss him. Both of them knew she planned to move if she got the job. But she also conveniently hadn't told him about the interview. It had felt too raw. Too soon after they were finding their friendship footing again.

It was okay she hadn't mentioned it to him, right? If they were in a relationship, she would have. But they weren't. She hadn't done anything wrong in not telling Hunter about the interview. Who knew if she'd even get the job? Rachel wasn't one to count chickens before they'd hatched.

Last night, she and Dana had shopped and gone out to dinner. It had been wonderful, confirming what Rachel loved about the city. But being in Fredericksburg had begun to cloud her thinking. She'd started to enjoy the peace and quiet, and look forward to the mornings when she'd sit on her porch swing and do her devotions. Drink a cup of coffee before heading over to Cash and Liv's. It had become the perfect beginning to her day, and she couldn't imagine giving it up.

When she'd first arrived back in town, she'd expected to hate every minute of the summer. But instead, she'd had plenty of good flood her life.

Up and down her emotions swung, like a yo-yo in a child's hands.

On Wednesday night, when she'd left the barn to take the phone call from Dana, she'd confirmed the details of the interview and then turned to find Bree standing behind her, her features an open wound.

"You're leaving?" Bree had questioned.

Rachel had moved slowly toward the girl, not wanting her to scram before she could explain. She'd assumed the kids knew her plans—that she was only back for the summer—but had they ever had that conversation?

"Bree, this job has been in the works for months. I thought you knew my move home was temporary."

"Yeah, I knew that, but I thought…" The girl's demeanor had hardened like chiseled stone. None of the soft, almost-there tears from the evening before had remained. "Never mind what I thought." Her arms had wrapped around her stomach as if forming a shield. "It doesn't matter."

Bree mattered, but what could Rachel do about it? She really wanted this job. But at the same time, she cared about the teens. Her family. Hunter. And that dog on her porch. She hadn't planned to fall for this place— these people—but she had. And then, this morning, she'd talked to the board about leaving them all.

Her phone rang, and Rachel checked the caller ID. She didn't recognize the number but answered, anyway.

"This is Rachel."

"Rachel, this is Lisa Trupe from the board." Pandemonium erupted within Rachel's rib cage. Should she rejoice or grab the box of tissues from the backseat? "We just finished meeting, and we'd like to offer you the position. Everyone thinks you'll be a great fit. We wanted to let you know before the weekend so you could think about it and hopefully get back to us by Monday or Tuesday next week."

Months of stress rolled from Rachel's back. She'd put so much of her hope into this.

"Thank you so much, Lisa, but I don't need time

to think about it." Did she? Hadn't she wanted this all along? Rachel had never doubted this was where God was directing her. But then, why did the thought of leaving Hunter fill her with sorrow?

She might want it all, but that wasn't how life worked. She couldn't have Hunter and the job. And that was assuming he was even still interested in her.

No. She couldn't let the thought of their renewed relationship sway her. Besides, Hunter had apologized for their kiss. He hadn't confessed any feelings for her. Rachel knew what she needed to do.

"Are you sure?"

"Yes, I'm sure. I would love to accept the position." Rachel answered emphatically, as though the strength of her voice could erase any remaining concerns and doubts.

They talked details for another minute, then disconnected. If this was what she wanted, then why was her stomach churning? She couldn't tell if it was nerves, excitement or dread.

The thought of telling Hunter about the job heightened that last emotion. She'd grown used to having him in her life again. If something came up, Hunter was on the top of her list of people to call. But what would her accepting the job do to them? How would he handle it?

She could wait a few days to spill the news to him, couldn't she? Take some time to let the decision sink in and figure out what to say.

Rachel pulled down her drive, and when she neared the house, her headlights illuminated a truck sitting next to her Jeep's parking spot. Hunter's.

What was he doing here? So much for time to process how to tell him.

Moose popped up from his resting place and moseyed down the front steps while she rolled into her spot and turned off the ignition. He greeted her with a *roo-roo* when she opened her door. "Hey, boy. I missed you, too." She ran her hands over his soft head and ears. Cash and Grayson had been checking on him while she was gone. Which meant Moose had likely had his fair share of treats over the last two days.

Rachel grabbed her overnight bag, slipped her fingers through the straps of her heeled sandals and crossed the grass barefoot. The dog moved back up the porch steps and walked toward the swing. And that's when Rachel saw Hunter slouched over in it, sleeping.

Moose sniffed along his jeans and down to his boots as if to show Rachel they had an intruder and he'd done a good job being a watch dog. Most likely he'd *watched* Hunter come up the steps and accepted a rubdown before both of them had conked out.

The warmth of the previously sun-kissed wood met her soles as she walked up the steps. At Moose's intrusion, Hunter opened his eyes and propped himself up. "Hey." His warm eyes met hers.

"Hey." She set her overnight bag and shoes by the front door, and he glanced around as if getting his bearings.

"Been here awhile?"

He nodded. "Fell asleep." His grin was sheepish. Adorable. "Obviously." He scrubbed a hand through his hair, and the dark blond strands stuck up in handsome disarray.

"Did we…" Her fingers found her gold R necklace and toyed with the pendant. "Did we have plans I forgot?"

"Nope. I just got done working and thought maybe you'd want to hang out. Grab dinner, catch a movie or go listen to some music in town. But then I sat down to wait for you, and…" He shrugged.

Rachel plopped onto the swing next to him, her decision to take the job weighing her down like a boulder strapped to her back. Hunter studied her, questioning, and everything in her wanted to lean in. Rest her head on his shoulder. Tell him how she suddenly felt confused about the job she wanted so badly, and it was all because of him.

What she wouldn't give for them to want the same things.

"You okay? What's wrong?" He laid an open hand on his jeans-clad leg, and like a fool, she put hers in it.

This man. What was she going to do with him? Even worse, what was she going to do without him?

She had to tell him. Rip off the Band-Aid. They were good, right? Surely they'd stay there. He would understand. He'd known all along this was her plan.

They both had.

Dread curled through Hunter as Rachel pushed her foot against the porch and set the swing in motion. Something was wrong. He could feel the tension coming from her, wrapping around him like a boa constrictor slithering around his chest.

"Were you out to dinner?" And, if yes, who had she been with?

"No."

He wasn't sure whether to feel relief or concern. When he'd opened his eyes a minute ago, her outfit had felt like a sucker punch. A fancy sleeveless shirt.

Dress pants that ended just above her ankles. High heels hooked in her fingertips. A bright blue, chunky beaded necklace in addition to the gold one she usually wore. Light pink sparkly polish on her toenails. His first thought was that she'd been on a date, and he'd been sleeping on her porch waiting for her. He'd wanted to kick himself.

So, if she wasn't at dinner, hopefully that meant she hadn't just been on a date. Not that he was allowed to care about that stuff. Not with their rules and relationship-defining decisions. But if she wasn't going to date him, he sure wasn't okay with her going out with someone else. Not that they'd ever had that discussion.

"So where were you?"

She stared straight forward as night fully descended and the first few stars began twinkling. It reminded him of one of Kinsley's drawings—a smattering of light in the midst of a black sheet of construction paper. "I was in Houston."

His lungs morphed into a balloon with a pinprick, the air slowly leaking out. "For the job?"

She nodded.

And she hadn't told him.

Maybe he'd rather hear she'd been on a date. Another guy he could fight and contend with, but the job? Not a chance. His feelings for her might be growing, but he couldn't give them wings.

He tried with everything in him to remember he wanted this for her. "What happened?"

"They interviewed me again this morning."

He was having a hard time taking a full breath, so he counted on the shallow, painful ones to pull him through.

"And they offered me the job." She'd been looking at her tan bare feet as she spoke, but now her gaze lifted to him, those green embers filled with more emotion than he could decipher. "I accepted."

It took him a minute to speak. "Congratulations." His voice cracked and he cleared his throat. "When do you leave?"

"The Monday after the parade."

A week and a half. Now it was his turn to stare out at the ranch. He'd known all along what her plans were, but that didn't fix the ache that had started right between his ribs.

He looked down at their hands. They were still touching. He'd offered her his hand as a comfort—at least, that's what he'd told himself—and she'd accepted. But now the simple gesture felt too intimate.

He needed to get out of here. Rachel was looking at him with wounded eyes—as if this was a choice *he'd* made—and he couldn't form the right words or thoughts.

Hunter stopped the swing and stood, the comforting warmth of her sitting beside him instantly gone. "I'm happy for you, Rach. I know how badly you wanted this." If he sounded rote, so be it. He was doing his best.

"Thanks." Her quiet response barely registered.

He felt a bit like a child who'd just had the ice cream on his cone fall to the dusty ground after his parent had warned him that very thing was about to happen. He should have expected this. She'd prepared him all along.

"You want to watch a movie?" She motioned inside. "Not that I have that much comfortable furniture…or we could play a game instead. I mean, you came over to do something, right?"

"I gotta—" *Get out of here*. He rubbed a hand across the back of his neck. "I have some things I need to do." Right. Even though he'd just been waiting for her for how long? But at this point, he didn't care about logic.

For once, it was him who needed to escape.

The next few days crept by with only one consistency: no Hunter. No contact from him on Saturday. At church on Sunday, Rachel somehow didn't see him. By that night, her curiosity at his lack of presence or texts was growing. And by Monday morning, she was thoroughly confused. Almost angry.

Hunter had said they were fine—that they were friends. But were they? Then where was he? Had her taking the job messed with their relationship?

He couldn't just disappear from her life without warning. He'd promised her a friendship and that's what she expected.

Rachel had stayed on the swing long after he'd left on Friday night, thinking. Praying. Hoping and trusting that she'd made the right decision about the job.

If she took Hunter out of the equation, she'd feel excitement. He was the one person making her question her choice. Well…him and her family. Val. And the teens. But the fact remained, no matter how close she'd grown to any of them, she still didn't want this life.

Being in Houston had been so refreshing. The city was bustling. Yes, she'd missed the quiet of the country. She'd missed her swing and being at peace with her thoughts. There was a lot pulling her here. But there was also a lot drawing her away.

Rachel busied herself all day Monday with Grayson and Ryder. But when she arrived home in the evening, the empty house haunted her. She felt…lonely. And that's when she knew what was happening. She missed Hunter. She missed him, and she hadn't even left yet.

Rachel could contact him. Or she could do the smart thing and start putting some space between them. Not let any more feelings grow in the short remaining time she would be home.

She paced the few steps from one side of her living room to the other, then threw her arms into the air with a groan of annoyance. Enough of this. She changed into workout shorts and a tank, snagged her running shoes and laced up, then tore out of the house.

Moose didn't even pretend to be interested in joining her. He gave one bark as she took off and tried to outrun her frustrations.

She was leaving.

Hunter had been reeling from the news for three days now. Rachel's announcement on Friday had sent him into a tailspin.

He'd come to a very unsettling conclusion over the last few days—one he hadn't wanted to admit, even to himself. Despite all of his attempts not to, he'd developed feelings for Rachel again. Or, more likely, they'd never truly gone away. They ran like a deep and wide river inside of him. A current he couldn't turn off. He'd tried over the years. Even convinced himself he'd accomplished that very thing. But the reason there'd been so much angst between them after she'd left was because he'd never stopped caring for her.

And sometime in the last few weeks, he'd started hoping she might change her mind about moving and want to stay. He hadn't even realized the hope had started flickering until it had been abruptly snuffed out when she'd told him she'd taken the job.

He half snorted, half laughed at his naïveté. What had he expected? She'd been very honest about the fact that she planned to leave from the first moment she'd stepped foot in this town.

Since Friday night, he'd been a mess. Trying to regroup and figure out how to get his feelings under control. He'd been working himself to the bone, thinking manual labor might dull the ache of his new discovery. Hadn't worked yet.

Hunter had come in from the ranch tonight and showered, then thrown on some clean jeans, socks and a navy blue T-shirt. Now he strode over to his fridge and rummaged inside. Leftovers would suffice for dinner. He heated up beef Stroganoff and took the bowl over to the island. His elbows landed on the countertop as he bowed his head for a quick prayer, then dug in.

When a knock sounded on his door, he didn't bother getting up. "Come in," he called out, scooping the last bite into his mouth before turning.

Rachel stood in the open doorframe. Hunter swallowed, then clamped his jaw to keep it from falling open. He scrubbed a hand over his face to make sure he didn't have any food hitching a ride and popped up from the bar stool, walking toward her. He wanted to crush her in a hug. He wanted to tell her he'd missed her over the last few days. Instead, he said, "Hey." Brilliant.

She was wearing a colorful tank top, black running shorts and tennis shoes.

Her breathing seemed labored.

"Did you run here?"

"Yep."

"You want to sit? Glass of water?"

"Sure."

He went into the kitchen while she crossed to the couch. He filled a glass and handed it off to her, then sat on the love seat, not trusting himself to sit next to her.

"I've never really seen your house. Besides when I picked you up. And then you were so crabby it took all of my effort and attention just to get you out of here." She flashed a sassy grin and scanned the first floor.

The kitchen and island were open to the living room. Upstairs he had three bedrooms. Three. Who knew what for? He'd thought for a family one day. With the way things were going, maybe he could use one as a craft room. He would have plenty of time in the rest of his unmarried life to take up a hobby. Knitting. Crochet. Scrapbooking.

"It's really nice."

"Thanks."

What was she doing here? Had she come with another announcement to throw his world off-kilter?

Her legs bounced, and she jumped up from the couch and walked along the island, then went back to her seat and dropped onto the cushions.

"Rach, what's on your mind?"

Surprise tugged on her features. "Nothing. I was just…out for a run."

Didn't ring true, but Rachel wouldn't give up information easily. She might not even know what she was upset about.

He'd always been good at getting her to spill, much like she'd done with him.

His heart squeezed. His Rachel, with all of the walls and hurt and toughness. She tried to keep up appearances. Act as if life hadn't thrown really hard things at her. As though she could handle it all. But he knew her inside and out. And now he'd broken through. She might not be staying, but he'd chipped away at her defenses until she'd let him in. She might not love him, but she liked him. She'd come to him.

Now he just needed to figure out why.

"I can't believe you went running in this heat."

"Me, either."

"Come on." He stood, offered her a hand. When she accepted, he pulled her up, too. "I'll drive you home. But first I have somewhere to take you."

Chapter Twelve

"Where are we going?"

Rachel's annoyance filled the cab of his truck as Hunter made the last few turns, and he tamped down his amusement.

"You'll see."

Whatever happened, she reacted strongly. If she shut down, it was with ten locked doors and a No Entrance sign blazing. If she let someone in, it was like seeing the sun up close and not getting burned. He liked her highs and lows. Her passionate opinions. He even liked the driven side of her that made her want to leave here— and him—and work somewhere else.

Hunter might not know what was going to happen between them, but in the last few days, he'd been drowning, forgetting that God's imagination was far greater than his. He would choose to have faith that God had a plan. That He loved Hunter and Rachel, and wanted good for them. Yes, Hunter would likely have to give her up all over again. And God's plan might turn out to be different than the one he would come up with, but he was still going to believe and pray and hope even if he didn't know what the future looked like. One day at a time. He could handle that, couldn't he?

He pulled into his friend's driveway, the fading evening light disrupted as his headlights splashed against the front windows of the house.

Hunter unbuckled and hopped out of the truck, met by the Texas heat that reached down his throat and closed like a fist. Rachel stayed in the passenger seat with the belt still on. "Are we going to visit your friends or something? Because I'm not looking my best." She motioned to her workout clothes.

"Nope, we're not. And you look perfect."

She rolled her eyes, and he fought a grin with everything in him. Hunter didn't need a Rachel-induced black eye any time soon.

"Come on."

Her hands tightened on the seat belt that still stretched across her chest, as though holding on would keep her from being ejected from the truck.

"Do I need to come over there and get you?"

She unbuckled lightning fast, the belt clinking against the metal doorframe as she got out.

When she reached his side of the vehicle, he swung the door shut and started walking. Rachel didn't follow, so he went back, grabbed her hand and tugged her along. Stubborn. Two could play at that game. Hunter didn't let go of her hand. If he only got to have her for another week, he might as well enjoy it. Touching her messed with him in ways a whole day in the hot sun without a drop of hydration didn't compare to. Surprisingly, she didn't fight to get away.

He went around the side of the house and found the wooden gate to the backyard, letting go of her hand in order to retrieve the key from under the rock to the right of the path. After popping the lock open, he ushered Rachel into the backyard.

Searching along the wall of the house, he found a light switch. The space sprang to life, a string of outdoor lights stretching from one end of the cement patio area to the other, swooping down and illuminating the pool. Clear, crisp inviting water beckoned.

"No way." Her tone brooked no argument, but Hunter toed off one boot then the other, stuffing his socks inside, while Rachel's voice grew louder. "Hunter McDermott, I am not getting in that pool. Are these people even home? Do they know you're here? Are you breaking and entering?" Her pitch increased to squeaking, breaking-glass level as he knelt and began untying the laces of one of her shoes. It must have taken her a second to process his actions, because he got it and her sock off before she started screeching and generally being feisty, trying to keep the second one out of his reach. For that shoe, he had to wrap an arm around her legs to hold her still and work quickly. But he managed to remove it and her sock, tossing them to the side.

When he stood and faced her, she looked like a mama hen whose babies had been attacked.

He made one last attempt to convince her, nodding toward the water. "You can't deny the appeal. It's two hundred degrees out."

"We wouldn't be alive if it was two hundred degrees out."

"It will feel amazing."

"No." Her ponytail swung back and forth with her head.

"In answer to your earlier question, this is my friend

Marc's house. They're out of town. Don't worry, I checked with him. That's who I was texting before we left."

"Great." Sarcasm dripped from the word. "I'm still not going in that pool."

"Okay." His arms relaxed by his sides. "You don't have to."

Her forehead puckered with doubt. "Really?"

"No, not really." She was standing near the edge of the pool—not her smartest choice—and he lunged, taking her out with something near a tackle and catapulting the two of them into the water. Rachel screamed so much on the way in he hoped she remembered to close her mouth.

She came up sputtering and splashing, and he grabbed her hands, holding them still. "Tell me that doesn't feel good."

"It doesn't feel good." At her rote answer, he dunked her. What else was he supposed to do? She was as stubborn as the day was hot. She surfaced fighting and lunged onto his back, trying to take him under. It didn't work.

At his laughter, she whacked him on the back and let go, swimming around to face him. "You're annoying."

"Thank you."

She huffed. "I'm sure my mascara is running everywhere."

He eased closer to her and slid his thumbs under her eyes, swiping away the black and washing the remnants on his fingers into the water. "There." He did it one more time. "You're fine now. Gorgeous as always."

Another eye roll. Would she ever believe him?

Rachel dipped her head back into the water and then stretched her neck from side to side. Letting go. Finally.

Now to get her talking.

"This job…how badly do you want it on a scale of one to ten?"

"Ten."

Ouch. Not even an iota of doubt or wanting to stay.

Her hands played with the water, creating miniature waves. "When I left here the first time, I had something to prove. I think I still do. But that's not the only reason. I've been praying about this, and I don't think God would have opened this door if I wasn't supposed to walk through it."

How could he argue with that?

Her head tilted. "Can I ask you a question?"

"No."

She splashed him and he scrubbed the water from his face with a grin.

"Did you ever date anyone over the years since I've been gone? I mean, I'm sure you did. But anything serious?"

Hello, loaded question. His chest heaved. He couldn't blame her for being curious. He'd asked her as much when she'd first come back and she'd answered him.

"Yes, I dated, but only one serious relationship."

"What happened?"

She wasn't you. And that's when he finally understood why that relationship hadn't worked out, why things—at least on his end—had fizzled. Nadine had been amazing. She'd had a young daughter, and Hunter had liked both of them, but love had stayed out of his reach. He'd broken up with her after he couldn't find a way for his feelings to grow, but he'd never grasped why until now.

"She wasn't the one." His answer hung in the air, snapping like an electrical wire above the pool, threatening to break and fall and electrocute them both.

"Hunter." Her voice was soft, almost mournful, causing his pulse to thrum sluggishly. "I want you to be happy. I hope you find the right one."

He fought to keep from saying something he shouldn't, to bury the emotion coursing through him. "I'm sure she's out there somewhere, crying in her soup because she hasn't found me yet." He opted for humor, and her bark of laughter warmed him.

"I'm sure she is." Now she sounded serious.

Rachel needed to stop being so nice. It was confusing, and he was going to kiss her again if she kept it up.

"I hope you find happiness, too." And he meant it. He'd just prefer if it was with him.

"Thanks." Her eyes crinkled at the corners, the light lashes casting shadows over her cheekbones.

"Can I ask you a question?"

"No."

Her answer mimicked his from earlier, and he chuckled. No one was as quick with a retort as Rachel. He splashed a light amount of water toward her, then continued despite her response. "Are you going to tell me what had you so upset earlier when you came over?"

"What do you mean? I was fine."

Her favorite claim. "Rach, I know you better than that."

He held on to her gaze with his and waited.

"It was just…" Her slight shrug made ripples in the

water. "I told you about getting the job and you just took off. And then I didn't hear from you." She sank lower in the pool, the jut of her chin dipping below the surface. "I didn't know if you were upset or if something was wrong."

She'd missed him. The knowledge rose up, shouting for attention.

"I just had a lot to do with work." *And I was figuring out what to do next about you. About the fact that I can't seem to want anyone but you, you stubborn, gorgeous, annoying woman who's leaving me. Again.*

The fact that she cared, that she'd missed him, was messing with every resolve he'd set to keep himself from doing something stupid—like easing forward to taste her lips again, or to say, *Hey, what if you stayed? How about that?* Just like the last time.

But he wouldn't ask. He couldn't. What had she told him? A ten. That's how badly she wanted this job. And he wasn't going to be the one to stop her.

The irony choked him. After all of these years, he was getting to her. She was opening up again. And now she was moving for sure.

They only had a small amount of time left together, and Hunter planned to spend every minute he could with her. Even knowing his heart was going to just shrivel and give up beating when she left.

She might as well take it with her when she went. He wouldn't have any need for it after she was gone.

"So you weren't upset that I took the job?"

Rachel wasn't sure why she cared so much. Or why she'd sought out Hunter in the first place. But now that they were knee-deep in this conversation, she wanted to finish it. To know.

"No." Some emotion she couldn't decipher flickered in his eyes. "I'm happy for you, Rach. I'm sorry I was MIA."

"It's okay. I don't know what came over me. I think…" The air in her lungs rushed out. "The thought of leaving has me pretty messed up."

"That's understandable. This is your home. It might not be easy to go." Hunter swallowed, his Adam's apple bobbing. "But that doesn't mean it's not the right thing for you."

Peace trickled in. "That's true." Her shoulders inched lower. "Thank you for talking this out with me."

"And for forcing you into the pool."

"No." She wrung her ponytail out. "Not for forcing me into the pool."

Except…maybe a little. Only Hunter could break through her defenses like this. He'd been her best friend when they were younger, and he was dangerously close to owning the position again. Though she hadn't said it, leaving him might be harder than saying goodbye to her nephews. How could she think such a thing? She could get arrested and thrown in aunt jail for a confession like that.

Rachel was losing the battle to stay detached. Who was she kidding? That ship had sailed weeks ago.

But now was not the time to be falling for Hunter again. *Pull yourself together, Maddox.* Her pathetic little pep talk didn't make a dent in her current frame of mind.

The noise of the gate opening made Rachel's head

whip in that direction. A police officer walked into the backyard, his flashlight—and thankfully nothing else—drawn and pointed at them.

"You kids need to get out of there. Trespassing is breaking the law."

Kids? Trespassing? She faced Hunter. Her concern was echoed in the pinch of his brow.

"We're not trespassing," he replied. "I can explain."

The flashlight settled on Hunter's chin. "Do you own this house?"

"No, sir, but my—"

"Then you can explain once you're out of the pool."

Rachel scowled at Hunter, lowering her voice. "I thought you said you had permission to be here?"

"I do. We'll get it straightened out. Don't worry."

Don't worry? Unfortunately she'd ridden in the back of a police car once before, and she had no desire to repeat the experience because Hunter had had a crazy idea.

Once she reached the tiled edge of the pool, Rachel lifted herself out, then followed the police officer and Hunter to the front of the house. Her apprehension lessened at the realization that he didn't have his emergency lights on. And that he made no motion to retrieve the handcuffs hanging from his belt, their metal gleaming in the headlights of the cruiser.

But he did open the back door of the police car. "Get in while we figure this out."

Rachel balked. She'd rather bare her innermost secrets to a group of nosy busybodies than get in that vehicle. But what was she supposed to do? Argue with the officer?

Hunter's hand slipped around hers and squeezed. Warm. Reassuring. "We'll work this out, but we don't need to make him upset." His voice registered just above a whisper, as calm as if they were deciding on which brand of cereal to purchase. "Just get in. It's okay."

But it wasn't. After one long exhale, she ducked and slid into the seat, and Hunter quickly followed.

When the officer asked them why they'd been in the pool when the homeowner wasn't home, Hunter explained. He got out his phone and relayed Marc's number to the officer so he could clear things up. Then they waited.

The air-conditioning in the police car was blasting. Rachel's hair was dripping, her clothes were soaked, her feet bare. She shivered.

Without invitation, Hunter wrapped an arm around her and tucked her against him. When she resisted, he cocked his head back far enough to meet her gaze. "Really? I know you're freezing. I can feel you shaking."

"I'm not." Her chattering teeth gave her away. Fine. She would soak up a little of his warmth. Rachel eased against him, his heat seeping through their wet clothes. She would stay here, crushed against his rock-hard chest, but she wouldn't enjoy it. Not one bit.

"This is a big deal, you know." Once again, she'd just backtracked miles in changing how people thought of her.

Hunter's hand slid up and down her arm. She was not going to admit it felt comforting. Was. Not. "It's not like Marc's going to press charges. They're going to figure out that I know him and that we weren't trespassing."

She ground her jaw tight. "And in the meantime, here

we are, sitting in the back of a cop car. It's like the old Rachel's back."

Again Hunter shifted so he could see her face. "The old Rachel isn't back, but so what if she is? I liked that Rachel. I like this Rachel. You're one and the same."

"I'm not." She certainly hoped she wasn't.

"Why don't you want to be that girl?"

Wasn't it obvious? "She was a screwup." With pretty much everything—life, school, family. Picking the worst guys. "I've worked so hard not to be her anymore."

"You're nowhere near a screwup. I'm not sure why you're so hard on yourself. We didn't do anything wrong tonight. And as for when you were a teenager, so what if you did a few things you regret? There's grace for that. No one thinks anything bad about you."

"The whole town does."

"Rach," he held her gaze, a seriousness unusual for him pulling on his features. "I think that might be in your head. I don't notice anyone treating you that way."

Had she really changed enough to convince everyone? Or had she only imagined they thought the worst of her when it wasn't necessarily true?

"People love you exactly as you are. You were great when you were a teenager and you're just as amazing now. And you're going to be really good at this job." Hunter squared his shoulders. "You're meant for this." His deep breath was audible, his tone somehow conveying pain and sweetness at the same time. "I'm proud of you."

She believed him, but she didn't know why the words hurt. Her emotions felt as though they'd been sent through a blender tonight.

But Hunter was right. They'd get this cleared up. It would work out.

She just didn't have any confidence she could say the same for the state of her falling heart.

Chapter Thirteen

"Whatever you do, don't fall off the float. And don't have any fun."

Hunter's directions caused the teens to laugh and Rachel to do the usual regarding his teasing—shake her head and fight the curve of her lips. It was the morning of the Independence Day parade, and the kids were jittery with excitement. One of them falling off probably wasn't as much of a joke as Hunter made it out to be.

Rachel and Hunter had only spent about twenty minutes in the back of the cop car on Monday before things had worked out exactly like Hunter had said they would. Turned out a neighbor had heard Rachel screaming when Hunter sent her flying into the pool. They'd known Marc was out of town and had thought some kids had broken into the backyard for a swim. But after talking to Marc, the police officer had let them go without issue.

She'd almost forgiven Hunter for the ordeal—not that she planned to admit that to him yet.

Rachel finished applying thick black lines across

Bree's cheekbones. A few of the girls had decided to dress as football players. There were other sports represented, too—volleyball, cheerleading, soccer.

At least the float had become about more than just football, but barely.

"Thanks." Bree's gratitude was short and not necessarily sweet. Since she'd overheard Rachel on the phone, she'd shuttered again. Not as badly as the first time around—she was still cordial. Polite. None of the angst from when they'd first met. But she definitely hadn't texted to request another chat on Rachel's swing. When Rachel had asked her about whether she'd talked to her parents, Bree had answered with, "Yep." She hadn't expounded on how the conversation had gone or if she felt any peace. The girl had closed down like a Chick-fil-A on Sunday.

Rachel hated that she was hurting Bree, but she wasn't sure what to do about it. Not like she could stay here just for the teen. She wasn't even letting herself consider that option in regard to her family. Or Hunter.

That thought—it was off-limits. She'd already made her decision. No going back now.

With her stuff mostly packed and her departure scheduled for the day after tomorrow, a big boulder had settled in her stomach. It was trying to drag her down, to drown her in doubts over her decision and sorrow over leaving everyone.

The whole lot of them were messing with her dreams of this job in Houston.

But she wasn't going to concentrate on any of that today. Because the day of the parade was finally here. It started in exactly twelve minutes, and Rachel only wanted to think about how hard the kids had worked and how great the float looked. Today was about celebrating their teamwork and even this town that had won over her affections.

Once all of the kids were stationed on the float and had the bags of candy they'd be doling out, she and Hunter climbed into the cab of his truck in order to pull the trailer.

He checked his rear and side view mirrors. The man might joke around. A lot. But she had every confidence he'd keep the kids safe.

"You ready for this?" His face softened as he glanced at her. He made her stomach do backflips and forward flips and cliff dives. Those dimples. She'd probably devoted a page or twenty in her diary to them when she was younger and hadn't wanted to admit to anyone that she thought the neighbor boy was cute. And...it had only taken her one second to veer off course. *We're not going there, today. Remember?*

She managed to nod in answer to his question. About time, too, because he was shooting her a look of concern/confusion.

"They did a great job."

"They did." The same innocent look of contentment Grayson wore when he found a new bug or when Cash took him out on the ranch was evident on Hunter's face, making Rachel pull her resolve tight around her. Two more days and she'd be gone—on to the next step in her life—and she wouldn't have to work at resisting her feelings for Hunter anymore.

She could do it, couldn't she?

She had to. Because if anything more happened between them now, it would only make leaving worse. And she didn't want to do that to either of them.

* * *

They'd survived the parade route without losing any kids and without any injuries, but Hunter was dangerously close to losing his mind. He'd dropped Rachel and the kids off near the festivities so he could drive the float home and leave it in the barn before heading back to town, but the scent of her still lingered in the cab of his truck. Sweet. Torturous.

He was afraid if he failed to stay away from her and she still left, he might just shut down and stop functioning. That would really make Dad mad, having to handle everything on his own without Hunter's help. Perversely, that thought cheered him. Deep down, he did love his father. He just didn't always understand him.

After unhitching the float, Hunter drove back into the packed town. Part of Main Street was still blocked off, and vendors dotted the blacktop, their colorful food trucks and tarped stands boasting homemade goods, American flags and festive trinkets.

He cracked his window and live music drifted in along with a rush of hot air. There'd been a slew of small local bands playing music all day, and they'd continue after dinner so people could dance the night away.

After searching for a spot nearby, Hunter gave up and parked blocks away, hoofing it to the area with long picnic tables spread between booths of food. He scanned for a familiar face and spotted Rachel sitting with her brother, Olivia and the boys. He made his way in their direction. When he neared, she looked up, and her smile lit with her greeting. All of that sunshine, just for him. She was going to kill him with it. Did she have any idea he'd fallen for her all over again? Or that he'd never really stopped?

Hunter shook off the melancholy that attempted to choke him. No pouting. This wasn't a sulking kind of night.

"I got you a plate." She motioned to the seat next to her and a paper plate covered by a napkin. Under it, he found a barbeque sandwich, the local sauce dripping from the meat. Chips were overflowing alongside.

He greeted Cash and Olivia, said hello to the boys then dug in.

They attempted adult conversation—the ranch with Cash and the upcoming volleyball season with Olivia. But the boys were too excited to do anything close to sitting still. They were keyed up, likely spinning from the large amounts of candy that had been tossed to the crowd during the parade. Cash and Olivia did their best to corral them into eating, but Hunter doubted more than a few bites were shoveled in between questions from Grayson.

How late do I get to stay up?

When are the fireworks?

And Hunter's personal favorite—*When can we get dessert?*

Ryder toddled along the seat, and Grayson climbed up on the picnic bench, then got down numerous times until Cash finally gave an exasperated sigh and stood. He swung Ryder onto his shoulders and reached for Grayson's hand. "Let's go pick out a piece of pie."

At Grayson's cheer and Ryder's clapping approval, Olivia stood and joined them. "We'll be back."

Rachel waved as they walked away, then faced Hunter. Tears glistened in her eyes.

"You okay?"

Her head bobbed but then changed directions. "No." She blinked back the moisture. "How am I going to leave them?"

It was painful not to plead his case. They all had reasons for wanting her to stay. Hunter was confident Cash and Olivia wanted her to live here just as much as he did. But they all quietly knew the same thing— the choice had to be hers. No one was going to impose an opinion on her. "You're going to be amazing. And you'll be back to visit."

Her eyelids closed and she nodded again. "You're right."

"Kind of prideful, if you ask me." At his teasing, her eyes popped open and she laughed. The sound made him happy and sad all at the same time.

"I meant the part about coming back to visit."

"I know." Hunter had cleared his plateful of barbeque in record time and now, much like Grayson, he couldn't wait for dessert. He pushed up from the bench, motioning for her to join him. "Let's go get something sweet." Hunter would gladly forgo sugar of the baking variety and choose Rachel instead, but unfortunately, that option wasn't on the menu.

She stood, her flowered sundress flirting above her knees as they gathered their trash.

By the time they'd stood in line and then finished their pieces of fresh strawberry pie, the band had switched and a new one had started. Kids were spread across a corner of the dance floor, shaking out their excess energy with crazy dance moves while the adults two-stepped. Cash and Liv were dancing, Ryder held between them while Grayson looked like he'd been two-stepping since he was born. He'd even asked a little girl to dance. A bit choppy, but still, impressive.

Rachel tracked him, her face glowing with pride and amusement. "I'm afraid he's starting young."

"Some of us do."

They stood next to each other, watching everyone spin past them for two more songs while a war raged within him. Should he ask her to dance? Did that qualify in the friend category? Or would she sense everything he wasn't telling her? And would Rachel even say yes?

He felt like a teenager again—minus the awkward voice cracking, thank the good Lord above.

When the smooth notes of George Strait's "The Chair" began, Hunter decided to man up and stop being a wuss.

"Seems like a waste to listen to all of this music and not dance to at least one song."

"It does seem like a waste." Rachel peered around him, straining to see who knew what. "I wonder who might be willing to dance with you, McDermott. I saw Patty Holster over by the popcorn stand." Patty was sweet all right. And she'd had white hair for as long as he'd been alive. Kind of like he assumed Rachel had been sassy since birth. "I think she'd love to—"

He interrupted her by pulling her onto the floor, and her words were swallowed up by laughter. Asking was overrated. In typical Rachel style, she completely baffled him by easing into his arms without complaint—almost as though she'd been waiting for that very thing. The woman was all things confusing, and he couldn't get enough of her. He wasn't sure what that said about him.

After a few times around, she let go of a sigh that

could only mean contentment. Her shoulders relaxed and her eyes closed as though savoring a bite of her favorite dessert.

She was going to be the death of him. And he no longer cared to fight it.

It was time for fireworks, and everyone was camped out on their blankets or chairs, looking for the best spot to catch every pop of color.

Rachel had helped Gray find a bathroom, and now she watched him scoot through the pockets of people until he reached his mom, dad and Ryder. He plopped into Olivia's lap, making everyone laugh. Liv said something in Cash's ear, and he kissed the top of her head. Sappy as always. Once the two of them had figured out they were perfect for each other, they'd been the kind of steady a person could use for a building foundation.

It wasn't the first time Rachel wished her parents could have met Liv. They would have loved her as much as Cash did. As much as Rachel did. The ache of missing her parents spread through her. She wanted her mom. Wanted to talk to her about Hunter. About the job. About everything.

Rachel could go for some wisdom right now.

Instead of going to sit with Cash, Liv and the boys, she leaned back against the building behind her. She'd let them enjoy this time as a family. They looked so peaceful, so right together. Would she ever have that? Or was she leaving that behind when she went to Houston on Monday?

Hunter appeared, settling beside her in comfortable silence. If Rachel let herself daydream, she could imagine herself married to the man next to her. They'd go home together after the fireworks. She'd live in this town she'd thought she hated, and she'd be content. Happy.

But would she? Despite her growing feelings for Hunter, she still wanted the job in Houston. She'd worked so hard for it. She couldn't just let it go now.

The fireworks started, the booming noise causing more than a few kiddos to cover their ears. Bits of red and white shot through the sky, dripping like spilled paint until it looked as though the sparks would stay lit all the way to the ground.

Rachel kept her gaze forward as long as she could. When she couldn't resist any longer, she glanced at Hunter. He wasn't looking at the fireworks. He was watching her.

The uneven thumping in her chest increased as she glued her eyes back on the sparkling sky.

Trouble. She'd called him the word more times than she could count. But now she was beginning to think she'd underestimated the kind of havoc he would wreak on her heart when she left.

After a few more minutes, the *pop-pop-pop* of the finale rang out as blue, green, white and red flashes of color all fought for space against the charcoal sky. A hint of smoke hung in the air after the last blast, and the crowd cheered before quickly starting to disperse.

She and Hunter were as close as they could be without physically touching. He had picked her up this morning for the parade, but it would make sense for her to catch a ride home with Cash and Liv. They'd drive right by her place.

Rachel could avoid the sensation flowing between

herself and Hunter. She could skip out on the turmoil this time around.

He nudged her shoulder with his. "Am I dropping you off?"

Yes. Her desires momentarily outweighed her maturity.

"I'll ride with Cash and Liv. There's no reason for you to drive past your ranch."

His lips pressed together. Finally, he agreed. "Probably a good idea. Let's find them, then."

They tried to ease into the crowd, but a stroller cut Rachel off, and she waited for it to pass. Hunter had paused to wait for her, and when she caught up, he snagged her hand and started walking again. He had a habit of doing that—always without permission—and she told herself it didn't mean anything. Usually he just wanted to direct her somewhere she didn't want to go, and it was his way of getting her there.

Tonight, he was simply making sure they stuck together in the crowd. But it didn't feel simple. And all of the other times he'd touched her or clasped her hand hadn't, either. His skin was warm and calloused—who knew she'd ever consider that an attractive quality?—and right at home against hers.

Somehow she needed to silence the teenager inside of her who clamored for one more kiss. The one who wanted to pretend she wasn't moving.

Who didn't care how much she got hurt.

If ever there was a night for Rachel to be mature, to cling to her last thread of dignity, this was it.

They caught up to Cash and Liv. Her brother had one hand linked with Grayson's, the other full of blankets and supplies. Liv held Ryder, who looked sleepy despite the recent noise level.

Cash greeted them. "You riding with us, Rach?"

"Yep." She turned to Hunter. "Thanks. I'll see you… tomorrow? At church?"

His head hitched in response, and then he was gone, disappearing with long strides into the crowd. Rachel took the blanket and diaper backpack from her brother. He scooped Gray onto his shoulders, and the four of them made their way to the car.

The whole walk, the whole ride home, Rachel told herself she'd made the right choice. Saying no to Hunter's offer to drive her was the smart thing to do. What would be the point of starting something now? It would never work between them. She was moving to a job she wanted in a town that offered so much more than this one, and she still had something to prove—if not to the people here, then to herself. And Hunter would always live here. His whole life revolved around ranching.

Even if the organ in her chest was barely beating from all of the abuse, she'd made the right choice.

It took Hunter forever and a day to get to his truck, and by then, the traffic was at a standstill. Now he was almost home. Finally.

He'd managed, somehow, to keep from kissing Rachel today. From telling her how he felt about her. But he was hanging by a thread. Hunter had no idea how he would survive tomorrow night at the going-away dinner Cash and Olivia were hosting. Or saying goodbye to Rachel on Monday morning.

No clue.

Loving her was a fire he couldn't extinguish. And he didn't want to—even if she was going to leave him.

It was a good thing Rachel had gone home with her brother. Hunter didn't have any resolve left when it came to her. Overnight, he'd shore up again.

Somehow.

He pulled up to his house, concern slithering through him at the sight of Rachel's Jeep. Was something wrong? He turned off the truck and got out, slamming the door. The sound reverberated in the otherwise quiet night.

Rachel had been sitting on his front steps, and now she stood. Her feet were bare, the strappy heeled sandals she'd worn earlier retired for the evening or, knowing her, left on the floor of the Jeep. She still had on the sundress that had messed with his mind all day. She looked gorgeous in it. But then, she looked amazing in anything.

With every step she took toward him, he fought two emotions—need and fear.

Once she reached him, she paused, mere inches separating him from everything he wanted and couldn't have.

The shyest look crossed her face. As if she'd come all this way and now couldn't say what she needed to.

"You okay?"

She nodded. "I just…" She shrugged in a helpless gesture, lips pressed together as if stemming her next words.

Before he could think, his hands were on her shoulders. Their gazes melded, tenderness passing between them. "Rach, tell me you don't want me to kiss you."

"I don't want you to kiss me." Not one part of him trusted her response.

For the first time all day, he let his guard down. "I don't believe you."

Her mouth barely had time to reach for a smile before his lips met hers. The pain of knowing he was losing her again wrapped into their kiss, and time and space stood still.

Her lips were sweet and soft, and he was afraid he'd never let her go.

Easing back, he rested his forehead against hers. "This is a stupid idea."

Her face broke into the kind of smile that held a secret. That could light up the night sky with electricity. "I know. It's idiotic. I'm sorry I came over."

"I'm not."

At his answer, he saw something in her shift. Soften. She propped her bare feet on the top of his boots, wrapped her arms around his neck and held on. He squeezed her close, nose buried in her fragrant hair.

When their lips met again, there was no hesitation in her kiss. She was all his, even if it was only for a moment.

He'd never loved her more.

Chapter Fourteen

"Give me that." Val snatched the veggie tray from Rachel's hand. "This is your going-away party. You're not supposed to be helping."

It wasn't exactly a party. More of a dinner. Olivia and Cash were hosting, and Lucy and Graham were in attendance along with their girls, Val and Brennon and Connor, plus Hunter. It was a madhouse, but it was the best possible kind. Rachel had spent most of the evening trying not to cry. She'd gotten everything she'd worked for, so why was this so hard? It was nothing like the last time she'd left. Colorado had been so far. Now she'd be much closer—a four-hour drive away. She could come back for a weekend easily.

But that wasn't making her feel better.

She was moving tomorrow, and last night she'd been kissing Hunter like she never planned to leave.

"What's going on?" Val set the tray on the table, studying Rachel much like she'd done with her chemistry homework in high school while the two of them were supposed to be working and Rachel had done anything but. They'd been friends long enough that Rachel knew better than to try to hide from her.

"I'm moving."

"Uh-huh. We've known that for a while. Tell me what's changed."

"Hunter."

People filled the first floor of the house, but between the loud conversations and wild kids, Rachel felt confident no one would overhear their hushed conversation in the corner near the dining room table.

"Oh." Her friend's face held a hint of amused *I knew it* with a side of concern. "He pulled you in, did he?"

Moisture pooled in Rachel's eyes. "It hurts that I'm moving away. I'm going to miss all of you."

"But especially him." Val's tone held no malice. "Do you…have you thought about the job? Do you still—"

"Want it?" Rachel's voice escalated with panic, and she dialed her volume back to a two. "Yes, I do." She was a mess. She'd never been so torn about anything in all of her life. Except maybe the last time she'd left. This ranked right up close to that experience. "What is wrong with me that I still do?"

"Nothing." Val's loose brown curls shook, her tone brooking no argument. "There's nothing wrong with you or your aspirations. I'm guessing you want to stay with him, too."

Fingers seeking the familiar comfort of her gold R necklace, Rachel slid the pendant back and forth on the chain. "It scares me, but I think so." Her mind spun at the truth she'd been avoiding. "But what can I do about that? How's that going to work? Part of me wonders if I'll ever forgive myself for giving Hunter up again. I've never felt about anyone the way I do about him. I told him we shouldn't get involved. I tried to stay away. To keep my distance." She paused and waited for Grayson and Lola to swing around the table and grab handfuls of pretzels before quietly continuing. "But it didn't work. Now what do I do?"

Compassion radiated from Val. "Oh, honey. I think you need to talk to him."

"But I don't want to," Rachel wailed with a childish flair, making them laugh, though hers was mournful. "I'm not sure what he's thinking, and I'm afraid to find out." Did he care about her as more than a friend? Was what they had real? Or just a mistake?

"The two of you didn't discuss any of this after your smoochy-smoochy last night?" Val made a tsking sound. "Kids these days."

"You and I are the same age!" Despite her misery, Rachel laughed. "And to answer your question, no we didn't. I just…left. I wasn't sure what to say. If it was just a goodbye, I'll always care about you kind of moment or something more. I needed time to process. But I'm realizing that I'm not okay with losing him again."

"Talk. To. Him." Huh. Val's counsel sounded strangely similar to what Rachel had advised Bree to do. But it was a whole lot easier to dole out than to follow.

"And say what?"

Baby Senna gave a disgruntled cry, and the voices in the room quieted for a second. Val waited, then continued once the hum of other conversations resumed. "Only you know the answer to that."

"I want it all." The selfish truth rolled from her tongue. "The job and him."

"Then tell him that."

"I can't. How will that help anything? How would that scenario ever work?"

"You'll be four hours away. Not impossible that you could date long-distance."

Rachel had thought about that option during her restless night. But to what end? Hunter belonged here—and although this life had grown on her over the summer and she was going to miss it, she still wasn't sure it was a fit for her. If she didn't go to Houston, she'd always wonder. She'd never know for sure.

Either way, Val was right. Rachel had to hash this out with him.

She grabbed a brownie from the table and took a bite, letting the sweet cocoa do its best to ease her tension. What would she do without Val in her life? They'd been friends a long time. Val knew all of her worst parts and loved her, anyway. She was the sweet to Rachel's sass. The two of them had always made a good team.

"I'm not sure you deserve the credit for that solution. Technically, I came up with what I need to say. You just listened while I processed."

"Whatever." Val tossed a baby carrot at Rachel. It bounced off the top portion of her black maxi dress and landed on the floor, making them giggle like they had so often back in their younger days. "Even counselors need a listening ear *and* some advice once in a while." Her friend's smile turned down at the edges, sadness seeping in. "And in case you're wondering, I'm going to miss you, too."

"Did you get two pieces of cake?"

Grayson stood before Hunter, hands on his hips.

He looked far more foreboding than any four-year-old should.

Hunter wasn't sure whether to tell him the truth or fudge, so he went for evasive. "Did you?"

"No. Mama said I couldn't have more than one. She said the sugars make me hyper." His nose wrinkled. "I don't know what that means but I don't like it."

"That's rough."

"I wanted Auntie Rachel to get a bug cake, so she picked a ladybug one for me. Still girly, but at least she tried."

"That was nice of her."

"Yup. Auntie Rach is the best."

Hunter agreed.

"Hey, are you two talking about me?" Rachel came from behind Hunter, joining the two of them.

He winked at Grayson. "We were discussing guy stuff."

The boy's mouth curved. "You wouldn't understand, Auntie Rachel."

She scoffed, then grabbed him up in a hug while he squealed and squirmed. "Hey, your mom says it's time for bed. Story time? It's our last night."

Rachel looked as though she was fighting back emotion. Grayson nodded, not seeming to notice his aunt's upset, and the two of them took off upstairs.

Cash was putting Ryder down, and Olivia had walked the other guests outside a few minutes ago. The front window framed the group still talking by their vehicles. Hunter had picked up Rachel on his way over, so he made himself useful and started clearing the table while he waited for her.

He'd just deposited a platter of veggies in the fridge when Olivia came back in.

"Hunter, you really don't need to do that."

"I don't mind." She took him at his word, which he appreciated, and the two of them worked quickly. By the time he heard Rachel's footsteps on the stairs, they'd made a huge dent in the cleanup.

"Gray's down. I'm not sure if he'll sleep, though. He's all ramped up from running around with the kids. Cash is going to try reading him one more book to see if it helps."

"Thank you." Olivia waved a hand. "He'll settle down eventually."

"What can I do?" Rachel came into the kitchen where they were working.

"Nothing. It's almost done thanks to Hunter."

"I don't deserve all of the credit." In fact, he'd rather have none of it.

Olivia smiled in answer and turned to Rachel. "I'm sure you have more to pack. Why don't you two head out?"

"I can help." Her voice wobbled, and in response, Olivia's eyes filled with tears.

Oh, boy. Hunter glanced around for an escape but didn't see any rocks he could crawl under. He needed to drive Rachel home, so he couldn't bolt before the waterworks started.

Olivia swiped under her lashes. "We are not doing this tonight. Hunter, get her out of here, already. She's going to turn me into a bumbling mess."

When he didn't move fast enough, Olivia raised an eyebrow at him as if questioning his snail-like pace.

Hunter wasn't one to make a woman upset if at all possible, so he obeyed.

"Yes, ma'am." He approached Rachel like he might a skittish barn cat. "Come on, let's get you home."

In response, she crossed her arms. "No. I'm going to help clean up."

Both women looked like their decision had been chiseled in stone, which left Hunter stuck in the middle. One had fed him, the other he loved. He went with the one who'd fed him, partly because it seemed like the right thing to do. Partly because he liked getting a rise out of Rachel.

Relying on his old standby, he bent and scooped Rachel up at the knees, swinging her over his shoulder. She whacked him on the back, complaining loudly. Something about a caveman. About how he couldn't just manhandle her all of the time. But of course he already was, so she'd pretty much lost that argument.

Olivia had a goofy smile on her face, and Hunter wasn't sure what that meant, so he thanked her for dinner and then swung Rachel around so that she faced her sister-in-law. Upside down and backward, but it worked.

Rachel thanked Olivia for hosting and then complained that she wasn't helping her escape from Hunter. After her upset earned a laugh from Olivia instead of assistance, Hunter headed for his truck.

He managed to make it through the door without bonking Rachel's head on the frame, and when he got to his truck, he set her down by the passenger side. Her hair was mussed from being upside-down, but it fell in beautiful disarray. Her back was to the vehicle, and his hands landed on either side of her. She still had tears glistening in her gorgeous green eyes.

Killing. Him.

"Rach, it's going to be okay." His hands slid to her face, cradling. "It's going to be okay."

He wasn't sure if he was repeating it for himself or for her. Maybe both.

"How do you know?"

"I just do." And he did. Hunter had been praying nonstop in the last week, and despite all of the turmoil he was about to face with Rachel moving, he felt peace. It was palpable, the knowledge that he had *no idea* what was going to happen next, but that God had a plan greater than he could imagine. Hunter was clinging to that belief.

He leaned forward and pressed his lips to hers. It was an assurance, meant to comfort. At least, that's how it started out. But then Rachel's fingers slid into his hair, pulling him under her current. How could she kiss him like this and not want to stay? He gave up on trying to stay afloat and let himself drown in her touch. If only he could spend the rest of his life doing exactly this. He didn't ask for much, did he?

After a few seconds, Hunter wrenched himself away. Caught his breath. "Rachel Marie Maddox, are you trying to get me seriously injured?"

Her eyes flew wide with innocence. "Why?"

"Your brother is going to come out here with a shot gun in a matter of seconds."

That, of all things, made her smile.

He ripped open her door and ushered her inside. The drive to her house was silent and fraught with tension.

Once they arrived at her place, he put the truck in Park. She reached over, turned the ignition off. "Come on."

He felt like a spider who could see the sticky trap coming, but refused to change courses. Stupid spider.

Still, he didn't resist. Hunter followed her out of the vehicle and up the steps. Moose stretched and stood, nuzzling both of them until he received the rubdown he was looking for. After he was satisfied, he curled back up on the soft rug Rachel had put out for him.

Rachel faced Hunter, her sadness painfully evident.

What was going on? Was it something besides the obvious?

"Rach, talk to me. What is wrong?"

Her hands jutted out, shoving against his chest but not moving him. "I don't want to leave you."

The words held in the air, a lightning strike of electricity. Hunter had to work to breathe in. Out. To not beg her to stay. He'd once promised her he wouldn't ask her to stay again, and he *would* honor that.

"I'm going to miss you." She sniffled.

"I'll miss you, too." There. That was safe. Truthful.

"I don't even know what I'm doing anymore. What I'm thinking. I feel so confused."

Warnings sirens flared to life in his mind.

She couldn't be considering not going, could she? How would that ever work? If it was because of him, she'd always wonder. He wouldn't be enough to hold her here, and then she'd leave, just like his mother.

She had to go. No matter how much he wished the outcome could be different. He knew how important this job was to her. What had she said to him that night?

A ten.

Any feelings she had for him at this point weren't enough. If she wanted to stay beyond a shadow of a doubt—if she picked this life—that would be different.

But she wasn't making that choice. Obviously. Because she was telling him she was going to miss him when she moved. Which meant she was still going.

Tears cascaded down her cheeks, each one inflicting a new stab wound. Hunter could handle just about anything, but Rachel crying might do him in. He'd much rather be the one hurting.

He allowed himself to slide thumbs across her adorable freckles and wipe away the moisture.

"What are we going to do? I don't know how to leave you. Do we try long-distance?"

He hadn't even thought of that. She'd only be four hours away. He could finally tell her how he felt about her. And they might be able to hang on for a little while. Schedule times to see each other. Make the trek back and forth. But eventually the truth would surface: it was never going to work. She wanted that world and he had a life here. Dating long-distance would only prolong the pain for both of them.

"We can't."

Hurt etched across her sweet face. "What do you mean, we can't?"

"We just can't." He couldn't be the person holding her back. How could she not understand that?

She was crumbling right before his eyes. And he was wounding them both. But better now than later. If they dated, he'd always be pulling her back here. They needed a clean break. A chance for Rachel to embrace the life she'd dreamed about without him in the way.

"You don't belong here."

The light in her eyes flickered. He wanted with everything in him to bring it back, but what he'd said was true. She deserved a better life than this. She should live in the city with all the conveniences she wanted. This town wasn't right for her.

He thought of his mom. Of all the days she'd been unable to get out of bed. The dark circles that had resided under her eyes. The number of times she'd turned the other way to hide her tears from him but he'd seen them, anyway. He held on to those memories for all he was worth, the reminder exactly what he needed.

"What did you just say?" Her voice was soft, sorrow seeping into every crevice.

"You don't belong here. You should go."

Hunter knew his words had wounded her by the fresh tears rolling down her cheeks and the way her face crinkled with pain. She'd softened so much since she'd come back. And now he was ruining all of it. He'd never have another chance with her. This was it. The end of so many years of wanting her, even when he hadn't realized his feelings were still there, lying dormant, waiting for a spark of hope to ignite them again.

She shifted closer to him, and he braced himself for a slap. Her hand did land on his cheek, but it was gentle. "I don't believe you."

They were the same words he'd said before kissing her. His eyes shuttered, overcome by her touch, by the last time he'd ever feel it. *Just go. Please, please don't make me do this.* He wasn't sure he had the strength to continue.

"You should believe me. We're not right for each other. I always knew you were moving." The words made what they'd had sound cheap, though it had been anything but. His voice was wooden, yet emotion still sprang behind his eyes. He needed to get out of here before she found out the truth.

He stepped back from her, from that questioning, injured look she now wore, and then, after allowing himself one more long drink of memorizing everything about her, he turned. He flew down the steps and across the drive to his truck as fast as he could, afraid that if he looked back, he'd be holding her in his arms, apologizing, before he could count to one.

He kept walking, even when he heard her sob, even when his heart tore in two.

He wasn't sure he'd ever be put back together again. And that was fine by him. Hunter would rather live with the pain of a thousand lifetimes than have her experience one moment of getting stuck in a life she didn't want.

Chapter Fifteen

The little ranch house looked sad and lonely in Rachel's rearview mirror as she headed down her drive for the last time on Monday morning. No lights left on. No Moose lazing on the porch. Rachel had already made a trip over to Cash and Liv's this morning to drop off the dog. Cash planned to deliver him to the shelter for her later today because she was too tormented to do it herself.

She'd only slept a few minutes last night in between horrid dreams. Most had revolved around her parents and that final fight with her mom. Some had trekked into Hunter land. She'd been crying out to him, but he'd had a hollow look in his eyes. He'd turned and walked away while her sobs had echoed to nothing.

A repeat of last night. Of course she hadn't thrown herself on the ground and engaged in an all-out toddler tantrum in front of Hunter. Rachel could turn off her emotions when needed. It was a skill that had served her well over the years. One she would use today as she said goodbye to Cash, Liv and the boys.

She'd heard nothing from Hunter this morning. He

had planned to come over to see her off with her family. But now she no longer expected to see him.

Rachel couldn't quit turning the conversation with him round and round in her mind. It had been so strange. She'd been confident Hunter felt something for her, like she did for him. But then he'd just pushed her away without giving them a chance to figure things out. And that hurt. So much.

Last night she'd let herself cry. Today, she needed to be numb to get through this last goodbye.

She pulled up to Cash and Liv's. They must have been listening for the sound of her Jeep, because they came out of the house and down the steps just as she turned off the ignition and got out.

Olivia peppered her with motherly questions, making sure Rachel hadn't forgotten any of the necessities she'd need to get by for the next few weeks while she slept on Dana's couch and hunted for an apartment.

Once she found one, Cash would help her move the rest of her stuff down.

Olivia stepped forward and wrapped her in a long hug. "Rach." She pulled away, face wrinkled with concern. "I don't know what's going on or what happened, hon, but I think maybe—"

"I should really get going." Rachel cut her off. It was something the teenage Rachel would have done, and she wasn't proud of it. But, then again, she wasn't as far from that immature girl as she'd like to think. Hadn't she just made another stupid decision in letting herself get attached to Hunter when she'd always planned to move?

Rachel bent to receive a tackle hug from Grayson, keeping her eyes closed so the tears wouldn't escape.

"Who's going to go riding with me, Auntie Rachel?"

She memorized his baby cheeks and soft lashes. How much more grown up would he look the next time she saw him? "Your dad will go with you. And your mom when she can. And I'll come visit." Except…she wasn't exactly in a rush to do that. Rachel was right back to where she'd started. She didn't want to be in this town.

She stood and accepted Ryder from Cash. He gave her a squirmy hug, then laid a palm on her cheek. She almost broke down right then and there. After kissing his pudgy hand, she shoved him into Liv's open arms, afraid she was never going to give him up if she held on a second longer.

Cash stayed facing her as Olivia and the boys walked back to the house. He had that analyzing look on his face—the one that said he didn't believe her. She remembered it well. He'd used it a lot when she was in high school.

"I know you're upset about something. This was supposed to be a good thing, you getting the job. This was what you wanted, right? What's going on with you?"

She concentrated on the house over his shoulder, the snap of the screen door as the boys and Liv went inside. "I'm fine."

"When Liv says something is fine it's never true."

That almost pulled a laugh out of her.

"Is it something with Hunter? I kind of thought the two of you…"

The beginning of a smile crashed from her face, and the flimsy dam she'd built around her emotions shattered. "What? That we'd get married and live on the ranch next to yours? That we'd be one big, happy family? It's not going to happen, Cash. Everyone knew I was leaving. We shouldn't have gotten so involved."

"We?"

Stink. She'd been thinking about Hunter.

"I need to go." Rachel hugged her brother. Her motions were stunted, and she pulled away quickly, needing to escape. Praying he would understand, she made a break for it, hopping into her Jeep. One wave later she was headed down the road. Just her and a whole lake of tears for company. Well, that was just fine. She was better off on her own, anyway. She could take care of herself. Getting involved with people always hurt.

She had once confronted Cash about that very thing with Olivia. He'd needed a little push to take the leap. And she knew he'd never looked back. Never regretted one single day. Rachel had learned that lesson watching him, and she'd been willing to shove past that fear. She'd wanted more with Hunter. She still didn't know what they would have done had he admitted feelings for her, but they would have worked it out.

But now? Now she didn't have to worry about anyone but herself once again. The thought should have brought relief, but it didn't. What had Hunter said last night? She didn't belong here. The words sent a shiver down her spine. She knew that. She didn't belong anywhere. But her stubborn heart hadn't listened to her numerous warnings. She'd begun to hope again. Silly Rachel. Didn't she know better by now?

Rachel would be fine on her own. She didn't need home or family. She had friends—or at least acquaintances. A new career.

She would be fine.

And maybe if she kept telling herself that, one of these days she'd even believe it.

Rachel had been gone six days—seven if he counted today. Hunter wasn't sure he'd managed a coherent conversation since. He'd forced himself to go to church this morning, hoping it would snap him out of the funk he'd fallen into. God hadn't left him yet, but He might be the only one sticking with Hunter.

He kept telling himself he'd done the right thing. Letting Rachel go had been the best thing for her. This way she could follow her dreams without interruption from him.

But he missed her so much it was all he could do to get up every day and keep functioning. All week he'd poured himself into work, hoping it might lessen the sting. He'd tried not to think about her, but that hadn't worked. Autumn had attempted to talk to him, to figure out what was going on, but he'd clammed up like Fort Knox. Or like Rachel.

The sermon had been on trust this morning. Hunter had thought he had a handle on that. But he couldn't shake the niggling thought that somewhere along the way, he'd missed that part of his faith. He believed... but did he really trust? If he had, wouldn't he have told Rachel the truth instead of pushing her away? They could have prayed over their relationship. Figured out what God had planned. His thoughts jumbled. Had he done the wrong thing? Hunter didn't know anymore, but it didn't matter. She would never forgive him for what he'd said, for the way he'd responded to her. And she'd probably never believe him if he did confess how he felt about her. He'd worked hard to gain her trust again, and then he'd thrown it all away.

He spotted Val in front of him in the church narthex, and before he could stop himself, he was touching her arm. Gaining her attention.

"McDermott." Her face held nothing but contempt for him, and he didn't blame her.

"How is she?" Val could be mad at him, but it would be worth it if he could get a little info about Rachel. "Is she okay?"

"No, she's not okay." Her voice snapped like the little white firecrackers kids threw to the ground on the Fourth of July. Strange coming from the usually even-keeled woman in front of him. "Why do you want to know, anyway?" Her eyes narrowed. "Why *do* you want to know? If you're so interested in her well-being, why'd you push her away?"

"She needed…" What could he say without giving everything away? "This was her dream." He cut himself off before he said too much. It might not be enough of an explanation for her, but it was all he had.

Brennon stopped next to his wife, his concerned look jutting between the two of them.

"Everything okay?"

"Yep." Their answers were simultaneous.

"I'm going to run and get Connor from the nursery." Val backed away as if she'd rather be next to a person with an infectious disease right now than him.

She headed for the steps, and Brennon watched her go before turning back to Hunter.

"How's the hole you dug?"

Hunter let out a noise that was half laugh, half disgusted sigh. "Excellent, thanks for asking."

"Listen, I think I have a way you can fix this. I just heard from one of the school board members that the high school is adding another guidance counselor this year. The money just came through, and they only have a few weeks to fill it. This is perfect for Rachel. Call her. Go see her. Convince her to come back. Not to sound selfish about the whole thing, but I'd really like my sweet, happy wife back."

Despite wanting his friend to have exactly that, Hunter wasn't about to do what Brennon said. That would defeat the whole purpose of letting Rachel go in the first place.

"At least tell me you'll think about it. You're a mess. Rachel's a mess. I don't understand what's going on in your head."

And he couldn't. Hunter didn't need Brennon knowing and then telling Val, who would then tell Rachel. Nope. Things had to stay as they were, no matter how much Hunter wanted a different ending. He'd come this far. He wasn't going to change his mind now.

"I'll think about it." Hunter could add that to his list of untruths.

Brennon took off to catch up with Val and Connor, and Hunter headed for the church doors. This time, it was his phone that made him pause.

It was a text from Autumn.

Remember we're celebrating Dad's birthday today with lunch at his house. I've got all of the food. (You're welcome.) So just come. And don't even think about skipping. I just saw you at church so I know where you are and how long it should take you to get there.

Perfect. Hanging with his family ranked nowhere on his want list for the day. Hunter had penciled in moping and kicking things. So much for that.

Could he use checking on Moose as an excuse to skip out on lunch? After Rachel had left, Hunter had headed over to the shelter and adopted him, hoping the pooch would give him something to focus on and lessen the sting of missing Rachel. No offense to Moose, because Hunter did have a soft spot for the big oaf, but the dog wasn't a worthy replacement for his girl.

And since Hunter had left Moose outside with water and food under a big shade tree, that excuse wouldn't fly.

He texted Autumn back.

Fine. I'll be there.

You'd better be.

I already said I'll be there!

Hunter shoved the phone back in his pocket. He was irritable enough to not want to celebrate anything—especially his equally grumpy father—but Autumn would never let him get away with that. He wasn't even sure why she wanted him there today. He wasn't exactly pleasant company.

Fear wound around his throat, choking him. After all he'd done in order not to turn into his father, he was sure acting and sounding a lot like him.

Maybe he already was him.

Scary thought.

Hunter went to lunch. He even ate lasagna, but he

wasn't happy about it. Except for when Kinsley climbed into his lap and tried to push his mouth out of a frown by manipulating his cheeks. He had a soft spot the size of the Grand Canyon for his niece.

At least Autumn waited until Kinsley ran off to play before launching her inquisition.

"What in the world is going on with you?"

The million-dollar question. He'd learned at least one thing about himself in the process of losing Rachel a second time—he was no good at hiding his emotions. After the first breakup, Autumn had known immediately something was wrong. And now? Felt like the whole town knew.

Except for his dad, who barely looked up from his slice of lemon meringue pie.

Autumn's husband, Calvin, was a quiet guy. Steady. Good to Hunter's sister. Not one for conflict, based on the way his eyes widened and scanned the room for an escape.

Hunter empathized.

"I don't understand why you just let Rachel go." Autumn's voice heated, scorching like cement under bare feet on a sizzling summer day. "I heard there's an opening at the high school for a guidance counselor. Are you going to let her know?" How did everyone know about this position but him? And why were they all pushing? Next thing he knew, even his dad would be weighing in.

Calvin stood. "I'll just…clear some dishes."

Hunter considered running for it along with his brother-in-law, but decided to tough it out. He'd have to face Autumn sooner or later. Might as well get it over with.

"I told you in the beginning we were only friends.

That was the plan. Right along with her moving." He was pleasantly surprised by how calm he sounded. Usually composure came easily to him, but it felt like his laid-back nature had hitchhiked a ride out of town with Rachel. He was afraid it might never come back—another thing that eerily reminded him of his father.

"So, no, I'm not going to let Rachel know about the job. She's a big girl. She can make her own decisions."

"Were you two dating?" Dad's gruff interest mystified Hunter, and it must have done the same to Autumn, because both of their gazes swung to him. "What?" He scowled. "Can't I have an interest in my son's life?"

Hunter clenched his jaw to keep from saying any one of the not-so-kind comments filtering through his mind. Since when did Dad care about what went on in their lives? Had Hunter entered some parallel universe? Or maybe he was still dreaming and hadn't woken up for church yet.

"No." His answer to his father's first question came out far more sad than angry. "We weren't."

Autumn attempted to say more, but Hunter switched the conversation to the ranch—despite his sister's glare—and Dad took it from there.

After a bit, Autumn and Calvin rounded up Kinsley to take her home for a nap. Hunter offered to finish cleaning up and sent them off. He made a trip into the kitchen and returned to find his dad still sitting at the table, studying him as though he could predict the next year's weather. A bit unnerving since the man rarely noticed anything about anyone but himself.

"Autumn is right. You should tell Rachel about the job, you know. She might be interested."

Hunter braced his hands on the table. Hung his head.

The pressure of Rachel leaving and everyone having an opinion about it felt like a precariously slippery ditch he couldn't seem to climb out of. Every time he tried, someone shoved him back down.

His dad didn't have a clue what he was talking about. And he needed to leave it alone. "Who are you to have an opinion about my life? You checked out back when mom left, maybe even before that, and you haven't been present since." The words were a landslide he couldn't get back. But part of him didn't want to. It might have come out without thought, but it was true.

Surprisingly, his dad didn't immediately have a retort. He simply released an audible breath, rubbing a hand across his forehead. "I know."

Hunter couldn't believe what he'd just heard. His dad never admitted fault. In business. In his personal life. Never.

"I wasn't there for you. I thought building a business, a ranch for you to take over one day would show you I loved you. I avoided the pain of your mom's troubles by concentrating on work." His dad's eyes filled with moisture—a sight Hunter had only witnessed once in his life. All of these years he'd wondered and hadn't asked. Well, now he was mad enough to let the words flow.

"Why did you do it? Why did you convince Mom to marry you when you knew she didn't want to live on a ranch? When she was going to be so sad? Why'd you beg her to stay? And then turn bitter when she didn't?"

His dad's brow pinched. "What do you mean?"

"You always told me Mom didn't want to ranch, but that you convinced her she'd eventually love it. If you hadn't pushed her—"

"We used to tell you that story because it was true.

Mom was a city girl. I did convince her to live here with me, to marry me, and she *was* happy."

"What? Mom was never happy here."

His father's features etched with anguish. "She was. When we were first married, she tried gardening. Canning. She got involved at church and began to feel connected. She did love it here, at first. But then…" Dad's fingertips dug into his closed eyelids. "But then she had Autumn. After, she struggled through some depression. It looked like she was going to get better, but when she got pregnant with you, it sent her into a downward spiral again. We tried so many things to help her. So many doctors. Medications. Prayer. Therapy. Nothing worked. It was like she'd stepped into a darkness and I couldn't find her. Nothing I did helped. She pushed me away, and I let her. I didn't know what to do."

Hunter's thoughts scrambled over one another like puppies in a pen. "But I always thought… I always thought that she'd given up her life for us and that it had broken her. That she'd been so despondent because you'd convinced her to marry you even though it wasn't what she'd wanted."

His dad's sigh was as long as the decades of hurt between them. "No, that wasn't the issue," he continued, voice quiet. "The story we used to tell you was true. I did convince her. I knew I couldn't live without her, but she was content here for a while. Until her illness. But you are right to blame me. I wanted to help her and I failed." His father pushed up from the wooden chair. Walked to the window. "I was so confused. So lost. I wrote her a letter once, thinking maybe since I was so bad at telling her how I felt, that writing it would help. Would remind her how much I loved her, no matter what."

The letter Hunter had found. Hunter couldn't believe his father was bringing it up.

"But then, like a fool, I didn't give it to her."

What?

"Maybe if I had told her more often how much I loved her. How much I wanted her here…maybe it would have made a difference."

"What do you mean you never gave Mom that letter?"

His dad's gaze snapped to him, filled with a heat that seared across Hunter's skin. "You knew about it?"

"I found it once when I was younger. It looked as though it had been read over numerous times."

His dad studied his hands and cleared his throat. Took a few seconds to steady his visually cracking composure. "I read it over the years. Punished myself with it after Mom left. Regretted not giving it to her. Being young and immature wasn't an excuse. I'd been prideful."

The creases in his dad's brow multiplied. "By the time I wrote that letter, she'd begun to take out some things on me. I didn't know what was happening. I just thought she didn't love me any longer. And so, instead of fighting for her, instead of giving her the letter or telling her how I felt, I let her go. I let her slip away one day at a time. I'll always regret it. I should have fought for her. I should have given her the letter and hundreds more, no matter how she was treating me or what I assumed she thought about me. I was hurt and wounded and I let it affect my decisions. It was so hard to lose her when we'd once been so happy. Watching her suffer and not being able to fix it. The more she struggled, the more I broke, too."

Hunter wanted to harden his heart against this man he'd never understood. But his grasp on that anger was slipping into sorrow. His father hadn't turned angry and bitter because his mom hadn't stayed or because he'd fought for her and lost, but because he'd never fought at all.

The opposite of everything Hunter had ever believed. Pain pounded in his temples. He'd been such a jerk to Rachel, and his actions had been based on false conclusions. How could he have been so foolish?

All of this time, Hunter had been wrong. He'd been self-righteous, assuming he knew what was best for Rachel. Driving her away from him when all he'd wanted to do was battle to keep her—even if he didn't know what that would look like. Why couldn't they date like she'd suggested? Why couldn't they have had an adult conversation and figured things out?

He'd been such an idiot. At this point, she must hate him. He'd hidden his true feelings from her—which sounded a bit like the story unfolding in front of him.

Hunter had always thought his dad was a jerk to his mom. That he'd ruined her life. But his dad had just been hurt and confused, and he'd done his best with a wife who'd changed. Who'd had an illness that nothing helped. Compassion for his father flooded him for the first time in his life. His dad wasn't to blame. Had never been. The man had held himself accountable all of these years for his mom's decline, and Hunter had been only too happy to join him in heaping on the guilt.

Hunter finally understood. Could finally forgive.

The question was, would Rachel ever do the same regarding his mistakes? The wall around her that had taken most of the summer to break through was back up. And if he knew her at all, she didn't have any plans to ever let it down again.

He pulled out a chair and dropped into it. "This changes so much. I didn't know…didn't understand." His dad's red eyes broadcasted the grief their conversation had induced. "Dad, I'm so sorry."

"For what? You didn't do anything wrong."

"For all of it. I should have…" Asked sooner. Had more faith in his father instead of blaming him.

"Me, too, son. Me, too."

Chapter Sixteen

During her first week in Houston, Rachel had accomplished very little except going to work and heading home to Dana's apartment at night. She was supposed to be hunting for a place to live. She was also supposed to be happy.

Dana had forced her to go out to dinner last night, and she had perked up a bit.

Until she'd crawled onto the couch and tried to sleep. She'd never been so exhausted in all of her life, yet was unable to find any rest.

Rachel walked to her Jeep in the school parking lot, the heat and humidity thick like warm, sticky Jell-O. It was Monday. Mondays were good for lists and plans. She'd hoped today was the day excitement over getting her dream job would kick in and she would stop thinking about Hunter.

Hadn't happened.

Instead, she'd had three parent meetings at school. What had they all been about? Getting their kids into Ivy League universities. None of their children showed any interest in that very thing, but parents were lining up at her door.

Rachel had taken this job so she could help students. She hadn't realized so much of her interaction would be with their parents. She'd assumed it would get better once school started and the kids were on campus. But when she'd broached that question today with her supervisor, she'd only confirmed Rachel's worst fears. It seemed at this school, parents were always going to take up a large chunk of her time.

And she was afraid that wasn't the only reason she couldn't find any joy in the job she'd wanted so badly. She missed her people back home. And home itself. But what was she going to do about that now? It was too late. She'd made a decision, and she needed to stick with it.

Her phone rang, muffled in her purse, and Rachel dug for it.

Val.

She wasn't going to be disappointed that Hunter's name didn't appear on the screen. Was not. And in that same vein, she also didn't miss his texts. Or his voice. Or the way he teased her constantly and made her laugh.

Rachel didn't miss any of those things.

She swiped to answer, infusing perkiness into her hello.

"Hey, I thought you'd be at work and I'd have to leave a message."

"Just walking out."

"I have some news for you."

"What about?"

"Hunter. Do you want to hear it? Or are you content as can be down there?"

Air leaked from her lungs. "I'm…not unhappy." But wasn't the opposite of happy exactly that?

Rachel unlocked her Jeep and got in, then started it and cranked the air-conditioning, trying to combat the heat that had swelled as the vehicle roasted in the sun all day.

"Hunter said something to me yesterday that I haven't been able to get out of my mind. He asked me about you. Asked how you were."

"He did?"

"Yep. And when he did, I said, if you're so concerned about Rachel, why'd you push her away? To which he replied, 'This was her dream.'"

What? "What does that mean?"

"I'm starting to think the reason Hunter reacted the way he did isn't because he doesn't care, but because he does."

A flutter started in Rachel's chest and she broke into a sweat. She adjusted the vents to pummel her arms and face with crisp, cool air.

"Then why would he say those things to me?"

"So that you'd go. Tell me this. How confident were you that he felt something for you—a lot for you—before he sent you packing?"

At times she'd wondered what he was thinking, but mostly Rachel had listened to her heart and observed the way he treated her. Deep down, she'd known that he had to feel something for her. "I didn't really doubt it." Not with the way he'd protected her and watched out for her. The way he was always there when she needed him. And his kisses…

"Maybe he didn't want to be the reason you didn't take the job. Did you tell him how badly you wanted it?"

Rachel's eyes closed. "Yes." A ten, she'd told him. Not even a sliver of a doubt. And then, in the police car that night, he'd encouraged her. Told her how amazing she would be at it.

"If he did this because of what you're saying, without telling me how he feels, then I want to hunt him down and hurt him." That immature teenage girl inside of her always popped up at the worst times. Perhaps, just perhaps, God would prefer she choose the less violent route.

"I know he never told you how he felt, but I could see it. We all could. And when you took the job—"

"Without talking to him first," Rachel continued Val's thought. She'd done the same thing to him. Pushed him away. "I self-sabotaged. I accepted the job without telling Hunter about it in order to protect myself. Yes, I still wanted it, but I was also scared that he might not love me the way I love him."

Love him. It had rolled right out, that truth. She should have known. Should have admitted it sooner. "Taking the position was a way to escape without finding out the truth. Because it would have hurt if he didn't feel the same. It does hurt. I'd assumed I'd learned this lesson watching Cash with Liv—that I was open—but I wasn't. I was running, protecting myself all along."

Rachel had also believed that the job would make her happy. Climbing another mountain, accomplishing another something. And for what? To prove she wasn't a troubled kid anymore? Who did she need to prove that to, besides herself? And she already knew the truth. God didn't have a list of things she had to check off in order to be forgiven or to start fresh. Her slate had been wiped clean yesterday. It would be wiped clean today. Same tomorrow. He loved her exactly as she was. Even the friends and family surrounding her loved her like that.

She'd thought the town had been waiting for her to mess up. But now? She was afraid it had all been her. Her judgments against herself. Her fears. It was time she learned grace didn't keep scorecards.

"I'm an idiot."

"You're not an idiot." No matter what mistakes she made, Val always had her back like a protective mama bear. "You were doing your best. And if you think there's a chance for you and Hunter, then there's something else I need to tell you."

Val proceeded to shatter Rachel's world further by telling her about the guidance counselor position at the high school in Fredericksburg, suggesting Rachel check into it. But even after they'd finished the conversation and Rachel had driven back to Dana's apartment, her mind was muddled.

It would be one thing if Hunter had wanted her to stay. Or he'd called to tell her about the job. But she and Val were simply guessing his feelings. What he'd told her—how he'd acted—wasn't anywhere near what they'd just discussed. And Rachel wasn't sure she could put herself out there again. She *had* attempted to talk to Hunter before moving—it might not have been the perfect scenario, since she'd already taken the job—but she'd tried discussing how she felt. And he'd shoved her away. The pain of that washed over her all over again. Felt like she was walking around bleeding for all the world to see.

Rachel could finally admit she loved Hunter. Always had. Always would.

The question she didn't have an answer to, was what she was going to do about it.

On Friday evening, Hunter stood outside Rachel's apartment door in Houston—make that her friend's place—and readied for a fight.

It had taken him a few days to process all his dad had revealed to him and to pray over his next steps, and he'd come to a very simple conclusion: he wanted Rachel in his life, and he'd do anything to make that happen.

His fist went up, then paused before connecting with the wooden door. *Wuss.* Hunter had thought about bringing Moose along for moral support—he'd known the dog would have pulled on Rachel's heartstrings and might have edged the score in his direction—but he hadn't wanted to force the animal to endure such a long drive in his truck.

He knocked, the sound reverberating in the pounding in his chest, and tried to run through everything he wanted to say.

The door flew open, revealing a much shorter woman than Rachel with dark hair and chocolate eyes.

"You must be Dana." He attempted a smile, but his nerves probably made it look like a wobbly spaghetti noodle. "I'm Hunter. Any chance Rachel's here?"

Recognition flashed on Dana's face, and she looked over her shoulder and called out, "Rachel, someone is here for you." Then she opened the door wider and motioned for him to come in. Bustling over to the kitchen counter, she grabbed a brown leather purse. "I was just… heading out." She bolted through the open doorway, then paused. "It was great to meet you." The nicety was followed by the sound of the front door slamming shut.

Huh. Was her departure a good or bad sign?

"Who is it?" Rachel came out from the bathroom, and at the sight of him, froze. She must have recently come home from work, because she still had on business clothes. Slim dress pants that landed just above her ankles and a flowing shirt. The turquoise color highlighted the green of her eyes. Her hair was down, and her feet were bare, the heels she'd likely taken off when she'd walked in the door haphazardly lying to his right. Her toenails were painted fluorescent pink. Hunter had never imagined he could actually miss something like knowing Rachel's current polish color.

She glanced around the living room and kitchen. "Where's Dana? You didn't add breaking and entering or kidnapping to your list of crimes, did you?"

Strangely enough, the sassy question alleviated his tension. Just being near her made him feel like he'd taken his first real breath in almost two weeks.

"She just left. Said she had to be somewhere."

Rachel's closed off body language told him her walls were up and functioning. On high alert for anyone who tried to breach them.

"What are you doing here, Hunter?"

She was beautiful, inside and out, and he'd been so stupid not telling her how he felt.

"I need to talk to you about something."

"You could have called."

"This wasn't a phone call kind of conversation." Besides, she wouldn't have answered. Didn't she realize he knew her better than that?

She shifted uncomfortably. "Okay."

He strode forward, hands landing on her arms, her skin soft and smooth to his touch. "I'm so sorry. Sorry that I let you go and that I didn't tell you I was crazy in love with you and always have been and not one thing on God's green earth is ever going to change that."

Whoa. That hadn't come out exactly as he'd rehearsed. Her jaw had gone slack, and he was almost certain a sheen of moisture appeared in her eyes. She blinked so fast he could be wrong, though.

When she didn't say anything in response, he stormed ahead.

"I have a whole long story that might help my behavior make more sense." He pulled her over to the couch and motioned for her to sit. Then he sat on the coffee table across from her and told her everything. About how he'd always thought his dad had convinced his mom to live a life she didn't want—and how that turned out not to be true. He explained how it had messed with him over the years. How it had convinced him to never ask anyone—including her—to stay in a life she didn't want. He told her about the letter. About finding out that his father had never fought for his mother.

"I wanted you to come to Houston because I knew this was a dream of yours and I didn't want to take that away. And that's still true. I can live without a ranch. But I can't live without you."

"What are you saying?" Her voice was a whisper, her eyes questioning. Still aching with hurt that he'd caused.

"I'll move here if you're willing to give us a chance. I'll work in a hardware store. Or on a ranch outside of town. We can do long-distance if you want, but that's only going to last for a little bit. And then I don't want things to dead end. So if we want a future together, I'm willing to move. I still want you to follow your dreams. I already talked to my dad. Told him I might need to sell back to him. He understands." His father had been so decent about the whole conversation that Hunter had almost checked for hidden cameras. But then his dad had sent him out of his office with a gruff "Get to work," and Hunter had known he was still in the right universe. The two of them were both making more effort in their relationship, though, and things were slowly changing.

"This is probably all coming out jumbled, but I'm trying to explain why I didn't fight for you. Why I let you go. I thought it was the best way to love you." He let out a slow exhale. "But I don't believe that anymore."

"What do you believe now?" Her voice was still quiet.

"That I love you and I want to spend the rest of my life with you and I'll do anything to make that happen."

She popped up from the couch and began pacing.

Not exactly the response he was hoping for.

After four turns, she paused in front of him. "It's not going to work for you to move here."

A boulder of disappointment crushed him.

"That wouldn't make sense because I'm not going to be living here."

What? What was she talking about? "Is something wrong with your job?"

She nodded. "It's not at all what I expected."

His heart drummed so hard he was certain he could feel it tapping against his rib cage.

"I'm sorry." And he was. He wanted her to be happy. Hated hearing that she wasn't. Yet, at the same time, hope rose up. "There's a position that just opened at the high school."

Her head shook. "No, there's not. They filled it."

How many times could his dreams be snuffed out in one day?

"From what I've heard, the person they hired is straight out of school. Young. Blonde." Her head tilted. "I should set you up with her."

He wasn't sure whether to sigh or growl or yell.

"Really? What's her name? I'll have to call her." Anger and sarcasm blended together, frustration causing his body to heat despite the cool air in the apartment. What was he going to do with this woman? How was he going to convince her that—

"Rachel Maddox."

Absolute silence reigned after her words.

And then he was standing, gripping her arms again. "You took the job? It was you?" She nodded, a smile inching across her face. "And you let me go on and on? Here I was thinking I might never be able to convince you to give us another chance and you'd already decided?" His voice had risen to a boom.

Her grin only grew. It was mesmerizing, but Hunter was doing his best not to let it distract him. He was mad at her. Or, at least, he wanted to be. She lifted one shoulder. "I thought you needed to grovel a little."

He scooped her up in a hug, and she squealed, her arms looping around his neck. "Hunter McDermott, put me down."

"Never." After not nearly long enough, he let her go slowly. She slid down until they were face-to-face again. "Does this mean you love me and can't live without me?"

Her lips pressed together, and she gave the sweetest nod he'd ever witnessed in his life.

"Say it."

She sighed and rolled her eyes, acting annoyed by his demand, but then she softened. Her eyes were so full of emotion that he knew what she felt, even without the words he couldn't wait to hear. "I love you. I'm never going to leave you. You're my home. And if Fredericksburg isn't right for me, you'll be the first to know." His breath caught. "And then we'll figure the next thing out together."

Every tense muscle in his body unwound. "You love me."

"At the moment. But you're really going to have to up your game, McDermott. I'm expecting flowers every day, and you're going to have to learn to cook, and—"

He cut her off with a kiss. It seemed like a good plan. One he'd need to use again in the future. His hands slid into her hair, the pain of the last two weeks ebbing away at the familiarity of her touch. He could just stay right here forever. Except…he needed info.

Hunter managed to wrench himself away from her, holding her at arm's length. "How did you know about the job? Val?"

She nodded. "I interviewed with the high school on Wednesday and they offered me the job right away. But then I had to decide what to do. I didn't want to leave my current school hanging, but I talked to my supervisor, and she understood my predicament. I guess she reads romance novels all the time, and she was almost giddy about us. I told her I wasn't sure we were going to work, but she encouraged me to take the risk. The person who was in line behind me for the job here hasn't found anything else yet, and they're going to offer him the position."

He tucked back a piece of her hair, and if his hand lingered against her cheek, sue him.

"I didn't know what you were thinking," Rachel continued. "Or how you felt about me. I only knew your actions showed me something completely different than your words, but you definitely threw me for a loop. Val told me what you'd said at church and we pieced together what we thought was going on." Her face grew serious. "But I was still scared. I wasn't sure what to believe anymore. So I prayed, and I asked Val and Cash and Liv to pray, and in the end…taking the job in Fredericksburg was the right thing to do. And so I decided to trust God with that—whether you wanted me or not."

"I want you."

At his words, a smile traced her lips. He barely refrained from kissing her again. But he needed more reassurance. He had to know she wasn't giving this up for him. "I thought you loved the city. You know how different it is. Are you sure?"

She traced soft circles with her thumb across the scar on his forearm—a gash that had required stitches a few years past. "I don't have any doubts. Ever since my parents died… I've felt like I didn't belong anywhere. Colorado was a pit stop. I made friends but never got too close. And even though I was starting to love it in Fredericksburg, I didn't let myself believe it could be home again. Leaving last time and going to school was the right thing to do. But that doesn't mean it's the answer this time. That quiet life I never thought I wanted… I was wrong. I already have a home. I just had to open my eyes to see it."

Relief was as sweet as lemonade on a scorching day.

"I was fighting against letting people in. Belonging. And I don't want to fight that anymore."

"So you won't hate living in Fredericksburg, let's say…on a ranch?" At his question, her eyebrows shot up, and he felt a full-fledged grin growing. "I mean, not that anyone is asking you to live on a ranch." Yet.

Her lips curved. "Because that would be a crazy idea."

Inching closer, he slid arms around the small of her back. "Absolutely crazy." And wonderful. "Have I told you I don't love you today?"

That earned him a laugh.

"That works out well, then, McDermott, because I don't love you, either." Her arms wrapped around his neck and tugged him down until her lips met his in a soft kiss. "Except I do."

"Me, too." And he liked the sound of her last two words a whole lot.

Epilogue

Rachel peered out the window of Mr. McDermott's home to the rows of white chairs lining the west side of the house and facing the ranch. A white tent lit with twinkle lights stood to the right, waiting for the reception to follow.

The ceremony was about to start, so everyone had taken their seats. Olivia was holding Ryder in the front row. The Redmonds were seated behind her, and across the aisle, Hunter's dad sat with Autumn and Calvin, who was holding their newborn son, Craig.

Rachel's favorite aunt and uncle had made the trip from Austin—her Aunt Libby had been a huge help with wedding planning. And some other friends from town were there, too—ones who had known her since she was a kid, and much like Hunter, stayed in her life through all of her ups and downs, mistakes and triumphs.

If there was one thing she'd realized over the last few months about the man she was about to marry, it was that his love for her had been consistent. Hunter had always known exactly who she was—even beneath any bad decisions she'd made—and he'd loved all the sides of her. He'd always believed in her. It was mesmerizing to watch his adoration unfold now that he no longer had to hold back. She could say without a doubt that his love had changed her for the better.

Bree and a small group of teens sat toward the back. After Rachel had returned to town, Bree had begun to open up again, even attending the Bible study that Rachel led one morning a week before school. Between that and stepping in as Olivia's new assistant volleyball coach when Val's mom retired from the position she'd held for many years, the last few months had raced by.

Rachel and Hunter had planned their outdoor wedding for early November—the weekend after volleyball season ended—knowing full well it might be raining or freezing and they'd end up doing the ceremony in the tent. But like a little smile from God, the day was gorgeous. Trees were brandishing their royal colors, and the sun had come out to play in all its glory.

The front door of the house opened and her brother stepped inside. "They're almost ready for you."

She abandoned the window she'd been peeking out of to meet him by the front door. The guys were wearing crisp, dark jeans, white shirts and camel vests—with cowboy boots, of course. Hunter had opted for the casual look—Rachel couldn't imagine him donning a tux—and she had no doubt her soon-to-be husband was going to look heart-stopping in the ensemble.

"You look really nice. Almost worthy of that beautiful wife of yours. I'm not sure I've seen you this cleaned up…maybe ever."

Cash jutted his chest out, tugging on the front of his vest. "I wore a suit for my wedding."

"That's true." Amusement traced her lips. "You did." She adjusted his orange calla lily boutonniere, which had slipped to one side.

For wedding colors, Rachel had opted for pops of orange, red, yellow and green. Val and Brennon were standing up with them, and Val had been tasked with the job of picking out her own bridesmaid's dress. She'd chosen a sweeping yellow one-shouldered dress that dropped to the floor with all of the drama the girl herself didn't possess. Perfection.

Rachel snagged her bouquet bursting with brightly colored calla lilies from the table by the front door. It looked amazing against her white, A-line, sleeveless dress. She eased her hem to the side, drinking in the sight of her shoes. Bright, bold green peeked back at her. She'd done her hair in a low side twist, opting not to wear a veil but to tuck in a sprig of greenery, instead.

"You look beautiful." Cash interrupted her love affair with her green satin, peep-toe pumps, and she found him looking at her with unguarded emotion that almost sent her free-falling down the same slippery slope.

"Thank you."

"I'm sorry Dad's not here."

"Me, too." Her eyes misted. "But I'm really glad you're here."

His creased cheeks spoke volumes. Of silent grief and the subsequent bond that flowed between them. "Me, too. Are you ready for this?"

"I am."

"So you really like this guy, huh?"

That got a laugh out of her, and the nerves that had started at seeing all of the people arriving calmed. "You know, I kinda do."

"And to think, only a few years ago I was working on letting you go. That whole saying about releasing things so they'll come back to you is true."

Humor tugged on her lips. "You're a dork."

"Aaand that sounds more like the sister I know and love." He grinned. "Have I told you how proud I am of you?"

"Not this week."

"You should be proud of yourself, too."

"I am. I think." Rachel had been working on letting go of needing to prove herself and trusting that God's opinion—His great love for her—mattered more than the past, present and future jumbled together. And she was happy in this town, with her family and friends, and with the man about to become her husband. She'd had no idea she could be so content with what she'd been fighting against for so long.

Music drifted through the open door, and Rachel placed her hand in the crook of Cash's arm. They made their way outside and down the front steps. About forty chairs were filled with guests for the simple ceremony they'd timed to start just as the sun began to set.

When they reached the end of the aisle, Rachel sought Hunter's gaze and found it wrapped around her as if no one else existed.

Lands, she loved him.

His dimples sprang to life as if her thoughts had been spoken out loud.

She and Cash walked down the aisle as Grayson

hopped on one foot up front, impatiently waiting to perform his job as the ring bearer, and Kinsley, their precocious flower girl, twirled in her white dress, both of them making the guests titter with suppressed laughter.

Gray had been full of questions about his important role for weeks. Though Rachel did think she'd convinced him that having a spider on the ring pillow was not the best idea.

Pastor Greg did the whole who-gives-this-woman part, and then her hand was in Hunter's and she was standing face-to-face with him.

"Hi."

His whispered greeting made her mouth curve. She was pretty sure they weren't supposed to be talking except to say their vows.

"You look…" His eyes filled with emotion, and he paused to swallow, causing his Adam's apple to bob. So, of course, the waterworks sprouted for her, too.

"Do not make me cry on my wedding day, Hunter McDermott."

That playful grin of his returned. "Yes, ma'am."

The ceremony went by in a blur. Rachel only knew she'd promised to share her life with someone she never wanted to live without. She was good with that decision.

"I now pronounce you husband and wife." Greg's head tilted toward them, his voice low. "Who knew that when Lucy Redmond suggested the two of you help with the float, we'd end up here?"

Rachel's mouth dropped open. Hunter's head shook in answer to her silent query, his cheeks creasing.

"I didn't know, either."

Both of them glanced in Lucy's direction. She was

sitting with Graham and her girls, absolutely beaming from the second row. Guess Rachel would have to thank her later for her meddling. Laughter bubbled in her throat. Leave it to Lucy to quietly stick her nose into their business and come out looking like a shining star.

Greg eased back, speaking in a louder voice. "Hunter, you may kiss your bride. And in case anyone is wondering, this is *not* a first kiss."

Laughter rang out, along with a cheer from their friends and family, as Hunter's lips met hers, his arms warm and strong around her. His whisper cascaded by her ear. "Time to head back down that aisle as a married woman, Mrs. McDermott." He inched back to look into her eyes. "Need a lift?" He made a motion, almost bending, as though he planned to scoop her up like he had before.

Her eyes shot to the size of dinner plates, and she whacked his shoulder in front of God and all of the guests. "Don't you dare!" The words hissed out and were met by a low chuckle as he straightened. Winked.

"I wouldn't dream of it. At least, not on our wedding day. But after…" He shrugged as if to say he couldn't control the future.

Her huff of exaggerated annoyance was negated by the smile that accompanied it. "What have I gotten myself into?"

"Only the best decision of your life, darlin'."

For once, she agreed with him.

"Ready?" He offered her his elbow, and she linked her arm through his as they faced the people who loved them and took their first step into the world as husband and wife. She couldn't wait to do life with Hunter by her side. Tears pricked her eyes as she contemplated the amazing man God had written into her story. He was more than she'd ever hoped for, a rock when she needed it, and most of all, he loved her with a devotion she almost couldn't understand.

She might not deserve him, but she planned to keep him.

* * * * *

WE HOPE YOU ENJOYED
THIS BOOK FROM

H HARLEQUIN
SPECIAL
EDITION

Believe in love. Overcome obstacles. Find happiness.

Relate to finding comfort and strength in the
support of loved ones and enjoy the journey
no matter what life throws your way.

6 NEW BOOKS AVAILABLE EVERY MONTH!

SPECIAL EXCERPT FROM

HARLEQUIN
SPECIAL EDITION

*When Laurel Hudson is found—alive but with
amnesia—no one is more relieved than Adam Fortune.
He will do whatever it takes to reunite mother and son,
even if it means a road trip in extremely close quarters.
Will the long journey home remind Laurel how much
they truly share?*

*Read on for a sneak preview of the final book in
The Fortunes of Texas: Rambling Rose continuity,
The Texan's Baby Bombshell by Allison Leigh.*

He'd been falling for her from the very beginning. But
that kiss had sealed the deal for him.

Now that glossy oak-barrel hair slid over her shoulder
as Laurel's head turned and she looked his way.

His step faltered.

Her eyes were the same stunning shade of blue they'd
always been. Her perfectly heart-shaped face was pale
and delicate looking even without the pink scar on her
forehead between her eyebrows.

Her eyebrows pulled together as their eyes met.

Remember me.

Remember us.

The words—unwanted and unexpected—pulsed
through him, drowning out the splitting headache and the
aching back and the impatience, the relief and the pain.

Then she blinked those incredible eyes of hers and he realized there was a flush on her cheeks and she was chewing at the corner of her lips. In contrast to her delicate features, her lips were just as full and pouty as they'd always been.

Kissing them had been an adventure in and of itself.

He pushed the pointless memory out of his head and then had to shove his hands in the pockets of his jeans because they were actually shaking.

"Hi." Puny first word to say to the woman who'd made a wreck out of him.

Still seated, she looked up at him. "Hi." She sounded breathless. "It's…it's Adam, right?"

The pain sitting in the pit of his stomach then had nothing to do with anything except her. He yanked his right hand from his pocket and held it out. "Adam Fortune."

She looked uncertain, then slowly settled her hand into his.

Unlike Dr. Granger's firm, brief clasp, Laurel's touch felt chilled and tentative. And it lingered. "I'm Lisa."

God help him. He was not strong enough for this.

Don't miss
The Texan's Baby Bombshell *by Allison Leigh,*
available June 2020 wherever
Harlequin Special Edition books and ebooks are sold.

Harlequin.com

SPECIAL EXCERPT FROM

LOVE INSPIRED SUSPENSE
INSPIRATIONAL ROMANCE

*They must work together to solve a cold case…
and to stay alive.*

Read on for a sneak preview of
Deadly Connection *by Lenora Worth,*
the next book in the True Blue K-9 Unit: Brooklyn *series,*
available June 2020 from Love Inspired Suspense.

Brooklyn K-9 Unit officer Belle Montera glanced back on the shortcut through Cadman Plaza Park, her K-9 partner, Justice, a sleek German shepherd, moving ahead of her as she held tightly to his leash. She had a weird sense she was being followed, but it had to be nothing.

Justice lifted his black nose and sniffed the humid air, then gave a soft woof. He might have seen a squirrel frolicking in the tall oaks, or he could have sensed Belle's agitation. Still on duty, she kept a keen eye on her surroundings.

"No time to go after innocent squirrels," she told Justice. "We're working, remember?"

Her faithful companion gave her a dark-eyed stare, his black K-9 unit protective vest cinched around his firm belly.

They were both on high alert.

"It's okay, boy," she said, giving Justice's shiny black-and-tan coat a soft rub. "Just my overactive imagination getting the best of me."

She had a meeting with a man who could have information regarding the McGregor murders. The DNA match from that case had indicated that US marshal Emmett Gage could be related to the killer.

The team had done a thorough background check on the marshal to eliminate him as a suspect, then Belle had been assigned to meet with him.

Justice lifted his head and sniffed again, his nose in the air. The big dog glanced back. Belle checked over her shoulder.

No one there.

She slowed and listened to hear if any footsteps hit the strip of pavement curving through the path toward the federal courthouse near the park.

Belle heard through the trees what sounded like a motorcycle revving, then nothing but the birds chirping. Minutes passed and then she heard a noise on the path, the crackle of a twig breaking, the slight shift of shoes hitting asphalt, a whiff of stale body odor wafting through the air. The hair on the back of her neck stood up and Belle knew then.

Someone is following me.

Don't miss
Deadly Connection *by Lenora Worth,*
available June 2020 wherever
Love Inspired Suspense books and ebooks are sold.

LoveInspired.com

Love Harlequin romance?

DISCOVER.

Be the first to find out about promotions,
news and exclusive content!

Facebook.com/HarlequinBooks

Twitter.com/HarlequinBooks

Instagram.com/HarlequinBooks

Pinterest.com/HarlequinBooks

ReaderService.com

EXPLORE.

Sign up for the Harlequin e-newsletter and
download a free book from any series at
TryHarlequin.com

CONNECT.

Join our Harlequin community to
share your thoughts and connect
with other romance readers!
Facebook.com/groups/HarlequinConnection

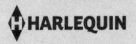